Praise for Patty Apostolides and her books

HELENA'S CHOICE

"A smooth journey in the past. Wonderful images, powerful feelings. Beautiful descriptions for the demanding. I found the story intriguing and unanticipated plot twists mind-blowing, a rare for this genre. Five stars from me."

– Christos Tsiaillis, Author

"The many specific details of daily life in both England and Greece show an author who is quite familiar with both cultures. She tells the story in a refined, elegant prose that is a pleasure to read."

– Rea Keech, Author

THE GREEK MAIDEN AND THE ENGLISH LORD

"This historical romance draws on the best traditions of English classics."

-Hagerstown Magazine

"I enjoyed your novel tremendously and recommended it to all the women in District #13!

– Melba B., Daughters of Penelope, District 13

"Lily's struggle to find identity and grasp her heart's desire spurs the reader to continue on to a satisfactory conclusion."

– Kristina Emmons, HistoryandWomen.com

THE LION AND THE NURSE

"Patty Apostolides' novel, which takes place on a "typical" Greek Island, Kos, is truly a proper follow-up to "My Big Fat Greek Wedding" although it comes from a different direction – Americans experiencing the Greek culture in Greece."

-Michael Bilirakis, former Congressman

"What impressionism achieved on the canvas, Patty Apostolides seems to accomplish on the printed page – and remarkable. A stunning achievement!"

- Nicholas D. Kokonis, Ph

BOOKS BY PATTY APOSTOLIDES

The Greek Maiden and the English Lord

The Lion and the Nurse

Lipsi's Daughter

Candlelit Journey: Poetry from the Heart

Helena's Choice

A Novel

Patty Apostolides

Helena's Choice

Cover art by Joanna Vasilakis, Jojo Haus of Design.

No man or woman born, coward or brave, can shun his destiny. - **Homer, *The Iliad***

It is no cause for anger that the Trojans and the well-grieved Achaeans have suffered for so long over such a woman: she is wondrously like the immortal goddesses to look upon. **-Homer, *The Iliad.***

CHAPTER 1

Oxfordshire, England
30 June, 1837

Helena Cadfield leaned out the window of the moving coach, delighting in the June breeze that brushed her face and teased her large hat. Above, the sky was a sea of blue, and in the hills, the cream-colored sheep grazed on pink heather. After being away for three years, she was content to be returning home to Cadfield House.

The carriage rattled across a stone bridge, waking the Pickets, an elderly couple who sat across from her.

Mrs. Picket pushed back the gray strands from her forehead and peered outside. "The clouds have cleared. Couldn't have picked a better day for traveling," she remarked.

"I can see the spires from here," Mr. Picket said. "Nothing like being in Oxford."

"Do you have family in Oxford, Miss?" Mrs. Picket asked Helena. "I'm sorry, what was your name again?"

"Miss Cadfield. My father is Dr. William Cadfield. Do you know him?"

"Yes, he treated my husband once, many years ago," Mrs. Picket said, smiling. "Where did you say that you were traveling from, Miss Cadfield?"

"Paris. I completed my term at Madame Guillard's boarding school."

"Ah, very nice. With your lovely features, you will probably have plenty of gentlemen suitors come calling."

Helena flushed, remaining silent. One person whom she looked forward to seeing again was Mr. Murphy, a medical student of Papa's. She was fourteen when he first visited her father to discuss his coursework one day. On returning from riding her horse, Helena had rushed into the house to greet her father. Next to him sat a young man with a boyish face. Papa scolded her lightly for her childish entrance, and then made the introductions. Later, when Mr. Murphy visited her father, he would tease her about her tomboyish behavior, pulling on one of her braids.

All these years Helena nursed a secret infatuation for Mr. Murphy. She wanted him to see her dressed in her fashionable clothes.

The coach entered the busy thoroughfare of Oxford, with its carriages, pedestrians, and wagons. The driver dropped them off at High Street and Helena bid the Pickets farewell. She spied Mr. Lindle seated on the Cadfield carriage and waved to him.

Still agile after all these years, he jumped down and strode toward her. "Welcome back, Miss Cadfield." He took her luggage.

"I'm glad to be back, Mr. Lindle."

Soon they were on their way to Cadfield House, passing Oxford's limestone college buildings with their manicured courtyards. The coach stopped to allow a group of young college men, their scholarly robes billowing behind them, to cross the street.

She remembered the times when she was young and Papa would walk with her there, telling her about each building and its history. She had wanted to go to college and be educated like her father, a physician, who took care of patients and lectured at the Anatomy School in Oxford during the school year. Women were not allowed to attend college, but that did not stop her from wanting to learn. After her father found her three years ago, sitting in on one of his lectures, dressed as a boy, he had sent her off to the boarding school in Paris. She had not seen him since then.

The carriage rambled past a great oak tree whose branches stretched toward her. The last rays of sun filtered through its green leaves while small birds flitted back and forth in its fold. Helena felt as if she had never left and was taking a ride around town.

The coach turned onto the familiar tree-lined path that led to Cadfield House. At the end of the row of trees stood the large, brick mansion surrounded by green bushes and luscious landscaping. Helena's heart swelled with pride. She wondered what Papa would say when he saw her dressed in the elegant Parisian dress with matching hat. Although her appearance differed from the gangly girl who climbed trees and dressed up as a lad to attend his anatomy lectures, she was still the same inside.

Nana met her at the door. A gray bonnet covered her head, while gray, frizzy strands waved about her small, wrinkled face. She had been Papa's nanny and later Helena's. She was like a mother to her.

Helena hugged her small frame warmly. "Hello, Nana. I'm so glad to see you."

"Miss Helena, welcome back. Let me have a good look at you!" Nana leaned back and stared at her with unshed tears. "My, my, you've grown into an attractive young woman," she said, with a high-pitched voice.

Helena gazed fondly at her nanny. "I may look different, but I haven't changed, Nana," she said. "I miss being at Cadfield House and reading my books, dressing casually and riding my horse straddle."

"You've always had that stubborn streak in you, wanting to do things your way," Nana said, shaking her head. "Pride goeth before a fall, and all those years at the boarding school doesn't seem to have done a bit of good for your pride."

Nana asked her about the trip, and Helena filled her in.

Mrs. Barton, the cook, came to the door. She was a large, imposing woman and towered over Nana.

"Welcome home, Miss Helena," she said, smiling, and then turned and scowled at Nana. "Where's your mind gone te, leaving the poor girl standing so long outside the house?"

"Oh, dear, where are my manners?" Nana said, appearing flustered. "Come in, Miss Helena, and tell us all about your adventures."

The house staff had assembled in a line to greet Helena as she entered the front hall. They had been patients of Papa's at one time or another. Mr. Barton, the butler, had a limp and walked with a cane, while his wife Mrs. Barton, complained of palpitations and a weak heart. Jon, the footman, stooped from the arthritis in his back, and Mrs. Rotcliffe, the housekeeper, had a skin condition where she would break out in rashes. They had helped Helena through scrapes and falls when she was a child. They had watched her ride her horses and host her father's teas. She often nursed them when the need arose while Papa was away, administering ointments, herbs, or advice.

They rewarded Helena with warm smiles. She asked them about their health, and after learning their news, looked around expectantly. "Is Papa here?"

"No, dear, I'm afraid he is not. He is still in Greece," Nana said, her voice wavering.

"Oh," Helena said. That familiar sinking feeling formed in her stomach. Papa would not be here for her birthday tomorrow. She held her breath for a moment, just enough time for her tears not to well up in her eyes. She had learned that trick in Paris. *Never reveal your emotions.* She had forgotten Papa's absentmindedness. She had forgotten that she had spent many birthdays without him.

"Miss Cadfield, would you like a bite to eat?" Mrs. Barton asked.

"I know how well you cook, Mrs. Barton, but all I want to do is rest," Helena replied. "Has Papa written to me?"

Mrs. Rotcliffe nudged Nana, her head jerking toward the library.

"Oh, yes, where is my mind these days!" Nana exclaimed, hurrying away. "He sent you a letter. It's in the library."

Moments later, Helena followed Nana up the stairs, holding her father's sealed letter in her hand. Nana chatted about the news, including the births, the marriages, and the latest scandals in Oxford.

They stopped in front of her room, and Helena's thoughts drifted to the letter in her hand. She wondered what news her father had for her.

"Oh, but here I am, such a chatterbox, and you, poor dear, must want to read your father's letter," Nana said knowingly. "We'll catch up on our news later."

"Thank you, Nana. I am glad to be back." Helena smiled at Nana's retreating figure.

The familiar scent of rosewater greeted her as she entered her room. Helena glanced around, feeling joyful. Everything was as she had left it.

She touched her favorite rose-colored bedspread that covered the cherry four-post bed. Nearby was the cherry table and the well-worn upholstered chair where she spent many a time reading in the evenings. The same cream-colored carpet sat in the center of the room, while the fireplace faced the bed. The heavy drapes, wide open, allowed the sun's rays to coat the chamber with a golden hue.

Helena stepped to the window and gazed at the beautiful garden with its rows of manicured roses. That familiar cozy feeling enveloped her as she pulled off her hat and sat on the bed. Then she remembered Papa's letter.

With a single-minded purpose, Helena ripped open the seal and read:

15 June, 1837

My dearest Helena,

I hope my letter will have arrived on or near your nineteenth birthday. How time flies! I still remember when you were a child, playing with your toys. I wish that I had been there to celebrate it with you. Three months ago, when I came to the village of Petri, near Nemea, my intention was to nurse your ailing Grandfather Nickos back to health, and then return home. Right before he died, he asked that I continue his efforts to rebuild his home. He had been digging the east side of the foundation. I agreed, and felt that your mother would want this also. Therefore, I hired twenty workers to help me dig the foundation. Progress is slow because of all the rocks and the heat.

Apparently, your grandfather had also begun digging part of that west section and had covered the hole. He was too ill to remember to tell me about it. After discovering it, I had a few workers help clean the area.

Just as importantly, a few days ago, after all the workers left for the day, I stumbled on a discovery of immense value in the west corner. After making my discovery, I took a few treasures and gave one (gold cup) to the archaeological authorities in Athens (though I have not given them all the details). I plan to return for more, but could trust no one here to help me.

I wonder whether I have stumbled on an important site, like a tomb or a palace, that may be linked to Homer's Iliad, where kingdoms like Agamemnon's and Dedemas's did exist, and wealthy vessels and jewels were housed in palaces and royal tombs. But I need not ramble on. Time will tell. I have signed the necessary papers to convert the property to my name. I also want you to come here and help me. If all goes well, we will become exceedingly rich.

However, as I write to you, dark forces have already stolen the precious treasures that I had stored in the cottage two days ago. They stole them while I slept during the night. I am having difficulty retrieving them. My inquiries have produced no results; either they don't know about them, or have decided not to tell me the truth. As a result, I have had to let go my workers because I do not trust them.

I understand that antiquities shops in Athens send their scouts around the region, renting land just to excavate and procure items. No rules are in place for such crimes. Therefore, chaos reigns. Those stolen pieces may already have left the country.

Meanwhile, I have been feeling unusually ill and weak these past two days, so I am writing to you from my simple bed in your grandfather's humble cottage. Please do not reply, since we have no postal service here. You will need to contact Mr. Avery to arrange for travel to Greece. I plan on going to Athens for supplies, and will notify you from down there, where we can meet.

> *Your loving father*
> *William Cadfield*

Helena was excited about her father's discovery and sensed that he was flustered and perturbed about the stolen treasures. She reread the letter, feeling elated about the idea of joining him in Greece and excavating for treasures. It had always been her dream to go with Papa on his archaeological digs.

As she went to fold the letter, she noticed some thick scribbling at the bottom of it, written in Greek. Helena's fine brows furrowed, as she tried to decipher their meaning. Her heartbeat quickened. She sensed that something was not right. She slowly translated it aloud.

"Dr. Cadfield was ill and I found him with this letter in his hand. He did not have time to send it. I felt it my duty to mail it to you.

> *We buried him today.*
> *May his memory be eternal."*
> *+ Elder James*

Helena's heart skipped a beat as the words sunk in. Her eyes grew wide and her lips trembled. She gave out a hoarse, painful cry and sank into the bed, fainting. In that darkest moment of her young life, in that black abyss of the never land, she dreamed this fateful dream:

> *Helena strolled on a ridge of a mountain, gazing at the breathtaking scenery. She wore a long, white dress. Her hair flowed freely around her. The sky was a sea of blue and the sun's brilliant rays warmed her soul. Resting under the shade of a fig tree, she picked the fragrant mint and white yarrow that surrounded her. The peaceful moment vanished when the ground shook mightily beneath her feet, and the earth cracked wide open. Helena shouted in fear. An ancient Greek palace thrust itself through the opening, its white columns reaching toward the sky. Under the arched entrance appeared her father, gesturing to her. She felt happy as she went to greet him. Then he disappeared and in his place stood a young, mysterious looking man.*
>   *"Helen," he said, extending his arm. "Helen." He was strikingly handsome and his voice was deep and resonated in her soul, yet she felt apprehensive. Why did he call her Helen? Her name was Helena. Where was her father? She did not want to go with this man.*
>   *He walked toward her and she screamed.*

"Miss Helena. Miss Helena."

Helena's eyes fluttered open. In the darkness of the room, a lighted candle wove its way toward her as if floating in air. Helena's breath caught in her throat when the candle was thrust in her face, followed by a black, crusty face that drooled. The whites of its eyes were bloodshot. It opened its mouth. Helena screamed.

The face screamed back, revealing a toothless mouth.

This screaming match brought in the housekeeper, who stood in the doorway holding candles and wearing her night robe and cap.

"What's going on here?" Mrs. Rotcliffe demanded. She marched into the bedroom and lifted her candle. "Is everything all right with Miss Helena?"

"Yes, yes, Mrs. Rotcliffe. Miss Helena had a bad dream," the black face announced in a high-pitched voice. "Could you light my candle, dear? Miss Helena blew mine out."

Helena stared as Mrs. Rotcliffe lit the candle of the owner of the black face, who happened to be Nana, looking tiny in that oversized robe and nightcap.

"*Yeeaaoo!*" Mrs. Rotcliffe exclaimed when she saw Nana's face. "No wonder Miss Helena's had a fright. Ye left that mud on yer face agin, haven't ye? Think it'd make yer skin younger."

Nana smiled sheepishly. "And what's it to you? Wouldn't hurt you none to use some."

"Well, I never!"

"Please, please," Helena said, trying to placate the two older women. Those two women always got on each other's nerves. "Everything is fine. I must have fallen asleep and had a dream. You may return to your rooms."

Mrs. Rotcliffe flounced out of the room in a huff.

Nana remained behind. "I came by earlier, but you had fallen asleep. When I heard your yelling, Miss Helena, I came down here as fast as I could. Looks like you had a bad dream."

Helena shut her eyes. "Nana, I saw Papa standing inside some structure. Then he disappeared." She rubbed her eyes.

"Tsk, tsk, my poor girl. Not good that your father disappeared. That is how it is sometimes. It vanishes when it gets interesting." Nana moved slowly toward the window and peered outside at the darkness. "It's almost dawn."

Helena's hand brushed against the wrinkled, tear-stained letter on the bed, reminding her of the horrible news. "Papa has vanished, just as in my dream," she said numbly.

"Oh, don't talk nonsense. You expected your father here and were feeling lonely, and it showed up in your dream."

With trembling arms, Helena picked up the letter for her to see, but Nana had her back turned to her. "Nana, I read his letter," Helena implored. "Papa is dea-!" She choked on the last word, the tears streaming down her face.

"It's like him to be absentminded," Nana said, chatting away, not having heard her. "Who knows when your father will finish the house in Greece? He loved your mother, I always said. He wants to fix the house because it reminds him of her. Too bad she died so young."

"Papa is dead!" Helena shrieked.

"Dead?" Nana turned and stared with her mouth open.

"He died, alone in his room, while writing this letter. The priest who buried him wrote on it to let us know." Helena covered her face with her hands, sobbing.

Nana rushed to embrace her. "My poor, poor Helena."

CHAPTER 2

2 July, 1837

Two days later, news of Dr. William Cadfield's death appeared in the newspaper, with a long list of his academic credentials and accomplishments, including the medical papers he wrote.

A strip of black crape dangled over the front door knocker of Cadfield House. Black crape even draped the mantles and picture frames, as well as the mirrors.

Soon a steady stream of people entered Cadfield House to pay their condolences. On that first morning of visitors, Nana was there to greet them. When Helena did not appear, Nana excused herself and hurried to her room. She found Helena in bed, dressed in her nightclothes and weeping.

Nana hugged her. "My dear, we have callers and they are asking for you."

"I don't want to see anyone," Helena said, sniffling. "Besides, I don't want to wear that smelly, black dress. It reeks of death."

Nana handed her a clean handkerchief. "Don't be silly, dear. The smell comes from those chemicals they treat it with. You'll only wear it when we have guests."

"I don't want to wear it," Helena complained, as she wiped the tears from her red eyes and dabbed her nose with the handkerchief. "I want to stay in bed."

"Look at you, thinking about yourself, while the whole staff here has been working hard for you."

Helena's eyes opened wide. "What have they been doing?"

Nana told her about Mrs. Rotcliffe scrubbing and cleaning the house, and waxing all the wood floors, while Jon put all the black drapes on the windows. "Mrs. Rotcliffe and I picked the darkest red roses we could find from the garden and put them in vases in the drawing room. Even Mrs. Barton prepared dainty pastries and little cakes for the guests."

"They're not black, too," Helena said crossly.

"Oh, no, no, they're made of cocoa," Nana replied, appearing flustered. "Anyway, your father would want you to serve tea when he wasn't around, and he wouldn't want you to stop now, would he?"

Helena was silent, knowing that Nana was right.

"Oh, I almost forgot to tell you, three men who knew your father are downstairs to see you," Nana said, beaming, "including Dr. Allan Murphy."

Helena sat up, her heart thumping wildly. "He's here?"

"Yes, and he is a physician now and has his own practice."

"All right," Helena said, sitting up eagerly. "Could you see to the china and the tea? I'll be down in a few minutes."

After Nana left, Helena's mind drifted to Dr. Murphy. She wondered what he looked like, and wished it were like old times, when he'd visit her father. *But Papa is no longer here.* It was different without him.

The tears poured down her face. How will she control her tears in front of these distinguished guests? *Didn't they teach you anything at the French boarding school?*

Sniffling, she removed the black, crape dress out of the closet and the matching black bonnet with veil. After putting on the starchy garment, Helena went to the mirror. She grimaced at her reflection and tugged at the snug collar. Her eyes appeared red and puffy from crying, and her face was pale. She splashed her face with cold water from the basin. Feeling refreshed, she dried her face, pinching it to give it color.

Next, Helena pulled up her long strands of hair, securing them under the black bonnet with hairpins, and then straightened the veil in the back. Sprinkling some rosewater on her clothing, she went downstairs.

Helena stopped at the entrance of the drawing room. The black drapes on the windows gave the room a somber feel, and her first impulse was to sweep them wide open, but she refrained, not wanting to attract attention. She saw Nana chatting away as she prepared the tea service, positioning the fine china cups and saucers on the tea table, and rattling a few cups as she talked.

Helena recognized Dr. Hood and Dr. Blakely, two of Papa's older colleagues, seated on the sofa with their backs to her. She fondly relived the old times when they visited her father and had lively discussions, while she sat nearby, a wide-eyed child, listening to them.

A burst of joy coursed through her when she spied Dr. Murphy seated across from the two older men. The boyish look that she remembered well had vanished, replaced by a lean face and full jaw. He looked up solemnly as she entered the room, but did not show signs of recognition.

"She received a letter from Dr. Cadfield," Nana was saying to the men. She handed Dr. Hood a cup of tea. "He complained of not feeling well. The words on the bottom of the letter, written in Greek, alerted her that he had died."

"I wonder about his illness," Dr. Hood said. His large head was bald, with wisps of white hair clinging on the back. With trembling hand, he lifted the cup of tea to his mouth. Much of the dark brew spilled on the carpet.

Nana rushed to clean the mess. He mumbled his apologies.

Helena greeted the men, curtsying with as much composure as she could find. They arose and bowed together, expressing their condolences. Dr. Murphy's face changed into something close to admiration as he gazed at her. They waited until she was seated before returning to their seats.

"Could you tell us more, Miss Cadfield, about what happened to your father? Did he say what his illness was? Did he have any symptoms?" Dr. Hood asked.

Helena relayed the news.

"Was there any confirmation of his death by any authorities?" Dr. Blakely asked.

Helena shook her head. "No. I plan to check with the attorney to verify his death. The Greek priest who signed the letter wrote that he buried him. I would assume that he was speaking the truth."

"You understood cursive Greek?" Dr. Hood asked.

"Yes," she replied firmly. She noticed the doubt creeping into his eyes. "My father spent many hours teaching me Greek when I was young. I was sure of what I read and it was signed by a Greek priest, for there was a cross next to his name."

The conversation lapsed into a momentary lull. Helena glanced at Dr. Murphy who had been quietly studying her all this time.

He coughed slightly. "Dr. Hood, I can testify that Miss Cadfield was a good student of the Greek language, for I happened to witness one of her lessons with Dr. Cadfield. She could read and write Greek remarkably well."

Helena smiled at Dr. Murphy. "Thank you."

Mrs. Barton bustled into the room, carrying a large tray of pastries and cakes, looking proud of her delicate creations. "Here ye are with some nice pastries." She placed the tray on the serving table in front of them and left.

Nana refilled their cups with hot tea while Helena served the concoctions, mindful of her position as the lady of the house. She could feel Dr. Murphy's eyes on her.

After some time, the two older men arose and politely took their leave, while Helena saw them to the door. After Helena bid them a "good day," she returned to the parlor.

Dr. Murphy rose from his seat.

He regarded her attentively. "I am pleased to see that you have grown into a handsome young lady," he said.

Helena blushed at his words, feeling pleased. "Coming from you, Dr. Murphy, I expected a teasing remark, and not a compliment."

His face turned red. "You are referring to when I used to tease you and pull your braids. Please forgive me, but we were both much younger then."

"You are forgiven," she teased.

"There is something I have much interest in and had been meaning to ask Dr. Cadfield about it. I wonder whether you would know the answer."

"Yes?"

"Where has he kept the human bones he discovered in Turkey last summer? He had promised to show them to me."

Nana's sharp gasp interrupted their conversation, followed by a loud rattling of cups.

Startled by Dr. Murphy's untimely request and Nana's response, Helena furrowed her brows, trying to recall the location of the bones.

"I remember he wrote to me about them. He used them in his anatomy classes to compare them with the bones of the modern-day cadavers, showing the differences in their nutrition. He had labeled them so one could tell them apart."

Nana collapsed in a faint. Dr. Murphy grabbed a bottle of smelling salts from his bag and revived her with them.

"I had forgotten how sensitive she was to these topics," Helena explained to him.

After making certain that Nana was all right, Dr. Murphy thanked Helena for the information about the bones, bowed, and left.

* * *

For several days, Cadfield House hummed with the stream of callers. Many people paid their respects and spoke with her, recalling all the intimate details of how Dr. Cadfield had treated them. "How are we going to get along without him?" they asked her, shaking their heads.

Their neighbors, the Cramers and the Barleys, visited. Also, the elderly tenants who had lived in the cottages all their lives, and the newly arrived young vicar. There was also the blacksmith, the farmers and merchants, and several other local people that Helena had never heard of. Even the Pickets, the couple she met on the coach ride, came to pay their respects.

The visitors kept Helena busy and distracted for a while, as she served them tea and pastries. Inevitably, the conversation shifted toward the morbid topic of her father's death and Helena would respond politely, almost stoically, to their intrusive questions. Only in the privacy of her room did she release her pent-up tears, mourning her loss in the bosom of her soft pillow.

When the visitors had stopped coming and Cadfield House became quiet again, Helena's attentions shifted to Dr. Murphy. He had changed from being boyishly exuberant into a more reserved man, which made it hard for her to warm up to him. She must remember that he was there because her father had died, and not because he was paying her a social visit.

Yet he complimented me on my appearance.

She wondered when she would see him again.

At night while in bed, Helena would think about the note from the priest at the bottom of the letter, hoping it had all been a mistake. She would picture the attorney shaking his head, saying that the letter was not enough proof of her father's death. Other times, she would see her father coming back to her, laughing and saying that everything was all right, and that the priest had mistaken him for someone else.

* * *

A couple of weeks later, Helena had a meeting with Mr. Avery, their attorney, who had an office in town. Having never dealt with him before, she did not know what to expect. He was a short, thin man with a stern face and spectacles perched on his long nose. She showed him her father's last letter and the writing at the bottom of the letter.

He gave her a long, searching look. "I regret to inform you that your father did not leave a will."

Helena was stunned. "Are you sure about this? He was a methodical person, always preparing ahead."

"If he did, I am not aware of it," he said. "In any case, this letter that you have presented me is inadequate proof of his death. I cannot proceed without a legal document."

Helena had already thought about it. "Could you send papers requesting verification of his death in Greece?" she asked.

He nodded. "I could do that, but I will need the location of his death. Based on past experience, from another client whose husband died in Greece, I would need to contact the local church for records of his death. What is the name of the village where your father died?"

"I believe it is called Petri."

"Petri?" he asked, appearing skeptical. "Never heard of it."

"It's near Nemea, in the vicinity of Corinth."

Mr. Avery scribbled the names down on a piece of paper. He arose. "I will let you know when I receive any news. Good-day, Miss Cadfield."

His cold dismissal left Helena feeling numb. Once settled in the carriage, she reflected on their conversation. She could not help feeling forlorn at the dismal news that her father did not leave her a will. How could Papa be so irresponsible in his duties toward her? What should she do?

CHAPTER 3

30 July, 1837

Two weeks later, Helena received a visit from the attorney. They sat in the parlor. She served tea, feeling nervous, while he shuffled through his documents.

Mr. Avery lifted a piece of paper and his black, beady eyes stared at it, while his glasses slid down his long nose.

"Ah, here we are," he said. His lips formed a thin line as he watched her. "Miss Cadfield, if you are ready, I'd like to proceed with this. I don't have all day."

Helena finished pouring the tea and placed the little cakes in front of him, knowing in her heart what the news was, but not wanting to face it.

She sat down and folded her hands on her lap. "Yes?" she asked shakily.

"I have here a document that verifies the death of your father. It came from Agios Giorgios, the local church of Nemea, near Corinth. The local priest's signature rendered it an official document. I had to use the services of a translator. That is the reason for the other paper. It will cost you more." He handed her the papers.

Helena trembled as she took them. One was in original Greek and the other one was its translation in English. She stared wistfully at her father's name and the date of his death written in black ink. She had somehow hoped he had not died, that it had been a mistake, but could not deny his death any longer. Her heart squeezed a few tears as she handed the papers back to him solemnly.

"I must contact Mr. Weldon, your father's cousin and the next heir in line to the Cadfield estate." He put the papers back in the black binder. "You do know, Miss Cadfield, what this means. Cadfield House and everything in it now belongs to Mr. Weldon. You will be at his mercy."

Helena's stomach heaved and nausea threatened to overcome her as she recalled scenes from her childhood when they visited Mr. Weldon and his family in London. He was the opposite of her father, overweight and a glutton, loving his mutton and drink, and prone to gambling. She wondered once more what would happen to her.

"And now, for the matter of paying for my services." Mr. Avery picked up a piece of paper and studied it. "The total amount comes to forty-three guineas, which also includes the amount your father owed me and the Greek document, and its translation."

Helena sucked in her breath at the high numbers. Never having done business with an attorney before, she did not know that he would be so expensive to deal with. It took her a moment to regain her composure. "Are there funds in my father's account to handle this outrageous cost?"

A frown creased Mr. Avery's face. "I regret to inform you, Miss Cadfield, that there are no funds left in his account. Dr. Cadfield did not pay me these past few months. Even worse, he had accumulated debts from his latest trips, which he expected me to settle. If I am not paid, then you will need to find another attorney to take care of your father's affairs."

Helena's hands became clammy and her throat closed tight. She could not breathe. "My father was in debt?"

"Yes."

As far back as she could remember there had been money by which to live comfortably. She had often wondered about the cost of her expensive Parisian school and the fancy clothing she wore there, and how much the house in Greece would cost her father to rebuild, but he had never indulged her that information.

"Forty-three guineas?" she asked, swallowing the bile that had risen to her mouth.

Mr. Avery coughed slightly. "I will also need to notify Mr. Weldon and prepare the necessary papers. That brings it to a total of fifty guineas."

Helena's body trembled with rage and her hands clutched her chair. She felt like shouting, "I shouldn't have to pay for you to notify Mr. Weldon. I think that should be his responsibility." Instead, she remained silent, just like they taught her at boarding school.

The sixty guineas that she had saved over the years from her father's monetary gifts had provided her a sense of security. She had lost her father, and now she was losing most of her savings. Her shoulders slumped forward as she was engulfed in a miserable sea of despair.

"I will go and fetch it," she whispered.

Helena returned with the money and paid him for his service. She had only ten guineas left to her name, but at least she did not owe him anything.

Mr. Avery's stern face softened a bit as he took the money.

The urgency from her father's letter regarding the discovery he had found in Greece was uppermost in her mind. The desire to go to Greece was even greater.

"Mr. Avery, I was wondering, after everything is settled, if any funds would be available for me to travel to Greece?"

"Impossible," Mr. Avery said, and shook his head. "All his assets are frozen until the legalities are straightened out with Mr. Weldon. I doubt if there will be anything left for you."

After he left, Helena's composure crumbled and she fled to her room in a torrent of tears. She stayed there for the rest of the day, feeling miserable and forlorn. Even when Nana visited her, she could not shake off her depressed state.

Several days later, Helena received a letter from Mr. Weldon. He was planning to arrive in two weeks with his wife and young son to Cadfield House. Helena paced the room feeling agitated, holding the letter in her hand. She was not ready for this change. She could not picture herself in the same house with these people. The security she once felt was vanishing, leaving a void in its place that threatened to swallow her up.

* * *

When the weather was fair, Helena would ride her horse, Tiger, out of the city, passing through green pastures and thinking about things. One day as she was riding, she thought about how she was going to find the money to help defray the mounting costs of managing Cadfield House. Her ten guineas had dwindled quickly after she paid off some of her father's overdue bills.

With five horses in the stable, of which three had been birthday gifts from her father, they could not afford to keep them all. Tiger was her favorite, and she could not see herself selling him. In a short time,

Helena found a buyer for two of the horses, which brought in enough money to manage the household's expenses until the Weldons' arrival.

One rainy day, Helena sat in her father's favorite chair in the library, rereading his last letter. The library was dark, except for the lantern next to her, and filled with the musty smell of books. She took off her shoes and wiggled her stockinged feet on the soft, maroon carpet, something that she always did when she was in deep thought.

She tried to remember the discussions she had with her father about Homer. She recalled how he had said that in Greece, the children read Homer's writings from a young age. He talked often about *The Iliad* in relation to archaeological digs that he wanted to conduct in Greece. He did not have a chance to find out the truth, not now. She arose and paced the room, her mind racing,

Could it be that Papa, such an educated and well-read man, believed that Homer's fantastic epic poem was true? True enough to link his world to our world? Was he chasing dreams? Maybe by finding the treasures on the property in Greece, it may have convinced him that there was some link to the ancient past, some truth to Homer's story.

A strong gust of wind interrupted her thoughts, rattling the loose window and pushing the pane open, releasing torrents of rain into the library. Helena ran to the window, wrestling with it and the raging wind, pulling it back to its position and securing it tightly. She glanced around the library, making sure the gale had not jostled anything out of place, and then wiped the rain from her face and clothing.

Trying not to be distracted, Helena took the lantern with her and perused the bookshelves. She knew that her father owned at least seven different copies of *The Iliad* and three old copies of the *Odyssey*, from different periods, translated by different authors. Unable to find them, she glanced around the room, wondering where he placed them.

Many leather-bound volumes that her father had attained over the years from his trips to Egypt, Turkey, and Greece were stacked in piles on top of his mahogany desk and under it, while others were perched precariously on the fireplace mantle.

Helena had tried once to organize her father's library, but he reprimanded her upon returning home from a trip and not finding what he was looking for. What appeared to her as chaotic clutter was what her father called "organized sections." Since then, she had left everything where it was.

After much effort, Helena found a copy of *The Iliad*. She turned the pages carefully, for they were crumbling along the edges. She read about the godlike Achilles, the sons of Atreus, the fierce King Agammemnon and his brother Meneleus. She read about the preparation of their ships for the battle against Troy in order to get beautiful Helen back. Although Homer's writing was not new to her, this translated version was. She read about goddesses that influenced people's decisions and made them do irrational acts, and she began to have doubts about what she was reading. How could there be any truth to this story when goddesses were involved? Goddesses did not exist in her monotheistic world. They existed only in mythology.

Another gust of wind whined loudly, accompanied by the angry rattling of the windows, piercing her concentration. She looked up, knowing exactly where to find that infamous crack on the side of the window that allowed the wind through. She had told her father many times to have it fixed, but he never got around to it. It became quiet again, except for the steady tapping of the rain against the windowpanes.

Helena pulled on a stray lock of hair, coiling it around her finger, engrossed in Helen and Paris of Troy's story. How could it be that all these men were fighting because of Helen? She thought about Helen's beauty causing men to desire her all her life, and found it difficult to believe that they wanted her only because she was beautiful.

Pretty women abounded in history. Some were sacrificed, like Agamemnon's daughter, Iphigenia, so that the ships could travel to Troy.

Helen's beauty was not the only desirable prize for this Trojan War to have taken place, thought Helena. She had much wealth and whoever won her, gained not only her, but power. Could the treasures that Papa found be linked somehow to Helen and Paris? When they escaped the palace of King Meneleus, they took the treasures with them.

Intrigued, Helena continued her reading. It dawned on her that Homer not only wrote about the idealized human figure, but also applied shameful, immoral acts to the Greeks. Her father once told her that the philosopher, Xenophanes, wrote that Homer tended to ascribe to the gods all shameful and disgraceful deeds.

She shut the book with a resounding smack. Her sensitivities could only handle so much of Homer in one day. She arose and began to pace the room.

Another thought entered her mind. Homer's adventurous tales, filled with warring themes and violent battle scenes, were intended only for male readers and not for women. She wondered how different the story would have been if written by a woman. Maybe it would have been filled with nurturing themes and love.

A sliver of light landed on Helena's lap, pulling her out of her reflective mood. Eager to get a glimpse of the afternoon sun, she went and opened the window. The storm had passed as quickly as it came, having swept the clouds away. It was remarkably quiet. She inhaled deeply, enjoying the earthy scent that permeated the air.

Her mind shifted to her boarding school roommate, Emily, whose letter she received yesterday. Emily proudly announced that she was engaged to Henrie, and confided her love and admiration for him. Helena felt happy for her, recalling how Emily increasingly spent her free time with Henrie those last months before graduation. Within weeks of meeting Henrie, Emily's personality had changed from a quiet, reserved girl to a glowing, confident and sometimes outspoken young woman. Emily would soon become a wife, loving someone and being loved.

Several young men had tried to court Helena in Paris, but she found them too shallow and foppish. She thought about Dr. Murphy and the compliment he gave her the day he came to pay his condolences for Papa, but there had been no other visit from him. She gazed out the window sadly, wondering if her fate was to become a spinster, chasing dreams and relying on family to support her.

The sun's rays filtered through the leaves of the oak trees that lined the side of the garden, yet there were no sounds of birds chirping, no rustling, no sign of life. Even the rose bushes and flowers in the garden were bowing their heads, as if they had been weeping. She sighed. Maybe she should not have been so cold and proud toward the young Parisian men after all.

A timid knock on the door had Helena scrambling to put her shoes back on. "Come in."

CHAPTER 4

Helena looked up as the door to the library slowly opened. Nana's head peeked through. Helena smiled, glad to see her. Nana had a knack for making her feel better.

"I thought I would find you here," Nana said, humming a tune that was familiarly off-key, trying to enter the library, wearing an outdated purple silk dress tucked in at the waist and expanded at the bottom. She turned one way and then another, and finally managed to squeeze through the door sideways. She bounced her way forward, almost tripping, exposing her hoop and generous layers of garments beneath the dress. She wore an equally ancient hat with drooping feathers.

Helena had seen her riffling through her trunk the other day, trying on her old clothing and reminiscing about the past. She suppressed a giggle. "Nana, are you going to a masquerade ball?"

"How did you guess, dear? I know we are still in mourning for your poor father, but my Jenny insisted that I attend her ball, saying that it is all right since I am not related to your father, although I felt like a mother to him. When Jenny speaks her mind, how can I not listen?" Nana gave her an apologetic look.

Helena pushed aside the gnawing emptiness that threatened to overcome her. With Nana gone, she wouldn't have anyone to talk to. Nana's daughter, Jenny, was a tall, brash woman, and her husband, Milton, was small and meek. They lived in Yorkshire, several hours away, and Nana visited once or twice a year. Although it was time for one of those visits, Helena didn't want her to go. *Stop being so selfish.*

"The ball is tonight?"

"Yes, my dear." As Nana nodded, the orange, drooping feathers from her hat tickled her nose. "I was waiting for the rain to stop, and, and, *Aaachooo!*" She put her hand in her pocket, sniffling. "I thought I had a handkerchief in here."

Helena handed her a clean handkerchief from her pocket.

After blowing loudly into the handkerchief, Nana folded it and gave it back to her. "Thank you, my dear."

Helena tried to remain calm and composed as she slowly took the handkerchief.

Nana's hand gripped hers.

"I hate leaving you alone like this," Nana said, fretting.

Helena knew that if she showed any sign of weakness, Nana would find an excuse to stay. She managed a smile. "I think the trip will do you good, Nana."

"Please don't stay up late reading. You know how bad it can be for your eyes, and remember to shut your window at night, so you don't catch a cold." Nana's voice trembled.

"Don't worry," Helena said, hugging her tightly and trying to refrain from crying. "I will be fine."

Nana pecked her on the cheek. "I must be off, then, or else I'll never hear the end of it. My Jenny has also invited Mr. Weatherspoon, an old bachelor friend of the family. You know he never married. He usually dresses up in his old naval uniform for these occasions which makes him look quite distinguished."

Nana's sheepish grin reminded Helena of the long-standing fondness that she had for Mr. Weatherspoon.

After Nana left, Helena tucked Homer's *Iliad* under her arm and left for her room. There was something comforting about this book. *Maybe because it had belonged to Father and that was all that was left from him.*

After resting, she dressed for dinner and sat in front of the mirror, gazing into her solemn, blue eyes. The tears slowly poured down her face. She combed her long, honey colored tresses, wondering once more, what was to become of her.

The next day, as Helena was reading in the library, someone knocked on the door. It was Mrs. Rotcliffe.

"Mr. Weldon and his family have arrived, miss."

Helena met them downstairs. They had been standing awkwardly in the hall waiting for her. Mr. Weldon was dressed in black, and so were his wife, Mrs. Lucinda Weldon and son, Mr. Willy. Helena greeted them civilly.

Mr. Weldon had not aged well. Too much food and drink had turned him into a stocky man with a red bulbous nose and large belly. A fashionable dress helped shape Mrs. Weldon's short, plump figure, while several jeweled necklaces adorned her large bosom. Their son was short for his nine years and stocky, with freckled face and unruly red hair.

"My, you have grown into a fine young woman. I almost did not recognize you," Mr. Weldon said, grinning and revealing wide gaps between his motley-colored teeth.

"Thank you," Helena said politely. A loud crash startled her. She turned and saw Willy grinning impishly at her, while scattered shards of a vase surrounded him on the floor.

Mr. Weldon bounded toward Willy and soundly pinched his ear.

"Ow!"

"You must keep your hands to yourself. Remember what I told you about knocking down vases. It costs us money."

"Yes, Father," Willy said, rubbing his reddened ear.

They moved out of the path of Mrs. Rotcliffe who was bearing down on them with her broom. It looked as if she was going to give Mister Willy a swat, but instead she gave him a look that could wither a rose, and went about sweeping up the vase.

"Let's not forget, Mr. Weldon, that Willy isn't the only child who has done damage," Mrs. Weldon said tightly. "I remember the visit that Miss Cadfield paid us with her father. She was about Willy's age, and a skinny little thing and always tripping over her feet and crashing into things. She must have broken at least two of our precious vases."

Helena blinked in surprise. She did not remember breaking any vases at their home.

"You must be tired from your trip," Helena said, feeling suddenly weary. "Dinner will be served at seven in the dining room." She directed the servants to take them to their rooms.

The next day, during breakfast, Mr. Weldon spoke to Helena. "As you know, it is my duty as the rightful heir to procure the property, since your father had no sons."

"I am aware of that, Mr. Weldon," Helena replied flatly. "Everything here is yours."

Mr. Weldon quickly assumed authority over Cadfield House with the aid of his wife.

The Weldons consumed Helena's every moment as they interrogated her about the silver, household inventory, livestock and servants. They acted as if they had every right to acquire everything in the house and on its premises, including her father's books that she had grown up loving and reading. Helena found herself spending more time in her room, feeling miserable and lonely. With Nana gone, she had no one to confide in.

One day as she walked down the hallway, someone jumped out from the corner, shouting, "Boo!"

Helena screamed, and then saw Willy standing there, smirking at her. She stared at him, feeling perplexed. Everyone came running to her aid.

"Naughty boy," Mrs. Barton said, shaking a finger at him. "If you were my son, I'd take you over my--"

"Now, now, Mrs. Barton," Helena said, having recovered quickly. She did not want Mrs. Barton getting into trouble for scolding the boy. Left to his own devices, and not having anyone to play with, this was probably Willy's way of getting attention. She went to him and patted his head. "He is only a boy."

He looked at her with a puzzled look.

"Would you like a chance to ride my horse, Tiger?" Helena asked him.

Willy's eyes became wide. "Tiger? Oh, that would be grand!"

"Right after breakfast. I promise."

The next day, Helena took Willy to the stable and helped him mount Tiger. She rode with him through the meadows and fields. She was pleased that Tiger accommodated the boy, but then he jabbed the horse with his shoe. "I want to go faster!"

Before Helena could reply, Tiger galloped ahead and when Helena caught up with them, she saw that Willy's face had turned white from fear and he was clutching the rein tightly.

Helena scolded him. "If you want to ride Tiger, then you shouldn't be pushing him hard. You might have fallen and hurt yourself."

The next day, Willy and Helena rode again together. Helena was pleased to see Willy handling Tiger more carefully.

A few days later, Mrs. Weldon entered the library while Helena was reading a book, and began clearing the desk of its books.

"Look at this mess," Mrs. Weldon said, muttering to herself and huffing, as she bent under the desk. She pulled out a stack of books and plopped them on the desk.

Helena coughed politely, making her presence known.

Mrs. Weldon turned around. There were blotches on her cheeks. "Oh, Miss Cadfield, I didn't see you." She brushed back her red, disheveled hair, appearing upset.

"Mrs. Weldon, are you looking for something?"

"These books, this mess will not do. We cannot invite visitors here with all this clutter. Why hasn't the housekeeper, what's-her-name, done anything about this?"

"Papa wanted them there," Helena said slowly, trying not to become upset. "Every book has its place. He never liked it when I moved his books."

"Maybe your father wanted them that way, but he is no longer here. I prefer the library neat and tidy, and so does Mr. Weldon."

"Very well. I will call Mrs. Rotcliffe to assist you," Helena said tightly.

The next day, when Helena entered the library, she found the table bare of books and polished, and the fireplace mantel cleared. To her dismay, the carpet where she would wiggle her toes was gone, revealing the wood floor, which creaked as she walked across the room. Her fears grew when she spied large gaps in the bookshelves. Missing were the rare books by Homer, several archaeological books, and books on philosophy and other subjects. She searched frantically for them, but could not find them.

At dinner, Helena asked Mrs. Weldon about the whereabouts of her father's rare books.

Mrs. Weldon shrugged her shoulders, waving her arm in the air. "I sold them to a bookseller. There were too many books. I felt that they would have better use where they are now," she replied.

Helena placed her fork down. She felt sick to her stomach. The books were all that were left of her father. Several of them were rare and irreplaceable. "Could you tell me the name of the bookseller that you did business with?"

Mrs. Weldon appeared surprised. "Why, I wrote it down somewhere."

"Even if you wanted to buy them back, you couldn't afford them," Willy said, with a derisive grin. "He paid Mama a lot-"

"Willy, that's enough," Mr. Weldon said sharply.

Helena excused herself, complaining of a headache, and then fled to her bedroom. She stayed there the rest of the evening, weeping.

Papa's collection of rare books was his passion. He had spent many years during his travels trying to locate these different books by Homer. She had assumed that Mr. and Mrs. Weldon would not want them and that they would be hers. How naïve she had been. She mourned that evening as though she had lost a loved one. Thankfully, she had that one book of Homer's still in her room. She decided not to tell the Weldons about it. They would sell it like they did the others.

The next day, when Helena visited the library, she stumbled on a meeting that Mr. Weldon was having with some men dressed in business suits. As she entered the room, their heated discussion stopped.

Mr. Weldon appeared upset. "Pray leave us, Miss Cadfield. We are having an important meeting," he snapped.

Feeling embarrassed, Helena excused herself and fled the room. Later, she thought about the meeting. The drawing room was the usual place to meet callers. It was a public place, but the library was closed off and private. She wondered if these men were debt collectors. The library was no longer her protected haven.

A week after the Weldons' arrival, Mrs. Barton gave Helena a letter from Nana.

"Would you mind telling us her news, Miss Cadfield?" Mrs. Barton asked Helena.

"I'd be happy to."

"Please come into the kitchen and tell us all about it. I don't want the Weldons listening in," Mrs. Barton said.

The staff joined Helena in the kitchen, and she read the letter and relayed its contents to them. "Nana enjoyed the masquerade ball, but had tripped on her dress while dancing with Mr. Weatherspoon and sprained her ankle."

There were exclamations from everyone.

"It seems she's all right, because Mr. Weatherspoon visits her daily to see how she is doing," Helena continued. "Jenny's oldest daughter is pregnant with her first child and she insists that Nana stay with her, saying she could become her nanny. Nana says she is not comfortable with the Weldons and feels this is the best course for her to take."

"Ah, she was complaining about the Weldons, wasn't she?" Mrs. Rotcliffe said knowingly.

"Nana invites every one of you to visit them in Yorkshire when you have a chance," Helena said, finishing reading the letter.

"I don't think her Jenny's going to like having us all up there," Mrs. Barton said, and everyone laughed.

Dinner became an extravagant affair, with much more food on the table than Helena had ever remembered. She heard Mrs. Barton grumbling about needing more help for the cooking.

Helena was relieved to learn that the staff would remain at Cadfield House. One evening, she overheard the servants saying, "Mr. Weldon had been renting in London, having gambled his house off and was in debt because of his gambling tendencies. Had to let go all their servants, I heard. Now look at them, they can't wait to get their hands on everything. They sold those books and the carpet from the library. Even some silverware is missing."

Helena began spending more time outdoors, dressed in her old garments, desperately trying to find peace. At first, she had ridden alongside Willy, but when Mr. Weldon started joining them on their excursions, she stopped riding. She settled for walking on the extensive grounds or spending time in the garden, where it was quiet except for the buzzing of the bees. A fountain sat in the center of the garden and near it stood a bench and a couple of statues. Time was nonexistent here, and she could rest her weary soul, nurtured by nature.

Here, Willy could not pounce at her from behind doors. He scared Mrs. Rotcliffe several times, and Mrs. Barton threatened him with a whack on the head if he ever did it again to her. He went bawling to his father about it, and Mr. Weldon ended up reprimanding Mrs. Barton, who was not happy at all. She grumbled all day after that episode.

Sometimes Willy would seek Helena out and she would talk with him about her father's expeditions and work. She would tell him stories and he would sit there listening wide-eyed.

He stopped pouncing from behind doors when she threatened that she would stop telling him stories. A bond had formed between them.

It seemed as if the Weldons were here to stay, but what was to become of Helena? The topic had not been brought up and she felt as if she were drifting. She needed to make a plan.

CHAPTER 5

One day, as Helena finished placing the rose clippings into her basket, ready to leave, she heard a rustling behind her. She turned toward the sound, facing the sun, thankful that her large straw hat shaded her eyes.

Her eyes quickly adjusted and she could make out the stocky frame of Mr. Weldon rambling toward her. She had never seen him in the gardens before. His face glistened with sweat, and his nose was red, showing signs that he had been drinking again.

"I thought I would find you here," he said. "Mrs. Weldon was asking for you."

"Then I will go to her," Helena said, determined not to be caught alone with Mr. Weldon. More than once she had noticed Mrs. Weldon's sharp glance if he so much as spent time with her.

"She is in no hurry. It's nice and quiet here, where we can talk. Eh?" He winked at her.

Helena eyed him suspiciously. He had taken everything that belonged to her. What else could he want?

"Let me mention, Miss Cadfield," he said, coughing lightly, "that Mrs. Weldon and I have observed that during our time here, you haven't had any gentlemen suitors calling."

Helena felt her face flush with anger. His remark felt too personal, too invasive of her privacy. She lowered her head so he could not see her face under the hat, then like a hunted rabbit, stood motionless, barely breathing. Her eyes settled on his dusty black shoes, creased with age. They were not the shoes of a wealthy man.

"Why is that?" he went on. "You are nineteen, old enough, and pretty enough. Haven't you had a coming out ball?"

"My father had promised me a coming out ball after I graduated from boarding school, but now that is impossible." Helena grabbed her basket and excused herself. She fled toward the house, not wanting to continue this uncomfortable discussion.

Helena found Mrs. Barton in the kitchen. "If you could please make rosewater from these, I would appreciate it," she told her, handing her some of the roses.

"Hmmm, what a nice scent," Mrs. Barton said, smelling them. "I'll have the rosewater made in no time, miss."

Helena entered the drawing room, intending to place the roses in the vases. She found Mrs. Weldon seated on the sofa, with her back to her. Her head of red hair was bent over as she sewed steadily.

Helena quietly carried the basket of roses to the back of the room, and began stuffing the flowers into the vases. She was still feeling perturbed by Mr. Weldon's conversation.

A cough came from the sofa.

"Ah, there you are, Miss Cadfield. I was looking for you. You seem to be disappearing on me these days," Mrs. Weldon complained. Her face was drawn, and she had the familiar red blotches, which meant she was perturbed. "Tell me, what are your plans for the future?"

"I wish to visit my mother's property in Greece," Helena replied. "I have been awaiting Mr. Avery's notification about the funds needed for the trip."

"Your mother's property in Greece?" Mrs. Weldon echoed, appearing surprised.

"Yes, she is Greek. She died when I was a child and my father took her back to Greece to bury her in the family grave. After the war, the only survivor was my grandfather. My father took possession of their property after Grandfather died. I need to claim it, for it belongs rightfully to me."

"What strange laws these Greeks have. Doesn't it rightfully go to the male heir?"

"It is different in Greece. Father said that the property belonged to my grandmother and was her dowry when she married. My mother was the only daughter. She would have been the rightful heir, but she died young, and now it belongs to me."

"Hmm," Mrs. Weldon said, wagging her head. "What with all the debts your poor father had, I doubt whether there will be any funds left for you to travel to Greece." She snickered.

Helena tensed, trying to ignore the woman's offensive remark. A thorn pricked her middle finger, drawing blood. She stopped what she was doing to remove the thorn. Successful, she pressed on the wound with her thumb until the bleeding stopped.

"I have another question to ask you. I have noticed that you have no young men calling. Why is that? You are a handsome girl."

Helena blushed, realizing that the Weldons had discussed this topic among themselves. "I have been away these three years and my father was to give me a coming out ball on my return."

"If only he knew what financial burden he has placed on our shoulders having you here."

"I was not aware that I had become a financial burden."

"Your father left no money for your care." Mrs. Weldon shook her head, her eyes flashing. "Do you realize how much it costs to clothe and feed you?"

Helena trembled with rage. *How dare she talk to me like this?* "If I am not mistaken, you have received not only my father's house, but also compensation from selling his rare books and his carpets, enough to offset feeding me." *There, she had finally spoken her mind.*

Mrs. Weldon's face turned a deep red. "You are an impudent and ungrateful girl, and we will see about that."

Helena bit her lip, trying to control her emotions. "Good day, Mrs. Weldon," she said with as much reserve as she could muster. She walked out of the room.

When Helena shut the door behind her, the tears came spilling down her face. She stayed in her room the rest of the day. She knew that her chances of living here were becoming slimmer and slimmer. She needed to become independent. But how? *By earning money.*

She wiped her tears and sat up, thinking. Should she apply for a governess position? Although she had little experience with children, she had bonded well with Willy, and had considerable knowledge from all that reading, plus the skills learned at the boarding school. Feeling hopeful, she mulled the idea in her head for quite some time.

In the middle of the night, Helena finally came to a decision.

* * *

The next morning, Helena crafted an ad for a governess position to post in the newspaper. She listed her skills. She had good penmanship, was well versed in several languages, played the piano, and had painted well enough at school to earn her high marks. That same morning, she took the carriage downtown and after inquiring around, found the newspaper building. Helena placed her ad with the clerk and paid her fee.

Later that day, Mrs. Rotcliffe came to inform her that Mr. Weldon requested that she meet him in the study. Feeling apprehensive, Helena went to him.

When she saw him seated in her father's large, comfortable chair, she choked back a cry. Instead of Papa's tall, lanky figure smoking a pipe, before her sat a bloated man with a bulging stomach.

"The reason I called for you, Miss Cadfield, is to inform you of news that involves your future. The attorney informed me this morning about the true state of affairs of your father's estate." He shook his balding head emphatically, while his fleshy lips, slightly turned down, were quivering in some secret anticipation of her reaction.

She immediately tensed.

"Since you have had no marriage propositions, and given your dire situation-"

"Dire situation?" Helena interjected. Her lips were trembling, and her heart was pounding in her throat as tears welled up in her eyes.

"Yes. I learned that my cousin William had acquired debts from his journeys, which came to a considerable sum of money."

Helena gripped the chair and sat down, for her legs threatened to buckle. The attorney had been right, she thought. "I hope I am not expected to pay them," she said bitterly.

"No, no, dear. We took care of that by selling a few items from the house. However, you must think about your future. Unfortunately, I cannot afford to have you remain here."

Helena was seething inside. She did not want to depend on Mr. Weldon for charity. *They are taking everything away from me, but not my dignity.* "I have already begun the process of seeking employment as a governess. If you know of a family needing my services, I'd appreciate you letting me know."

He coughed politely. "I will check into it."

"Thank you. I don't want to *burden* you any further."

Helena had the satisfaction of seeing Mr. Weldon's face turn red.

CHAPTER 6

That afternoon, while Helena was in her room reading and contemplating on things, Mrs. Rotcliffe paid her a visit.

"Miss Cadfield, I thought that you'd might like to know that Dr. Murphy is here, dear," she informed her.

Helena felt suddenly happy. "Please tell him I'll be right down," she sang out. *He came to see me after all.*

Feeling giddy with excitement, Helena hummed as she quickly made herself presentable. She was about to sail down the stairs and rush into the drawing room, as she used to when she was younger, but she remembered her lady-like manners. Gaining her composure, she walked slowly into the room.

Dr. Murphy sat with Mrs. Weldon on the sofa, having tea. He immediately arose when Helena entered the room. He smiled at her, and then bowed gallantly.

Helena curtsied, her heart thumping wildly. "Dr. Murphy, it's a pleasure to see you again," she said, smiling warmly.

"Miss Cadfield," he said, gazing steadily into her eyes.

"You two know each other?" Mrs. Weldon asked.

"Yes. Dr. Murphy was Father's medical student and would often visit Cadfield House."

"How nice. We called for Dr. Murphy because Willy awoke with a fever this morning," Mrs. Weldon informed Helena.

Helena swallowed her disappointment. *He came for Willy, not me.* "Is he all right, Dr. Murphy?" she asked, feeling concerned about the boy.

"We must see about getting his fever down."

"Father used to say that bedrest and liquids are the best medicine," Helena said.

"Yes, I am aware of that, Miss Cadfield. He is resting and I told Mrs. Weldon to give him plenty of liquids," he said, smiling at her.

She smiled back as he picked up his cup and sipped his tea.

"Would you care for some more tea, Dr. Murphy?" Mrs. Weldon asked.

He placed his cup back down and arose. "No, thank you. I really must be going. I have several patients to attend to. I will return around seven to check on Mr. Willy."

"We hope you could stay afterwards for dinner," Mrs. Weldon promptly offered.

"Thank you, I would be delighted."

Dr. Murphy bowed and left.

Helena felt disillusioned that he didn't stay and converse with her.

"There goes a fine young man," Mrs. Weldon said to Helena. "He seems to have taken an interest in you."

"He only came because of Willy," Helena said.

Mrs. Weldon wagged her head knowingly. "Yes, but his face glowed when he saw you."

Helena blushed, feeling pleased with her comment. "I will check on Willy." Without waiting for a response, she fled to the boy's room. She found him sleeping and touched his forehead. It felt hot.

"Willy. Willy," she said.

He slowly opened his eyes and smiled at her dreamily. "Could you please, miss, read to me?" he whispered.

She smiled. "My pleasure. I'll fetch a book from the library."

A short time later, Helena returned with a thick tome of *Aesop's Fables*, and sat by his side, reading it. When she finished the story, she found him sound asleep.

Mrs. Weldon entered the bedroom carrying a tray of tea. "How is he?"

"He still has a fever. I tried reading to him, but he fell asleep," Helena whispered to her.

"Thank you, dear. You are good for him."

Afterwards, Helena tended to the roses, feeling oddly light-hearted and uplifted. The intoxicating scent from the red petals, accompanied by the swallows chirping merrily in nearby bushes and trees left her in even better spirits. Did she feel this way because Mrs. Weldon had complimented her about Willy? *No, it was more than that.* Mrs. Weldon had noticed Dr. Murphy's reaction to Helena when she entered the room. *It was significant enough for Mrs. Weldon to comment on it. That meant he had some feelings for me.* Helena was looking forward to seeing him later in the evening.

She brought a bunch of cut roses into the parlor. Mrs. Weldon sat on the sofa, steadfastly occupied with her needlework.

"You know, Helena, I met Dr. Murphy's mother at a dinner party the other day. She is a widow and I hear that she is wealthy. She is looking for a young woman to marry him off. He is twenty-five, and won't remain a bachelor. Mark my words."

Helena became alert. She had been interested in Dr. Murphy for many years. The thought of marrying him excited her, but a nagging thought had presented itself lately. She needed to find out what had happened to her father's discovery in Greece. If she married Dr. Murphy, she doubted that he would allow her to travel to Greece to take care of her father's business, especially if he had a thriving practice. He would want her by his side.

* * *

That evening, while Helena read to Willy in his bedroom, Dr. Murphy arrived with Mrs. Weldon.

After greeting them, Dr. Murphy checked the boy. "I hope you enjoyed the story that Miss Cadfield was reading to you."

Willy nodded slightly, appearing flushed from the fever.

Dr. Murphy gave him a spoonful of medicine.

"How is he, Dr. Murphy?" Mrs. Weldon asked.

"The medicine should help him. If it gets worse, I might have to bleed him. All we can do is wait and see," he replied.

At dinner, Dr. Murphy sat next to Helena. They were quiet for a few minutes, focusing on their food and the conversation at the table.

At one point, he turned and spoke to her. "How have you been faring, Miss Cadfield?" he asked softly.

"Well enough," she replied, surprised by his question and at the same time, pleased. *His question shows that he has some interest in me.* She was about to smile at him but caught Mrs. Weldon eyeing them. Helena stiffened. She was not going to give her that satisfaction.

"It's different without my father," she replied, focusing instead on cutting the mutton in her plate.

"Yes, I understand."

"I remember how pleased he would be when you asked him tough medical questions," Helena said to him. "He'd talk about you afterwards to his colleagues, telling them that you would go far."

Dr. Murphy chuckled, his eyes glowing. "I didn't know he felt that way about me." He took his glass of wine and drank from it with relish.

"It seems as if your medical practice is doing well, Dr. Murphy," Mr. Weldon said.

"I admit that I enjoy it, although it doesn't leave me much time to do anything else."

"Papa used to say the same thing, and decided to take fewer patients. That way he had enough time to teach at the Anatomy School," Helena said.

"Yes, I know. Then he went off during the summers on his archeological expeditions," Dr. Murphy said. "You probably didn't see much of him then."

"I was used to it," she said, shrugging. "I found things to keep me occupied during the times he was away."

"Miss Cadfield would make an excellent wife for a doctor," Mrs. Weldon tittered. "Isn't that right, Dr. Murphy?"

Helena blushed at the woman's bold remark.

Dr. Murphy gazed earnestly at Helena. "Indeed, Miss Cadfield would make any man a good wife."

Helena felt warm emotions coursing through her body. *What did he mean by that sincere remark? Does he have the same feelings about me as I do of him?*

His sparkling eyes and boyish smile had returned.

"You are teasing me," she said, blushing.

"On the contrary. I meant every word I said."

Dr. Murphy turned and focused his attention on Mr. Weldon, discussing the politics of the day, leaving Helena to muse over his words.

After dinner, Dr. Murphy promised he'd return the next day to see Willy.

* * *

The next morning, Helena was up early. She had not slept well the previous night, thinking about Dr. Murphy. As she ate breakfast, she pictured his smile last night. His reserved look had vanished, and his handsome, boyish face had come alive. She knew that she was reliving the times when he'd visit Papa and tease her.

Last night, he had rekindled the old flame in her heart.

Although the idea of Dr. Murphy courting her was attractive, Helena had nothing to offer him but her youth and her looks.

She visited Willy to see how he was doing. His energy had returned and he was more talkative. Soon, Dr. Murphy arrived with Mr. and Mrs. Weldon.

After Dr. Murphy greeted Helena, he proceeded to check Willy with his stethoscope. He then took his pulse.

"I am pleased to say that it's a matter of a few more days before you will be up and about," he told the boy.

"I'm hungry," Willy whined.

Everyone laughed.

"Thank you, Dr. Murphy. That's a sign that he's on the path to recovery," Mr. Weldon said.

"He is young and has a strong constitution," Dr. Murphy replied, as he placed his stethoscope in his bag.

"Please join us for tea in the parlor before you leave," Mrs. Weldon said. "Meanwhile, I need to see about my son's breakfast." She left the room with Mr. Weldon.

Dr. Murphy picked up his bag and sauntered with Helena out of the room and down the hallway.

"Dr. Murphy, I wish to apologize for Mrs. Weldon's comments last night," Helena said.

"You do not need to apologize. It happens often to me," he said, laughing. "Ever since I became a doctor, the matrons have pushed their daughters on me. Even my mother has invited families with daughters for dinner in the hopes of marrying me."

For some reason, the idea of all these women and their daughters vying for Dr. Murphy's attentions perturbed Helena.

"Oh," she said. Her eyes became wide. *How could I handle all this competition?*

They walked down the stairs together.

"I'm sure you probably have several young suitors seeking your attention," he prodded, his eyes gleaming.

"It's not at all the case, particularly when one is still in mourning," she mumbled, feeling miserable. *He doesn't know about my financial situation?*

They reached the entrance to the parlor.

He looked at her, smiling in that familiar playful manner. "Would you accept suitors if you were not in mourning, Miss Cadfield?"

Helena felt her cheeks become hot. *Why does he like to tease me? Why doesn't he come out and ask me that he would like to be my suitor?*

"Why do you ask, Dr. Murphy? Were you thinking of becoming my suitor?" Helena teased back.

He chuckled. "*Touché.*"

"Mrs. Weldon is expecting you for tea. Please excuse me, but I have something to attend to," Helena said tightly, and left without waiting to hear his response. She could not ignore the mixed feelings about Dr. Murphy and the inner tugging that had formed in her heart.

She needed to think carefully about her future.

* * *

The next day, one family responded to Helena's ad, but at the interview, she discovered that they had four children, all under the age of eight, and the pay was low. The following day, another family summoned her for an interview. Helena was appalled at the conditions of employment. There was no housekeeper and the house was messy. The mother's uncouth behavior toward her two, unruly children left Helena shaken. Even worse, the pay was lower than the first family. Her dream of going to Greece was appearing dim.

The Weldons received an invitation to dine at the Murphy's house a day later. Mrs. Weldon informed Helena that she was also invited.

Helena had misgivings about going to the dinner party with the Weldons. She did not know what Mrs. Weldon would say and felt uncomfortable being put in the same category as all the other women vying for the young Dr. Murphy, yet her curiosity got the better of her, and she agreed to go.

CHAPTER 7

The day of the dinner arrived. Helena dressed in her black dress, and took extra precautions with her hair. That evening, as she left with the Weldons for the dinner party, it began to rain. The rain had strengthened by the time their carriage rolled to a stop in front of the Murphy mansion.

Upon descending from the carriage, Helena's foot stepped into a mud puddle, splashing her dress with mud. Mortified, she fled into the mansion.

Once inside the lobby of the house, she tried to fix her hair and clean the mud stains from her black dress and shoe. The footman led them to the parlor. Mrs. Murphy sat on the sofa, dressed in expensive attire and jewelry. Her pinched face exuded a mixture of reserve and boredom. As introductions were made, Helena noticed Mrs. Murphy eyeing her with a calculating look. Helena felt herself blushing under her scrutiny as her eyes settled on her dirty dress.

Mrs. Murphy informed them that her son had been called away to see a patient and would arrive later. She turned her attentions on Helena.

"Why haven't I met you before?" she asked her.

"My father, Dr. Cadfield, sent me to a boarding school in Paris. I was away these three years."

A sign of respect akin to admiration settled on the older woman's face. "I did not have the pleasure of meeting your father, but my son showed much progress while under his tutelage," Mrs. Murphy said. "He was quite affected by your father's death, I might add."

"Indeed, we all were," Mr. Weldon said.

Small talk ensued between the Weldons and Mrs. Murphy about Dr. Cadfield and their relation to him.

A well-dressed couple arrived a short time later with their daughter, an attractive young woman. She wore the latest fashion, and her cream-colored dress had lace trim and sported a low front. She had dark, shiny hair, a rosy complexion, a small, pert nose and small hands.

Mrs. Murphy introduced them as the Balfreys. Helena bowed civilly and kept her features composed. *Just like they had taught me at the boarding school.*

When she looked up, Helena caught herself staring at the dazzling diamond necklace that hung around Miss Balfrey's neck. It was real. It meant one thing. *This family was wealthy and I am not.*

Helena didn't know what to do about it. A knot had formed in her stomach.

Mrs. Murphy's face became expressive as she complimented Miss Balfrey. "The last time you were here, you played piano superbly. You must entertain us later, my dear," she told her.

Miss Balfrey blushed and smiled. She nodded her pretty head, her shiny curls bouncing.

The dinner was uneventful. The conversation, dominated by the older people, left the young people listening quietly.

When Dr. Murphy arrived, he appeared a little flustered, apologizing for his delay. Occasionally, someone asked him a question and he responded politely.

Helena realized that Dr. Murphy was a quiet and reserved person in social settings. Not much of a conversationalist, he preferred to be absorbed in his thoughts. She was feeling awkward by his reserved stance.

Afterwards, they went into the music room and Mrs. Murphy asked Miss Balfrey to play the piano. She performed a Mozart piece competently and with grace. Dr. Murphy stood next to her, turning the pages of the sheet music. He seemed to be gazing at her admiringly. When she finished, he warmly congratulated her on her playing.

"Please play us another piece," Dr. Murphy said, smiling warmly at Miss Balfrey and touching her shoulder as she looked up at him sweetly.

Helena felt the bile rising up in her throat when she saw Dr. Murphy's obvious display of familiarity toward Miss Balfrey. At that moment, he glanced at Helena with an amused look. Helena blinked. She couldn't believe her eyes. *He is teasing me, just like he did years ago.*

Afterwards, Mrs. Murphy asked Helena if she could play the piano. She obliged her, playing a few Bach pieces and realizing that she was also on display. Dr. Murphy stood by her side, just as he had with Miss Balfrey and congratulated her just as warmly.

Helena sensed everyone's eyes on them as he led her back to her seat, her hand placed on his arm.

By the time that they left the Murphy residence, Helena realized that Dr. Murphy had not spoken to her other than to commend her on her piano playing.

The next day, after breakfasting in her room, Helena sat sewing by her window. She felt particularly empty, as if all her emotions had vanished and she was left with an aching feeling that settled in her bones. How could she ever compete with Miss Balfrey, who was not only beautiful, but rich?

It was obvious that Mrs. Murphy was checking the eligible girls for her son. Even worse, Dr. Murphy had not shown any particular interest in Helena over Miss Balfrey.

In a short period of time, Helena had lost her father, her house, and her wealth. Was she losing Dr. Murphy, too?

The radiance of a solitary ray of sun filtering through the morning gray clouds, tempted her to stop and observe it, but even that could not lift her spirits.

Around ten o'clock, Mrs. Rotcliffe stopped by to gather her breakfast tray. As she was leaving, she informed her that the Weldons had gone out with Willy for a visit. "I thought ye might want to know."

After a few minutes, Helena stopped her sewing and gazed out the window. The clouds had remained, but the sun had vanished. She sighed. Nothing was going right. There had been no more responses to her ad. Should she place another ad?

Mrs. Rotcliffe entered the room. "Dr. Murphy is here to see you, miss."

Helena's heart leapt to her throat. This was the last person she expected to see this morning. She tried not to show her excitement. "Please tell him I'll be right down."

Helena dressed carefully into a suitable dress, and checked herself in the glass mirror. She caught herself fixing her hair nervously, trying to look her best. "Why am I doing this? I don't want to encourage his attentions, or do I?"

She was confused about her runaway feelings. She knew deep down that she still had feelings for him, yet his mother's interference with his life was a concern, and even more pressing was the need to take care of the property in Greece. What was she to do? She went downstairs, not knowing what to expect.

At the very least, she would remain civil and pleasant.

He greeted her warmly. He seemed less reserved and more his usual charming self.

"The Weldons are out visiting," she informed him politely.

"Good. I didn't come to see them, but to see you," he said, his eyes twinkling.

Helena blinked, feeling awkward. She ordered tea, trying to guard her emotions.

"I apologize that I arrived late last night and did not speak with you at the dinner party," he said. "My mother invited the Balfreys. I had nothing to do with it."

Helena smiled. "I understand your mother's concern in finding you a prospective wife."

The tea service arrived and Helena served the tea and cakes.

Dr. Murphy thanked her and cleared his throat. "Miss Cadfield, I came to see you for an important reason."

Helena placed her teacup down. The solemn tone of his voice set her heart racing. "Yes?" she asked.

He took her hand. "I know that you are still in mourning, but I already received permission from Mr. Weldon to court you." He bent down and kissed her hand warmly.

"Dr. Murphy," Helena said, feeling hot all over at his sudden show of emotion. This typically reserved man had a hidden side to him. His expressive gesture reminded her of the young, hotheaded Parisian men, eager to kiss her.

She pulled her hand away and arose shakily.

"Please forgive me for my boldness," he said ardently. "I have been thinking about you ever since you returned from Paris."

Helena paced the room nervously, trying to regain her composure.

She had to tell him.

She stopped her pacing and faced him. "I thank you for your compliments, but when my father died, he left me no will."

He appeared thunderstruck, almost angry. The color had left his face and his eyebrows were furrowed. "You tease me," he muttered darkly.

"No, it is true. As a result, Dr. Murphy, I am penniless."

He crossed his arms, appearing angry. "That is difficult to accept, given that your father was such a distinguished person," he retorted, "and from what Mr. Weldon told me, you were-" Then he stopped, as if thinking.

Helena's senses were suddenly alert. Her stomach formed a knot. "Mr. Weldon? What did he say?"

Dr. Murphy shook his head. "I'd rather not say. But it does pose a problem for you."

"If I wish to marry?" she said bitterly, realizing that Mr. Weldon might have concocted some lie to Dr. Murphy, implying that she was wealthy.

A shadow formed on Dr. Murphy's face. He remained silent.

"The Weldons want to marry me off so I would not be a burden to them, but I have other plans," she said.

"Please make yourself clear, Miss Cadfield."

"I must travel to Greece to see about the property I inherited. Since my father did not leave a will, I must go and claim it before someone else does. I cannot become involved in any relationship until I take care of that first. I hope you understand."

Dr. Murphy's mouth had formed a thin line. He arose stiffly.

Helena felt her face flush. She stood there, staring at him, the very same person whom she had dreamed about for so many years. He appeared so serious, so much older.

"You were always a headstrong girl, going after whatever you wanted," he said reproachfully.

"Maybe you're right, but I have to do it, for Papa's sake, and for my mother's sake," she said earnestly. "I do plan to return once it is taken care of, hopefully within the year, and if you still-"

"Want to court you?" he finished.

She nodded.

He became thoughtful. "Very well. I will be here when you return." He bid her a civil goodbye and walked solemnly out the door.

Helena stood there, trembling and wondering if she was the most foolish woman in the world to let him leave.

Mrs. Weldon came running in, appearing excited. She asked if Dr. Murphy had paid her a visit.

"Yes, he did."

"How exciting! I bumped into his mother earlier today, and she said that he was interested in coming here to talk with you. Tell me, did he make a proposal of marriage?"

Helena shook her head numbly.

"I am much vexed! I wash my hands of you," Mrs. Weldon cried.

* * *

A few days later, Mr. Weldon summoned Helena to the study.

"I have good news. Today, we received a letter from Mrs. Stirling, who is married to my wife's brother and lives in London. She has alerted me that they are having difficulty finding a governess for their daughter. Therefore, I am arranging for you to take a position there." He looked at her, appearing pleased.

"I am grateful for your aid in this matter. May I ask what the age of the daughter is?"

"Fourteen." He handed her a sealed letter. His smug look was that of a man who had done his duty as a relation. "Here is a letter of recommendation that I have prepared in case the family is not in when you arrive. Make preparations to leave as soon as possible."

CHAPTER 8

Athens, Greece
19 August, 1837

Aristotle Mastoras rode on top of the carriage on this brisk, August morning, heading for Athens. In the distance, he could see the Parthenon standing at the crest of the Acropolis hill, towering above Athens, welcoming him home. He inhaled deeply the carefree air that had a life of its own and savored the view as they passed fig and olive trees that graced the rugged terrain of Greece.

Two months ago, Dr. Kostakis, whom he met at a conference in Egypt, had invited him to work for the Archaeological Society in Athens. He had accepted the offer, but had to wait for his graduate degree. Once it arrived, he contacted Dr. Kostakis and they arranged to meet.

He had finally arrived.

The ancient marble columns that once housed the statue of Athena were a welcoming sight and caused his heart to swell with pride. It brought back memories of when he was a child and used to climb the Acropolis hill, playing contentedly among the ancient marble ruins. Everything changed once the war against the Ottomans broke out and he had left Greece hurriedly with his grandfather.

They entered a large, paved road that led into Athens, and soon the carriage was maneuvering its way through the crowds of people, horses, and shouting merchants. Ahead, Aristotle could see Hadrian's Arch standing tall above them as they rolled to a stop at the Plaka. He jumped down from the carriage, paid the driver, and grabbed his two bags. He strode across the dusty pavement of the main square.

Aristotle gazed around him expectantly. All the stores were open, and men of all ages were milling around him. There was much commotion as merchants sold fruits and vegetables from their wagons, shouting out prices to customers. The young Greek men were dark and handsome and wore the modern clothing of the day, while the older men were dressed in the colorful national costume. People were busy shopping and haggling with merchants over their wares.

"Move out of the way," someone called out authoritatively.

Pushed to the side with the others, Aristotle looked up curiously at the group of fair-haired men riding past them. Dressed in polished uniforms, they skirted around the people in the street. They must work for the King, Aristotle thought. He had heard about young King Otto, who had arrived from Bavaria several years ago to rule Greece.

After they left, Aristotle noticed workers constructing a building across the street from where he stood. His eyes followed the group of sun-soaked men, with their colorful scarves wrapped around their heads, sweating and working like ants, as they dug, loaded and carried stones on their backs toward the pile on the side of the building. Slowly they worked, to preserve energy. He was no stranger to that backbreaking work. He would need workers like these for his new job, hardworking and methodical.

Aristotle pulled out the creased letter from his pocket to verify the directions that Dr. Kostakis wrote him. He had met him a few months earlier at the archaeological conference in Egypt and they had talked extensively. He had corresponded with him since then, and they had arranged to meet this morning, but he was late. In a few hours, it would be evening.

Aristotle turned to face the row of shops and buildings, looking for the Kostakis sign. In front of him was a coffee shop with a newly painted sign and two old men sitting outside. A quick glance to his right revealed his destination, an old, decrepit building, scarred by musket fire during the war. It had seen better days. The faded sign above the door read *KOSTAKIS*.

Yet Aristotle stood strangely still, his gaze riveted on the two old men sitting in front of the shop, drinking coffee. Something about them demanded his attention. Was it the way they were dressed in the national costume? Their golden vests gleamed in the sun, while their full white skirts covered the top portion of their spindly legs, encased in white stockings. They were boasting about their heroic exploits during the war against the Ottomans.

"And when they came through the door, I let them have it," one of the old men shouted, his arm slicing the air. "There must have been at least twenty of them. We Greeks squashed those Turks like insects."

He wiped his luxurious, white mustache with gusto and took another swig from his cup, ready to continue.

Aristotle remained rooted, listening intently, mesmerized by the vividly described scenes. The past threatened to overwhelm him. The last time he had been in Greece was when he was ten years old, sobbing and running for his life with his grandfather up into the mountains, hiding from the ferocious Ottomans who had attacked their town. These terrible memories of his childhood, buried deep in his psyche, popped up only in the form of nightmares that had haunted him for years.

"God had been with us and wanted us to live, my friend," continued the old man, "but he wasn't as kind to the others, poor souls. May they rest in peace."

"Ahh, your courageous acts can never be forgotten, Barba Manolis. Our country is free because of men like you," said the other old man. "Now I must leave you. I need to take care of some work." He arose, shuffling away with as much dignity as his old body could muster, his white skirt flapping behind him, his body bent slightly forward.

Aristotle had been watching all of this with fascination. He caught the man called Barba Manolis studying him. His eyes were the color of faded blue skies under brows of white clouds, and his long, white mustache curled at the ends.

Flushing under the intense scrutiny, Aristotle felt as if he were a child, caught eavesdropping.

Several boys brushed past Aristotle, running and laughing, without a care in the world. He smiled at them, enjoying their laughter. A small boy ran smack into him. Aristotle grabbed him, chuckling and righting him up. He was around four or five years old, with big brown eyes and a mop of straight black hair.

"Manolaki, look out for the man!" The old man shouted at the boy. "Sorry, Mister, my grandson doesn't watch where he is going!"

Aristotle grinned, patting the boy on the head. Manolaki rewarded him with a bright smile, his eyes large and trusting, before he ran off toward his friends.

The old man extended a large, tobacco stained hand, introducing himself as "Barba Manolis."

They shook hands. The old man's grip was surprisingly firm. There was something sincere and familiar about this man. Maybe his mustached grin reminded Aristotle of his grandfather.

"Please, sit and have coffee with me, *Kyrie*," Barba Manolis said, gesturing toward the empty seat next to him.

Aristotle appreciated the respectful manner in which the older man had addressed him by calling him *Kyrie*, or Mister.

"My name is Aristotle Mastoras." Aristotle flashed him a smile. "I would like to join you, but I am late for a meeting."

A look of surprise dawned on Barba Manolis's tanned, weathered face. His eyes glistened. "You wouldn't happen to be my friend Aristotle's grandson, from the Mastoras family? I swear you are the spitting image of Aristotle when he was young."

The old man's revelation shook Aristotle to the core of his being. In Germany, it took years to build friendships with the reserved Germans. Besides, he had always thought that all family and friends in Greece had died in the war. That was not the case. One man knew his grandfather. One old man was enough to make his heart sing with joy.

"Yes," Aristotle replied.

"*Eeeaaoouu!*" Barba Manolis slapped the table with force, causing his cup to rattle. Letting out a cry of happiness, he arose shakily, almost teetering, and hugged Aristotle with gusto. "This is a happy day for me! I grew up with your grandfather. We were the best of friends, almost like brothers."

Aristotle sensed the strong emotion coursing through the old man as he embraced him. He knew that he could not leave for his meeting yet. Dr. Kostakis would have to wait.

Barba Manolis sat down, holding on to the table for support, his eyes red and his smile shaky. "Where is he, what happened to your grandfather? Tell me your news."

"My grandfather and I moved to Germany shortly after the war broke out and the rest of my family was lost." Aristotle paused to keep back the emotions that threatened to overwhelm him. "Uncle Elias, my father's brother, lived there, and helped my grandfather open a grocery store. Grandfather did quite well. I attended the university in Munich, and graduated with a doctorate in philology."

"Oh, so you are a university man," Barba Manolis said with respect. The next words he spoke were almost a whisper, as if he was afraid of learning the news. "And your grandfather?"

"He was planning on returning to Greece early this year, but it took time to find a buyer for his store. He died suddenly of a heart attack before he could sell it. Unfortunately, I was in Egypt." A burning ache drummed through his chest. He remembered the loss as if it were yesterday instead of four months ago.

"Achh, too bad. We were the same age." A sad expression settled on Barba Manolis's weathered face. He rubbed his left leg. "Excuse me, friend, but this old wound doesn't let me forget. I have your grandfather to thank for saving my life. I must tell you the story." He looked at Aristotle expectantly. "But you will come and visit me for dinner, eh? We will catch up on our news then. I will tell my son to have a plate ready for you tonight. This is a great day for me."

"But-"

"No buts," Barba Manolis interjected, raising his hand and looking offended. "Tonight, I am expecting you." He gave him the directions. "I live fifteen minutes from here. Where are you staying? Not at your old home? I have been there. It's a pile of stones, ruined during the war."

"I just arrived, and plan to visit it one day and rebuild it," Aristotle replied, grinning at him. He liked the old man.

"Good. We have much to talk about, but it can wait until later." Barba Manolis patted him on the back, his eyes moistened. "Now I will leave you to go to your meeting. I don't want you to be late." He winked at him and they shook hands.

Aristotle strode toward his destination, feeling the old man's eyes on him. He had sensed Barba Manolis's sadness upon hearing the loss of his grandfather, but realized that these old men, these fighters of freedom, did not cry in public. He had never seen his grandfather shed a tear.

CHAPTER 9

Aristotle entered the Kostakis building, and found Dr. Kostakis pacing the hallway with nervous energy, his hands behind his back. He was a short, heavyset man with a beak nose.

When Dr. Kostakis saw him, he raised his arms excitedly and sped toward him. A film of sweat was evident on his broad brow, while the worried look on his face disappeared.

"Dr. Mastoras, I am so glad to see you. I was worried you had changed your mind."

"You need not worry," Aristotle said, laughing. "I'm sorry I was late. My carriage broke down and it took the driver a few hours to fix it."

"I know, I know about these things. I met today with Mr. Pittakis and he was asking for you, and finally you have arrived. We need our young men to be here, helping our country, don't you think?" Dr. Kostakis said, shaking his hand energetically.

"Thank you for your warm welcome. I am glad to be back in Greece."

"What is your decision? Will you remain here or do you plan to return to Egypt?"

"I plan to stay here and rebuild my family home. I have informed my German colleagues of my intentions."

"Good! Egypt is not the only country with antiquities. We have much to do here!" Dr. Kostakis exclaimed.

"How is the Archaeological Society progressing? Any new excavations?"

Dr. Kostakis smirked, bending his head to the side as if to see Aristotle better and lifted his eyebrows. "Trying to organize this takes time, and much work is needed in cleaning and repairing the structures on the Acropolis. Last summer, we had Mr. Hansen and Mr. Schaubert finish rebuilding the Temple of Athena Nike (Victory), up on the southwest part of the Acropolis. Now we must work on restoring the Parthenon, which has seen tough times. Can you believe that the

Ottoman Turks stored gunpowder in it? That's not the only thing, a Turkish mosque sits right in the center of it, and it must be removed."

"Has King Otto shown any interest in all of this?"

Dr. Kostakis smiled cynically. "My dear Dr. Mastoras, King Otto was too young when he came here. What did a seventeen-year-old prince from Bavaria know about running Greece? He has never been in charge, but his Bavarian regent, Joseph von Armansperg, has been holding the reins all this time. Did you know that Mr. Makroyiannis, the president of the Athens city council, proposed a constitutional law at a banquet earlier this year? The next thing one hears, the city council dissolves and Von Armensperg places him under house arrest. Can you imagine that?" He paused to take out a handkerchief from his pocket and wipe his sweating forehead. "Meanwhile, the King is expected to take office in December. Let us see what he will do."

Aristotle raised an eyebrow. "It looks as if other forces are controlling this country."

Dr. Kostakis wagged his head in exasperation. "Yes, and at the end of the day, the Greek people will demand their due. We have no constitution. We cannot live without a constitution, is that not right?"

"Yes, our country definitely needs one," Aristotle said.

"I must tell you another bit of news. Three years ago, they brought an architect from Bavaria, Klenze was his name, to repair the Acropolis, but he wanted to remake it. The nerve of the man! He would have destroyed valuable structures. There was much outcry and we got rid of him. Now we are free to move forward."

"Will you be leading the projects?"

Dr. Kostakis appeared flustered. "Oh, no, not me. I have no experience in excavating. I teach classics at the university and am passionate about our Greek heritage, but Mr. Pittakis, who leads the society, knows more about these things. One day I will arrange for you to meet him."

"That would be good."

"Meanwhile, our members have been more than enthusiastic in wanting to see this society move forward and have even donated pottery. We have so many vases and broken fragments, that I do not know how we will ever be able to organize them. I am storing them until we decide what to do, but listen, I want to show you a new discovery. You may leave your bags here. They are safe. Follow me, please."

They walked down the hallway, their footsteps crunching on the soiled floor. The building was old and dingy, with no windows and no sign of life.

"Excuse the appearance of this building. I inherited it recently and am doing repairs on it. We are using the basement to store our findings for now. In the future, we hope to get enough money for a new building."

They entered the stairwell and walked down the dark steps. Aristotle's eyes adjusted to the darkness. "Tell me about this new discovery."

"It comes from a private collection."

"Private?" Aristotle's eyebrows shot up. He was intrigued.

"Private excavations are rarely publicized, and whatever the Greeks find in their back yard, they do not want us knowing about it. Eventually, these discoveries make their way to the antiquities shops or collectors and that's how we learn about it. But this collection is from Dr. Cadfield, an Englishman."

"Dr. Cadfield?" Aristotle said, remembering the physician who was also an amateur archaeologist. "I met him a couple of years ago in Egypt. He wrote an article on some excavation that he had conducted and gave a talk about it." Aristotle felt excited at the prospect of meeting him. He remembered Cadfield's probing questions and thoughtful replies. "I would be interested in seeing him again."

"I'm afraid that is impossible," Dr. Kostakis said firmly. "He is dead."

"How can that be? You said that he donated the artifact."

"Wait. Let me finish. Earlier this year, Dr. Cadfield came from England to nurse his Greek father-in-law from an unknown sickness, but the old man died. Dr. Cadfield ended up staying there to rebuild his wife's home, which his father-in-law had begun. The property is in Nemea, near Corinth."

"Nemea," Aristotle said, trying to recall the name. "I believe Nemea was a sanctuary for the Nemean Games in the sixth century BC., and according to legend, Hercules slayed the lion there."

"Yes, and legend also has it that Hercules founded those games, which were held in honor of Zeus every two years. You know your history well, Dr. Mastoras."

Aristotle nodded.

"Now, while digging the foundation, Dr. Cadfield made the discovery of this artifact. He gave it to me to safeguard after I returned from the conference in Egypt. Shortly afterwards, he became ill and died. I have tried to learn more about him. They called him '*O trellos yiatros apo tin Anglia.*' The crazy doctor from England."

Aristotle was quiet. "I am saddened to hear this. He was a good man. But why did they call him crazy?"

"The peasants can be superstitious over anything. They believe that some dead soul, angered by his excavation, did not want him digging up his ancestors. Others thought he was crazy to continue digging the foundation after what happened to his father-in-law. 'Let the spirits rest,' they said. Who knows what these superstitious villagers were thinking." Dr. Kostakis shook his head. "They even say that they've seen his ghost wandering around the site."

They entered the cold, damp basement, which consisted of a rectangular room that had an earthy smell to it. A flat board covered most of a small, dirty window. As a result, little light entered the room, barely enough to see.

"I found that window broken yesterday and nailed some wood there until I have it replaced. It leads to the back of the property. A small courtyard, nothing much, but someone can get in through the unlocked gate. Luckily, I had the foresight to lock up Dr. Cadfield's discovery."

Aristotle's eyebrows went up. "Is it that valuable?"

"Only you, Dr. Mastoras, are qualified to determine its value. When I heard your talk at the conference in Egypt, I knew that you were the right man to lead the project. I am not trained in these things," Dr. Kostakis said, shrugging his shoulders.

"Remember, I have no experience in digging up Greek archaeology."

"You told me this already. Your education as a philologist, studying Greek philosophy and antiquities along with your practical experience as an archaeologist, are sufficient. Educated men in this field are difficult to find."

Three, long wooden tables lined the center of the room. Large, earthen pots filled with broken pottery sat along the wall, a chaotic testimony to the society's lack of help. On the dusty tables lay various artifacts. Aristotle's quick assessment revealed them to be items of little or no value, and common in antiquities.

"What you see here were all donated and found practically on the surface. Come with me."

Aristotle followed him to the end of the room where a table, shoved against the wall, brimmed with pottery fragments. Dr. Kostakis asked him to help pull the table to the side. As they did, its feet scraped the floor and a few clay fragments tumbled unto the floor, shattering into tiny pieces. Aristotle stooped to pick them up.

"Don't worry about them. See what I mean? We are running out of room. I need to get more tables."

Dr. Kostakis pointed to the door previously hidden behind the pile. "Dr. Cadfield's discovery is inside that locked room. Come." He unlocked the door. It creaked as he pulled it open.

Aristotle followed Dr. Kostakis's short frame into a smaller room, sensing the anticipation in the older man's steps. Inside the dark, damp room was a small table. A wooden box sat on top of it. Aristotle placed the lantern on the table and observed Dr. Kostakis remove a key from his pocket and unlock the box.

"I've hidden it here so as not to attract attention. I wanted you to see this first before anyone else," Dr. Kostakis said. He opened the box and carefully retrieved something wrapped in a white cloth and held it up for Aristotle to see.

CHAPTER 10

"Incredible!" Aristotle whistled his appreciation when he saw the beautifully crafted gold cup with images of bulls circling it. On the one side was a strong youth handling one of the bulls. Around the cup's top edge, the boldly etched angular inscriptions caught his attention. He sucked in his breath in amazement, studying them closely.

"Yes, isn't it?" Dr. Kostakis said.

"Dr. Cadfield found this in Nemea? Where in Nemea?" Aristotle asked, his thoughts racing to what he had learned in his studies at the university. He did a rough calculation in his head regarding the cup's value.

"To my knowledge, he discovered it on his property on a mountain in Petri, near Nemea, this summer in June. His crew unearthed it while digging the foundation of his house."

Aristotle continued to study the gold cup closely, admiring the inscriptions under the light of the lantern, trying to decipher them.

"What do you think, Dr. Mastoras?"

"This is fantastic. A master artisan definitely designed the cup. The bull suggests influence from the Minoan culture, a time in ancient Crete when King Minos reigned. This cup could be thousands of years old. The inscriptions are unique and may have phonetic implications, where the symbols may represent sounds. I will have to study them further. I don't think I have seen anything like them before."

"That is why I have asked you here. I will need your help and expertise to continue the excavation on his property. I am sure we will make more discoveries there. Since no one has come forth to claim it, we have started the process in claiming it for the state."

"Very good. Do you mind if I copy the design? I want to study it further," Aristotle asked. His fingers fumbled in his pocket, and came out clutching a pencil and folded paper.

"No, no go right ahead."

Dr. Kostakis held the gold cup nestled in the cloth, while Aristotle smoothed the paper carefully over the design, then with his pencil, traced the design on the paper. He felt his palms sweating.

"It's possible that there are more treasures like this at that site in Nemea," he said to Dr. Kostakis. "Could you turn it around so I could see the back?"

Dr. Kostakis twisted the vessel, revealing the man and the bull. Around the edge were more hieroglyphic writing. "I stored it in this cloth to keep it clean and also covered from prying eyes," he said.

"Hmm. Good idea. Closer to the lantern, please. I need more light," Aristotle commented, watching the older man oblige his request. He traced the back design on his paper.

"So, tell me, Dr. Kostakis. Do you know how deep Dr. Cadfield's men dug into the ground?"

"Close to nine feet. I have witnessed antiquities unearthed during these types of excavations, but never a treasure like this." Dr. Kostakis shook his head, his eyes opened wide.

"You are right about that." Aristotle finished the drawing. "Thank you."

Dr. Kostakis wrapped the gold cup in its cloth, placing it reverently in the box, and then locked it.

They left the little room. Dr. Kostakis secured the door, and Aristotle helped him put the table back in its place, his mind racing in all directions at what he saw. Although he had experience with Egyptian hieroglyphs, these inscriptions were different. Was it possible that the Minoans had designed their own language? His nerves were taut with excitement, as he realized what this could mean. Could these inscriptions have been the beginning of the Greek language?

They walked up the stairwell to the first floor.

"Dr. Handal, my mentor at the university in Munich would be interested in this. I would like to consult with him about the hieroglyphic writing on the cup. This writing is different than what I observed in Egypt," Aristotle said.

"Unfortunately, we must keep this secret at all costs for the moment. Mr. Pittakis is the only other person who knows about this. He would be interested in learning what you have to say," Dr. Kostakis said tensely.

"You can try to keep something like this secret, but people do talk. Dr. Cadfield's workers knew about this. Eventually it will get out."

"Yes, and we are aware of that, and that is why I have locked it away," Dr. Kostakis countered, his voice rising. "We are counting on you to help us keep our treasures here. We do not want to see them sold to other countries by foreigners, like Lord Elgin. You remember how he took such valuable pieces to England. The Ottoman Turks allowed him to purchase our ancient statues, as if they belonged to them. The English have yet to return them to us."

Aristotle nodded in agreement.

"Not even King Otto should know about this yet. We have bled enough," Dr. Kostakis continued.

Aristotle understood the implications of Dr. Kostakis's words. If King Otto learned about it, what would stop him from transporting these statues to Germany? Greece needed every opportunity to move forward. What better avenue than through the discovery of ancient treasures? He was thrilled and uneasy at the same time, yet knew that he trod on uncharted territory. His graduate thesis on Egyptian hieroglyphs was a result of four years of research and open communication with his German professors and other experts at the university. His work passed through several layers of checks and counter-checks by other experts. Before arriving in Greece, he had received his doctoral degree. This was the first time in his twenty-seven years that he would be in charge of such a project.

"I will do the best I can," Aristotle said. "We are fortunate that Dr. Cadfield gave it to the Society."

"Yes." Dr. Kostakis nodded emphatically. He appeared apologetic. "Unfortunately, we cannot pay you at this time. The revolution has carried a heavy price, not only of human resources, but also material wealth."

"I am well aware of the situation here. I accepted your offer in Egypt, knowing the conditions of payment. I am interested in helping my country," Aristotle reassured him. Many people had perished, including most of his family, and the whole country was in ruins, and struggling to get back on its feet. By Greece's standards, he was a wealthy man, having inherited his grandfather's riches from Germany.

"Of course, as we discover more treasures, that will generate much interest, and therefore funding," Dr. Kostakis said.

They had reached the front entrance and Aristotle retrieved his luggage. "The treasures of Greece are a valuable connection to our past, and we need to do everything in our power to unearth and protect them."

Dr. Kostakis smiled at him as he opened the door. "I agree with you, but we need money and leadership. We lack both."

Outside, the sun's rays felt inviting. The square was quiet, with very few people. The air inside the basement had been stale and Aristotle had developed a headache. He had been so eager to get here that he had not eaten all day. He took a deep breath, inhaling the fresh air.

They strolled toward the direction of the coffee shop where he had met Barba Manolis earlier.

"I cannot claim that I fought for our freedom, as did our brave people of Greece," Aristotle said. "I was young then, but because of our heroes, I am free to speak these words on Greek soil. These heroes paved the way for the rest of us, and now we must move forward with the rest of Europe."

"I am totally in agreement," Dr. Kostakis said. "We were once a great and powerful country, but now look at us; we are in debt and grovel for food, and ask for favors from other countries. We have much catching up to do with the rest of Europe. While Europe was advancing these four hundred years, we were living in servitude to the Turks."

They stopped in front of the coffee shop. The tables and chairs were gone.

"We must have more of these philosophical discussions," Dr. Kostakis promised. "Meanwhile, I have reserved a room over the coffee shop. My brother, Demosthenes, owns it and is waiting for you."

"Good, but we haven't discussed yet the need for laborers."

"Yes, yes. I already have three Albanians picked for you, Alexander and his two sons. They are strong and willing, and eager to work. Of course, we have no funds yet to pay them," Dr. Kostakis said, shrugging.

"Albanians?" Aristotle asked. "What about the Greeks? Don't they need the work?"

Dr. Kostakis sighed. "The Albanians moved in after the war and have settled here. I tried to hire Greeks, but somehow, they learned that we do not have resources, and are afraid we won't pay them.

Besides, they also like to talk, and I do not want this discovery to get around. The Albanians keep to themselves."

Aristotle flung his head back, laughing. "Clever Greeks, eh? How sure are you that the Albanians would be willing to work without pay?"

"These Albanians are poor and any promise of payment is better than nothing. They will even work for food." Dr. Kostakis took out a handkerchief from his pocket and wiped his forehead nervously.

Aristotle guessed what had happened. As a representative of the Archaeological Society, Dr. Kostakis must have approached the Albanians for work, and promised eventual payment. Since they probably were desperate to work, they did not negotiate payment terms.

"Hmm," Aristotle said, thinking. His grandfather had left him enough money to live comfortably, and the grocery store in Germany was for sale. If sold, it would net him enough money to rebuild his family home. Yet this discovery was too important to ignore. It needed exploring.

"This is what I will do," Aristotle said.

Dr. Kostakis looked at him expectantly.

"I will work it out with them so that they are paid for their efforts, even if it's only a few drachmas. I will do this until we find treasures and the funds begin arriving."

"Thank you, your honorable gesture is greatly appreciated," Dr. Kostakis said, appearing relieved, as he pushed the coffee shop door open.

The store was dark and nearly empty. A pungent scent of smoke hung in the air. Two men sat in the back, smoking and talking at a table that held a lantern. Aristotle followed Dr. Kostakis to the back, where he made the introductions.

Demosthenes had the same beak nose as Dr. Kostakis, but was taller and thinner. "Welcome, Dr. Mastoras. I have reserved a room upstairs for you," he said, putting out the cigarette and extending a tanned hand.

"Thank you." Aristotle shook his hand.

Demosthenes turned to Dr. Kostakis and slapped him playfully on the back. "Stay for some coffee, *adelfe* (brother)."

"As much as I would like to, I am already late. Mrs. Kostakis and I have been invited to dinner," Dr. Kostakis said, glancing at his pocket watch. "Dr. Mastoras, I will stop by at eight tomorrow morning and take you with me to the university, so we can discuss further details with Mr. Pittakis."

After Dr. Kostakis left, Aristotle followed Demosthenes up the dark flight of stairs to the second floor. There were two rooms on each side of the hallway. They turned left. His room was on the right, facing the back of the building. When he entered the room. he noticed immediately the window, and a small table and chair, sitting underneath it. Against the wall, to his right, sat a wooden bench with folded linen and a wool blanket. That would suffice. He had slept in worse conditions.

He walked to the window, and opened it, allowing fresh air to enter the room. "Could I possibly get some water?" he asked.

Demosthenes returned with a pitcher of water and a basin. He placed them on the table and gestured apologetically. "I am sorry that I have nothing more to offer. I know you are a man of importance, but we've seen difficult times."

"You don't have to apologize." Aristotle dug into his pocket, pulling out several drachmas. He dropped them into the man's hand. "Here. Is this enough? I arrived today and need to go to the bank."

"Thank you, it is more than enough," Demosthenes said, beaming and bowing his head as he headed for the door.

"I almost forgot. I was wondering if you know where Manolis Papadouris lives?" Aristotle asked. "I have been invited to his house for dinner but don't know how to get there."

"Everyone knows Barba Manolis. He is one of our decorated heroes. I will send for Yianni to guide you. He is my cousin and an excellent guide, and knows all the parts around here. He can show you around," Demosthenes said, appearing excited, as he hurried away.

Aristotle drank some water, undressed, then washed and rested. Soon, sleep overtook him. When he awoke, the sun was beginning to set. He had enough light to shave his day-old stubble. His stomach grumbled as he pondered everything that had occurred that day. He concluded that the war had changed Greece and its people, but there was hope, as people like him returned to the country with money and ideas.

He sifted through his luggage, then slipped into a clean pair of pants, wondering if his guide would show up.

Someone pounded heavily on his door.

"I'll be right there," he said.

The pounding resumed.

"One minute!" Aristotle shouted, pulling out a shirt from a bag, and stuffing it in his pants. There was one thing he didn't like and it was to be rushed into dressing. Barefoot, Aristotle yanked the door open, and the person on the other side literally tumbled into the room.

"Oh, a thousand apologies," the man said, righting himself. He was a stocky fellow, with a round, tanned face. A dirtied red and orange bandanna was wrapped around his head and partly covered his oily black bangs. He saluted him sharply.

"Yianni Kalosvaltis, at your service! My cousin Demosthenes said you needed a guide, Dr. Mastoras?"

"Yes," Aristotle replied, looking for his socks. "As you can see, I'm not finished dressing." He started to put them on. "Can you help me get to the home of Manolis Papadouris?"

"Yes, yes, of course I know him. Who doesn't? He is one of our heroes," Yianni said, grinning proudly. "He is a few minutes away, on the other side of the Acropolis. I will take you with my wagon. I know these sights blindfolded."

CHAPTER 11

Several minutes later, Aristotle and Yianni sat in the wagon as it rambled up the hill heading toward Barba Manolis's house. The sun had set and the night had descended upon them. Aristotle combed back his wind-ruffled hair with his fingers.

The rocky road jostled the wagon, and the wheels creaked heavily, as he stared at the stars that filled the black sky like diamonds. He remembered gazing up at them when he was a boy and would sleep outside with his family on hot evenings. A familiar ache in his heart formed at the thought that he no longer could see his family. It stayed with him as he listened to an owl hooting its lonely call.

Farther up the road, in a nearby house, people were singing a mournful song. He cocked his head to the side, trying to make out the tune.

"Do you hear them? That's the wine talking," Yianni said, wagging his head in the direction of the house. He crooned softly for a while. "Ahh, life! So many people are still mourning their dead from the war, and many are poor, but we Greeks have pride, and would rather eat greens and walk barefoot than go begging in the streets like those gypsies. *Tsk. Tsk.* Our king dresses and talks like a Greek, but builds all those buildings for his German staff and does not do anything for the poor Greeks."

"I have wondered why a German was placed in charge of our country," Aristotle admitted.

"Ahh, don't get me started on that topic. They killed our Greek president, Kapodistrias, in order to bring the German in."

"That's a little farfetched," Aristotle retorted. "Everyone knows that Kapodistrias died under the hand of another Greek."

They turned a sharp curve, and Yianni pulled on the leash abruptly. "*Brrr!*" he shouted to the mule. "We're here," he announced, and then jumped down.

Aristotle peered around in the dark, trying to find the house.

Yianni busied himself taking care of his mule and wagon. "Please go ahead. The path is there to your right. I have to make sure my mule is fed or he will bray all night."

Aristotle jumped down and walked along the stone path that led to the house. Soon, he saw the lights in the house. The sweet scent of a nearby fig tree perfumed the air, and his mouth watered. As a boy, he used to help his mother pluck the ripe fruit off their fig trees to make jam, and would chew the juicy fruit, savoring them, until his little belly was full. How long had it been since he had eaten a Greek fig and heard his mother's voice?

He blinked back the tears at the memory, surprised by his emotions. It had been years since he had allowed these buried memories to surface. A knot formed in his chest. He hesitated before knocking on the door, waiting for his composure to return. Would it ever return? He inhaled the scented air, and knocked.

A small woman in her early thirties greeted Aristotle at the door. The warm scent of food wafted toward him as he introduced himself. He felt comforted by her smile. She introduced herself as Despina, Petros's wife.

"Welcome, Dr. Mastoras. My father-in-law has been eagerly awaiting you." Despina's eyes were warm and friendly.

Yianni arrived and greeted her in a familiar manner. She directed them through the house and to the back courtyard. Several lanterns lighted the area, revealing Barba Manolis seated at a table with his grandson Manolaki and another man. Grapevines formed a canopy over them. The breeze ruffled Aristotle's locks of hair and swept through the bushes and flowers that bordered the courtyard.

"*Opa*! There you are." Barba Manolis arose eagerly and went to Aristotle. He enveloped him in his large arms. "I am glad you came. We were getting ready to have dinner." He turned and greeted Yianni. "I am glad to see you again, my friend."

"I brought him to you, Barba Manolis," Yianni said, beaming.

Barba Manolis introduced his son, Petros, to Aristotle. He was a smaller version of his father.

"I have heard many stories about your grandfather, Dr. Mastoras," Petros said, rising and shaking his hand. "I am sorry to hear about his death. May his memory be eternal."

Barba Manolis gestured for Aristotle and Yianni to sit down. They made small talk until Despina arrived with the roasted lamb and baked manestra in tomato sauce, an orzo dish. A few minutes later, she returned with a tray of little round spinach pies and a plate of fried eggplant. Slowly the table filled with a plate of mizithra, a soft, Greek cheese, a bowl of small, black olives, and freshly baked bread. When finished, she sat next to her husband at the table.

Barba Manolis said a short prayer, bowing his head. He looked up." K*ali orexi.* Eat. Eat. There's plenty here for everyone."

Aristotle placed the soft eggplant, swimming in olive oil, on his crusty bread, and then chewed it, enjoying the textures and flavors of the soft, sweet meat of the eggplant and the crusty bread. He proceeded to eat the rest of the savory meal with gusto.

Barba Manolis took the carafe of dark-red wine that had been sitting next to him, and poured it into their glasses. "This year we had a good harvest," he said, appearing satisfied and wiping his mustache in anticipation. "The weather was just right, not too much rain, and the grapes grew plentiful." He lifted his filled glass. "Let's drink to Dr. Mastoras, who has honored us with his presence tonight."

"Thank you. I am glad to be here." Aristotle smiled. He lifted his glass and slowly drank the strong, sweet wine. "Hmm. The wine is quite good, but it cannot match your hospitality and the delicious food."

"My wife is the best cook," Petros said, smiling at Despina, who dipped her head down, blushing at the compliment.

Barba Manolis asked him about his lodging and Aristotle told him where he was staying.

"Yes, I know Demosthenes well, but you can't stay there forever. Are you going to reclaim your house? Many people are returning and fixing their homes," Barba Manolis said.

Aristotle nodded. "I have thought about it." That had been his grandfather's dream, but he remained in Germany so Aristotle could finish his studies at the university in Munich. For his doctoral thesis, Aristotle had spent the last three years in Egypt, excavating with archaeologists. He was finally in Greece, with his doctoral degree, but without his grandfather.

Barba Manolis talked about the goings on in the area. "Ever since King Otto arrived, we have had new roads and buildings built in Athens. The progress is remarkable. I wish your grandfather was here to see it. I truly miss him."

"You were good friends," Aristotle prompted.

"We were close, like brothers. He saved my life, you know, the night they attacked our town," Barba Manolis replied. "There were about thirty of us, mostly older men, including me and your grandfather. We had just fought in a neighboring village, and were returning home on foot. All our horses had been lost in the battle and we had to carry the wounded. I could still remember thinking how fortunate we were that we had the full moon that night to guide our way back home.

"As we approached our neighborhood, someone shouted that he saw fire ahead. Fear drove our poor tired bodies, and we raced toward our homes like lunatics. The dirty Turks had set everything on fire and like thieves stole our hopes and dreams, killing our families."

Barba Manolis shook his fist ferociously in the air, his eyes red. "I fought the Turks like a madman, desperately trying to get to my family inside the burning house. I danced with death a dozen of times that night. When I finally entered my house, a Turk came from behind and pierced me with the sword. I awoke in much pain, and learned that I had lost my wife and two daughters. They lay there before me, unrecognizable. I had been too late." Barba Manolis blew out a loud sigh, shaking his head sadly. "I prayed for God to take me right there and then."

Aristotle was silent, feeling compassion toward the old man who was trying to gain his composure. Tears sprang to his eyes as he remembered his own mother, serving the family meals, her voice singing out to him and his younger sister Fotini, who was only six when the war broke out. Fotini's charming laugh, head of blonde curls, and bright eyes were what he remembered, and how she was always tagging along, holding her doll. She would have been twenty-one this year, and probably married with children.

"Father, you didn't lose everything," Petros reminded him gently. "You have me and my family. Look at Manolaki, the spitting image of you."

The old man's eyes rested on the boy's face, and he smiled. "My Manolaki," he said in an affectionate tone.

"*Pappouli*," the boy replied, his eyes large, as he chewed his meal and smiled back at his grandfather.

"Thank God, my son Petros was away in England at the time, studying at the university and was spared from all of this." Barba

Manolis stroked his bushy eyebrows, pausing to reflect. "Aristotle, if it weren't for your grandfather, I would not be here, talking with you."

"Tell him how Mr. Mastoras fought so many Turks, Pappouli," Manolaki said, tugging his sleeve.

"Be patient. I'm getting to that," Barba Manolis said, cutting a piece of lamb. "Eat, everyone, before it gets cold." He nudged Aristotle, gesturing toward his plate.

Aristotle rubbed his stomach, unable to eat after listening to the story. "This is delicious, but-"

"Nonsense. I will treat you like my own grandson. Eat!" Barba Manolis scolded, but his eyes were twinkling. "Look at Yianni, he doesn't need encouragement."

Everyone laughed at Yianni, who had emptied his plate and was reaching for seconds.

"Eh?" Yianni said and chuckled with everyone as he filled his plate. "Dr. Mastoras, do you remember those people singing those songs on our way here?"

Aristotle nodded.

"I know a song like the one they were singing, but it is about the *Panagia* (Virgin Mary), and freedom." Yianni started singing softly, his voice low and husky. Everyone at the table became quiet.

"Panagia, watch over our sons
Who fight for our freedom.
They are so brave and so young

As the dove flies high above
Be with them on their journey.
Be with them always.

And where are you now,
My dove, my country,
My Greece, our sons?

Panagia watch over us
As we mourn the deaths of our sons.
For Freedom plays with our hearts."

The beautiful melody and the lyrics were haunting. At one point, Barba Manolis and Petros joined in, and Aristotle felt the painful longing of his lost family reach deep into his bones. He remembered how his mother used to pray to the *Panagia* when he was young.

When the song ended, Barba Manolis continued speaking, his eyes shining. "I swear, Yianni, you have a good voice."

"I always liked to sing, ever since I was a child," Yianni said, stuffing his mouth with food. He washed it down with wine.

They quietly ate their meals.

"Aristotle, did you know that your grandfather had the strength of Hercules?" Barba Manolis said. "He was so strong, that I saw him grab two Turks in each arm and throw them like rags on top of each other. On that dreadful night where I lay almost dead, burning from a fever, he came and took me to a shelter, where there were other wounded Greeks. Your grandfather forced the doctor to drop everything and care for me. I had lost so much blood." Barba Manolis shut his eyes and sighed. "I never saw him again. I thought he had died. I had always wanted to thank him for saving my life."

Despina arose and began to clear the table. Little Manolaki fidgeted in his seat and taking his fork, began striking his plate, making a ringing sound.

"Sshh," Barba Manolis said to him, his finger on his lips.

"See, *Pappouli*, I am playing a tune," Manolaki said, his face flushed. "Do you know what it is?" He proceeded to strike the plate with enthusiasm.

"Despina, come and get the little one. He is tired," Petros called out.

Despina came to Manolaki. "Come, my love. Time for bed. Say good night."

The child went and kissed his father and grandfather, and smiled sleepily at Aristotle and Yianni as they bid him goodnight. Despina scooped Manolaki in her arms and carried him away; his flushed angelic face rested on her shoulder.

"How old were you when the war began, Dr. Mastoras?" Yianni asked. He filled his empty glass with more wine.

"Ten," Aristotle managed to say. "I remember Grandfather taking me to town because he wanted to do some shopping, and Fotini, my little sister, had wanted to join us, but Grandfather told her to stay and keep Mother company. I promised her that I would play with her later. That same day, while we were away, the Turks swept through the village, massacring everyone, including my-" His voice caught in his throat as he was about to say parents and sister. He clenched his jaw and tried to overcome the turbulent emotions that threatened to overwhelm him. All these years he had blocked these thoughts from his mind. It was time that he faced them.

"You don't have to continue," Petros said gently to Aristotle.

Aristotle shook his head. "I'm all right. Grandfather learned the news in time and took me away to Mount Parnes. We traveled that night, walking for hours, and I was afraid and hungry. I wanted to be home, with my family. Grandfather did not tell me the truth about what had happened to my parents and sister, giving excuses that he could not find them and that they would probably join us later. The next few days, we slowly hiked through the mountains, making our way out of the country, heading for Germany."

"You walked all the way?" Yianni asked, looking incredulous.

"Part of the way, and after we left Greece, we hitched rides."

"Why did your grandfather choose Germany?" Petros asked.

"My father's brother lived in Munich and owned a grocery store. We worked in Uncle Elias's store for a few years, and later, Grandfather bought his own store."

Yianni chewed his food, shaking his head. "Ah, those memories. How can I forget the revolution? I was eight then, too young to fight. My father died in the fighting, and my mother and two sisters and I fled to Patmos Island, where she had family. I returned four years ago looking for work," he said.

"We have a new country, a new beginning. We cannot forget the past, but we need to move forward," Petros said.

"*Brrrrr*," Yianni said, shaking his head angrily. "King Otto is for King Otto. He doesn't know what the Greek people want."

"I have been compensated for my deeds in the war and even been invited to the banquets that the king gives," Barba Manolis said, his eyes flashing.

"Father and his comrades are considered heroes. We have everything we want. Even I have a job under the king," Petros said.

"All I know is that we don't need a foreigner running our country," Yianni mumbled, slurring his words. He hiccupped.

"So, Petros, what type of work do you do?" Aristotle asked, trying to steer the conversation away from Yianni, who seemed to have imbibed a little too much wine.

"I am a tutor. I teach the King's staff the Greek language, and any other language deemed necessary."

They talked about Petros and his duties.

"And you, Aristotle, what are your plans?" Barba Manolis asked.

"I'll be working on an assignment for the Archaeological Society."

"Bravo, you are doing the right thing. We need to place our treasures in museums. They don't belong in other countries," Barba Manolis said.

The entrance of a young woman interrupted their conversation. Aristotle stared at her. She was beautiful and slim-hipped, with a long braid hanging down her back. Her carriage was straight, and she gracefully carried a tray of pastries.

"*Kallostine.*" Despina greeted the young woman, kissing her on the cheek. "We have guests." Despina took the tray and placed it on the table, and then made the introductions. "This is my sister, Magdalene."

Magdalene smiled. "I am pleased to meet you."

Her voice was soft, like Despina's, and she nodded serenely toward Aristotle and the others.

"I am sure you would like to try the delicious baklava," Barba Manolis said to Aristotle, wiping his mustache in anticipation. "Despina's family owns the bakery in town. They make the best pastries."

"How can I resist such a tempting offer?" Aristotle answered.

Despina smiled as she cut the sweet baklava and placed it on the plates. The honey-soaked layers of crusty dough encased a mixture of chopped walnuts and cinnamon. "You get the first piece, Barba Manolis, because I know how much you love this. Magdalene, please serve the rest. I forgot the figs." Despina hurried into the kitchen.

"They don't make them like this in Germany. Eh, Aristotle?" Barba Manolis winked, nodding his head toward the beautiful girl as she served the baklava.

Aristotle smiled warmly at the girl as she handed him a plate of the delicious pastry. He liked that she was shy. His best friend's sister, Miss Greta Heinz, who lived in Germany, was the opposite. When she learned that he was leaving for Greece, Miss Heinz teased him that she would visit him there. Sometimes her bold behavior was disconcerting, and he didn't know when to take her seriously. She flirted with everyone and at the same time, acted as if they were engaged, although he had never proposed to her.

Magdalene was a Greek beauty in a class of her own. Their fingers brushed. "Did you help make this, Magdalene?"

The young woman nodded shyly, but her almond shaped eyes were large as she took him in. "We bake these all the time in the bakery," she replied softly.

Despina returned with a plate of figs and sat next to her sister. The two women talked quietly as Barba Manolis ate the figs and Aristotle munched on his honeyed baklava. Too quickly, the delicacy ended. Despina immediately asked if he wanted another one.

"Thank you, but we must be going," Aristotle said, rising. "Yianni?"

Yianni had been staring at Magdalene with a sweet expression on his face. "Yes, boss."

Aristotle turned to Barba Manolis. "I am thankful for your warm hospitality and opening your home to me."

"Come tomorrow evening if you have some time. We can play some backgammon."

"I will surely return."

CHAPTER 12

London
1 September, 1837

Helena stared out the window of the carriage. They had entered Grosvenor Square. The clouds had gathered overhead, blanketing the sky with a dingy gray. The weather reflected the internal state of her heart, caused by the loss of her father and leaving Dr. Murphy behind. They stopped for well-dressed pedestrians out on a stroll, and then passed a couple of stately carriages parked in front of elegant buildings.

Immersed in that world once, she was witnessing it from the outside. She pictured Dr. Murphy finding out that she had left for London to become a governess to the Stirling family. She wondered what his reaction would be to the news. Would he try to contact her? Would he try to convince her to return to Oxford?

The carriage turned into a side street, interrupting her daydreaming. She gazed at the handsome town homes, including the one where the Stirlings lived. Her heart began to pound rapidly as she pictured Mrs. Stirling's show of surprise when she arrived at her front door, for there had been no time to send a letter informing them of her arrival.

The carriage rolled to a stop in front of a stately brick building, similar to the others that lined this street. It featured several tall windows and a small lawn with clipped shrubbery.

"Here ye are, miss." The coachman jumped down and helped her with the cumbersome luggage. After she paid him, he tipped his hat and was off, the carriage clattering down the cobbled street.

Helena's shallow breathing formed a mist in the air. There were no signs of life in the Stirling house, and no evidence of lights flickering through the windows. Her worst fears threatened to choke her. What would she do if the Stirlings were not there? Where would she stay?

The wind teased her dress, making it swirl around her ankles, while her knees felt weak and ready to cave in. She was hungry from the journey and chilled through and through, for she had not had the sense to dress warmly enough for the trip. She pictured herself at Cadfield House, seated in front of the hot fireplace having tea with her father, conversing on a number of interesting topics. The scene was a pleasant one.

She remembered where she was and shook the image from her head. She was living a dream that no longer was true, and must remember the reason for being here.

A fine mist of rain accompanied Helena's ascent up the steps of Stirling mansion. The heavy, leather bags, containing all her belongings, swiveled around her, threatening to topple her. Once at the top step, she banged the knocker.

When the door opened, Helena found herself staring at a liveried footman who appeared cross. He was fair-haired, and had ruddy cheeks and a square jaw. He looked her up and down in obvious disdain.

Helena became uncomfortably aware of her travel-stained clothes and the stray hairs jutting from beneath her worn hat. She straightened herself.

"I would like to see Mrs. Stirling," Helena said, trying to portray a confident demeanor.

"Ze family is not here, miss. You may leave your calling card," he replied.

Helena gathered that he was German, for she recognized the accent. She tried not to show her dismay. How could she proclaim that she was the new governess if the family was not even here to accept her? What was she to do? She blindly thrust Mr. Weldon's letter of recommendation into his hand, hoping he could read English.

The footman stared down at it with a perplexed air, as if he did not know what to do with it and looked at her. After what seemed like an eternity, he opened and read it.

Helena trembled at the thought that the door would shut in her face and all her hopes dashed to the ground. She did not want to return to Mr. Weldon, begging him to take her back. She had too much pride.

A woman's guttural voice called out angrily from inside the house. It sounded as though she were telling him to get in from the rain in German.

The footman thrust the letter back into Helena's hands and picked up her luggage, muttering something under his breath. They entered the warm quarters of the residence. Her hopes rose. Having made entry into the warm house was a step in the right direction.

He stopped in the lobby. His square face showed no recognizable signs as to what was going to happen next.

Helena looked around her. In the center of the lobby was a stairwell. Its damask-line walls were the color of royal red, making the lobby seem unduly dark, but the paintings on the walls and gaslights helped lighten the atmosphere. Some paintings were landscapes and others were portraits, she presumed, of ancestors.

"Please, remain here. I vill tell Mrs. Grady of your arrival." He walked up the stairs with undue ceremony and disappeared out of sight.

Mrs. Grady did not take much time in appearing. Her keys clinked with every step she took. The housekeeper had a wrinkled, small face but lively step. Her beady gray eyes squinted at Helena, causing her face to crinkle up even more. Her movements reminded Helena of Nana.

"The family isn't expected until late tonight," she announced with the voice of authority, her foot tapping the floor impatiently.

"I understand that Mr. Stirling is looking for a governess for his daughter," Helena ventured, her voice trembling. "I have traveled all the way from Oxfordshire based on the assurance of the position." She showed her the wet letter.

Mrs. Grady sniffed as she took the letter reluctantly. "Mr. Stirling is quite selective, ye know, and has already gone through three governesses in the past year."

Helena had no experience being a governess, and Mrs. Grady's statement did little to boost her confidence.

Mrs. Grady read the letter. Her pinched features slowly softened until there was a hint of a smile around her thin, pressed lips. She nodded, appearing pleased. "Why didn't ye tell me Mr. Weldon sent ye? His wife, Mrs. Weldon, is the sister of Mr. Stirling." She gave Helena a broad smile, handing the letter back. "Follow me, Miss Cadfield. Someone will bring your luggage."

A rush of relief filled Helena as she followed the housekeeper up the long, narrow flight of carpeted stairs. Mrs. Grady continued about the goings on of the German footman, Hans, and his wife Helga, who was the cook, and who had come from Germany because Mrs.

Stirling was from there, and of the time schedule and the necessity to be in bed by a certain hour.

After they reached the top floor, they walked down a long, dark hallway past several closed doors. She informed Helena that these were the servant's quarters.

"Mind ye, Hans and his wife have the largest room on this floor." She sniffed. "Me room is smaller than theirs is and I have more seniority than the two put together. The Misses brought them with 'er from Germany, and Mr. Stirling will do anything she says. I've been with the family since Mr. Stirling was a lad, but that don't count with Mrs. Stirling and she wouldn't have it any other way. German is a language they want Miss Stirling to learn, and French, and Greek. I presume you know all them languages?"

"Yes," Helena replied. In addition to her father teaching her those languages, she had polished her French at the girls' school. She felt awkward because she knew not to confide in servants, for whatever she tossed her way would soon become juicy gossip for the other servants' ears.

"Below us is the schoolroom, which used to be the nursery, and where Miss Stirling now has her lessons." Mrs. Grady stopped in front of a door at the end of the hall. "This is the room where the governess stays." She lit a candle, and then opened the door.

Helena followed her into the dark chamber, their shadows dancing on the wall from the flickering candle. A mahogany bed sat in the center of the narrow room and to its left was an unlit fireplace, while to its right was a curtained window with a table nearby.

Helena shivered at the tiny room, feeling a strong urge to turn around and leave, to head back home, back to its spacious, well-lit rooms, and gardens, and birds chirping in the trees. How could she live here?

Yet where is my home?

As if reading her mind, Mrs. Grady advanced toward the window and swept the curtains open, allowing a glimmer of grayish light to filter in from the window. "Hmm, the rain has stopped," she announced, sniffing and peering outside.

Helena joined her. Her window faced a long row of brick town homes. They were tall and elegant, with several chimneys smoking away. Below, she could see the carriages ambling down the road. There was no garden or fields.

She turned to face the small wooden table with a washbasin and pitcher. Above it, a round mirror hung on the wall. To her left, an open closet revealed two simple dresses, one gray, and the other a mousy brown color. Like uniforms, they hung there, a testimony to the previous governess who had spent time in the schoolroom with her charge.

"The last governess left in a hurry and some of her belongings are still in the closet." Mrs. Grady wrinkled her face, as if she smelled an offending odor.

"Oh?"

"She had mighty fine airs, she did. She was a redheaded beauty and barely eighteen. I saw trouble when I saw her. I said she wasn't going to last long, not with those flighty ways of hers, and I was right. Her mind wasn't on her charge, but on flirting with Mrs. Stirling's brother, Mr. Felix, who was visiting, but decided to stay indefinitely. Two weeks didn't pass before she was let go because of him." Her eyes had formed into two slits.

"I assure you, Mrs. Grady, you have no fear on that end," Helena replied with as stern a voice as she could manage. "I am here for one purpose and that is to be a governess."

"I wasn't referring to you, miss. Mr. Felix goes for the flirting, attractive ones, he does." Mrs. Grady snorted.

Helena felt slightly bothered by the woman's remark. *Am I that unattractive?*

A male servant arrived with the luggage and placed them in the room, and left.

"Take this opportunity to rest. I don't think they'll be seeing you anytime tonight, given the late hours they keep. Tomorrow you will meet with the Missus and then begin the day with Miss Stirling. She is a bundle of energy and cannot sit still." Mrs. Grady stood at the door. "I'll have the maid bring warm water and light the fireplace. Oh, and I'll bring your meal shortly."

"Thank you, Mrs. Grady. What time should I make my appearance?"

"You will breakfast at eight in your room. I will take you down to the drawing room at nine. My room is next to yours if you need anything."

After Mrs. Grady left, Helena turned and stared at herself in the mirror. Her normally glowing face was pale and drawn. Dark shadows circled her eyes, showing evidence of her recent mourning and sleepless nights. Her hair was displaying its usual signs of disarray and her nose was embarrassingly red from the cold. Her normally full mouth was set into a thin, determined line, like a soldier marching into battle.

She frowned at her reflection. There was no sign of contentment or the promise of happiness in her blue eyes, but instead, a much older woman than her nineteen years stared back at her. She had aged into a woman overnight. She looked at least thirty, and her features were plain and stern.

No wonder Mrs. Grady had made that comment.

Helena removed her hat and cloak, and then went and gazed sadly outside the window, remembering riding her horse, Tiger, in the luscious green landscape outside Oxfordshire. She'd fly through the wind, feeling joyful, as the fresh, clean air filled her lungs. There were only townhomes here. She glimpsed the setting sun spreading itself thin like butter over the tops of the homes she faced.

She thought about the Greek property and wondered how long it would take to earn her fare for the trip. Mr. Weldon had not mentioned the pay for her services. If all went well, she hoped she would have amassed enough money for the trip and for her expenses in a few months.

It seemed too long a time, especially if there were treasures waiting to be discovered. Once she found the treasures, then all her worries would disappear. She pictured herself being wealthy and returning to Oxford to marry the handsome Dr. Murphy. Would he still be available? Would he want to court her then?

A short time later, Mrs. Grady brought the meal on a tray. "There you are, Miss Cadfield."

A maid followed Mrs. Grady into the room, carrying a bucket of warm water in one hand and a bucket of coal in the other. The two women caused much commotion as they moved around the small room, taking care of their tasks and chatting away.

Mrs. Grady talked incessantly, seeming to take great pleasure in criticizing the cook, saying that the chicken was overcooked because no one knew what time the Stirlings would arrive, so the cook had begun the dinner early, and "now look at how stringy the chicken looks."

Helena did not see anything wrong with her portion. Although the chicken breast was small, it looked perfectly fine to her. She kept silent, nodding and glancing hungrily at her plate, hoping Mrs. Grady would get the cue that she preferred to be alone. The maid finished lighting the fire, and curtsied and left.

Mrs. Grady took one last look at the offending chicken, sniffed, and then shut the door behind her.

Helena promptly began eating. The act of chewing the chicken was a reminder that she was feeding her starved body. The crusty bread with butter proved to be quite delicious, while the pickled relish more than made up for any inconveniences in the meal. The black tea was hot and soothed her throat on this cold evening, and the heat from the fireplace was warming up the room.

Afterwards, with much deliberation, Helena presumptuously unpacked her clothing. Although she did not have an interview yet with the Mistress of the house, she felt that she had already passed inspection through Mrs. Grady. She shook each of her three dresses, smoothing the creases that had formed in the luggage and hung them in the closet next to the other two governess dresses.

Helena combed and braided her hair, and then changed into her night robe. She retrieved the *Iliad* from the luggage. She brought it along to save it from the clutches of the Weldons.

The bed was uncomfortably small, and as a result, her feet dangled over the end. Attempting to find a comfortable position, she propped her knees up and settled the book on them. Immersed in the story, she pictured handsome Paris wooing beautiful Helen from her home in Sparta while her husband, King Menelaus was away, and looting Menelaus's treasures, and taking her to Troy with him.

Helena was beginning to doze off, soothed by the warmth of the cozy fireplace, when the clattering sound of a carriage awoke her. She lay alert in bed, listening to the voices and commotion in the house.

The Stirling family had arrived.

A sharp pounding on the door startled her. She shot up in alarm, clutching the blanket close to her. Helena pictured Mrs. Stirling's brother barging in here, thinking the previous governess might still be here. She was about to call out, but her voice was unwilling to cooperate, and she dumbly watched in dismay as the door swung open, realizing too late that she had not locked it.

Helena blindly groped for the blanket, staring at a girl, whom she presumed was Miss Stirling. She was small in stature and looked younger than her fourteen years. Obviously, she had raced up the stairs as soon as she had gotten here, for she was panting from the exertion and still wore her brown overcoat, hat, and mittens. Her black hair lay limp under her hat. Her small, dark eyes appeared cross and defiant as if Helena had offended her in some way. In the dimly lit room, her face had a scornful expression, with shadows etched on her face one minute, and flitting around the next.

"You're the new governess, aren't you? Answer me this minute!" She shouted in a high-pitched voice, stomping her foot, acting as if it were perfectly normal to barge into people's rooms in the middle of the night and yell at them.

How could Helena answer the little Napoleon, when her whole body was trembling like a shaky leaf, and she was clutching the blanket, trying to maintain a sense of respectability? How could she maintain her professionalism while dressed in her nightclothes and with her hair in braids like a schoolgirl?

Helena pulled the blanket protectively over her body, trying to gather her wits about her, wondering if the girl was in her right mind. A governess was supposed to be calm and in charge, and should always have the upper hand, she thought.

"Yes. I am Miss Cadfield. I presume you are Miss Stirling."

"Only to people who are not family. My family calls me Catty, which is short for Catherine."

She stepped into the room with a decisive air, studying Helena contemptuously. "I don't want a governess. That is why the others left. You won't last here, either, because they all say that I am difficult. So why bother? You can leave first thing tomorrow."

Helena ignored her caustic remark. "I would have liked to have thanked you for your warm welcome, but unfortunately your bad manners prevented me from saying so."

This seemed to catch Miss Stirling off guard and her face changed, almost appearing older than her years, into a grave and thoughtful look, before she resumed her defiant pose. "I'll be fifteen soon. I am too old for a governess."

"Well, that's for your parents to decide," Helena replied smartly.

"I will tell Mother that you aren't nice to me, and we'll see about that." Miss Stirling tossed her head back and stuck her tongue out at Helena, and then ran out the door, leaving her agitated and unnerved.

Helena scrambled out of the bed and ran to the door, locking it, her heart pounding. Her hopes of working with this girl were dashed to the ground before she even had started. She had no experience dealing with children. There were no cousins, or nephews, or even nieces to play with. This interaction with Miss Stirling did little to help build her confidence.

Helena did not know what to do next. She sat on the edge of the bed, her mind racing for solutions. She bit her lip, knowing there was no other alternative. *I have nowhere else to go.*

She must follow through with this.

CHAPTER 13

The next morning, before nine, Mrs. Grady came and took Helena to the drawing room. Helena carried with her a copy of *The Iliad* for Miss Stirling's Greek lessons.

"I hear ye had a visit last night from Miss *high and mighty*," Mrs. Grady grumbled. "She woke everyone, she did."

"Yes."

"She's done that before. Should've told ye to lock the door. What that girl needs is a wallop, a good-sized wallop." Mrs. Grady smacked her wrinkled lips, looking as though she were envisioning the act, and then grinned foolishly, revealing crooked teeth. "There's a bet on that ye won't last a week here." She chuckled, giving her a knowing look.

Taken aback by her comment, Helena secretly wondered on which side she had placed her bet. They walked quietly down the stairs.

"Will I be seeing Mrs. Stirling?"

"Yes, ye'll be seeing her."

Helena felt deflated by the conversation and remained quiet. If Mrs. Stirling was anything like her daughter, Helena's chances of remaining here were slim. Her feet felt quite heavy, and she dreaded the meeting.

Upon entering the parlor, Helena was introduced to Mrs. Stirling, an attractive young woman, around five and twenty, who greeted her with a smile that revealed perfect white teeth.

Mrs. Stirling had a flawless complexion, a small pert nose, large blue eyes, and golden-brown ringlets. Her slender figure was clothed in a fashionable dress that showed to her advantage.

Helena's fingers automatically smoothed the creases in her dress, feeling as if her simple attire was dowdy. She joined her on the sofa. She could not picture Mrs. Stirling as the mother of that contemptible child she met last night. They were like night and day, both in looks and in character. Helena glanced around for a sign of her pupil, and to her relief, saw that she was not present. She relaxed slightly, placing her book to the side.

Mrs. Stirling's blue eyes twinkled, as though she were amused. "Miss Cadfield," she said with a slight, German accent, "Mr. Weldon has the highest regard for you and your late father. He mentions in his letter that you impressed him with your education in several subjects, particularly the languages. You do speak German, do you not? *Sprechen zie Deutsche, ja?*"

"*Ja, ich spreche Deutsche.*"

Mrs. Stirling clasped her hands in delight. "*Sehr gut.* I am so delighted that you speak German."

They continued the conversation in German, with Mrs. Stirling talking affectionately about her home country, people, food, and customs. She asked Helena whether she had ever been to Bavaria, and Helena told her that she had not, but that she had learned German from her father.

Helena realized after a while that Mrs. Stirling wanted only to talk about herself and her country. She quietly listened, straining to understand all the German phrases spewed in quick succession. Helena learned that the young King Otto of Greece was from Bavaria, and that Mrs. Stirling's relatives were the first staff to move to Greece with Prince Otto when he became monarch there. They worked there in many capacities.

"Even my husband recently was assigned a position under King Otto, with help from my relatives," Mrs. Stirling said.

Helena's heart skipped a beat when she heard about Greece. "Mr. Stirling is in Greece?"

"Yes, he has been working there temporarily."

When Mrs. Stirling paused to take a sip of tea, Helena toyed with the idea of asking her whether she planned to go to Greece, but decided not to ask so early in the interview. Instead, she politely changed the subject, and talked about her daughter.

"I had a chance to meet your daughter last night," Helena began, studying her face for any sign of surprise, but was not rewarded that satisfaction. She continued. "She entered my room without permission and appeared cross that I was here."

"Oh yes, that is Catherine all right," Mrs. Stirling said, looking at Helena as if conspiring with her, as though they were the best of friends. She sighed. "Of course, you do not know why she is the way she is. She has not behaved well since her mother passed away two years ago."

Stunned by the news, Helena tried to regain her composure. *Mrs. Stirling was not the girl's mother.* That explained everything. Helena was no longer upset with the child, but feeling sorry for her, for she knew how it felt to lose a parent.

"You see, I met Mr. Stirling in Bavaria over a year ago. He had traveled there with some friends. Well, he knew English and his German was not that good. When we met at a dinner party, he was so happy that he could speak English to me. You see, I had taken lessons in English and could speak it well. We spent some time together and fell in love, and then he proposed." Mrs. Stirling blushed prettily. "Of course, I accepted and left my country and came here, and we married quietly, but Catherine is such a headstrong and difficult child, and will not listen to anyone but her *vater*. She has been straining my nerves so much lately." Her lovely hand, slightly bent at the wrist, fluttered to her forehead, and she tilted her head to the side, batting her eyelashes and sighing.

Helena secretly wondered if she had ever been in the theatre; she reminded her of someone acting the part.

"Mr. Weldon mentioned that you were looking for a governess for her," Helena prompted, anxiously wondering whether they still wanted a governess. "That is the reason I came here. I was interested in the position."

"*Ja*! That is so. Unfortunately, the previous governesses did not do well at all. They were too young and flighty. Catherine needs an older, more mature person." Mrs. Stirling studied Helena for a moment or two.

"I am quite mature for my age."

"I can see that. I think you would do fine."

Mrs. Stirling told her that her responsibility was to teach Miss Stirling the languages, embroidery, dancing, and painting. Helena was to eat alone in her room unless the family called for her to dine with them.

"You will receive eighty-eight pounds a year, paid monthly."

Helena did a quick calculation in her head. That came to a little over seven pounds a month. *I would have to work at least four months to earn my fare to Greece.* Four months seemed like a long time. She would have to be careful with spending her money. She thanked her, trying not to show her disappointment.

Mrs. Stirling nodded pleasantly. "I am happy it worked out." She rang for Hans, and asked him to fetch Miss Stirling and to prepare the carriage for her.

He informed her that Miss Stirling had gone for a walk with Mr. Helzig right after breakfast and had not returned yet.

"Thank you, Hans," Mrs. Stirling said.

He bowed and left.

"Oh, dear. My brother Felix is such a nice fellow, but I'm afraid he has spoiled her ever since Mr. Stirling left for Greece." Mrs. Stirling pouted slightly.

"Then I will await their return."

"Meanwhile, I have some things that need to be mended, and I will have them brought to your room. Now if you will excuse me, I must be off to town."

* * *

Helena sat near her window sewing the stockings from the basket that Mrs. Stirling had given her. A growing pile of neatly folded stockings had formed on the table. Most of them were gray and black, and there was an occasional blue one. She had not expected to be doing this. Feeling a little resentful, she sighed and rubbed her aching neck. *Where was that girl?* She threaded her needle, and then grabbed a thick wool stocking and began sewing again. Sensing resistance, she jabbed through the thick, scratchy material, stabbing her thumb.

"Ouch!" Helena jumped up, dropping the stocking. She sucked the bleeding thumb, pacing the room, her anger and resentment growing. Was she to be sewing stockings all day, cooped up in this tiny room? She searched for a clean handkerchief and wrapped her thumb with it.

A clap of thunder startled her. Helena rushed to the window and gazed outside at the swollen, gray clouds that threatened rain again. It was two o'clock and still no sign of Miss Stirling or Mr. Helzig.

Helena looked at the stockings in the basket and blinked back her tears. She had been sewing since nine thirty this morning. Except for Mrs. Grady who had popped in an hour ago with tea and crumpets, Helena had been alone, waiting for her charge to return.

She missed her daily rides in Oxford and reading the books in their library. She missed Nana's cheerful presence each morning when she came into her bedroom to open the curtains. She missed Dr. Murphy, too. Helena sighed. Why did her father have to die? Then she remembered her mother and grandfather. *Why does anyone have to die?*

Helena finished mending the stocking, being careful not to press on the injured thumb. She cut and tied the thread, and then folded and placed the stocking on the pile on the table.

Mrs. Grady visited her. "Best if ye come quickly, miss. Mr. Helzig arrived with Miss Stirling. Ye can't leave them to their devices. He said they went walking to the Serpentine, and then shopping. Don't know whether I trust him. He's as bad as she is," she mumbled.

Helena followed the housekeeper down the stairs.

"All me time is spent cleaning up after her, and now him. I'm behind on me other work, 'tis a crime, I say." Mrs. Grady's keys jingled with every step she took. "They's got puddles on the floor from all that rain, and I'm down on me knees cleaning it up."

"Is this the way things are always here?" Helena ventured.

"Oh, no, miss, not when her father is around, it isn't, but once he's gone, everyone does what they's wants, including Mrs. Stirling." Mrs. Grady gave a loud sniff. "What Miss Stirling needs is a firm hand. If you're too soft, like the other governesses, you won't last long here. Mark my words."

Helena heard shouting and laughter coming from the drawing room.

"Right in there, miss, they are," Mrs. Grady said, with a gleam in her eye as she opened the door to the drawing room before hurrying off to finish cleaning the floor.

CHAPTER 14

Helena entered the room and shut the door behind her, taking everything in, her heart sinking. The room looked as though a strong wind had passed through it and had tossed everything around. Scattered here and there on the floor were several pillows, shards of broken vases, and a toppled end table.

Catherine had her back turned to Helena. Her hair was wet and stringy from the rain. She was shouting and waving her arms up and down excitedly at Mr. Helzig, who stood to the far left. They were the only ones in the room, and were evidently intent on their game and had not seen Helena.

Struck by Catherine's exuberance, Helena wondered at the positive change, and then she saw Felix Helzig. Even with wet hair, he was fair and exceedingly handsome. He had a fine nose, blue eyes, and a firm chin. Now she understood why the other governesses had fallen for him, but Helena was different.

Catherine threw an object at Felix. It sailed over the sofa, and he caught it easily. With a flip of the wrist, he threw it with greater force back at her, laughing all the time. She giggled, ducking just in time, thus moving out of its path.

"Ha, you thought I'd catch it," Catherine shouted triumphantly at him.

Helena's quick reflexes saved her from the hurling object headed her way. She sidestepped in time, avoiding collision with them. A resounding crash behind her made both Miss Stirling and Felix turn her way. Both their grins froze on their faces. Helena gazed sadly at the torn book that lay on the floor. Its victim, the broken pieces of a vase, lay next to it.

She felt her face become hot, realizing what had happened. The book that lay before her was none other than her father's precious *Iliad* that she had brought down earlier in the day and had forgotten there. She picked it up slowly, carefully smoothing back the twisted pages, and then picked up a few shards of the ceramic vase from the floor, trying to regain her composure.

"Miss Cadfield! Miss Cadfield!" Miss Stirling shouted, running toward her, laughing. "The maid can clean it. Give me back that book."

Helena clutched it instinctively to her chest, trying to preserve what little dignity she had. "I brought down this important book for your lesson," she said, her voice shaking. "It's a very important book indeed, and written in Greek."

She was unprepared for what came next, for Miss Stirling thrust her impish, laughing face close to her face while her busy fingers tried to ply the book from her hands. Unable to achieve it, for Helena was stronger than she was, she began tickling her. Her deceptive fingers probed and poked Helena's waist with impunity. Helena could not help herself and laughed uncontrollably at her antics, trying to move away from her prying hands, but Miss Stirling was like a leech. She wrestled the book away from Helena's hands, and turned around ready to throw it back to Felix, but he was already there to grab it from her hands.

Felix wrapped his arm around Miss Stirling's shoulders in a brotherly fashion, as she lunged forward once more for the book tucked under his arm. "I will hold you dear niece and tickle you until you make the proper introductions to this lovely creature," he said.

Helena felt herself blush at the compliment, for he reminded her of the French men who tried to flirt with her when she was a student in Paris. She had made sure that her appearance was anything but lovely, particularly after she heard about his affair with the previous governess. Her hair was pulled back severely, and her somber, black dress emphasized her pale face. The last thing she wanted was to encourage this kind of flirtatious talk in front of Miss Stirling.

Mr. Helzig's pale blue eyes, shrewd and calculating, did not match his smiling face. She steeled herself, feeling slightly annoyed because deep down inside, she knew that he toyed with her emotions. She did not care for it one bit.

Helena noticed Miss Stirling's demeanor change like quicksilver. Her lips had become a thin line of contention, and the cranky, angry girl returned from last night. Miss Stirling made the introductions sullenly, her eyes lowered.

Helena curtsied politely, and Felix bowed gallantly back.

Helena turned to Miss Stirling. "Your stepmother informed me that I am your governess. Since I have been waiting all day to begin language lessons, I'm afraid we will have to start them at this late hour."

Miss Stirling's face darkened, and her brows crossed. "I want to begin them tomorrow." She challenged Helena with a defiant look.

"Why waste your time closed up in a room upstairs? Your company will be more appreciated here," Felix said playfully to Helena.

Miss Stirling's body tensed as she twisted out of his hold, her eyes looking downward. In that brief movement, Helena realized where the girl's affections lay.

"Thank you for the compliment, but Miss Stirling's education is my priority," Helena answered. "May I have my book back?"

Mr. Helzig dutifully handed her the book. Helena tucked it under her arm, and then seized Miss Stirling's hand, opened the door, and marched past Hans, who shot up, his face a bright-red color. He had apparently been listening at the door.

"Let go of my hand!" Miss Stirling shouted.

Helena's grip remained strong as she pulled her up the stairs. From the corner of her eye, she could see Mr. Helzig standing at the foot of the stairs laughing at them.

"In Greek, you would say *Afise to heri mou, se parakalo*, which means please let go of my hand," Helena said firmly. "If you repeat that correctly back to me, I will oblige."

"I don't want to learn Greek!" Catherine screamed.

All the servants had lined up next to Mr. Helzig, including Mrs. Grady, and were staring up at them with smirks on their faces. Helena wondered if they were checking to see what she would do next. She knew that they had put a bet on whether she would last a week in this household. She was determined to show them that she was in charge.

Helena pulled the feisty girl up the stairs, panting from the exertion. They were almost there. "Just think, knowing the Greek language will give you the opportunity to share secrets so that no one else knows what you are talking about," she said.

Catherine scowled. "I don't want to learn Greek."

"Then we will also learn another language. How about Pig Latin?"

"Pig Latin? Is that pig talk?" Catherine snorted. "I don't want to talk like a pig."

"This is a special language that few people know about."

Helena now had Catherine's undivided attention as they entered the spacious schoolroom. It had two windows, a large table and two chairs, a bookshelf that held several books, and many drawing and painting materials, among other things. She shut the door behind her, and then let go of the girl's arm. She leaned against the door, trying to catch her breath and making sure the girl would not make a dash for it.

"Thomas Jefferson used Pig Latin when he was young, and it's easy to learn. All you do is move the first letter of a word to the end and add an 'ay' to it. For example, your name Catherine would be atherinecay and my name Miss Cadfield would be *Issmay Adfieldcay*."

Catherine wrinkled her brows, appearing puzzled. She suppressed a giggle. "*Elixfay Elzighay*," she said, and broke out giggling. "*Issesmay Arleyfay.*" Another bout of giggling ensued.

Helena smiled. "Since you don't want to learn Greek, how about French?"

Catherine stopped her giggling and crossed her arms. "I don't want to learn any languages."

"What do you want to learn? How to play throwing a book?" Helena asked lightly, trying not to let her anger show. She lifted *The Iliad* that she had been carrying, her heart bleeding at the torn pages that lay before her. "I don't think that will go far in this life."

"I know many things. I know French and German," Catherine said, her eyes flashing.

"All right then, let's see what we have here." Helena looked through the collection of books and chose the book of folk and fairy tales written in German by the Grimm brothers. "Come, sit next to me." She sat down at the table and patted the chair next to her.

Catherine did not budge. She stood there, her arms crossed.

Helena spoke to her in English. "Learning is a lifetime endeavor. Everything around us is an opportunity to learn. Your lessons will not be limited to the classroom. We will spend time taking walks and learning not only the languages, but also about history and other cultures, like ancient Greece."

Catherine sniffed.

Helena opened the pages, leafing through it slowly. "Please join me so you can hear me," she said quietly.

Catherine sighed, and plopped down next to her.

Helena stopped at a certain section. "Have you read the *Frog Prince* yet? This was one of my favorite stories when I was young."

"I'm half way through the *Frog Prince*! Here, let me show you where I'm at."

Helena handed her the book.

Catherine leafed through several pages until she found the chapter. She read a few words in German, stumbling over them, and then gave back the book. "Read to me, but promise you'll go slowly."

"Thank you." Helena read slowly in German, pronouncing the long words carefully. "Next day, when the King's daughter sat at the table with her father, eating from her golden plate, something was heard coming up the marble stairs, splish-splash, splish-splash."

"It's the frog!" Catherine cried. "He's come after her."

Helena nodded, enjoying the rapt look from her student's face. She continued reading in German. "What does the frog want of you? asked the King. Oh, dear Father, when I was playing by the fountain, my golden ball fell into the water and this frog fetched it up again because I cried so much. I must tell you that I promised him to be my playmate. I never thought that he would come out of the water."

As Helena read the rest of the story, she aided Catherine in the pronunciation and explained the meaning of several words. "The frog turned into a handsome prince with beautiful eyes, who after a short while, became with her father's consent, her dearest friend and playmate."

Catherine grew starry-eyed as she listened intently.

Helena closed the book when she finished. "And that is the end of the story." She checked her watch.

"Read me another story," Catherine said, grabbing her arm.

Helena smiled. Although Catherine was fourteen, at this moment, she resembled a much younger child. The yearning in the girl's voice touched her.

"Tomorrow, if you promise to meet me after breakfast, we can resume our reading," Helena said. "Now you must change and get ready for dinner."

And that is how Helena started her first day as a governess in the Stirling residence.

CHAPTER 15

Athens, Greece
3 September, 1837

Aristotle and Yianni rode on mules carrying supplies, leaving Athens and heading west on the dusty road. Though the breeze was crisp, the sun's rays warmed their bodies. They traveled lightly, with the idea of locating the Cadfield site in Nemea, scouting the property, and returning to Athens for more supplies. They also needed to hire workers.

Yianni appeared familiar with the terrain as they ambled toward their destination, his tanned, round face seeming content beneath his bright red bandanna. They passed carriages, men on horseback, and wagons. Slowly, they left the busy city of Athens. Once outside its boundaries, they found little signs of life.

Riding through the plain, they passed a few olive orchards, bushes and uncultivated farmland. It appeared desolate and quiet, except for the occasional ringing of bells from the shepherds guiding their flocks of sheep. The sloping gray mountains remained in the distance to their right, with more mountains looming ahead. Periodically, they came across damaged buildings and homes, turned into piles of stone and rubble. Yianni pointed them out to Aristotle as remnants of the revolution. To their left, the immense Saronic Gulf's blue water glistened under the sun's bright rays.

Soon, they stopped near the edge of the bank for a break.

As they took care of the animals, Aristotle thought about the events of the previous days. He had met with Dr. Kostakis a few days ago and finalized the plans for the site. He was to be in charge of the excavation project at the Cadfield site, as well as buying the supplies and paying the workers.

He also had found himself back at Barba Manolis's house the previous afternoon with Yianni. Aristotle played backgammon with Barba Manolis. When Magdalene had arrived, and helped serve dinner with Despina, Aristotle quickly sensed Barba Manolis's attempt at matchmaking, through his winks and gestures afterwards. Although Aristotle was attracted to the young woman, she was shy and kept her eyes lowered. She was beautiful, but rarely talked or showed any interest in his conversation, which left him feeling nonplussed. Typically, women tended to be interested in him. He wondered if she secretly had a beau.

Yianni's lively singing interrupted Aristotle's thoughts.

"I've gone through this area so many times, boss," Yianni said, watering the mule. "I know it by heart."

"Hmm, that is good," Aristotle said, removing the bag of food and jug of water from the saddlebag. "Tell me, Yianni, do you know anything about Magdalene, the sister of Despina?"

"She's a pretty girl," Yianni replied, winking. "I know that she will be engaged soon."

"She will?"

"You are looking at him," Yianni answered, then continued singing his happy tune. "Ah, life is wonderful when you have your health and a job, and no one is firing at you from behind those trees, because you believe in another religion. Now that I am earning some money, I decided to propose to Magdalene last night."

Aristotle was startled to hear Yianni's confession. For some reason, he could not see him marrying Magdalene. "You did?"

"Yes, but she is too shy." Yianni scowled. "As soon as I talked with her, she lowered her head like a lamb. I like my woman to be like that, meek, but-" He paused, as if thinking.

Aristotle cocked his eyebrows. "But?"

"She is too young, only sixteen, and not ready for marriage." Yianni began whistling. "I can wait for her to grow up, boss."

Magdalene's reserved nature had placed her several years older in Aristotle's mind. *She was definitely off limits.*

After they washed, they sat under a tree to eat their meal of bread, cheese, and olives.

"How about you, boss? Do you have a woman?"

Aristotle's thoughts turned to Greta Heinz. He had met her years ago in Munich, when Ludwig, his college friend and her brother, had invited him over for dinner one day. She was fair, with exquisite features, and clear blue eyes that beckoned and challenged at the same time.

"There's Miss Heinz, my best friend's sister in Germany," Aristotle replied thoughtfully. "I've known her since she was twelve. She used to say that when she grew up she would marry me, but that was many years ago. I have watched her develop into a beautiful young woman, pursued by many beaus. She dances superbly and plays the piano well."

Yianni whistled. "Sounds like a good catch. Have you proposed to her?"

"I was always busy with school and work, and saw her mostly as a younger sister, although I admit that lately I was beginning to feel differently about her." Aristotle drank some water. "On the day of my departure, she promised that she'd pay me a visit with her brother."

"She is interested in you, boss."

"Yes, but she made it clear that she will not leave Germany," Aristotle replied wearily. He had entertained the idea of courting her after he received his graduate degree, but this trip to Greece had put that idea to rest.

"But how will you manage it if she comes here and you two marry?"

Aristotle shrugged his shoulders. "When I decide to marry, my wife will have to live here in Greece with me," he said firmly.

Soon, they were back on the road. They traveled through an uninhabited, barren plain with broken down buildings.

"Look at all these ruins. Greece's freedom came with a heavy price tag and that's hard to forget," Aristotle said.

"We are left behind, so we must make the best of it."

Several hours later, they stopped for the night at the inn just outside Corinth. It would be too dark to travel through the hills that led to Nemea. After dining, Aristotle and Yianni sat at the dining-room table studying the map.

Yianni pointed to an oil-stained area with his dirty finger. "Boss, we are here. We continue through these hills and then here is Nemea, a valley that sits at the base of the Arcadian mountains. Petri is behind it, and the closest village near the Cadfield site, a few kilometers on the other side."

The next morning, they left for Nemea, traveling through a number of hills and villages. Three hours later, when they passed through a valley and reached the foot of the mountain, they stopped for another break.

"Boss, did you know that there is a mountain region up north, in Trikala, that is purely Greek, called the *"agrapha,"* which means unwritten? People who live there have never shown their faces in Athens. There's a good reason for it."

"They were hiding from the Turks?"

Yianni nodded. "The mountains also make good hiding places for the *klephtes* (thieves) and bandits."

"I am aware of them."

"Make sure you never carry much money or treasures on you, and have a good reason to be there, or else," Yianni joked, his arm making a slicing motion across his thick neck. He took a swig of water from his jar and wiped his mouth with the back of his hand.

"I spent time up in the mountains escaping the Turks with my grandfather when I was young. I learned then that the Mastoras name held weight," Aristotle said, remembering the respect the bandits held for his grandfather. "They won't harm us."

Yianni wagged his head knowingly. "These are different times."

They continued their ride, and reached a small, sheltered village that sat in the valley near the foot of the mountain. It contained a small store, a coffee shop, a village well, and a few homes nestled within walking distance of the town. Several buildings were damaged, including the coffee shop where musket fire had ripped part of the side off.

Yianni stopped and took out his map. "It is here somewhere, boss," he said, scratching his head and looking at the map.

Aristotle saw an old, weathered man sitting in front of the *cafenio*, drinking coffee. "Let's ask him for directions," he told Yianni.

They rode up to the man. Yianni greeted him. *"Yiasou Barba."*

"Eh? What did you say?" The man stood up, looking bewildered, gesturing toward his ear. "I lost my hearing during the war."

Yianni shouted his greeting. "We are looking for Nikos Kallodaftis's house."

The old man looked at him keenly, his interest apparently aroused. "God rest their souls," he said. He pointed with his trembling arm at a grove of trees behind them. "Go straight, and there, where the almond trees are, on your right you will see a dirt path. Follow it up the hill, until you see the house on your left."

The two men thanked him and rode ahead.

They found the dirt path, almost invisible to the undiscerning eye, and continued their journey up the mountain, passing almond trees, and a grove of olive trees. Birds chirping in overhead branches provided a cheerful chorus, while clusters of red and yellow wildflowers along the path, swaying with the gentle breeze, greeted them as they passed by.

At some point, the path disappeared into a dark, woodland area that jutted against the wall of the mountain. They had reached a fork in the road. To their right was a small, meandering path lined with bushes and trees on each side, and to their left, another small, wooded path.

Yianni stopped and scratched his head, as if thinking. He turned around and shrugged his shoulders. He unfolded the map once more and looked at it. "It must be here somewhere," he said.

"Who goes there?" someone shouted.

Aristotle gazed around him, trying to pinpoint where the shout came from.

"Boss, look," Yianni said, pointing upward. "I told you we need to be careful! Bandits!"

Aristotle looked up. Above the wooded area, on the cliff of the mountain, three men on horses were pointing muskets at them.

The men disappeared before Aristotle could say anything. He breathed a sigh of relief, but it did not last. Yianni jabbed him on his side, his head nodding backward.

Aristotle turned around. The bandits had arrived.

CHAPTER 16

Armed and dressed in dark clothing, the swarthy young men wore black bandannas wrapped around their heads. They sat confidently on their horses and regarded him suspiciously. His heart pounded in his chest as he studied them. *I must remember not to show any signs of fear.*

"What are you doing here?" one of them sneered.

"We are here on business for the Archaeological Society," Aristotle replied firmly.

"A foreigner," another bandit said, and spat on the ground. He lifted his weapon and shot at the ground in front of Aristotle.

Aristotle felt sick, as if someone had punched his stomach. His mule, startled by the shot, became agitated. Aristotle pulled forcefully on his leash, trying to control him, while Yianni's mule ran off.

The three bandits laughed as Yianni and Aristotle tried to gain control of their mules.

"*Brrrr!*" Yianni shouted at his mule. He finally turned the mule around and stood there, a pained look on his face.

Aristotle sensed the immaturity of the bandits. They were firing their guns, trying to prove their might. "I'm not a foreigner. I was born here in Greece. I am looking for Dr. Cadfield's site," he said calmly. He gazed at them steadily.

"So, you are looking for Cadfield's site," the third bandit said, sneering. Quiet until now, he jumped down from his horse, swaggering toward him. He was the oldest of the three and was darkly handsome, except for a scar that marred his cheek. He held his musket skillfully in his right hand.

"Yes," Aristotle replied.

"It was never Cadfield's site! Nikos Kallodaftis owned it," the scarred bandit said, raising his weapon slowly.

Aristotle's whole body was taut. He was ready to jump off his mule if the man fired. From the corner of his eye, he could see Yianni edging his mule nervously closer to him. He must remember to buy a firearm next time, if there was a next time.

"Yes, but after he died, Dr. Cadfield who was his son-in-law, owned it. He is also dead," Aristotle said matter-of-factly, as if he were having a conversation with a friend. "Now the Archaeological Society is claiming the property."

The scarred bandit aimed his musket at Aristotle. "You will be dead, too, if you don't leave."

Aristotle locked eyes with the bandit, not yielding. "My grandfather also fought bravely in the Greek revolution. He was a mighty fighter. Aristotle Mastoras was his name."

There was a moment of silence as Aristotle eyed the scarred bandit.

The bandit's face slowly formed a smile, which seemed genuine. "I heard about your grandfather. He is a legend. My family and I fought in the war too, brother. They call me Phillipa. Phillipa Mavros." He lowered his weapon and threw it to one of the men, who caught it. He swaggered toward Aristotle and shook his hand. His handshake was firm.

"Meet my younger brothers, Markos and Nikos." His arm swept toward the bandits sitting on their horses.

They smiled widely at Aristotle.

Aristotle nodded slowly.

"But now that we have you here, we cannot leave without asking for something. You see, we must make a living." Phillipa's grin was wide as his eyes settled on the watch that hung on a gold chain on Aristotle's vest. He opened his rough palm, while his other hand rested on the handle of the knife that sat firmly in its belted sleeve. "Come, you have that watch to give us, I am sure."

Aristotle tensed. The watch had belonged to his grandfather. He clenched his fists as Phillipa came forward and reaching up, grabbed his watch, gazing at it, ready to pull it away. He gripped Phillipa's hand in a vice-like hold. "Not so fast. This was my grandfather's watch. I have a proposal to make first. One that will earn you money."

"What is it?" Phillipa slowly removed his hand.

"I am looking for people to watch the site for me. It needs to be protected from-" Aristotle was about to say bandits, but held back.

"From whom? Nobody comes up here," said Phillipa, scowling.

Aristotle knew that he was taking a chance in hiring these bandits, but he knew that they could be loyal to a cause. "That is for me to decide. Are you interested?"

"Dr. Mastoras, look," Yianni interrupted, making the sign of the cross and pulling his mule closer to him. His face was breaking out into a sweat. "Crossing the path of a priest brings you bad luck."

Aristotle turned and saw a lonely priest ambling toward them, carrying a bag in one hand and using a cane. His long, black gown billowed around his thin frame, and his white, feathery beard flowed down his front. His kind, weathered face graced a wide smile when he saw them.

"Greetings," the priest said. He turned and looked at the bandits. "How are you, my brothers?"

"*Figame*! We are gone. He will bring us bad luck." Phillipa scrambled away and jumped on his horse. He vanished with his brothers up the mountain, back where they came from.

Aristotle laughed heartily as his hand rested on the watch. He must make sure to keep it hidden from now on. "Come now. You don't believe in those tales about priests having powers."

Yianni nodded his head knowingly toward the bandits. "They seem to think so, boss."

Aristotle and Yianni dismounted from their mules and went to meet the priest. The priest appeared happy to see them. They made introductions. Aristotle learned that he was a priest-monk, and his name was Elder James.

"I was returning from the village and was headed to my humble quarters when I saw you," Elder James told them. His beard quivered as he talked. His eyes were lively, taking everything in.

"Father, may I ask you a question?" Yianni asked. "Why did those bandits flee when they saw you?"

"Don't worry about them. They think I have the power to bring bad luck to them because I visited Nikos Kallodaftis when he was sick, and then he died that evening."

Yianni's eyes bulged like a frog's as he stepped back, his face breaking out into a sweat. "Yes, but they also carry weapons."

"Don't fear the person who can hurt your body, but the person who can hurt your spirit," Elder James replied. "What brings you this way?"

"We have come from Athens and are looking for Dr. Cadfield's house," Aristotle replied.

Elder James appeared reflective. He made the sign of the cross, then reverently touched the cross hanging from a chain on his neck. "I met Dr. Cadfield. He is the British man that died on the Kallodaftis property. I presided over his funeral. God rest his soul."

"Yes," Aristotle said. "Our map shows his house to be somewhere around here."

"I'm afraid it is on the other side. When you get to the fork in the road, you swerve east," Elder James said, pointing to their left. "The brothers live above here. You must be careful not to bring anything of value up here or they'll snatch it from you."

Aristotle pondered over the priest's words. "But what if they are given a job and earn decent money?"

The priest appeared thoughtful. "That is rare here, but it might change things." He nodded, smiling. "You must be tired from your trip. Come to my humble home for some tea and respite from the sun."

"Thank you for the invitation," Aristotle said, following him. Then he turned and saw Yianni looking worried. "Come, Yianni."

Yianni reluctantly tethered the animals, and followed Aristotle and Elder James through the shady and cool woods.

The one-room hut, hidden behind the trees, was made of makeshift logs and a dilapidated thatch roof that was ready to cave in. Decaying stumps of trees surrounded the small hut.

"Please have a seat," Elder James said, pointing a long, bony finger at the stumps. "I will make some mint tea. It grows wild here." His long, wrinkled fingers plucked some green leaves from a bush nearby, and then he disappeared into the hut.

Aristotle and Yianni were quiet, waiting for the monk to reappear. The sun filtered through the trees.

A peaceful feeling engulfed Aristotle and put him in a contemplative mood. Birds chirped overhead, accompanied by the rustling of leaves. He looked around him, savoring the tranquil setting.

After a few minutes, Elder James returned with a small tray containing cups of tea and a small plate of hard biscuits.

Aristotle sprang up and helped him serve it, then sat back down. He sipped the hot, mint tea. He dipped his biscuit into it, but stopped when he realized that the priest was saying a prayer of grace. He waited until he had finished, then resumed his eating.

Yianni snatched a couple of biscuits with his burly hand and munched on them noisily, and gulped his tea.

"As you can see, I live here alone. I rarely have visitors. My wants are few and I am content with being close to God."

"Tell me, Elder James," Aristotle said, "what brought you here?"

"It is a long story, my child. I fought in the war against the Turks and saw much destruction and devastation. My heart was heavy after I lost all my family, and I visited Mt. Athos in search of peace. Through much prayer and repentance, I turned to God. Through the grace of God, I have found peace here." He sipped from the bowl, looking contemplative. "Dr. Mastoras, you are not a doctor of healing, but a master of languages, and your degree is related to that." He looked up, searching Aristotle's face.

Aristotle was pleasantly surprised to hear that. He glanced at Yianni, who shrugged his shoulders, as if saying, "I did not tell him."

"Yes, that is correct," Aristotle replied. "I am looking to help the Archaeological Society unearth antiquities from our long-lost Greek civilization that is thousands of years old. That is what I plan to do at the Cadfield property."

Elder James made the sign of the cross. "There are many mysterious things that we do not know about. Digging up dead people's bones sometimes stirs up things we do not want to know."

Aristotle was quiet. As he finished his tea, he noticed the time. "Thank you for your hospitality. We must be going."

"I should be thanking you. You have taken the time to talk with an old, foolish man. May you go in peace."

They took the single path back to the fork in the road, and then continued in that direction, steadily climbing. The path eased into a larger dirt road so that they could easily ride side by side. They reached a ridge of a mountain.

The view was uplifting as Aristotle gazed at the blue, cloudless sky, and the olive trees that studded the lime-green hills. Below, the verdant valley spread far. Off to the distance stood the majestic mountains that had stood the test of time, and like good friends, faithfully greeted the sun each morning and bid it farewell each evening.

Ahead was the small, stone cottage. They had reached the Kallodaftis and Cadfield property.

CHAPTER 17

The cottage faced an expansive, stone-paved courtyard, with a stone well in the center. To the right was the stable, and beyond the courtyard, farther to the right, was a woodland area that sloped upward, joining the wall of the mountain, and providing shade at certain times of the day.

Aristotle followed Yianni as they turned right and entered the courtyard. They would have a ready supply of water when needed. He jumped off his mule, eager to look at the site.

Yianni took the mules to the stable.

To the left, and behind the cottage, was the excavation site. Aristotle had glimpsed it on their way in. Eager to see it more closely, he walked toward it, toward the open space ahead, with the blue sky encompassing everything above him and beyond. He walked with the spring of Hercules, the curiosity of Pandora, and the weight of Atlas on his shoulders. He felt invincible up here, as if nothing was impossible, and yet at the same time, he felt the full weight of his responsibility to the Archeology Society. He breathed deeply of the fresh air, enjoying the feel of the wind skimming his skin and the hot sun on his upturned face. He knew that this moment had been waiting for him.

Almond trees lined the wide, stone-paved path on the left as he trudged forward, looking to get better glimpses of the excavation site. He passed a stone veranda with a large table that sat on his right, behind the cottage. A whitewashed stone boundary wall encased the veranda.

Then he reached the excavation site.

Aristotle's eyes combed the immense, marble foundation, the rubble and few columns that remained from the damaged mansion. It was a magical world, opening like a lovely rose petal, and promising endless possibilities and potential. He walked on the dusty, marble pavement that surrounded the foundation, sidestepping several piles of stone rubble, his shoes crushing small stones.

In front of him, on the east side of the foundation, was a long trench about a meter deep, with signs of digging. He continued his exploration. The two white columns at the far west corner must have marked the entrance point into the house.

He skirted the rubble piles and reached the waist-high stone boundary wall that lined the back of the property. Below, was the tree-studded valley. The air was crisp and cool, and the sound of goat bells in the distance alerted him to a shepherd passing through. The quiet that followed filled him with serenity. He knew that he was going to like working here.

Yianni joined him. "Isn't this wonderful, boss?"

"Yes," Aristotle answered, "but one thing puzzles me. This property is isolated and located high on the mountain, so how did the Turks know to come up here to fight?"

"The church below, Agios Giorgios, was important during the revolution," Yianni said, pointing toward the valley. "The mighty fighter Kolokotronis and his group had gone to Agios Giorgios, and then as the Turks marched past this area, they ambushed them. They fought hard and cut back the Turk's strength. I heard that this family also fought in that ambush."

"Now I'm beginning to understand how they were targeted." Aristotle cut across the veranda looking for an entrance into the back of the cottage. "Let's try getting into the cottage."

He noticed that the back of the cottage had one shuttered window, but no back door. "No back door," he muttered. "It's a bit inconvenient if we're coming from the veranda."

They walked to the front of the cottage. The front door opened easily.

A musty smell hung in the air.

"Let's get some fresh air in here," Aristotle said, wrinkling his nose.

Yianni opened the two windows and swung open the shutters.

The cool, mountain breeze swept through the room, replacing the musty smell with a fresh scent of mint.

Aristotle found a key on the table. He pocketed it and looked around.

A wooden table with piles of books sat in the center of the room. The opened books lay on top of each other, as if someone had been reading them, while more books were stacked on the side. Next to the books on the table was a plate with crumbs and moldy cheese, and a cup of dried coffee. A tall, wooden bench sat underneath the front window. A large, metal washbasin filled with dirty dishes, sat on the bench, with a drain pipe that led to the outside.

A small room to the right held a stone oven and a storage space with linen-filled shelves. Beneath the shelves, were a pile of cut wood and some broken pots, filled with artifacts.

"Boss, look." Yianni pointed to the cot.

The cot still held the impression of Dr. Cadfield's thin body, and Aristotle paused solemnly for a moment to reflect on him. He had been a learned man, pursuing the highest ideals and writing about his archeological research and findings. He was someone that Aristotle would have wanted to spend more time with, to have discussed archeology and philosophy over tea.

"May he rest in peace," Aristotle said.

Aristotle mentally made a note to remove all the old linen and replace it with fresh linen.

Two weeks later, Aristotle sat in the trench on the east side of the foundation, digging and scraping the ground with the Albanian, Alexander Bejko, and his son Armand. They were working steadily, and Yianni was sitting next to them, scratching the mound of dirt with a knife. Dr. Kostakis helped find the two Albanians, who spoke passable Greek. Yianni also had become his personal assistant.

Aristotle taught them and Yianni how to work carefully, making sure they did not damage anything. One false move and they could easily chip into a valuable artifact.

Settling into a routine, Aristotle had worked with quiet intensity, keeping a vigilant eye on everything. They had uncovered mostly pottery fragments and small metal tools. He knew that he needed to hire more help for this painstaking work.

He had been staying in the cottage on the days that he worked here. Since their arrival, he and Yianni built a makeshift wooden hut in the woods behind the stable for Yianni's sleeping quarters.

Aristotle wiped the sweat from his brow. The setting sun made it difficult to detect the various shades of dirt under his chisel. This delicate work needed plenty of light, where every little corner and crevice was available for scrutiny.

He took a swig of water from the ceramic jar and wiped his mouth with the back of his tanned hand.

"Time to begin cleaning," Aristotle told the workers.

After the men finished their work, he paid them their daily wage of two drachmas each.

Alexander looked at Aristotle. "I will bring you some food that my wife has cooked."

Aristotle thanked him. The camp in the hill below served as sleeping quarters for the Albanian family. Alexander's wife, Miranda, and two daughters took care of their needs in the camp.

Aristotle watched as they walked down the hill. He went to the cottage to wash.

Soon, Alexander had returned with a pot of goat stew. He kept Aristotle company as he ate.

"Alexander, I will need more workers. If you know of men needing work, send them over on Monday when I return from Athens. I will pay each person two drachmas a day and no more. If we find valuable objects, then their pay will rise."

The word apparently spread and in a few days, a workforce of close to forty Albanians had formed, ranging from children to grandparents.

Lucas Vratsis, a former Greek employee of Dr. Cadfield also showed up with his two sons, Stephanos and Giorgios, ready for work.

The Albanian camp had grown.

CHAPTER 18

15 September, 1837

The weeks flew by at the Stirling house, and Helena continued to battle with Catherine over her lessons. Just when Helena thought the girl was cooperating, she would do something to ruin it. She would either be late for breakfast, or pretend to be sick, or would be gone for hours with Felix. Catherine was not interested in anything other than herself. Helena wondered how she could get through to her.

One morning in the middle of September, Mrs. Stirling received a letter from her husband that caused a stir in the household. That day, Helena overheard the servants whispering the family would be moving.

"Tis a shame for us to be let go like that. Where are we going to find employment?"

Helena became worried when she heard this. Did that mean that she would also lose her position? She steeled herself for the inevitable.

That afternoon, Mrs. Stirling called for Helena in the parlor. Helena was feeling particularly anxious about the meeting. With clammy hands, she entered the room. She found Mrs. Stirling seated on the sofa, and they greeted each other.

"Miss Cadfield, I received news from Mr. Stirling that his temporary employment in King Otto's court has been extended, which means he will work there permanently. He wants us close to him. We plan to leave for Greece in a fortnight, and will have to let go all the servants."

Helena felt a sinking feeling her stomach. This would have been the perfect opportunity for her to travel to Greece with them.

Mrs. Stirling smiled at her. "You would be interested to know that Mr. Stirling felt that Catherine would benefit under your care. Would you be able to come with us to Greece?"

Helena was thrilled at the opportunity to travel to Greece with them and had difficulty hiding her excitement. "Yes, I would like that."

"Good. We will be leaving from South Hampton on the steamer for Malta on the twenty-eighth, although I don't think I am ready, for I still have much packing to do. The trip is long and tedious. From Malta, we will take the French packet ship to Athens." She paused, looking perplexed. "You had said that you also knew Greek? That is important, because Mr. Stirling wants Catherine to be fluent in both the French and Greek languages."

"Yes. I learned to speak the language mostly from my late father, who was a Philhellene and had spent time in Greece. You see, my mother was from Greece, and I am interested in going there to see about the property he left behind."

Mrs. Stirling's eyes flew open in dismay. "You do not plan to leave us and live there?"

Helena hesitated, feeling her palms become sweaty. She did not want to lose this chance of going to Greece. "That is not my intention, I assure you," she began slowly. "I presume that I will have some time off during the weekends or holidays, so I can visit my property."

"Oh, that would be fine."

* * *

A few weeks later, on a cold, early October afternoon, Helena, Mrs. Stirling, Felix, and Catherine arrived in Malta with the steamer. They safely boarded the French packet ship docked at the port, and soon were headed to Greece. It had been a hectic time getting ready for the trip, but they had managed somehow to pack everything in time.

The tumultuous sea, and fierce winds and rain, kept Helena confined her to her tiny cabin. Mrs. Stirling rarely left her cabin, except to give something for Helena to do. Felix also kept to his cabin.

Whenever she could, Helena checked on Catherine and found her mostly in bed. Helena tried to cheer her up and coaxed her to eat a bite of the food that had been sitting there all day, but the girl would have none of it. She rolled over, looking pale and sickly.

When the weather was calm, Helena strolled around the ship, gazing out at the water that reflected the sun and glistened like tiny, crystal diamonds. Hardly anyone moved about the ship, except a few crew members. Feeling refreshed, she would return to her cabin, licking the salt from her lips.

On a cold, cloudy afternoon, the packet ship arrived in the harbor of Nafplio, Greece. Helena had coaxed Catherine outside and they stood at the rail, looking out at the breathtaking views. Little boats, docked on the side, bobbed from the wind. Helena's body shivered in anticipation of what awaited her. She could see the splendid mountains in the distance. She was only hours away from her family's property in Nemea.

Catherine clutched the rail tightly, appearing weak and pale. "What is that?" she asked, pointing to the fort that had materialized. It sat on a small island in the middle of the bay.

"I believe that's Bourdzi Island. On it is a Venetian fort built in the fifteenth century."

"Is that another castle?" Catherine asked, pointing toward the fortification on the cliff above the port of Nafplio.

Helena remembered reading about it in one of her father's books. "Yes. It's the Castro of Akronafplia and Palamidi. Nafplio has a long history and many rulers. The Byzantines, Venetians and Turks ruled here, and now the Greeks. Because of the battles in those days, they built their cities on top of hills with fortified walls. Greece has many such cities, and they are called *acropolis*. There is the famous Acropolis in Athens."

"I already know about the Acropolis in Athens," Catherine scoffed. "Father told me that President Kapodistrias was assassinated at Agios Spiridon, one of the churches in Nafplio. May we go see it?"

Helena shuddered at the idea of visiting the scene of a murder. "I don't think we will have time."

Catherine sulked, but it didn't last long. She became excited as the ship docked at the port. Mrs. Stirling and Felix joined them.

Catherine waved excitedly to someone standing in the distance. "There's Father."

When they disembarked, Mrs. Stirling and Catherine rushed ahead to meet Mr. Stirling, who was waiting for them. He wore a business suit, was medium height, sported a thin mustache, and had an exceedingly large head. Catherine clung to her father, not letting him go. Helena's watched with increasing melancholy as Mr. Stirling showered his family with affection, hugging and embracing them. *I miss Papa.* She wondered how it would have been if he and her mother were there to greet her.

Mrs. Stirling introduced Helena briefly to Mr. Stirling, who nodded his greeting and looked at her keenly through his spectacles, as if gauging her character. Helena flushed under his scrutiny.

Mr. Helzig seemed excited to see him and talked animatedly about his career while Mr. Stirling switched his attentions back and forth between him, Mrs. Stirling, and Catherine.

Helena gazed around her at the bustling port. It was teeming with tanned men in colorful clothing, shouting in Greek, while unloading cargo from the ship. To her right, stately buildings lined the side of the dock. Up ahead, uniformed men, fair-haired and dignified looking, rode silently past them on horseback. They were probably German.

Two closed carriages appeared.

"Miss Cadfield, Miss Cadfield," Mrs. Stirling called out. Mrs. Stirling, who had been pale and unwell throughout the trip, appeared refreshed, with a glowing face.

"Yes, Mrs. Stirling?"

"We have no room for you in our carriage, so you will travel in the carriage with the luggage."

Helena watched numbly as Mr. and Mrs. Stirling, Felix and Catherine climbed into their carriage. She collected her belongings and climbed into the other carriage.

The two carriages slowly left the port of Nafplio. They ambled through the paved roads of the city and eventually entered a rocky, dirt road, making the ride bumpy. The area was not lush green as in Oxfordshire, but a mixture of lime green and dusty brown. At one point, they passed almond and olive tree orchards.

The road opened, revealing a hilly terrain spotted with bushes. In the distance, the gray mountains stood like silent sentinels. As the carriage turned the bend, she could see tiny, white homes dotting the landscape of the mountain, which had not been discernible minutes before. Green vegetation surrounded the homes. She dreamed of Nemea, wondering where her family's property would be.

In the distance, a broken-down temple sat atop a high hill. Helena stared in wonder at it, her imagination running wild, thinking about its age and wondering if it were a palace, for a king like Menelaus, or a temple made for a goddess. She guessed that they were somewhere near Corinth.

A heavy clap of thunder startled her. She shivered. Above, dark clouds had quickly formed. Another clap of thunder, followed by lightning, caused the driver to pick up speed and surge forward. She held on tightly. Soon, droplets of rain coated her window. The muddy roads forced the carriage to start and stop, as it plowed onward.

Within minutes, they stopped at The Corinthian Inn, which stood on the side of the main road. The inn, a large, two story building, faced a smaller building one story high, probably the stable. Another carriage and several horses were already there.

Helena spied the Stirling family fleeing into the building. She jumped out of the carriage and dashed in the rain, joining them inside the entrance. She shook the rain off their clothing.

"We will stay here for the night because the wet roads are dreadful," Mr. Stirling announced.

Helena dutifully followed the family into the large dining-room. A long, rectangular table ran down the center of the room, flanked by benches on each side. Three tanned men sat at the far corner, eating and drinking. They wore red and blue bandannas and spoke in some dialect of Greek. Helena caught one of the men staring at her, and he grinned at her. She looked down, blushing. She must be careful to observe the ways of the people here.

Her father used to tell her that the women in Greece were "*semni*" which meant they didn't stare at men, and they were not supposed to attract attention to themselves.

Mr. Stirling spoke to the owner and made the necessary arrangements. They sat at the other end of the long table, and soon the meal arrived. It consisted of roasted lamb and baked potatoes, crusty bread, black olives, cheese, and wine.

Afterwards, the restaurant owner, Stathis, informed them that he had three available rooms with one bed each. "We have other lodging for the servant."

It took a moment for Helena to realize that the servant he was referring to was none other than herself. Feeling the heat of indignation rise to her face, she collected her luggage and silently followed the owner's wife, Sophia, outside.

The rain pounded them as they hurried to the nearby building, which had three doors.

Sophia opened the door to the far left. "You will stay here the night," she barked, going inside, carrying the lantern. She placed the lantern on a long, wooden bench covered with hay. The bench spanned the back wall, and was a meter wide and a meter above the ground.

Shivering, Helena entered the dimly lit room. The stench made her grab a handkerchief from her pocket and dab her nose discreetly with it. "It smells like a pigsty here."

The sound of children crying caught her attention. She looked around with growing consternation. At the far corner, she could make out the huddled shapes of two women seated on the dirt floor, their two children running around them, crying. The women were thin, and their simple garments and shawls were the only protection they had from the cold. The children were dressed in ill-fitted clothing and were barefoot.

Sophia yelled at the women, "Take your children outside next time if they need to relieve themselves. The outhouse is out there."

Silence reigned as the two women grabbed and subdued the children, clasping them closely to their bosoms.

Sophia opened a shuttered window, allowing the cold wind, sprinkled with water droplets, to sweep the stench from the stifling room. "Here, that will help with the smell."

Helena shivered from the cold.

"Where will I sleep?" Helena asked, looking around her in dismay.

"There," Sophia said roughly, pointing to the long bench.

CHAPTER 19

Sophia picked up the lantern to leave. "Shut the window when you sleep. The cold night can be deadly."

"Are there any candles for light?" Helena asked Mrs. Sophia, trying to keep her voice steady and calm. She took out a few coins from her pocket, showing them to her.

Mrs. Sophia grunted, pocketing the money. Her face and slow motions revealed her antipathy as she grudgingly placed the lantern on the bench and left, shutting the door behind her.

Helena turned and saw the women's eyes going over her wool topcoat. She nodded shyly to them, and then swept the dirt and hay off the bench, wondering if they kept horses here, for the smell of manure was powerful. She wiped her grimy hands, realizing too late that there was no water basin. Helena had heard about the poverty of Greece after the war, but had not realized its severity until tonight.

Taking her handkerchief from her pocket, Helena stuck it outside the window, soaking it with rain. She shuddered as the wet wind smacked her face and rattled the opened shutters. It was biting cold. She squeezed out the excess drops from her wet handkerchief and washed her face and hands with it. After she had finished, she shut the window, shivering, then turned to greet the women.

"*Kalispera.* Hello. My name is Miss Cadfield," Helena said in Greek, smiling timidly.

They responded in a strong Greek dialect. It took a few moments for Helena to understand what they were saying. She learned that Mrs. Roula was the mother of Litsa, and they were traveling from their village in Argos to Athens to meet with Litsa's husband, who had left a month earlier to sell wares there. Roula, the older woman, had lost her husband in the war.

"I am hungry!" whined the boy, tugging at his mother's shawl. He was around four years old.

"*Ssst!*" hissed the mother, wrapping her arms around him. She murmured into his ear, rocking him.

His younger sister began to whine as she complained about being hungry also. Tears formed in her huge, dark eyes and rolled down her thin cheeks. Her grandmother pulled her close to her and rocked her also, crooning to her.

"Your father has a nice meal planned for us when we get to Athens," Mrs. Roula told the children.

"If you will be good children, he will give you twice as much," Litsa told them.

Helena caught Mrs. Roula winking at Litsa. Her heart sank. They were lying to the children. The children became quiet, digesting what she had said. The girl began to suck her thumb and laid her head wearily on the bosom of her grandmother. She stared solemnly at Helena with those large eyes.

Helena felt her heart tug at the scene before her. Apparently, the two women had too much pride to ask for help. Helena wished that she had saved some of her bread from her meal to give to them. How could she sit there and let them starve like this? Raised by a physician, Helena knew what would happen to them if they did not get nourishment.

It only took a moment for her to decide what to do.

Helena opened the door and marched toward the nearby building, the indignation rising in her. The raindrops that spilled on her face were refreshing, but did not quench the burning heat that had arisen in her chest. A new picture was forming in her mind of Greece, where the ravages of war were becoming increasingly apparent. Desolation and despair filled her young heart as she pictured the untold suffering that had occurred on this soil after the war. These women and children represented those who lived in poverty, scrimping and toiling for a bite of bread.

There must be some food from the restaurant that she could take to the women.

Helena entered the inn. Two newcomers sat at the long table in the dining area. The rest of the customers had retired for the evening. Helena observed them eating their plentiful meal. Both men sported beards, and one was taller and well built, while the other man was overweight. From their clothing, they appeared to be laborers. She searched for Sophia and found her busy in the kitchen.

"*Kyria* Sophia," Helena called out. "Could I bother you for some more food?"

Sophia stopped what she was doing and looked at her suspiciously. Her eyes narrowed and she wagged her head knowingly. "Are you trying to feed those beggars in the khan? Don't bother. We get them daily. We can't be feeding every poor person who comes here, or we'll become poor ourselves."

Helena felt as though she had been slapped in the face. "My dear lady, I did not ask for charity. I would be willing to pay for their food."

Stathis appeared on the scene. He gestured angrily at Helena, his face turning red. "Look here, the restaurant is closed for the evening."

"But the children are hungry," Helena protested.

"May I be of assistance?"

Helena turned around to the sound of a man's deep voice. He was the tall, bearded man who had sat eating at the table with his plump partner. He stood there, looking expectantly at them, his strong arms crossed over his wide chest. He appeared powerful and virile. She caught herself staring at him and then dropped her eyes in confusion. Why would a common laborer want to help her?

"This servant wants to play the saint and feed those beggars in the khan," Sophia sneered, wagging her head. "They cannot even pay for their nights' rest."

"Whether they are beggars or not, they are people, and their children are hungry," Helena replied firmly. "Maybe it's not their fault that they are under these difficult circumstances. They must have something to eat. I came to get them some bread. Anything. I would gladly pay for the food."

The bearded man nodded authoritatively to Sophia. "*Kyria* Sophia, get me a clean plate."

Helena blinked at the man's command.

Sophia stared at him as if he had offended her, then sighed and obliged him. She muttered darkly as she handed him a plate. Helena watched as the man placed all of his untouched food on the clean plate and then grabbed his partner's plate.

His partner sputtered his protest, his mouth full.

"Be quiet, Yianni," the bearded man laughed, pulling the plate away from his partner's grubby hands and scraping the food into the receiving plate. "You have enough fat on you to feed off of for days. We can make up for it in the morning."

Helena's heart soared as she watched him carry the laden plate of lamb, bread, olives, and cheese to her. He was remarkably handsome, even with the beard. His beautiful dark eyes were steadily observing her and they had a glow about them.

"Is this to your satisfaction, miss?" the man asked.

"Yes, thank you. How much do I owe you, kind sir?" She reached into the pocket of her dress, where she kept some money. She only had a few coins, but she needed to do this.

He shook his head. "Compliments from…the restaurant."

Helena looked up in surprise and recognized the dawning sign of respect in the man's eyes, something that she had witnessed with her father's students when he lectured to them.

Sophia coughed, her face turning red.

"You have done a good deed, indeed, sir," Helena told him, wondering what his name was. No one had come forth to introduce him, as was the custom, and she was too shy to ask him. She took the plate, mindful of his fingers brushing hers and his eyes taking her in. She saw him glance at her disheveled hair and her face. He smiled at her and she felt her face become hot.

"You are mistaken," he said softly. "*You* have done the good deed, miss."

Trembling slightly at the raw magnetism this man evoked, Helena bowed with as much grace and dignity as she could gather, taking the meal to the hungry family.

When Helena presented the food to the two women, there were outcries of joy.

"May God bless you, miss. You are an angel," Roula said, beaming at her.

The transformation in the two women was miraculous. Helena watched them as they said their prayers, thanking God for the food. They fed the children first, then themselves. There were smiles and tears at the same time. Helena soaked it all in, grateful that she could help, even in this small way.

The two women chatted the rest of the evening asking Helena questions. She told them about life in England. Soon, the children became quiet after their stomachs were filled, and huddling next to their mother, dozed off.

Helena went to the window to close the shutters. She noticed that the rain had stopped for the moment and the clouds had shifted enough so she could see the brilliance of the half moon. She heard some movements outside. Stathis, the innkeeper, was talking quietly to someone. She paused, unable to comprehend the conversation, yet recognizing the deep voice of the bearded man.

"Who was the young lady?" the man asked quietly.

"I don't know, sir. She's only a servant of the noble family," Stathis replied. "They will be gone tomorrow, to Athens."

Once the conversation ended, she heard the clinking of keys and the sound of a creaking door.

"Are you sure you are out of rooms?"

Helena smiled and suppressed a giggle as she pictured the bearded man looking in disgust at his room, which was next to their room.

"Yes," Stathis answered. "I apologize for the condition, but this is the only one left. The noble family visiting from England is using the three rooms in the inn. They will be gone tomorrow. A room will be available then."

There was a quiet response followed by silence.

Helena moved her two valises and clothing on to the bench, to soften the hard surface.

"Sleeping on the floor is not healthy for the children. They might catch cold," Helena remarked to the women in Greek.

"How do you know so much?" Mrs. Roula asked, placing the empty plate on the floor.

"My father was a doctor, and he taught me many things."

"Ah," Litsa said in admiration. "You come from a learned family, yet how is it you are treated like a servant?"

"It is a long story," Helena said. The differences between her existing life and her previous life were significant, and she did not want to relive the pain. "More importantly, let us place the children on the bed."

"We are not paying customers, *Thespinis* (Miss)," Roula admitted. "We will settle here for the night." She patted the cold, dirt floor.

"Nonsense," Helena retorted. She scooped up one of the sleeping children. "There is room enough for all of us. Please help me settle the children."

The two women arose and obediently helped Helena carry the sleeping children to the bench. She realized that they did not have outer clothing or bedding to keep them warm from the cold night. Helena rummaged through her luggage and yanked some dresses from it. She covered the two children with them and gave the women some wool clothing.

"Cover yourselves with these," Helena said. "I will shut the shutters to keep the cold out."

The two women thanked her profusely. They snuggled next to the children on the bench, with curled backs against the wall.

At the window, Helena could hear the soft tapping of the rain falling again and smelled the damp, musty soil. She was about to shut the window and shutters when she heard a man singing. She stood there for a moment trying to make out the German tune, one that she did not recognize. She wondered if the bearded man was singing it.

The lantern went out and the room became dark.

With a sigh, Helena shut the window and secured the shutters. Fully clothed and wearing her stockings and shoes, she eased herself on the bench, and rested her head on her valise. The wall was cold and damp against her back. The rain had picked up and she could hear the raindrops pounding the roof. Her sleep was fitful and she dozed on and off.

During the night, a dripping sound awakened Helena. To her dismay, she realized that her clothing was wet and she was shivering from the cold.

The roof was leaking.

Helena jumped off the bench and landed in a puddle of water. She stepped aside, only to step on a soft, furry body.

"*Eeeaaaouu!*" Helena screamed, shuddering from fear.

The offended rodent squealed and scurried away.

The children began to cry.

A frantic pounding sound on the door followed.

"Is everything all right in there?" a man called out in Greek. The door flew open before Helena could answer.

Shivering, her heart pounding, Helena stared at the bearded man standing in the doorway, holding a lantern. He was drenched. The rain formed rivulets down his beard. He must have heard her screaming.

"Hello? Are you alright?" he demanded.

"Yes," Helena managed to squeak. Her teeth began to chatter. "I, I must have gotten wet. The roof leaked and it awakened me and I jumped off the bench, I mean the bed, and landed on some poor creature."

"Probably some rat. I'm afraid these are not ideal lodgings. I think they keep their cattle here. Sorry I cannot offer you my room. It's not much better than this one."

Mr. Stathis barged into the room. "What is going on here?" he demanded. He had thrown his coat over his pajamas and was holding a lantern.

The small room had filled with the women, the whining children, the tall, bearded man, and Mr. Stathis.

"The roof is leaking and these poor women and children are getting soaked," Helena said. "I think the children should sleep in warmer quarters. Don't you have better rooms for them? *Aachoo!*"

Helena's sneeze caught her unawares. She searched for her handkerchief in her coat pocket and dabbed her nose with it.

"We are used to it," Mrs. Roula said, clutching her crying granddaughter to her, rocking her. "We have slept outside often when the weather is warmer, but because of the rain we came inside."

"If you do not give them better sleeping arrangements, I will report this establishment to the King personally," Helena insisted. "We have connections with the King!"

Mr. Stathis's eyes became round as saucers. He scratched his head. "Well, let me see. There is a small room next to the dining-room, used for storing olives."

"Give them the room," the bearded man growled.

"All right, all right," Mr. Stathis said, raising his arms in surrender.

"Now I will excuse myself," the bearded man said.

"Thank you, sir," Helena called out, as the bearded man slipped away. She wondered what his name was, but her manners precluded her from asking.

Mr. Stathis turned to Helena. "They can sleep with you in there so long as they don't touch anything. Just for one night."

A short time later, Helena and the women and children had moved to drier quarters. The marble floor was clean, and the storage room dry. It held a few large barrels. The women were thankful as they settled in the corner of the room with the children, who were already asleep.

The door shut and the darkness enveloped them, except for a sliver of light coming from under the door. Unable to sleep in her wet clothing, Helena fumbled through her luggage, shivering and pulling out some clothing. She changed and then curled up on the floor, resting her head on her valise. She had a difficult time sleeping, thinking about the kind man who had helped her. He not only was handsome, but talked in a cultivated and dignified manner, which belied the way he was dressed. Could he have been raised in better conditions, like she had, and had also fallen on hard times?

Then Helena thought about how the women were going to get to Athens. "Mrs. Roula, how are you going to Athens?" she said aloud in the dark.

Mrs. Roula was silent, but Litsa spoke up. "We will walk," she said simply.

Helena digested this bit of information. She could picture them walking hours on end with the children and not having food or water to drink. She shuddered at the thought that something might happen to them and the children.

"I am travelling alone in a closed carriage. You can travel with me. We will get up early, and you will get into the carriage and wait for me and I will bring you some food. No one will notice, for they will be in the other carriage. We'll drop you off when we stop for a rest."

"*Panagia mou*, what am I hearing? Are you sure?" Litsa asked her, hope entering her voice.

"Quite sure."

"God must have sent you," Mrs. Roula said, sniffling.

Soon, Helena could hear the soft snoring sound of one of the women, and the worried sound of one of the children sucking their thumb.

At least the room was warm and comfortable.

CHAPTER 20

The next morning, Aristotle awoke to the piercing call of the cock's crow. He stretched his sore body and sat up on the wood bench, feeling stiff. He scratched his beard, then his chest. His throat felt dry. Last night he had rushed out in the rain when that young woman screamed in the next room, and he had returned drenched, requiring a change of clothes. Although used to sleeping in all kinds of situations because of his work, Aristotle normally would have fallen asleep quickly, but her beautiful image had kept him up last night.

He turned and saw Yianni, who was still sound asleep. Dr. Kostakis's recommendation of using Yianni as a guide proved to be a good one. Yianni not only provided the transportation of the artifacts back to Athens to be stored in the storeroom and gave useful tips on the geographical, political and historical landscape of the country, but he also was a loyal assistant.

This last trip, they were returning from Athens to Nemea with much needed supplies and had stopped at the Corinthian Inn after the unexpected storm burst on them. Yianni told him that if it continued to rain, the narrow dirt road leading up to the Cadfield site would be slippery and difficult to handle with the wagon loaded with supplies, and they would need to remain at the inn until the rain stopped and the sun dried the mud.

Sounds of people moving around and conversing in the courtyard made Aristotle rise eagerly. He found himself at the window, excitedly opening the shutters like a boy. Still early and damp, a surge of cool morning air embraced him, entering the stale room. His fingers touched the wet windowsill as he leaned forward, gazing outside at the gray morning. The road was drenched, yet he knew that once the sun rose, everything would be dry later in the day.

Aristotle hoped to get a glimpse of the woman he had met last night. He had not thought of introducing himself and neither did he know her surname. Her behavior had intrigued him, for she acted too proud for her position, speaking her mind and offering to pay. She was also attractive even with her unruly hair and her travel-stained clothes. Her spoken Greek was too clean, too crisp, as if she had learned it from a book; this implied that she must have had some education. He recalled her lovely, blue eyes, wet with unshed tears, when she spoke about the hungry children. He guessed that she had been raised under better conditions, and unfortunate financial circumstances had forced her into employment.

Mr. Stathis had informed him that the Stirling family was from England and headed to Athens, where Mr. Stirling worked in King Otto's court.

Aristotle's eyes adjusted to the two dark shapes of the carriages, their creaking wheels burdened by their loads. They were rolling away. Too quickly, the carriages blended into the grayness of the landscape. A sense of disappointment enveloped him.

Would he ever see her again?

Aristotle thought about his recent meeting in Athens with Mr. Pittakis and Dr. Kostakis from the Archaeological Society. The outcome had been a mixed one. Mr. Pittakis told him that he had shown the gold cup to the society members and they were interested in the project, yet no money was forthcoming when they saw that Aristotle had not found anything else of value. Mr. Pittakis had suggested to Aristotle to have the Cadfield site guarded daily, in case any more valuables showed up.

He also mentioned that they were having another meeting again on Friday where more members would be present and it would be good for Aristotle to attend and bring any artifacts he may have found. In addition, King Otto had learned about the excavation and the gold cup and wanted to meet him.

"King Otto will give a court ball at the end of October, and you have been invited," Mr. Pittakis had told him. "You will meet the king then. He is interested in your excavation."

Aristotle wondered if the Stirlings had been invited to the ball, and if so, might bring the governess along. The possibility of seeing her again in a few weeks made him feel better.

He checked his watch. He needed to awaken the snoring Yianni, whose exposed hairy belly moved up and down rhythmically.

Aristotle tapped Yianni on his shoulders. "Yianni, time to get up. We have work to do."

Three other people sat in the dining area having breakfast when Aristotle and Yianni entered the room. The innkeeper served Aristotle and Yianni a hefty meal of eggs, crusty bread, olives, goat cheese and coffee. When they finished, Aristotle searched for the innkeeper in the kitchen, intent on paying the fare. He asked about the two poor women and the children from last night and learned that they had left earlier that morning.

Upon his return, Aristotle saw Yianni's pockets bulging with several pieces of bread.

"In case I get hungry," Yianni explained. He then grabbed a few more. "For the mule."

"You're fortunate that the innkeeper didn't see you," Aristotle admonished him.

Although the sun was beaming strongly on them, the roads were still muddy from the rain last night and their progress was slow. Aristotle rode his mule, while Yianni sat on the wagon, whistling a lively tune, followed by chatter as they headed toward Nemea. They were going slowly enough to carry on a conversation.

"You know, boss, what will we do if someone steals the ancient objects we find? How do you know they are not putting them in their pockets and not telling you? Do you trust those bandits to keep an eye on everything? How do you know whether or not they're the ones stealing--?"

"Yianni, could you please do me a favor?"

"I know, I know, boss. You want me to mind my business." Yianni stuck his thick finger in his ear, scratching it vigorously and grinning sheepishly. After a few moments of this athletic activity, he whistled for a while, then taking out a chunk of bread from his pocket, began chewing it.

"When are you planning to move back to your own home again?" Yianni asked.

"One day soon," Aristotle said. "I have started the process of rebuilding my house. Barba Manolis is keeping an eye on it for me while I am away. Meanwhile, I need to take care of this project."

They passed through a shady grove of mulberry trees, where the sun had not reached, and the road was unusually wet. The mule stopped in front of a large puddle and lowered his head, drinking the water.

Yianni began to whistle wildly at the mule, rising and tightening his reins. "Come on, *Mulari*, don't do this to me. *Eh. Brrrr.*"

Aristotle watched in fascination as Yianni's attempt to pull the mule away from the puddle failed. The animal was stronger and stood his ground, glaring at Yianni. He bent his legs, lowering himself into the large puddle and plopped down, oblivious to Yianni's frantic shouts.

Yianni jumped down from the wagon and marched to the front of the mule, his face red. "You will not get any food today if you don't get up!" he shouted at the mule, shaking his finger at him as if he were a child. The mule turned and stared at him, then curled his lip and showed his teeth, as if he were laughing at Yianni.

Yianni scratched his head. He looked at Aristotle. "What should I do, boss? This mule's only weakness is that he loves water puddles."

"Here, why don't you entice him with some of that delicious bread you brought along?"

Yianni winked and smiled knowingly. "You're right, boss. That's his other weakness." He thrust his hand into his coat pocket and removed two crusts of bread. Walking forward, he flaunted it in front of the mule's face. "Tsk, tsk, come on, here's some food."

The mule rose swiftly, heading for the bread, his teeth bared.

Yianni lost his balance and plunged into the muddy puddle, dropping the bread. The mule plopped back down in the puddle and feasted on the wet bread, then nipped Yianni's pockets for more bread. Yianni emptied his pockets, looking disgusted.

"I think next time we should travel by horse," Aristotle remarked dryly, jumping off his mule and helping Yianni get up. "Come, let's get you cleaned."

He poured some water from the jug on Yianni's hands.

Yianni washed his face and hands as best he could and they continued on their journey.

CHAPTER 21

Soon, they had reached Nemea and were ambling through the city, heading to its outskirts, toward the village of Petri. When Aristotle saw the town square, with the familiar water fountain in the center, he knew they were almost there. One of several villages hit heavily during the revolution by the Ottomans, Petri had a crumbling grocery store, a coffee shop and a handful of homes in varying states of disrepair.

Aristotle had witnessed much rubble and ruin on his way here. Homes leveled during the war forced many to flee to the mountains, the islands, or even to other countries. Others moved into the broken-down khans, or small buildings, built by the Ottomans for travelers. Some families, like Dr. Cadfield, had returned in hope of rebuilding their homes.

They found the narrow, dirt road that led up to the site. It had been difficult to find at first, because the almond trees had hidden it. Now Aristotle knew it well.

When they arrived at the site, Aristotle could hear the Albanian workers singing, even the children; Aristotle recognized the patriotic Albanian song, reminiscent of their homeland. It seemed to help lighten the monotony of the work.

To the right was the stone cottage where Aristotle had been staying. Aristotle took care of his mule and then helped Yianni unleash the mule from the wagon and feed him. Yianni headed for his small wood hut behind the stable.

Aristotle walked toward the foundation. Lucas Vratsis, his Greek foreman, stood in a ditch inside the foundation, in deep discussion with Alexander Bojke, the Albanian worker. Lucas was a thin, wiry man in his late forties. A mountain man, he lived an hour away on the other side of Nemea. Lucas could speak the rough dialect of the Albanian workers, which helped Aristotle.

The work on the site improved dramatically with so many workers, but so far, there had been no valuable discoveries.

"Lucas," Aristotle called out, waving to him. "I need help unloading the supplies."

Lucas looked up and waved back. "Yes, *Afenti*." He signaled to his sons to help them unload the wagon.

The two lads hoisted the crates on their backs and followed Aristotle to the cottage. After they left, Mrs. Bojke, Alexander's wife, and four other Albanian women lined up at the door, carrying food. They provided him with goat cheese, bread and boiled eggs.

"I have something for you, Mrs. Bojke," Aristotle said. He gave her two large bags of flour, three bottles of olives and three bottles of olive oil. This exchange had worked well. He would provide the supplies, and she would bake for him.

"And for you, Mrs. Selmani, here are the apples and dried figs for your lovely desserts." Aristotle handed them to the widow. She thanked him. Her seventeen-year-old daughter, Lule, was with her and smiled sweetly at him.

"For your daughter, I have honey and walnuts, to put on the goat yogurt that I hope you bring me soon." He handed them to Lule.

"I'll make some yogurt tonight and bring it first thing tomorrow morning, Dr. Mastoras," Mrs. Selmani promised, smiling as she left with her daughter.

Lucas entered the cottage, removing his hat. "*Yiasou, Afenti.* How was the meeting in Athens? Did the Archaeological Society agree to fund this project?"

"I was counting on their support, but Mr. Pittakis, the head of the Society, is concerned that we found nothing important. They will not fund our project if we do not produce anything of value," Aristotle replied.

"Much time is needed to dig through all this earth," Lucas said, scowling.

"Unless we find any treasures soon, I will have to let go of the workers by the end of the week."

Lucas sucked in his breath. "End of the week, eh?"

Aristotle nodded slowly.

"I had better get back to work," Lucas said.

A few minutes later, Phillipa and his brothers arrived.

"Greetings," Aristotle said to the brothers. The bandits grinned. They seemed to have taken a liking to him. They had arrived a week ago, taking turns watching the property when he was away. They did not press him for any watch or item to steal, now that he promised to be paying them on a regular basis.

"So, what brings you here?" Aristotle asked.

"We came to get paid," he said proudly. "We kept a good watch while you were away those two nights and saw nothing suspicious. Not even Lucas and his sons."

"Lucas and his sons?" Aristotle asked, feeling surprised.

"They are thieves," Phillipa growled and spat on the floor.

His two brothers spat on the floor also.

Aristotle remembered hearing once that it took a thief to catch a thief. "Did you see them steal anything?"

"No, but around here they have a bad reputation. Why did you hire them?" Phillipa asked.

"Lucas claims he worked for Dr. Cadfield and seems to know what he is doing," he said thoughtfully. "Besides, you will be keeping an eye on them."

"We will," Phillipa said, chuckling wickedly.

"Wait right here." Aristotle entered the cottage and searched for his coin bag, which he had hidden in a safe place.

He paid the bandits. "Is that enough?"

They nodded, appearing pleased.

"Meanwhile, I will need more regular attendance from you. Come daily instead of the weekends. I do not need all three at the same time. You can do shifts. One will guard from eight to four, and the next from four to eleven, and the next from eleven to the morning."

Phillipa's eyes gleamed. "Are you expecting to find many treasures, eh?" He poked Aristotle and laughed.

"The Society has asked me to guard the site more carefully, and that is what I am doing."

"You can count on us. We'll be your eyes and ears," Phillipa said, beaming at him.

"Good."

They shook hands. Aristotle had learned that shaking hands with the Greeks was as good as signing a contract. They stood by their word.

CHAPTER 22

Afterwards, Aristotle joined the workers, determined to see results. He wore his khaki work clothes and khaki hat. He stood there for a moment, watching them steadily chip away at the hard surface with knives and sharp tools. They used sieves to sift the pile of dirt that had formed from the digging. They carefully brushed bigger objects, such as pottery shards, ornaments, and metal tools. Once they filled the baskets with these items, the children and young men carried the baskets to the women for washing.

Aristotle moved around the site, doing various jobs. He had identified the different layers they were digging by studying the pottery, since it was commonly used throughout the centuries. From his guess, the layers they had dug were only a few hundred years old. He knew that one had to dig much deeper to find older artifacts. Other than small pottery fragments, tools, and tiny animal bones, there had been no sign of valuable items.

This had troubled him for a while, as he wondered where Dr. Cadfield had found the gold cup. He had toyed with the idea of digging elsewhere on the foundation, hoping to discover valuable artifacts, but that required more time and money.

Phillipa had arrived. He wore a menacing look on his face as he swaggered back and forth, staring meaningfully into the workers' baskets, his hand on his weapon.

Several hours later, Aristotle stopped his work and arose. He pushed his mighty shoulders back, trying to fight the ache that had formed in his back. He took a swig of water from his ceramic jar and brushed the sweat off his brow. The sun was hiding behind some gray clouds. This delicate work needed plenty of light, where every little corner and crevice was available for scrutiny.

"Lucas, tell everyone to start cleaning," Aristotle called out.

Afterwards, the workers lined up in front of Aristotle, waiting to receive payment. Their bandanas, encasing their sweating heads, formed a moving flowerbed of red, yellow, and orange colors.

Aristotle paid Yianni first, then Lucas and his sons, and Alexander Bejko and his sons, and then everyone else. Their faces creased into smiles, as he dropped the money into their dusty palms. They were not a handsome people, with angular features, but they were willing to work. Even the children received a lira for their efforts.

"Do you want to join us later for dinner?" Alexander Bejko asked him.

"Not today. I have to attend to several things. Maybe Yianni might be interested."

"For sure, boss," Yianni said, smiling as he watched Alexander and the other workers leave.

"Meanwhile, get Lucas to help you bring the containers filled with the new finds of the day to the veranda. I want to look at everything more carefully."

Yianni headed for the site, humming a tune.

Aristotle gazed at the dusty-clothed workers as they walked wearily down the tree-lined road to their camp. They were not as jovial as usual. He realized that Lucas probably had told them the news about being let go if nothing valuable showed up.

Aristotle felt he had matured these past few weeks. This project was a challenge and a new experience for him. In the past, he was under the direction of his father, grandfather, and then professors who mentored and guided him through the university. Now, he had become a leader, a provider, guiding the actions of dozens of people daily.

He retrieved water from the nearby well, went inside the cottage and cleaned himself, then ate some cheese, bread and olives and washed it down with wine. He could hear the men moving the crates and containers. Soon, he sat outside on the small veranda and Yianni joined him. They began sifting through several boxes of artifacts and logging them in a book. Although this laborious task was time-consuming, it provided essential cataloguing of everything they had found.

"Where is Lucas and his sons?" Aristotle asked.

"They left early with the others."

Aristotle was surprised to hear that. Normally Lucas would hang around and help with the cataloguing. "Hmm, then who helped you move the crates?"

"Phillipa and his brothers. They left to eat down at the camp," Yianni told him. "I think Phillipa goes down there to spend time with Mrs. Selmani's daughter."

"He should have told me that he would be leaving the grounds," Aristotle said. *I must remember to talk with him about it.*

* * *

The day was full of pleasant surprises for Aristotle. It appeared that Lucas had relayed the information to the workers the previous night regarding cutting back on help due to lack of finds. Many workers came up to Aristotle with artifacts that they said they had found on "another site," and Aristotle duly bought the items. When he pressed for more information, the workers were silent, shrugging their shoulders. Aristotle marked the objects as coming from Nemea.

The word spread quickly that Aristotle was paying money for the antiquities. The following day, several Greek villagers from the surrounding vicinity, and even Corinth, stopped by the site and showed him some valuable items that they or a family member had found on "our site," hoping to receive payment for them. By that evening, he had amassed a few large metal tools, several pieces of gold jewelry, inscribed stones that included a broken stele (slab), and a number of Corinthian vases and other vases of varying sizes.

Aristotle was amazed at the outcome. The jewels and stele were between one and two thousand years old, intriguing him. This area and neighboring sites would be something to consider pursuing in the future, but for now, he must focus on the Cadfield site.

After everyone had left for the day, he sat at the table on the veranda with Yianni and Phillipa, reviewing the artifacts and valuables.

Phillipa whistled his appreciation as he picked up a gold necklace, his eyes gleaming. "You must have paid a pretty price for this one. Who sold it to you?" He handed it to him.

"Lucas. He said that Dr. Cadfield had given it to him as a present," Aristotle replied, gazing thoughtfully at the gold necklace with its lace designs and emerald jewels embedded in it. He had been surprised to receive this piece of treasure from the foreman. Although he had enough money to pay him, it set him back.

"Don't believe everything he says. He probably stole it," Phillipa warned, leaning back in his chair, his eyes narrowed.

"I cannot accuse him without evidence," Aristotle said carefully. "That is why I hired you, Phillipa, to keep an eye on things."

"From now on, I'm going to check the workers' pockets when they come to you for payment."

Aristotle was surprised at the man's suggestion. "What makes you think that we have thieves here?"

Phillipa arose. "If you had lived here as long as I have, you would know what I am talking about. You are too naïve. You should not trust anyone here." He winked and swaggered away.

The next day, as the workers lined up to get paid, Phillipa searched their pockets.

Lucas grumbled at first, as he watched. When it was his turn, he became furious and shouted at Phillipa. "Here, you don't need to do that. We're not thieves!"

Phillipa promptly showed him his gun. "Take it up with the Archaeological Society. They're the ones that requested it."

"Well I don't like it!"

Aristotle tensed at the scene. The workers' eyes were riveted on Lucas, and since he was the foreman, there was a real possibility that they would also follow his lead.

"If you don't like Phillipa going into your pockets, then you can do it," Aristotle told Lucas calmly. He did not want any trouble.

Lucas put his head down, as he pulled his pockets out. There was nothing in them. Phillipa then searched his sons.

After Aristotle paid them, Lucas left angrily with his sons without speaking to anyone.

When it came to searching the women, Phillipa scowled, looking uncomfortable. Instead, he asked them to pull out their pockets. Nothing came up. When Lule's turn came, Phillipa grinned boldly at her, as she obliged the request. "You're a lovely girl, you know."

This caused Lule to blush as she fled toward her mother.

Although Lucas returned the next day with his two sons, he was unusually quiet. He continued to do his job as usual, but his mood was dark and his eyes shifty. Aristotle made it a point to talk with him normally, but Lucas only gave him nods or grunts, avoiding eye contact. Aristotle knew that Lucas had felt insulted by Phillipa's searches, but he was taking it too personally. His actions hinted at a personality that was deeper, more sinister than Aristotle had initially assumed. Could there be some truth in what Phillipa had said about

Lucas? But where was the proof? The necklace he had sold to him? Dr. Cadfield was not around to prove if Lucas was telling the truth or not.

* * *

Thursday afternoon, after the workers had left, Aristotle and Yianni prepared the wagon containing the artifacts and valuables. As they wrapped the valuable artifacts in several layers of cloths, Aristotle checked his logbook to make sure they had everything. They laid them carefully inside the large vases that sat in the wagon and filled the top of the vases with hay, capped them, and covered everything with a large, wool blanket, tying them with ropes. They finished by throwing hay over everything as a camouflage.

He retrieved the valuables from the locked cottage and brought them along with him, keeping them in a safe place. He was reassured that he had left the site guarded well with Phillipa and his brothers.

Aristotle locked the cottage. "We will return Monday," he told Phillipa.

Aristotle and Yianni stopped overnight at the Corinthian Inn. There were no other travelers that night, so the rooms at the inn were available. They placed the wagon in a sheltered place under a large tree, in case it rained.

That night, while in bed, Aristotle ruminated once more on the course of action he would take. He would store the valuable objects with Dr. Kostakis until the Archaeological Society held their monthly meeting in a few weeks. He hoped to sell them at the meeting. He would also sell a small portion of the items to an antique dealer, just enough to help pay for the workers and supplies.

He should also seriously think about digging other areas of the foundation soon.

CHAPTER 23

26 October, 1837

On a cool day in late October, Helena and Catherine sat on the marble-paved veranda of the Stirling House in Athens, going over the French lessons. The limestone mansion was three stories high and had five bedrooms.

A fig tree spread its branches over them, providing shade. A nearby potted jasmine's scent beckoned to Helena, and she snipped the white delicate flower relishing the sweet aroma.

A tall, whitewashed wall surrounded the veranda, and was lined by an array of potted red geraniums. Behind the wall were the stables, and often Helena would think about going for a ride, like she did in Oxford, but she learned from Mrs. Fournos that the Greeks frowned on women riding alone.

Catherine's hair hung limply, brushing her thin shoulders as she bent forward and read the sentence. "Jew swiss enchantee," she said, moving her lips in a painstakingly slow manner.

"Not quite. *Je suis enchante, Mademoiselle,*" Helena said, emphasizing the pronunciation and pointing to the section in the book. "Now try it again, and this time I want you to read the whole page."

As Catherine labored over her words, Helena became reflective. When they arrived three weeks ago from England, she had penned a letter to Nana, giving her the Athenian address. She had not heard from her yet. She missed her talks with her nanny.

Another day, when Catherine was out shopping with her mother, Helena had slipped away and met with Mr. Poulopoulos, an attorney in town. She told him about her father's property, and he asked if her father had left a will. She shook her head.

"We will need to convert the title of the property to your name, and there are papers to fill out. You also have to prove that you are the next of kin. All this will take time and money. You will need at least twenty-five drachmas to get started."

"I do not have that much money," she mumbled. Mrs. Stirling had not paid her for her services yet.

He looked at her with kind eyes. "I will try to work with you, Miss Cadfield. I know you are an orphan, so I will do it for half the money."

Helena thanked him, feeling elated.

"Have you had a chance to visit the site in Nemea?" he asked her.

"No, not yet. I'd like to travel there soon, but am trying to gather the money for it."

"Make sure you get a guide to show you the way. It's a two-day trip, and you might get lost."

A week ago, Helena pawned a gold locket that she had in her possession and paid the attorney, which started the legal process of attaining the title.

The sounds of pots and pans clanking interrupted Helena's thoughts. Mrs. Fournos, the heavy-set housekeeper and cook, who had a hint of a mustache on her upper lip and a robust voice, was shouting.

"Didn't I tell you not to put the bowl there?" Mrs. Fournos shouted from inside. "Now look what happened. It broke!"

"I didn't put it there!"

Helena recognized Koula's voice. She was Mrs. Fournos's niece and worked as a maid, but was slow and clumsy, which caused constant strife between her and Mrs. Fournos.

"Well, then, who did? *Kyria* Marika?" Mrs. Fournos bellowed.

Helena smiled. "*Kyria* Marika" was an imaginary figure who always received blame whenever something bad happened.

The door to the veranda burst open and Koula ran toward Helena, shrieking and cowering behind her. Although a year older than Helena, she acted much younger. Short and plump, she had a plain face and black, braided hair that hung down her back.

Mrs. Fournos followed her, holding a broken bowl in her hands. "*Tora tha theis ti tha sou kano, mori!*" (You'll see what I will do with you!) When she saw Helena, she stopped, appearing embarrassed. "Miss Cadfield, look at this bowl. Now I will have to pay for it."

"I tell you I did not do it," Koula said from behind the chair.

"Well, if Koula didn't put the bowl there and you didn't either, then you have nothing to worry about," Helena said calmly.

Mrs. Fournos mumbled something and returned to the house.

Koula kissed Helena on the cheek and bounded into the house. They resumed the lesson.

Although the girl had grasped the language quickly, applying the necessary inflections of voice with just the right nasal emphasis, she would often make fun of the French language, exaggerating the words. This time, Catherine read it perfectly.

"*Qu'est-ce qe le temps, s'il vous plait?*" Helena said, asking about the time.

Catherine rolled her eyes and tightened her lips in resistance. She ground out the words.

"Remember to purse your lips," Helena said, pursing her lips, and causing a giggle to erupt from Catherine. She repeated the French words, letting them roll off the back of her throat. "Now do it properly."

"Why do I have to do it again?" Catherine whined. "I know it already." She pursed her lips too much, as if kissing the air, and rolled her eyes, mimicking the phrase impishly.

Helena refrained from giggling. She knew that if she did so, there would be no end to Catherine's bantering. "Remember, you said you wanted to convince your father that you knew enough French to join them at the court ball, and it is only three days away."

Catherine promptly continued her lesson with renewed energy.

Koula arrived and handed Helena a letter.

"Thank you," Helena said, taking it and looking at it curiously. The last time she had read a letter was from her late father. Her heart leapt with joy when she recognized Nana's writing.

"You may be excused," Helena informed Catherine.

After Catherine left, Helena eagerly opened Nana's sealed letter. She was surprised to see several pound notes folded inside.

Helena read Nana's shaky handwriting.

My dearest Helena,

Oh, how time flies now that I am getting older. I received your lovely letter, and I'm excited about your trip to Greece. I hope they are treating you well. I am coping with living with my daughter Jenny. As you know, I remained here to be the nanny of my granddaughter. She is such a joy.

I do miss seeing you, Helena, with your sweet smile and logical ways, and always checking out for me, but I must tell you the news before I forget. Today I received Mrs. Barton's letter and it concerned you. Mr. Barton apparently found a letter on Mr. Weldon's desk, and you know he normally doesn't pry into such things, but because it had been opened and your name was mentioned, of course, he had to look. He was only able to get the first few sentences in when Mr. Weldon's unexpected arrival made him drop it back on the desk. When he returned later to the study, the letter was gone!

All he knows is that there is some problem with the Stirling family's financial situation. In that letter, they were requesting money from Mr. Weldon because the Greek government had not paid them yet, and when they left London, they were up to their necks in debt. The voyage to Greece came from borrowed money, and they have no money to pay the servants, including you! That is all Mr. Barton could decipher.

The Stirlings are in debt, my dear. I knew it, and who knows when they will pay you for your services. Enclosed, I have sent you some money to help you on your journey. All the staff that knew you at Cadfield House gave a little, God bless them! Mr. and Mrs. Barton gave the most, and your father had also sent five pounds for your birthday before he passed away for me to buy something with it, but I forgot about it and now I found the money in one of my pockets. How silly of me! Now you will need it even more.

If I could, I would journey to Greece to be with you. I would! Make haste, my dear, to your new home. Write me your news.

P. S. I heard that Dr. Murphy called to see you at Cadfield House after you left so suddenly. He was disappointed at the news. I sent Mrs. Barton your address in Athens to give to him. Don't be surprised if you receive a letter from him soon.

With love,
Your Nana

Helena reread the letter, feeling pleased to learn that Dr. Murphy came to see her, and at the same time shocked that the Stirlings were without funds. She realized that the honor system that she had grown up with, where people kept their promises, had vanished. Her assumptions that the Stirlings would treat her with respect were naïve. She had been hoping the Stirlings would pay her and give her a day off so she could visit the property, but it never came. Why had she been so blind before? At this rate, she would never be able to visit her family property.

She counted the pounds in her hand. There were ten notes. "Oh, sweet Nana and Father, and the good old staff," she said.

Mrs. Fournos approached her, carrying a tray of tea and biscuits.

Helena hastily stuffed the letter and money in her pocket.

"Here you are, Miss Cadfield," Mrs. Fournos said, placing the tray on the table. "I know you like your tea in the afternoon. I made these biscuits this morning."

"Thank you," Helena said, pleased with this special treatment. Mrs. Fournos rarely went out of her way to make tea for her.

"I hope you let Mrs. Stirling know that I did not break the bowl," Mrs. Fournos said anxiously. "I don't want them to charge me for it. I have yet to be paid and cannot afford this."

Helena reassured the woman that if it were to come up in discussion, that she would defend her.

At dinner, Catherine performed her French dialogue. Pleased with her progress, her father officially allowed her to attend the ball on Saturday. The matter of the broken bowl was not brought up.

Helena decided not to mention the matter of her payment. Not yet.

CHAPTER 24

Friday afternoon, Helena and Catherine sat on the veranda doing lessons. Helena half-listened to the girl's droning voice, gazing dreamily at the flourishing red geraniums near the wall. Her mind shifted once more to Dr. Murphy and Nana's letter with the ten pounds. It had incited her to want to leave the Stirlings immediately and head for her family property.

She had spoken to the stable boy and discreetly inquired about prices for horses and guides, and discovered that the ten pounds would not be enough for hiring a guide, renting a horse or mule, and paying for food and drink. She sighed at her dilemma.

She felt pressed to go to Nemea and seek the treasures that her father wrote to her about. Once she became wealthy, she would not have to work as a governess and would return to England and marry Dr. Murphy. That was her plan.

Helena needed to find the right time to speak with Mrs. Stirling about getting paid.

Koula arrived, interrupting their lesson. "Miss Stirling, you have visitors," she said.

"I wonder who it is?" Catherine asked, jumping up eagerly and heading to the front of the house.

Helena followed her. She recognized Felix Helzig, who bowed politely. Standing next to him was a beautiful young woman with blonde hair swept up under her elegant hat. She was clothed in the latest fashion, with her dress emphasizing her slim figure. Next to her stood a tall, fair man with blue eyes. He wore spectacles, which gave him a studious look.

"Meet my cousins, Miss Greta Heinz and her brother, Dr. Heinz, newly arrived from Germany. They are staying with Uncle Gustav," Mr. Helzig said in English.

"This is my governess, Miss Helena," Catherine said.

Dr. Heinz and his sister bowed in greeting.

"I am pleased to meet you." Helena curtsied, acutely aware of Dr. Heinz gazing in admiration of her.

Helena recognized their names. Mr. Gustav Heinz, Mrs. Stirling's uncle, had helped Mr. Stirling find work in King Otto's court. Highly esteemed by the Stirlings, Mr. Heinz and his wife had visited a couple of times for dinner. They lived farther down the road in this exclusive neighborhood of fine homes. Everyone in this area worked in some capacity for the court.

"Ludwig and I thought we would take Greta and Catherine for a ride to see the Acropolis. You are welcome to join us, Miss Helena," Mr. Helzig said.

"The carriage fits only four, Felix," Miss Heinz retorted in German.

"Very well then, Felix, would you be kind enough to sit on top with the driver, so Miss Helena can come along?" Dr. Heinz promptly replied in German.

Helena had understood every bit of this German conversation, and her cheeks felt hot. This Miss Heinz was not friendly, yet Helena knew that Miss Heinz's rudeness was probably because she saw her as a servant, and servants didn't ride in carriages with their masters. Helena threw caution to the wind and promptly accepted Mr. Helzig's invitation.

"Miss Stirling's parents are not here, and I would be pleased to come as a chaperone," she said to Mr. Helzig. "I will fetch our bonnets."

Everyone had already entered the closed carriage when she returned with the bonnets. Catherine and Miss Heinz sat together, so Helena took the seat next to Dr. Heinz, conscious of his eyes on her. She handed Catherine her bonnet.

The carriage made its way up the gentle slope and the road flowed into the Plaka. They entered the busy marketplace. The vendors, dressed in colorful clothing, shouted and haggled, selling their wares. The Greek men were dark and upright, and many were richly dressed in Greek costumes. Helena could not help admiring them. They were an expressive people, so different from the polite, aloof Englishmen. She also spied small groups of foreigners walking about, gazing around and looking awkwardly out of place.

Helena was excited as they drove toward the area. She had wanted to visit the Acropolis but had not had anyone to go with.

"How are you finding life in Greece, Miss Helena?" Dr. Heinz asked Helena in English.

"Very well, thank you," Helena replied shyly.

"Where does that lead to?" Miss Heinz asked, pointing to the main road ahead.

"I think it goes to Corinth," Felix replied. "I was told by Uncle Gustav that King Otto had it paved. Most roads were dirt roads before he came."

The carriage stopped to let some pedestrians cross the road.

"Greta, I believe I see Aris!" Dr. Heinz cried in German. He commanded the driver to stop, and then leaned outside the window and called out to a tall man who was walking by.

Helena looked past Dr. Heinz at the man named Aris. He was well dressed and striking in appearance. Something about those expressive eyes reminded her of someone, but she could not place him. Miss Heinz appeared happy to see him and chatted animatedly to him in German.

The man smiled, appearing pleased to see Miss Heinz and her brother. "When did you two arrive in Greece?" he asked Dr. Heinz.

"Yesterday, and I wrote to you about it," Dr. Heinz said, smiling. "Didn't you get my letter?"

"I was out of town and returned today. How long will you be staying?"

"At least a fortnight. Our uncle is looking to find a job for Ludwig with King Otto's government," Miss Heinz announced.

Dr. Heinz winced. "Only if I receive a good offer would I consider it. My work in Egypt is still ongoing."

"Good, good. We must get together," Aris said.

"We are planning to visit the Acropolis. Miss Stirling and her governess are with us, as well as Felix, Miss Stirling's uncle," Miss Heinz said.

Helena saw Aris glance around in the carriage. His gaze settled on her. She shyly receded from his view. His bold gaze puzzled her. *Did she know him?* She felt her cheeks flush from his stare.

Then she heard his deep voice and immediately recalled the voice of the man at the Corinthian Inn that night they stayed there. *Could it be him?* Without the beard, he looked handsome and more refined. Did he recognize her as the governess? Why would he be interested in a lowly governess? With that thought, she glanced away.

"Would you care to join us, Aris?" Dr. Heinz asked him.

"Thank you, my friend, but I am expected at an important meeting. We must get together another time."

"Aris, are you going to the court ball tomorrow? We will be attending it," Miss Heinz asked him.

"Yes, of course. I will see you then," Aris smiled at her.

Miss Heinz badgered him about visiting him. "I promised you that I would come, and here I am," she teased.

"What are they saying? I cannot understand them," Catherine asked Helena.

"It's not polite to eavesdrop," Helena said to her in English.

Dr. Heinz looked with amusement at Catherine. "You will learn soon enough. My sister keeps nothing back," he said in English.

After Miss Heinz's conversation with the man ended, the carriage rolled ahead.

"Too bad that Aris can't come with us to the Acropolis," Miss Heinz said in English, her face glowing. "If anyone knows about these things, he does."

"You forget, dear sister, that I attended the same school as he did," Dr. Heinz remarked dryly.

Helena wondered what relationship Miss Heinz had with the handsome Aris.

CHAPTER 25

The carriage dropped them off at the foot of the Acropolis, and they began walking up its south slope. To actually be here and see it in person was an exhilarating feeling for Helena. She saw an immense open stone theater to her left, and stopped to gaze at it in wonder. Mr. Heinz and Catherine stood nearby.

"That stone theater is the Theater of Dionysus, dedicated to Dionysus, the god of song and wine," Helena told Catherine.

"Yes, and it's over two thousand years old," Mr. Heinz offered.

Helena nodded. "In the fifth century, every spring time, they would have choral performances and a theatrical festival."

"They wrote plays in those days?" Catherine asked.

"Oh dear, yes. Haven't you heard of the playwrights Euripides, Sophocles, and Aristophanes? They wrote comedies and tragedies that were acted out at the festival," Helena replied.

"The festival was really a competition, and the judges would decide on the best plays. The victor wore a garland on his head and marched through the streets of Athens in a procession," Mr. Heinz offered.

Catherine shook her head. "I didn't know that."

"The origins of theater began here in Greece," Helena said. "It was popular in those days and could seat more than fifteen thousand people."

"Why don't they have theater here anymore?" Miss Heinz asked.

"I understand that they have been making renovations," Mr. Heinz replied.

"Maybe one day, when it's fixed, they will resume the theatrical festival," Helena said hopefully.

"What is that over there?" Catherine pointed to another, smaller amphitheater.

"The Odeon of Herodes Atticus," Mr. Heinz replied. "It was used for music concerts and could fit five thousand people."

"Herodes Atticus was a wealthy patron of the arts and built this amphitheater about seventeen hundred years ago, in memory of his wife," Helena said to Catherine.

They stared at it silently.

Catherine looked around. "Where are Felix and Greta?"

"I believe they went ahead," Mr. Heinz replied.

Catherine ran up the hill, and Helena hurried after her. The steep and stony hill made her breathless. When she reached the others, they were resting under the cool shade of a tree.

After a short break, everyone climbed to the top of the Acropolis.

The warm wind was fierce and tugged Helena's dress in different directions. She focused her attention on the white columns of the Parthenon that jutted majestically toward the blue sky. Reading about it in a book did not compare with seeing it in person.

"Look at this, Miss Cadfield," Catherine said, pointing at the lifelike, sculpted maidens that stood on the porch of the Erechtheum.

"They are called the caryatids," Helena informed her.

"Remarkably beautiful," Mr. Helzig said, joining them. "I see a resemblance of Miss Cadfield in their faces."

Helena blushed and looked down shyly. Miss Heinz and her brother joined them.

"What lovely creatures. It seems as if they are holding the building up with their heads," Miss Heinz said, studying the caryatids. "Wait, one is missing."

"Dear sister, must I remind you that Lord Elgin took the caryatid statue back to London with him along with other Greek marbles, at the beginning of the century, before the war?" Mr. Heinz informed her.

"They should all be returned to their rightful place," Helena said.

"I agree, but it cost Elgin a fortune to transport them to England. The cost to transport them back is just as formidable," Mr. Heinz said.

Helena realized the implications of his words. Greece was struggling economically to get back on its feet. How could they afford to pay for the marbles to be returned to them?

Mr. Heinz turned and pointed to a small building with four columns in the corner. "That must be the Temple of Athena Nike Apteros. They restored it recently, I heard."

Helena nodded. "Apteros means without wings," she said to Catherine. "They didn't want Nike to have wings so that she wouldn't fly away."

"That's silly. She was only a statue," Miss Heinz scoffed.

"In those days, statues were larger than life," Helena replied.

The group walked toward the Parthenon with its many columns. Catherine continued to hover around Mr. Helzig, bantering with him. Helena also noticed that Dr. Heinz and his sister were conversing in German. They probably did this when they wanted privacy, and switched to English when discussing mundane topics. Should she let them know that she spoke German? She decided not to. It would complicate matters if they discovered that she had been listening in on their private banter.

Not wanting to lose the opportunity to teach her young charge, Helena spoke to Catherine.

"Miss Stirling, the Parthenon is the building where the statue of the goddess Athena was housed. The goddess Athena is supposed to have come out of the head of Zeus and represents victory and wisdom. Her statue was as tall as the building and made of ivory and gold, and she wore a helmet."

Catherine gazed in wonder at the building, her mouth wide open.

"Also, can you see the way those columns appear straight? It is an illusion." Helena said to Catherine.

"If you look carefully, you will see that the center is slightly wider than the edges," Dr. Heinz offered.

"I see that," Catherine said, nodding. "Up close, they don't appear straight, but from afar they do."

"Very good, Miss Stirling," Dr. Heinz said to her. "It seems your governess knows a few things." He glanced at Helena with admiration.

"Everyone could see that they are not straight," Miss Heinz said, laughing. "You don't need to read a book or be an archaeologist to see it. What do you think, Felix?"

Mr. Helzig regarded Helena with admiration. "I hadn't noticed them before."

Miss Heinz sat on the marble steps of the Parthenon with her brother and Mr. Helzig. They began chatting in German.

"Would you like to see more?" Helena asked Catherine.

"I'm going to sit here. I'm tired." Catherine plopped down on the steps next to the others.

"We have done a considerable amount of walking," Helena admitted, sitting down next to her. She held onto her bonnet with one hand, for the wind was fierce and threatened to pull it away.

Below, she could see the broken city of Athens, sprawled on the plain. The contrast between the Acropolis, with its glorious past, and the war-ravaged city below was unnerving. The war had done much damage to Greece, yet the Greeks were free to move forward. They had a considerable amount of work ahead of them to match the glory of the past.

Would they ever achieve it?

Helena noticed the main road leaving Athens. A light feeling overcame her as she imagined herself riding down that same road one day, heading toward Nemea and her family home. Would that day ever arrive?

A short man dressed in a uniform approached them. He appeared harried. "Please, ladies and gentlemen, do not sit on the steps."

Helena jumped up, apologizing. The others joined her. The group walked away from the man, past the columns and toward the exit. They returned to the carriage at the bottom of the hill.

Dr. Heinz discussed archaeology with Helena all the way back home. "You seem to know much about archaeology, Miss Helena," he remarked.

"My father was an archaeologist and often discussed topics like these."

"I didn't know that," Dr. Heinz exclaimed. "Tell me about him. Where is he?"

"He died recently," Helena began.

"Oh, he's dead," Miss Heinz interjected, making a face. "I don't like hearing about dead people."

"Yes, let's not talk about dead people," Catherine pleaded.

Helena was surprised to hear that, especially coming from Catherine. The girl's sad demeanor struck Helena that she was probably still mourning her mother. She smiled at her, patting her hand.

Helena steered the topic away from archaeology. She asked Dr. Heinz and his sister questions about life in Germany. They happily complied, telling her about their beautiful forests, castles, and traditions.

Although Helena felt tired when she entered the house, she was thrilled that they had visited the Acropolis and its buildings.

After Catherine left to wash and rest, Helena went to her room. As she changed her clothing and washed, she reflected on the outing to the Acropolis. She had enjoyed it immensely. Dr. Heinz and Mr. Helzig were perfect gentlemen, although Miss Heinz could have been more cordial.

More importantly, the unexpected meeting with the man called Aris, had stirred something inside her. He must have recognized her also, the way he had stared at her. Intrigued by him, she dwelled on his handsome image awhile longer, remembering how distinguished he had looked.

Why was she feeling this way?

Then she remembered that she was a mere governess and no longer the daughter of a gentleman. Why would he be interested in her when he had obviously formed some relationship with Miss Heinz?

What about Dr. Murphy? Hadn't she nursed his image all these years while in Paris? Why was she suddenly thinking about the man named Aris? Was it because he helped her at the inn by giving his plate of food for the women, or by coming to her aid later that night? Or was it his good looks and deep voice?

Too tired to think, Helena took a nap.

After she rested, Helena went downstairs for dinner. The Stirlings were away and she dined alone with Catherine.

CHAPTER 26

Aristotle strolled through the Plaka, toward his destination. He had been surprised to see Miss Heinz and her brother arrive in Greece so quickly. If he did not have to speak at the Archaeological Society meeting this afternoon, he would have gladly joined their group to visit the Acropolis.

He also was surprised to see in the same carriage the mysterious and captivating governess of Miss Stirling. She had stared at him curiously. She was even lovelier than he remembered her and had an innocent, shy look about her. The governess's carriage, manners, and reserved stance were indications of good breeding and education. She was probably there as a chaperone for Miss Stirling.

The governess did not recognize him at first, for she showed no sign of awareness at his steady gaze. Yet he glimpsed a glow in her eyes when he began speaking, as if she recognized his voice. While Miss Heinz conversed with him, he glanced once more in the direction of the governess and saw that she had averted her gaze, retreating into her shell. This simple act, although disappointing to him, elevated her in his eyes. She had class.

It had been a long day for Aristotle. He and Yianni had left Corinth early in the morning and arrived over an hour ago. Aristotle had no time to rest, but had only enough time to quickly wash and dress for the meeting at Mr. Pittakis's house. This going back and forth was taking its toll on him. He was fortunate to have both Lucas supervising the operations when he was away, and Yianni's assistance. Yianni proved to be loyal, valuable, and trustworthy.

Aristotle had arranged for Yianni to bring the wagon with the artifacts directly to Mr. Pittakis's residence and wait for him there. He strolled down the road, enjoying stretching his legs after all those hours of riding. Even the horse and mule would be out for a week, needing their rest. If they were to return in a few days, they would need fresh animals.

Keen on presenting to Mr. Pittakis and the members the recent artifacts that the workers and villagers had sold to him, Aristotle's mind went over everything he would discuss. He stopped and looked around, realizing that he had almost passed the side street. The house was around the bend and down an alley of residential homes. He had been there once before.

He turned and made his way down the cobbled alley. As he approached the residence, he spied the mule and wagon, and Yianni leaning against the wagon, munching on an apple. He winced. He had forgotten to tell Yianni to dress better; he still wore the travel-stained clothing from this morning.

Aristotle waved to him and Yianni waved back.

"Everyone is almost here, boss. We're going to sell many items, I can tell."

"Good. Yianni, wait until I give you the signal to bring them in."

When Aristotle entered the lobby, he was led into the elegant parlor with its fine furniture and Oriental carpeting. There, he greeted Mr. Pittakis and Dr. Kostakis, along with Mr. Heinz and Mr. Stirling who had recently joined the Society, and three other members, Mr. Laoutos, a wealthy merchant, Mr. Kappas, a poet, and Dr. Renagis, a scholar. Several chairs had been brought in, and some people were seated, while others were enjoying the refreshments on the side table. More people, comprised mostly of older gentlemen, arrived.

Dr. Kostakis took Aristotle aside and asked him what he was going to present. Aristotle told him about the artifacts. Then he showed him the gold necklace. "This is extremely valuable. Please keep it in the safe room with the gold cup. It belongs in the same period. I am thinking about selling the other artifacts to the members in order to help pay for the cost of the workers."

"Good," Dr. Kostakis said, appearing pleased.

After wrapping the gold necklace carefully in its cloth, Aristotle placed it in a small bag and gave it to Dr. Kostakis, who put it inside his coat.

"Make sure that you mention that the artifacts are superfluous or *achrista*," Dr. Kostakis said to him in a low voice. "Those are the only antiquities that we are allowed to sell. A law passed in 1834 concerning antiquities, states that in order to sell them, they have to be useless. I know not if everyone follows those rules, but we don't want to get into trouble."

Aristotle nodded, understanding the older man's concerns. He went outside and called Yianni, and they brought the artifacts inside. Dr. Pittakis had a table ready for them and they set the pieces on the table.

"Thank you, Yianni, you may go and wait for me outside. I won't be long," Aristotle said.

More people, comprised mostly of older gentlemen, arrived. Mr. Pittakis stood next to the table, greeting everyone.

Aristotle counted seventeen men.

"We can start," Mr. Pittakis informed Dr. Kostakis.

"Good afternoon, gentlemen. Please take your seats," Dr. Kostakis said. "Most of you here have met Dr. Mastoras, but for those who do not know him, he has a Ph.D. in philology from Germany, and has worked as an archaeologist in Egypt. The Archaeological Society is pleased to have him lead an excavation in Nemea."

People clapped politely as Dr. Kostakis gestured to Aristotle to come and speak.

"Thank you, Dr. Kostakis, for the introduction," Aristotle said. "The property is located on a mountain in Nemea, in the town of Petri, and belonged to the Kallodaftis family. Later, Dr. Cadfield, a physician and archaeologist, inherited it. The Archaeological Society received a valuable gold cup from him several months ago, just before he passed away."

Exclamations were heard. Aristotle had caught their attention.

"Since our project began many weeks ago, we have found only a few artifacts of value," Aristotle said. "It is still early to tell if we are on the right path, however, upon inquiry, we learned that a number of villagers possessed artifacts that had been discovered in different regions of Nemea and its surrounding areas. We collected them and brought them to you."

Clapping ensued, and Aristotle paused, gazing at the faces that looked in admiration at him. He gestured toward the artifacts on the table. "These are considered superfluous, because there are so many of them and were considered *achrista,* or worthless, to those who sold them to us."

Everyone laughed and looked at each other knowingly.

Aristotle held up a Corinthian vase and explained its design and year. He then held up several other artifacts, one at a time, and talked about them. After he finished his talk, he bowed to the clapping.

Mr. Pittakis went to him and shook his hand, smiling and thanking him. He turned and faced the group. "We are very fortunate to have Dr. Mastoras. He not only brings much knowledge and experience to the Archaeological Society, but has also offered to pay for the excavation until we get funds. So, if anyone is interested in having a closer look at them with the purpose of adding them to your collection, please see Dr. Mastoras. All proceeds will greatly aid the excavation."

Everyone seemed interested and approached the table.

"How much is this vase?' Mr. Laoutos asked Aristotle, pointing to a vase.

"How much would you be willing to pay for it?" Aristotle countered.

Mr. Laoutos silently stroked his chin thoughtfully.

Another person examined it. "How about one hundred drachmas?" he offered.

Aristotle was about to answer when Mr. Laoutos said, "One hundred fifty drachmas."

The two men kept raising their prices. When they reached three hundred drachmas, the other gentleman shrugged his shoulders and walked away.

Mr. Laoutos gladly paid the sum.

Others came forth and Aristotle sold more items.

Two hours later, Aristotle was pleased with the outcome. Only a few objects remained, which he planned to sell to the antiquities dealer. He had successfully earned enough money to keep his workers employed for quite a while longer.

* * *

Later that evening, after everyone had retired, the Stirlings remained in the parlor. The lit fireplace cast a soft glow on the couple. Mr. Stirling sat in the armchair reading a book and his wife sat nearby on the sofa doing her needlework.

Mrs. Stirling looked at her husband. "Have you heard any news from your sister in Oxford, Mr. Stirling?"

"Not yet," he replied, looking up. "It is too soon." He resumed reading.

"Oh."

He glanced at her, and put his book down in his lap. "What is it? You appear worried," he said to her.

"I have been thinking about paying the staff," she said, sighing. "Miss Cadfield has been working hard and so have the others. How are we going to pay them?"

He took his glasses off and rubbed his eyes. "As you know, the court has been slow in paying me. I looked at the books today and the news was not good. I wonder, dear, remember those emerald jewels that I brought you last year, after we were newlyweds?"

"*Ja*? Don't tell me that we need to sell them?"

"If we don't, then we cannot pay our creditors or the servants. Those jewels will tide us over for a while."

"If it is needed," she said, sighing and lifting her lovely shoulders.

"Don't worry, once I am paid by Otto's government, we will be in good shape and I can buy you more."

"I have received so many pretty gifts from you anyway. I will not miss them." She gave him a bright smile.

He went to her. He kissed her forehead, and then caressed her shoulder. "That is why I love you. Thank you, my dear. I will take them tomorrow morning to the shop."

"Come, sit by my side," she said, patting the sofa where she sat.

They were quiet for a few moments, as he sat close to her, caressing her hand.

"Mr. Stirling, I forgot to ask, how was your meeting at the society this afternoon?"

He told her about the young man, Dr. Mastoras, and how he brought ancient artifacts to be sold there. "Did you know, my sweet, that this man is working on a project in Nemea, and that the property belonged to the late Dr. Cadfield? Tell me, is Miss Cadfield a relation of his? I was here in Greece when you hired her."

"*Ja*, she is. Don't you remember when your sister wrote and said that they had moved to Cadfield House in Oxford? After Dr. Cadfield died, Mr. Weldon inherited the property because he was the next heir in line. Miss Cadfield did not receive any monies from her father and needed employment. Since we had let them know that we were looking for a governess for Catherine, they sent her here and so I hired her."

"Yes, there were so many governesses coming and going, that I couldn't keep track of them. Hmmm. Do you realize that since Miss Cadfield is the daughter of Dr. Cadfield? She is the rightful heir to the property in Nemea and is rich?" Mr. Stirling said, looking at his wife meaningfully.

"Rich? How can that be?"

"Today I learned that her property in Nemea has netted a priceless gold cup, thousands of years old. They are excavating to find more treasures like that one."

"Ahh, I see now why you are interested in Miss Cadfield," she said, and smiled at him knowingly.

"From now on, we must be kind to her," he said, patting her hand. "We must treat her like family."

They became quiet once more.

"Mr. Stirling, now that Catherine will be attending the ball, I wondered if she could bring along Miss Cadfield?"

He coughed nervously. "My dear, I forgot to tell you that today I had mentioned to Mr. Heinz that we would be bringing Catherine, and he told me that hardly any women go to these balls. The majority of people there will be men."

"But we had promised Catherine that she could go."

"Yes, but what will the men think?"

Mrs. Stirling arose, appearing flustered. "I spoke with Mrs. Heinz the other day and she will be going with their niece, Miss Heinz. Surely if they can take her, we can take Catherine and Miss Cadfield."

CHAPTER 27

1 November, 1837

Late Saturday morning, the day of the ball, Mrs. Stirling summoned Helena into the parlor.

Helena was pleasantly surprised when Mrs. Stirling presented her an envelope with her payment. She thanked her, putting it in her pocket.

"I also feel that you should accompany Catherine to the ball tonight. I want to be free to enjoy myself without having to worry about her, and she is remarkably quiet when you are around. You seem to do her good."

Helena blinked at the sudden change of events. One minute, Mrs. Stirling had been ignoring her, and now she had paid her and even asked her to go with them to the ball. A small feeling of hope entered her heart.

"Thank you, Mrs. Stirling, I am grateful for the invitation," Helena said, "but I don't have any dress to wear for the ball."

"Oh, not to worry. I have some dresses from which you can choose," Mrs. Stirling said, smiling.

When Catherine learned that Helena was coming to the ball, she bounced around the room. "Now I'll have you to talk with and won't have to worry so hard about my French."

"What about Miss Heinz? Won't you have her as company?"

Catherine became silent. "She will be too busy dancing with her beaus and will leave me all alone." She sidled up to Miss Cadfield and grabbed her by the arm, gazing up at her with an anxious look. "Will no one care to dance with me, Miss Cadfield?"

"Surely your father will dance with you, and there's always Mr. Helzig, too," Helena said, smiling fondly at her. "And with your pretty dress, I am certain that some nice young men will want to dance with you."

Catherine smiled, appearing satisfied.

Later that morning, Mrs. Fournos presented the birthday cake to Miss Stirling, and they celebrated it in the dining-room with Mrs. Stirling, Helena, and Koula, singing her the birthday song in Greek.

Helena had sewn two handkerchiefs with Catherine's initials on them, which earned her a grateful peck on the cheek. Miss Stirling's parents hugged her and gave her a white dress as a present with matching white slippers and a white hat with yellow flowers. Catherine was thrilled with them. She put them on and paraded around the house, preening and modeling the gown.

When Helena entered her room later, she found two silk dresses on her bed. She touched the soft fabrics, marveling at the beauty of the gowns. The dress she favored had a creamy white color, with pearls stitched around the trim and down the large sleeves. The dress fit her but was short. She examined the hem and found that she could lengthen it. She started working on it.

Koula came by later, carrying white slippers and a pair of long, white gloves. "Mrs. Stirling said you could wear these."

That day, Catherine chattered away, apparently in an unusually cheerful mood, as Helena helped her prepare for the event. She told Helena that the king and queen were to be there, as well as several dignitaries and members of the court. She also mentioned that Felix would be there. "I wonder if he will recognize me all dressed up." She gazed at herself in the mirror, her eyes glowing. "Oh, and I believe Greta's beau, Aris will be there. She is head over heels in love with him."

Aris?" Helena asked, her heart quickening. She had thought about him quite a bit after that meeting, and had been excited when his eyes sought hers in the carriage. His steady gaze was real. He had looked straight at her and had shown signs of recognition.

Catherine turned and looked at her. "Yes, you remember him. We saw him yesterday when we were going to the Acropolis. Greta told me that she's known him for a long time, and that she's going to marry him."

He is Miss Heinz's beau and you have Dr. Murphy. "Oh? Is he German, too?" she asked lightly, trying not to sound disappointed.

"Well, no, and yes. She told me that Aris is Greek, but grew up in Germany. He can speak German, English, Greek, and French quite well. He's very smart. Here, can you help me with the buttons?"

Helena silently buttoned the girl's dress in the back, trying to get him out of her mind by focusing on her task. "All done."

"How do I look?" Catherine asked, whirling around.

"It's beautiful on you, but a little too long. You don't want to be tripping on it. I'll sew it up in no time." Helena got a needle and thread and several pins, and kneeling on the floor, began to pin and sew the hem. She listened to Catherine's chatter, but her mind drifted back to Aris. *Was he really Miss Heinz's beau?* She realized Catherine had asked her a question.

"Hmm?" Helena asked, taking the pin from her mouth.

"Did you have a coming out ball?"

"No, and it did not bother me one bit. My father died before I could have one."

Koula entered the room carrying an envelope in her hand. "This is for you, Miss Cadfield. From England."

Helena thanked her and took the envelope. Her hands became clammy when she saw Dr. Murphy's name on it.

"Another letter from your nanny, I suppose?"

Helena didn't answer Catherine, but tucked it in her pocket and continued working on the dress. She did not want to share Dr. Murphy with the inquisitive girl.

Afterwards, Catherine preened in front of the mirror as Helena combed her hair and made ringlets to frame her small face. She placed a delicate bouquet of gardenias on the side of her head. "There, you look *tres belle.*"

"*Merci,*" Catherine replied prettily. "I do look beautiful. I have never seen anything like it. Oh, thank you." She hugged Helena.

"That is sweet of you, dear. Please be careful not to mess your hair. Now I need to leave you," Helena said. She went to her room and hastily opened the envelope.

Dear Miss Cadfield,

I hope this letter finds you well. I stopped by one day to visit the Weldons and inquired about you. You can imagine my surprise when I learned about your recent departure to London to work as a governess for Mr. and Mrs. Stirling. I entertained the idea of visiting London for some business there, and calling on you at the same time. Upon returning to Cadfield House to inquire about your London address, the Weldons were away, but luckily, Mrs. Barton provided me with your new address in Athens. I was not surprised to learn about your trip, since you were so determined to visit your property in Greece. May I ask how long you plan to be there? Are you still employed with the Stirlings?

My work is coming along nicely, although it is not the same without you. Maybe I should become adventurous like your father and travel the world. Alas, my work does not permit me to do that so I must settle with hearing about your adventures in Greece.

Please write back and let me know your news.
Yours truly,
Allan Murphy

Helena sat there in a daze, realizing that Dr. Murphy had meant what he had said about waiting for her. She looked at the time with consternation. It was too late to send him a letter. She would write to him tomorrow, after the ball.

After washing, Helena slipped into her cream-colored dress. She pulled up her hair and created some curls at the top. Where was Nana to help her? She gazed at herself in the mirror, marveling at the transformation. Was she that beautiful? Her skin glowed with radiant health and the cream dress brought out the blue in her eyes.

After she put her slippers on and her long white gloves, Helena twirled around, her arms outstretched, picturing the handsome Dr. Mastoras dancing with her. She stopped, feeling ashamed of her bold thoughts. She should be thinking instead about Dr. Murphy. *Besides, why would Dr. Mastoras want to dance with the governess? He already had Miss Heinz.*

As she left the room, she felt as if she were back in Paris, going to a social function with her classmates, but it was not the case. She was no longer a student, but a governess, and she must remember that.

Mrs. Stirling was dressed even more beautifully, with expensive jewels around her neck. It hardly seemed possible that the Stirlings were in dire financial straits.

Catherine ran up to Helena, clasping her hands and jumping up and down. "Oh, Miss Cadfield, you look stunning!"

"Thank you, and so do you. Now please calm down. It will do you no good to mess your curls."

"You have done a wonderful job with Catherine," Mrs. Stirling told her.

"Thank you." Helena also thanked Mrs. Stirling for the dresses.

"You can keep them, if you like. I have so many."

Mr. Stirling arrived and appeared pleased with the results. Everyone was in a good mood as they left for the ball.

CHAPTER 28

Earlier on Saturday, Aristotle visited an antiquities dealer and sold the remaining artifacts that he had purchased from some workers in Nemea. With new money in his pocket, he felt especially cheerful.

Freshly washed and shaved, Aristotle dressed for the ball. He wore a fine, dark suit, with a shirt made of crisp, white linen and an equally white cravat.

Later, when he walked into the large ballroom, he scanned the room. Predominantly a male group, only a few elegantly dressed women graced the ballroom. Many Greek men outfitted in the traditional Greek costume, including Barba Manolis, stood to the side.

Barba Manolis appeared happy to see Aristotle and took him to meet his old friends. Many knew of Aristotle's father and grandfather.

Barba Manolis's son, Petros, was also there, and was dressed conventionally in a suit and white linen shirt. Several men were dressed in the German uniform. The King and Queen had not arrived yet, and everyone was waiting for their entrance.

While conversing with Petros, Aristotle spied the Stirling family entering the ballroom. He recognized their daughter, but was that lovely creature next to her the governess? He stood there, amazed at Miss Helena's transformation. She looked exquisite in that ball gown.

"How is your work coming along, Dr. Mastoras?" Petros asked. "I understand that you are in charge of the excavation site near Nemea."

The question interrupted Aristotle's thoughts. "Ah, yes," he said, nodding his head and then briefing him on the project.

Petros introduced another person to Aristotle, who also worked in King Otto's court. They discussed the economic viability of Greece for a while.

Mr. Stirling joined them. "I am impressed with the objects of antiquity that you presented to the Archaeological Society yesterday,

Dr. Mastoras. I was surprised to hear you call them useless. Why was that?" Mr. Stirling asked Aristotle.

"Dr. Kostakis informed me that a law was passed a few years ago, stating that antiquities must be considered useless before they could be sold. These objects may appear valuable to you because you have never seen them before, but since there are so many of them, they do not have the value that a rare object has."

"So you assessed them as useless," Mr. Stirling said, laughing. "Very clever."

Everyone laughed.

Mrs. Stirling joined her husband, greeting Dr. Mastoras. He bowed politely.

"My daughter tells me that you are Greek, but you were raised in Germany, Dr. Mastoras?" Mrs. Stirling asked in French. "What part of Germany?"

Aristotle recognized the polite conversation. "We lived in Bavaria with an uncle."

"How delightful. I was born in Bavaria," Mrs. Stirling said. She began to speak to him in German, telling him about her country and culture. "I have tried to get Mr. Stirling to return to Bavaria for a trip, but he is tied down here. On the other hand, Miss Stirling has expressed interest in visiting Germany."

"Your wife is right, Mr. Stirling, you must visit Bavaria again," Aristotle told him.

"I would like to, but my job is too demanding at the moment," Mr. Stirling replied.

Aristotle noticed his friend, Ludwig Heinz, and his sister approaching him. He was glad to see them. Miss Heinz was beautiful, as always.

"There you are, Aris," Dr. Heinz said to Aristotle in German, patting him on the back.

"I'm pleased you came," Miss Heinz said, placing her hand on his arm. "I have so much to tell you."

"That's all she talked about today, whether she would see you or not," Dr. Heinz teased, laughing.

"Oh, stop it, Ludwig. I was not," she said, blushing.

Aristotle stayed awhile with them, chatting in German. It felt like old times as they talked and joked. Several old men wearing Greek costumes walked past them.

Miss Heinz's demeanor changed as she gazed at them, her brows arched. "Why do they still wear those frightfully old clothes?"

"Probably because King Otto likes to wear them himself," Aristotle responded dryly.

Miss Heinz giggled. "You make me laugh so."

Dr. Kostakis arrived and asked Aristotle to join him. He introduced him to a group composed of Mr. Pittakis and members of the Archaeological Society, two bankers and a scholar.

They asked him if he had any more artifacts to sell, and Aristotle told them that he had sold most of them, but that he would keep them in mind for future acquisitions. They were interested in archaeology, but knew little about it, so Aristotle did the best he could to educate them on the topic. Now he understood why Dr. Kostakis had wanted him to work for them. So far, he had met no one from the society, other than Mr. Pittakis, who knew anything about archaeology.

King Otto and Queen Amalia arrived and began circling the room, speaking to everyone in French. King Otto, a handsome man, was dressed in a Greek costume and his wife was dressed in the latest fashion. They approached Aristotle's group, accompanied by their entourage, and Dr. Kostakis introduced Aristotle to them.

"Dr. Mastoras directs the archaeological excavation in Nemea," Dr. Kostakis said.

King Otto seemed deeply interested, nodding his head. "Have you found any valuable items?" he asked Aristotle.

"So far, our results have netted nothing of importance, your Majesty."

"*Eh*? I'm sorry, what did you say?"

Aristotle repeated his word, shouting in his ear.

"You need not shout," King Otto said, appearing flustered.

"I apologize. Some pottery and tools that we have found are stored here in Athens, under Dr. Kostakis's care."

"Ah, *oui*. Good, and isn't there a gold cup?" King Otto's eyes were kind, but piercing.

"Yes, and we are hoping to find more like that."

"*Tres bien*."

The King and the Queen continued making the rounds.

The musicians began to play, and the floor filled with the older men dressed in Greek costumes, looking fierce and proud at the same time as they formed a dance line.

Miss Heinz approached Aristotle, smiling prettily. She asked him to dance, and he graciously complied. It did not surprise him that she took the lead. She had always been an assertive, confident person, and always seemed to be chasing him. He usually liked to do the chasing when it came to women. Miss Heinz led him to the line that consisted mostly of Germans in uniforms. He noticed that the King and Queen had formed their own line.

Barba Manolis stood in a line consisting of aged men dressed in Greek costume. Aristotle gazed proudly at the fighters, knowing what sacrifices they had made for their country. If his grandfather had been living, he would have joined this group proudly. Barba Manolis waved for him to join them. Aristotle stared at him, and then looked at Miss Heinz.

"I think we are in the wrong line," he said firmly, taking her hand and pulling her toward the group of Greek warriors.

The music was a lively Kalamatiano dance.

Aristotle tried to show Miss Heinz the steps. "Eight steps to the right, and then four to the left," he said.

She bumped into him awkwardly. "Oh, you dance it well. I'm afraid I don't know this dance."

"That's all right, half the people in this room don't know it either," Aristotle said, chuckling, looking at the Germans who were trying to learn the dance.

Their line moved forward in a semi-circle, and the old warriors, fierce looking men with large mustaches and strong noses, took turns leading the line, their steps agile. They periodically leapt high into the air, their hands slapping their heels, and then landed like cats.

Miss Heinz giggled when she saw the men leaping into the air, their billowing skirts revealing stockinged legs. She was the only woman in their line. She stood out like a butterfly, and he secretly wondered if the old men were dancing to impress her

After the dance, Aristotle escorted her back to her group. He noticed that a number of men dressed in German uniforms were gazing at her. A couple of them were heading their way. He dropped her off with Mrs. Frieda Heinz.

CHAPTER 29

Helena strolled outside with Catherine and Mr. Helzig. Lanterns surrounded them, bathing them with a soft light. The cool night air was a refreshing respite after the hot ballroom.

"Would you care to dance with me the next dance?" Mr. Helzig asked Helena.

"Thank you. I would enjoy it, on the condition that you dance with Catherine afterwards," she replied. She felt someone staring at her and turned to look.

Mr. Stirling had arrived with the man named Aris. To her consternation, her heart started beating rapidly. *What was happening to her?* She had seen him dancing with Miss Heinz, and they had seemed happy together. She stiffened and raised her chin, trying to regain her composure.

The two men approached their group.

"You were right, Dr. Mastoras," Mr. Stirling was saying, "it's much cooler out here."

Helena was surprised to hear Mr. Stirling address Aris as Dr. Mastoras. Was he a physician?

"I have not had the pleasure of being introduced formally to everyone," Dr. Mastoras said pleasantly to Mr. Stirling.

Mr. Stirling introduced him to Mr. Helzig and Miss Stirling. He then turned to Helena. "Miss Cadfield is my daughter's governess."

Helena curtsied politely while Dr. Mastoras bowed. She was puzzled to see a cool expression settle over his face. *Was he not used to being introduced to governesses?* Feeling indignant at the thought that he was arrogant, she flushed.

Strains of a minuet filtered outside.

Mr. Helzig approached Miss Helena. "Miss Helena, I believe this is our dance," he said to her, taking her arm possessively.

"What about Miss Stirling?" Helena asked him. "I can't just leave her."

"Dr. Mastoras, why don't you dance with my daughter? I know she's been dying to show off her skills," Mr. Stirling said.

Catherine blushed and curtsied. "Je swiss enchantee."

"I would be delighted to dance with you," Dr. Mastoras told Miss Stirling, bowing politely.

As Catherine took Dr. Mastoras's arm, she turned to Mr. Helzig. "Don't forget, Felix. You promised me a dance. Aw revwar."

"All right, the next one," Mr. Helzig answered, turning red.

Mr. Helzig escorted Helena to the dance floor. "I have waited for this moment for a long time. You are a vision of beauty tonight."

Helena blushed. It had been a while since she had received such compliments. Mr. Helzig was well versed in that area.

* * *

When the minuet ended, Aristotle took Miss Stirling to her parents, feeling perturbed. He needed to learn one thing. When he had a moment alone with Mr. Stirling, he took him aside.

"I was surprised to learn that the name of your governess was Miss Cadfield," Aristotle began, trying to keep his composure. "Am I to presume that she is the late Dr. Cadfield's daughter?"

Mr. Stirling nodded solemnly.

Aristotle sucked in his breath. "May I ask why you kept this fact hidden from me?"

"I only discovered this last night," Mr. Stirling said, shrugging his shoulders. "Miss Cadfield was hired while I was here in Greece. The transaction occurred between my sister, Mrs. Weldon, and my wife. When I learned that you were working on Dr. Cadfield's property, I made the connection that she might be related to him. Last night, my wife confirmed the relation."

"Is Miss Cadfield aware of the excavation being conducted on her property?"

"I'm afraid I don't know. It never came up for discussion."

"Thank you. Please excuse me," Aristotle said tensely, nodding slightly and leaving. He must deal with this new dilemma.

* * *

Catherine made her way toward Helena. She was breathless and excited. "Oh, this Aris is so handsome and he danced the minuet beautifully," she said, glancing around the room. "I wonder if Greta saw us. She would have been so jealous."

"That's not a nice thing to say."

Catherine's face fell. "No, it isn't. Every time I try to catch her attention, she is always with a different beau. How could she look at anyone else when she has Aris as her beau?"

"Maybe it's because she isn't serious about him, and by the way, you should address him as Dr. Mastoras."

"Oh, that is so old," Catherine scoffed. She looked around and became excited. "Oh, look, Aris, I mean Dr. Mastoras, is coming here. Do you suppose he wants to dance with me again?"

Helena saw Dr. Mastoras approaching them. "I don't know, dear."

He bowed and she and Catherine both curtsied.

Helena's her heart raced, when he didn't turn his gaze on Catherine. Instead, he looked at Helena with a single-minded purpose. "Miss Cadfield, may I have the pleasure of the next dance?"

Helena blushed furiously. She was excited that he had singled her out, but Dr. Murphy's letter earlier that day burned in her mind and heart. She couldn't trust her heart with this man. Besides, she was waiting for Mr. Helzig to claim Catherine for a dance.

Helena stole a glance at Catherine, whose face was crestfallen. "Thank you, but I'm waiting for Mr. Helzig to claim the next dance with Miss Stirling."

Dr. Mastoras stood there, appearing handsome and dignified. "I will wait, then."

They did not wait long. Mr. Helzig soon arrived. "Miss Stirling, could I have this dance?" he asked Catherine, bowing.

"*Merci. Je swiss enchantee.* I am delighted that you kept your promise to dance with me, Felix," Catherine said, smiling at him and taking his arm. They left for the dance floor.

"Miss Cadfield, will you do me the honor of dancing with me? I need to speak to you," Dr. Mastoras said.

Helena blushed as she accepted his hand.

Dr. Mastoras escorted her to the dance floor. He was a smooth and sure dancer, and they moved well together. He leaned close to her and Helena felt the warmth of his breath against her cheek.

"I must admit that I was surprised when I heard your name," Dr. Mastoras said softly in her ear.

Helena was confused. "Oh? Why is that?"

"I knew your late father, Miss Cadfield. You have my condolences. I once met him at an excavation site in Turkey."

Helena became excited. "Yes, he liked to travel the world and conduct archaeological digs."

"I had the deepest admiration for him."

Helena smiled at him, feeling warm all over when she saw his eyes shining with admiration. *He knew my father.* She wanted to ask him so many questions, especially since he was an archaeologist, but the music precluded a decent conversation.

After the dance, an old man dressed in Greek costume came and spoke to Dr. Mastoras.

"Miss Cadfield, let me introduce Barba Manolis. He is an old friend of my family," Dr. Mastoras said.

"It is a pleasure to meet you," Helena said in Greek, bowing politely.

"Ahh! Likewise, Miss Cadfield," Barba Manolis said, shaking her hand and beaming.

They conversed for a few moments in Greek.

"You speak Greek well," Barba Manolis said, smiling.

"Thank you."

After Barba Manolis left, Dr. Mastoras turned to Helena. "Before you go, Miss Cadfield, have I permission to call on you at the Stirling house tomorrow morning at ten?"

Helena gazed back at him, excited and stimulated by his request. His handsome, dark eyes bored into hers, sending warm signals down her spine and making her knees feel suddenly weak.

"Yes," she said breathlessly. She turned and spied Mr. Helzig gaining on them quickly.

"Miss Cadfield," Mr. Helzig said, appearing flustered. "Miss Stirling has been pestering me for another dance. I will not have it."

Helena excused herself and fled toward Miss Stirling.

CHAPTER 30

2 November, 1837

The next morning, Helena awoke early. She lay in bed, reliving the events of the previous night's ball. Dancing the waltz with Dr. Mastoras was like floating on air. They had moved effortlessly together and she did not want it to end. She had never danced with Dr. Murphy and felt guilty for enjoying this dance with Dr. Mastoras. *Was it that easy for her to fall in love again?* Was Dr. Mastoras's magnetic personality seducing her, as it did Miss Heinz?

Her guilt feelings were appeased when she reminded herself that by dancing with him, she had learned that he had known her father. Perhaps he could help her understand about the treasures her father had discovered.

She jumped out of bed eager to greet the day. She was expecting Dr. Mastoras to pay her a visit at ten and she must look her best. Slipping into her gray dress, she noticed how drab it looked on her as compared to the beautiful dress that she had worn the previous night to the ball. The ball dress had made her feel special. *Remember, you are the governess, and you should dress like one.* Sighing, she made an extra effort this morning with her hair.

Then she spied Dr. Murphy's letter on the table. Feeling guilty, she promptly wrote him a letter. She thanked him for his letter, and wrote her news and about her life with the Stirling family. She would send it off tomorrow.

The Stirling family was still asleep when Helena descended the stairs at nine o'clock. Mrs. Fournos and Koula were not around. They usually went to Agios Nikolaos church on Sunday mornings and would return by eleven. Helena knew that the family would be getting up late today because of last night's ball.

Helena went to the parlor and swept the curtains open, inviting the sun to flood the room. She picked up her needlework from the sewing basket and sat on the sofa working quietly and waiting for Dr. Mastoras.

She wondered if everyone would still be asleep when he arrived at ten. What would she say to him? What would she serve him if Mrs. Fournos had not returned from church yet? She glanced at the clock several times. It was marching slowly today.

Mrs. Stirling entered the parlor a half hour later and greeted her. "Is Catherine still asleep?" she asked.

"Yes. I checked on her earlier and she was still asleep."

Mrs. Stirling joined her on the sofa and began her needlework. "She is like her *vater*. They both like to sleep in on Sundays. I guess Mrs. Fournos is not back from church, yet?"

"No, Mrs. Stirling. She comes at eleven on Sundays," Helena reminded her.

"Oh, that's right. Would you be kind enough to make some tea, then? I have a headache from last night."

"Surely." Helena went into the kitchen.

Sunday mornings were becoming Helena's tea mornings. Mrs. Stirling had told Helena once that the way she made the tea reminded her of England. Helena hummed as she placed a few of Mrs. Fournos's Greek *koulourakia* on the plate.

After serving the tea and cookies, she sat down.

They sipped tea for a few moments.

"Mrs. Stirling, I wanted to mention that a gentleman will be visiting me today."

"Oh?" Mrs. Stirling asked, looking surprised. She placed her teacup down. "And who will be calling, may I ask?"

"Dr. Mastoras. Mr. Stirling introduced him to me last night at the ball. I am expecting him at ten."

"Oh, dear," Mrs. Stirling said, her cheeks turning red. "I must tell you something about him before he arrives, Miss Cadfield."

"What is it, Mrs. Stirling?"

Mrs. Stirling shook her head prettily, making her curls bounce. "I'm afraid this man does not have good intentions." She looked sincerely into Helena's eyes.

Helena was disturbed by this. "What makes you say that?"

"My dear, this is not a personal visit that he is making. First of all, he is almost engaged to Miss Heinz, my cousin," she tittered. "She told me the other day at the ball that she will be marrying him."

Helena felt embarrassed by Mrs. Stirling's remark. Had Mrs. Stirling read her mind? She had honestly hoped this would be a personal visit, but given the amount of time Dr. Mastoras had spent with Miss Heinz at the ball, she could not deny his interest in that woman.

"I presumed that he was calling because he knew my father," Helena said flatly, trying to maintain her composure.

"It is more than that. It came to my attention recently that he has been hired by the Archaeological Society to dig on your *vater's* property. He is an archaeologist."

He is an archaeologist. Helena was stunned. "He's digging on my father's property?" she cried, spilling some tea on her lap. Placing the teacup down, and grabbing a napkin, she dabbed at the spill.

"*Ja.* They are digging it and taking all the buried treasures."

Helena felt her skin crawl at what she heard. This man was digging on private property without her permission. *How dare he?* "This is quite a shock."

The image of the handsome Dr. Mastoras was swept into a mire of mud, and Helena did not know how to handle it. How could she have been so naïve? He was coming here to inform her about his disturbing role in confiscating the treasures off her property.

"I am sorry if it upset you, but I felt that you must know about it, Miss Cadfield."

"Thank you, Mrs. Stirling, for advising me on this important matter. I should have visited the property as soon as we had arrived, and would have been able to do something about it then."

"Yes, I'm afraid so," Mrs. Stirling said contritely. "I had no idea that your father left you with so much…responsibility. Maybe we can all go up there in our carriage soon and visit the place. Would you like that?"

Helena smiled at her. Mrs. Stirling was appearing friendlier and friendlier to her. "Thank you."

"Meanwhile, if you'd like, Mr. Stirling and I could be present when Dr. Mastoras visits. Here in Greece, as in England, single women do not entertain gentlemen alone," Mrs. Stirling said slowly, looking at her with meaning.

* * *

At eleven o'clock, Helena still sat in the parlor, anxiously waiting for Dr. Mastoras. He was late. Mrs. Stirling had gone upstairs.

She had thought about what Mrs. Stirling had told her. Was she telling the truth about Dr. Mastoras? If so, Helena felt ashamed of her uncontrolled emotions when she was around this man. She must treat him civilly, like one of Father's colleagues.

Someone was at the door and Helena shot up. Could it be him? She hurried to the door.

Mrs. Fournos and Koula had arrived from church.

"Is everyone still asleep?" Mrs. Fournos asked Helena. "I'll begin preparations for breakfast."

Helena went upstairs to see about Catherine. By twelve o'clock, the whole Stirling family had awakened and eaten breakfast and there had been no sign of Dr. Mastoras. After breakfast, Helena and Catherine had moved to the veranda to paint. The veranda had become Helena's favorite place. They prepared the paints and canvas, and put on their aprons.

"Let's paint the red geraniums in those white pots today," Helena told Catherine, pointing to the bright crimson flowers sitting in their pots, lining the white wall.

"Oh, yes! That would be wonderful," Catherine exclaimed, setting her canvas in front of her.

Helena worked quietly, periodically checking Catherine's painting. The girl not only liked to paint, but also did it well. This was one time that she didn't whine or complain, but was content and happy. She had changed so much in such a short time, and Helena had become attached to her.

Dr. Mastoras's image came to mind, and Helena became embroiled with her thoughts again. Her heart stirred in different directions after her talk with Mrs. Stirling this morning. The disturbing thought that he was working to remove the treasures from her property caused her anguish. Yet, when she danced with him last night, he had swept her off her feet. The thought made her feel exhilarated again.

"How does this look, Helena?"

"Hmm. What?" Helena looked at the girl.

"Did I put too much paint on this one?"

"That looks very nice, Catherine," she said, nodding her approval. "Remember to touch the tips of the flowers with a darker color so as to separate them from each other."

CHAPTER 31

Dr. Mastoras sat in the parlor with the Stirlings. After twenty minutes of polite talk, he arose. *Where was Miss Cadfield?* "I thank you for your hospitality, but I must be leaving," he said, bowing stiffly.

"Must you be going already?" Mrs. Stirling asked, appearing concerned. She rang for the maid, but she didn't come. "I wonder what happened to Miss Cadfield?"

Mr. Stirling rose also. "Surely, she should have been here by now."

Mrs. Stirling rang again.

The maid finally arrived, looking flustered. She curtsied.

"Koula, where have you been?" Mrs. Stirling asked, looking vexed. "I've been ringing for you all this time."

"I had to clean the stables and feed the horses. The stable boy did not come today."

"And where is Miss Cadfield? Dr. Mastoras has been waiting here for her all this time."

"Oh, I forgot," Koula said, turning red. She pulled a note from her pocket and gave it to Aristotle. "For you, sir."

Aristotle took it and read it out loud:

Dr. Mastoras,
We are painting on the veranda in the back.
It is difficult to get away. Would you mind meeting me
there?
Thank you,
Miss Cadfield.

"Take Dr. Mastoras to see Miss Cadfield at once," Mrs. Stirling told Koula.

The maid led him down the hallway toward the veranda, where Miss Cadfield was painting with Miss Stirling.

"Aris," Catherine cried, clasping her hands together and appearing pleased. "What are you doing here?"

"Good afternoon, Miss Stirling," he said. "I came to speak with Miss Cadfield about something."

* * *

Helena's heart skipped a beat when she heard his name. She had handed her note to Koula a long time ago. She had assumed that he had not come.

Helena turned and saw him staring at her. He was impeccably dressed and exceedingly handsome. He smiled, and all her reservations about him melted away.

"Dr. Mastoras," she said breathlessly, curtsying.

"Miss Cadfield." He bowed.

Feeling mortified that her emotions betrayed her resolve to be cool with him, Helena became stiff and said in a reproachful manner, "I had expected you at ten."

"I apologize for my tardiness," Dr. Mastoras said softly. "I stayed up late because I hadn't seen Dr. Heinz in a while, and we had much catching up to do. As a result, I arose late this morning."

"I see." *He probably hadn't seen Miss Heinz for a while, either.*

"I wanted to speak to you about an important matter."

Helena wiped her hands and brushed back the strands of hair from her face. "Miss Stirling, could you leave us for a few minutes? You do not need to put your supplies away. The visit will be short and we can resume our activity afterward," she said.

"Yes, Miss Cadfield," Catherine said, bowing politely and looking subdued. She left, then glanced back at them knowingly, and giggled, fleeing into the house.

"Miss Cadfield, are you aware that the Archaeological Society has been excavating on your father's property in Nemea?" he said quietly. "I am the director of the project."

Mrs. Stirling was right after all. "Mrs. Stirling informed me just this morning, and I admit that it distressed me. How could you do such a thing?" Helena cried. "Just take over someone's property?"

"After your father gave the gold cup to the society, it captured the society's interest," he replied calmly. "Dr. Kostakis approached me at a conference in Egypt and told me they needed someone to continue the excavation. Unaware that Dr. Cadfield had a daughter, they have begun the papers to claim the property."

"I've started the papers to claim the property as the rightful heir. I want you and your crew off my property immediately," Helena said firmly. Inside, she was raging. The property was all that was left of her family, and she was going to fight for it.

"Now listen to reason, Miss Cadfield. I know you are upset that this happened. I would be too, if it were my property."

His gentle words stirred something deep in Helena. She sensed that his words and accompanying silence were an act of compassion rather than one of indifference.

She stared at the red geraniums, which for some reason gave her a feeling of peace. So many things had happened to her these past few months; she had lost her father and her home, and everything in England, and now people were taking her Greek property away from her. *It was not fair.*

"Dr. Mastoras, what would you do if you were in my position?" she asked, trying to keep her voice from trembling.

"I would do what you are doing," he said slowly. "I would file the papers to convert the title to my name, then go from there."

Helena turned to look at him. He appeared sincere.

"I suggest that you not let go of our services. You still need to hire a crew to excavate it and for it to be guarded. If you don't, then you risk having thieves loot the property," he continued.

"Miss Cadfield," Catherine called out, waving to her from the doorway.

Helena turned and saw her. "Yes?"

"*Ouyay aidsay ehay ouldway ebay eavinglay ortlyshay* (You said he would be leaving shortly)."

"Oh, my. We'll be but a minute," Helena replied.

"Miss Cadfield, I suggest that you visit the property," he said earnestly. "We can work together on this."

Helena listened as he talked further about the project. She was surprised to learn that he had been funding it from his own pockets. He was making it hard for her to dislike him.

"I appreciate you trying to work with me. I wonder if the Archaeological Society will accept me as the owner or will they give me a difficult time?"

"You can set up a meeting with the society and talk with them. I believe that they will work with you."

"I honestly haven't been able to find a way to get to the property," she said, sighing. "They frown on women traveling alone and my funds are limited to hire a guide."

"We are leaving tomorrow morning for the property in Nemea. If you'd like, you could join us."

The temptation to see the property with the aid of Dr. Mastoras was great. His eyes were twinkling, and his offer irresistible. He was a man, and she was a woman, and she knew how tongues would wag if she made this long trip alone with him.

"I appreciate your offer, but may I ask who else is going with you?"

"Yianni, my assistant. I can arrange for you to travel on the wagon with him. Do not worry. You will be treated properly. You have my word; besides, there are other women working there."

Helena's fingers pressed into the folds of her dress nervously as she thought about his proposition. "I usually do not make decisions so quickly. Also, I have obligations here that I cannot ignore."

"I understand," he said, appearing uneasy. "We can just forget it."

"No!" she said, not wanting to lose this opportunity. "It is not that I do not want to go. Actually, I would like to go." She paused to gather her thoughts. "But I would need to speak first with the Stirlings."

"The decision lies ultimately with you," he said firmly. "I will stop by tomorrow morning at six, in any case."

After Dr. Mastoras left, Helena resumed painting with Catherine, who asked many questions about Dr. Mastoras.

"If you must know, we discussed business," she told her. "It had to do with my property in Nemea. I need to visit it."

"You will go away and forget about me," Catherine complained, rushing into the house.

Was Catherine jealous of the attention that Dr. Mastoras was giving her? Was it possible that the girl had sensed her own thoughts about leaving?

Helena retreated to her room. She reflected on her conversation with Dr. Mastoras. As soon as she said about speaking to her employer, Helena had regretted it. He appeared disappointed. Was she using that excuse to hide her eagerness in going with him? And how was Catherine going to manage without her?

When she went down for dinner, she had made her decision. She found Mrs. Stirling sitting alone at the dinner table and informed her of her desire to travel with Dr. Mastoras to see her father's property.

"When are you planning on going?" Mrs. Stirling asked.

"They are leaving tomorrow morning."

Mrs. Stirling's eyes flew open. "So soon? Why don't you wait and we can all go together?"

"Dr. Mastoras has stressed the importance of my going there as soon as possible. I may lose everything if I do nothing."

"How long do you plan to stay there?"

"It will be only for a week."

"Oh, that is good, for Catherine's sake."

"Thank you, Mrs. Stirling," Helena said. "I think Catherine has formed an attachment to me."

"Yes, she is fond of you, as we all are. Now don't you worry about Catherine. She *vill* be fine for one week."

Helena was thrilled at what she heard.

Mr. Stirling and Catherine arrived at the dinner table.

Mrs. Stirling relayed to them the news about Helena. Mr. Stirling seemed surprised, but his wife smoothed everything with her talk, emphasizing that Helena would return in one week.

Catherine, on the other hand, pouted throughout the dinner and retired early to her room.

After dinner, Helena visited Catherine in her room. The girl was lying in her bed, and her eyes were red and puffy from crying.

Helena went and sat on the side of the bed and touched her shoulder. "Dear, you didn't finish your dinner."

Catherine buried her face in the pillow. "I'm not hungry."

"If you're not hungry because of my going on this trip, then you are a foolish young lady."

Catherine turned and stared at her, her eyes pleading. "I don't want you to go. Not now. Just when we were having fun."

"It is important that I go, but it will only be for a short while and I will return to you," Helena said softly.

Catherine sat up, sniffling. "You promise?"

Helena patted her on the hand, realizing how attached Catherine had become to her. "Dr. Mastoras said that we will return in a week. I'm sure he will honor his word."

"Why can't I come with you?"

"I don't think your parents would approve of it. Besides, I don't know whether there will be a place for you to sleep there."

"Oh, that would be wonderful. We can sleep outside, under the stars."

"Catherine, you are being silly. The nights are cold up in the mountains." She arose. "Now, it is time for you to go to sleep. Let me help you get ready."

Minutes later, Helena tucked Catherine into bed.

"What will I do without you?" Catherine said sleepily. "What if you don't return?"

Helena promised her that she would return, and that one day she and her family could visit the Cadfield site. She then hugged her goodnight.

Catherine finally seemed at peace as she shut her eyes.

CHAPTER 32

3 November, 1837

The next morning, Helena found Mrs. Fournos in the kitchen, preparing breakfast for her.

"I know how you like bacon and eggs," Mrs. Fournos said, smiling at her as she stirred the crispy bacon in the pan.

"Thank you." Helena took out the letter from her pocket that she wrote to Dr. Murphy. "Could you do me a favor, Mrs. Fournos? Could you please mail this letter? I wanted to mail it before I left for Nemea." She handed it to her.

Mrs. Fournos wiped her hands then took the letter and nodded. "Today I will mail it."

After Helena finished eating, Mrs. Fournos handed her a bag filled with food for the trip. She also gave her a vessel filled with water.

"Take these with you," she said. "You will need them for the trip. May Panagia be with you."

Thanking her and bidding her farewell, Helena went and stood outside in the darkness of the early morning, shivering not from the cold, but from excitement. For so many months, she had wanted to visit her family property in Nemea, and she finally had the chance to do it.

The sound of clopping hooves alerted her that someone was approaching. The dark shape of a wagon materialized in front of her with Yianni sitting on it.

"She is here, boss," he told Dr. Mastoras, who rode on a mule next to him.

"Good morning, Miss Cadfield. I am glad you will join us. I hope we are not too early," Dr. Mastoras said, smiling.

"No, no, that's quite all right. I am eager to get to Nemea."

Yianni helped her up the steps and into the wagon, and took care of her luggage.

They maneuvered their way through the winding streets of Athens. It was quiet and hardly anyone moved about at this early time, except for a lone shepherd or a farmer bringing his crops into the city to sell.

Once outside the city, they picked up speed. Slowly, the sun began to rise above them. The rough road, rattling wagon, and creaking wheels, made it difficult to have a conversation with Dr. Mastoras.

Helena sat there, taking it all in. The large, sloping mountains on her right formed a protective wall that led toward her home. The activity on the road increased, and they passed several riders, wagons, and a few carriages. Three hours later, they swerved to the left, down a path, past some fig trees, and stopped at a bank on the Saronic Bay.

"We will take a break, Miss Cadfield," Dr. Mastoras informed her.

Yianni helped her down from the wagon.

Dr. Mastoras jumped off his mule and tethered it to a nearby tree. Pulling a blanket from the wagon, he spread it on the ground next to Helena. "You can rest here while Yianni and I take care of the animals."

Helena thanked him, feeling grateful for his concern, but at the same time felt sore from the rough ride. "I'd prefer to move around and stretch my legs first, if that's all right."

"Fine, but don't go too far."

Helena walked toward the water. Millions of diamonds danced on the sun-kissed water, making for an enchanting experience. She washed her face in the cool, refreshing water and shivered. She pulled her wool coat close to her, feeling an inexplicable joy course through her body.

She strolled along the bank, gazing at the splendid view of the bay. In the distance, she could see the shapes of tiny fishermen in their tiny boats bobbing up and down. She wondered if they had caught any fish. She could make out an island in the bay, which she presumed was Salamis Island.

Being this close to nature reminded her of the times in Oxford, where she galloped through the fields and stopped at streams to rest, with no one around but the birds and the fish in the streams.

Feeling refreshed, she returned and sat on the blanket that Dr. Mastoras had placed on the ground. He arrived shortly, and stood there, tall and confident. "May I join you?"

Helena nodded and moved to the left, close to the edge of the blanket as he eased himself down. She sensed the warmth of his body next to hers. She glanced furtively at him, appreciating his fine profile.

Yianni plopped down next to them. "All done, boss," he announced, proceeding to munch on an apple.

"What is your impression of Greece, Miss Cadfield?" Dr. Mastoras asked.

Helena was thoughtful. "It has many sides to it, with its raw beauty, its once glorious past, and its potential for growth. Yet the war has produced much destruction and loss." She looked at him. "You see, Dr. Mastoras, Greece has a soul, and it has been wounded from the war. It will take time to recapture the beauty and glory of its past."

"You not only speak Greek well, Miss Cadfield." Dr. Mastoras nodded appreciatively, "but have grasped what has happened to the country. Yes, Greece has been wounded, but the Greeks are survivors."

"Like Grandfather."

"Did you ever meet him?"

"Four years ago. He visited us in England. He was a good storyteller and I learned about my family in Greece. He told me how beautiful and virtuous Mother was."

"Your grandfather built a small, stone cottage on his property with his own hands. He lived there until his death," Dr. Mastoras said.

"I know about it. My father tried to convince him to live with us in Oxford, but he did not want to leave his home."

"How did your parents meet?" Dr. Mastoras asked her.

"My father met Grandfather while studying the archeological terrain of Corinth and its neighboring sites, and Grandfather invited him over to their house for dinner. He fell in love with my mother and they married quickly, and he brought her back to England with him. When she died of pneumonia, Papa returned her to Greece to be buried in the family grave."

Feeling as if she had said too much, Helena awkwardly pulled the jug out of her bag and drank some water, not wanting to continue.

After a period of silence, Dr. Mastoras arose somberly. "We need to get moving if we want to reach Corinth before dark."

They resumed their journey.

CHAPTER 33

Aristotle spied the ancient columns standing grandly in the distance like a beacon. They had arrived in Corinth. A few minutes later, they rolled to a stop in front of the Corinthian Inn. Aristotle dismounted and walked over to Miss Cadfield, who sat in the wagon appearing puzzled. He informed her that they were going to sleep there overnight.

She appeared surprised to hear that. "Is it necessary to stay here? I was hoping that we'd reach the property tonight."

"The mules are tired and the unpaved roads and hills make it difficult to travel at night."

The innkeeper, Stathis, greeted Aristotle and told him that he had three rooms available. They followed Stathis up to their rooms.

After Aristotle deposited the luggage into the appropriate rooms, he suggested to Miss Cadfield that she wash and meet him in the dining room.

He went into his room and was pleased to see a washbasin and a pitcher of water on a small table. He washed, shaved, and changed into clean clothing. For some reason, he wanted to look good tonight.

The dining room had three other travelers, all men, quietly supping.

Aristotle sat at the table. Yianni arrived shortly after. After a few minutes, Miss Cadfield arrived. She appeared also to have washed and changed into a new outfit.

Soon, they were enjoying a meal of lamb soup, bread and an eggplant dish

While eating, Aristotle stole glances at Miss Cadfield as she daintily ate her meal. When she finished, she set her silverware down, wiped the ends of her mouth with a napkin, then folded it and set it aside. Everything she did was methodical and calm, revealing the manners of a well-bred woman.

"This is the same inn that we stopped at with the Stirlings. We were traveling from Nafplio to Athens and got caught in the rain," Miss Cadfield told Aristotle.

"Yes, I remember that night," he said, smiling.

She glanced at him inquisitively.

"You were that young lady that demanded food for the poor women and children, and I helped you accomplish that."

She blushed. "It was noble of you, and I thank you."

"Yes, and I helped, too!" Yianni cried, then continued slurping his soup.

"Thank you, Yianni," she said.

Yianni beamed from her compliment.

"Miss Cadfield, did you recognize me that day in Athens, while you were in the carriage with Dr. Heinz and his sister?"

A deep shade of pink spread on her cheeks. "Not at first, but when you spoke, your voice was familiar," she admitted, tilting her head slightly to the side and studying him. "My initial assessment at the inn was that you were a common laborer because of your attire and lack of beard."

Yianni laughed. "Haha, boss. That is funny."

Aristotle stroked his chin thoughtfully, glad that he had shaved. "I'm afraid that we archaeologists have two sides to us, part intellectual and part laborer."

After his meal, Yianni excused himself and went up to his room.

"You know, I am enjoying this trip," Miss Cadfield admitted to Aristotle. "For the first time in a long time, I feel free. Just the idea that I will be at my parents' property tomorrow excites me. I honestly don't think I can sleep well tonight."

"The same goes here," Aristotle said, rising. "I usually take a walk after these long stretches. Would you care to join me, Miss Cadfield? It would be good to stretch our legs a bit."

Their eyes met.

She blushed, looking pleased. "All right," she said.

They strolled outside into the crisp night air.

The moon was full, and lit the leaves of the trees and the bushes around them with vivid strokes that produced an eerie, glossy row of dark green covering with black undertones. The hooting sound of an owl was their only companion. The lights from the inn slowly faded as they strolled toward nowhere in particular.

"There were many a time after my grandfather died when I'd walk alone in the evenings in Egypt, thinking," Aristotle said, gazing up at the stars. "The stars were bright, just as they are tonight."

"What did you think about?" Miss Cadfield asked.

"Oh, about everything, about life, and how lonely it could be sometimes," he said, shrugging his shoulders. "You know, I never told this to anyone, but I dreaded the nights when I was younger, for that's when the ghosts would come and haunt me."

"Ghosts?"

Aristotle nodded. "The ghosts of my mother, father, and sister. They had died during the war, and visited me in dreams, reminding me of the past. I was ten when the revolution happened." He told her how he and his grandfather escaped in the middle of the night.

"I am sorry to hear that. I also lost my mother when I was young, and more recently my grandfather and father. My Nana has been supportive, but other than her, I have no one." She became reflective. "I think life does not stop here. Our loved ones are up in heaven looking down on us. We are left behind and must live our lives fully."

He gazed at her. Her eyes glowed liked stars under the moonlit night. She seemed so ardent, approachable, and loveable. "Yes, we must live our lives fully," he said softly.

A strong yearning to pull her close to him, overcame him. Bending forward, desiring to kiss her on the lips, his kiss met her soft cheek instead.

She had turned her face slightly away.

Aristotle paused, staring at Miss Cadfield's hidden face. He awkwardly moved away.

"I think we should be going back," she said tightly.

His hands that had worked so hard these past few years, confidently attaining his doctoral degree, now fumbled their way into his pockets. Feeling disturbed about his runaway emotions and the irresistible effect she was having on him, he inwardly admonished himself. *I must seem incredibly forward to her.*

She turned, appearing stiff as a rod, and marched back to the inn.

CHAPTER 34

Early the next morning, after breakfast, Helena and the two men continued their journey, heading southwest. All morning, she had been silent, thinking about Dr. Mastoras's attempt to kiss her last night. It was her fault for accepting to walk with him in the middle of the night, with no chaperone. What had she been thinking? A part of her was upset, but another part of her liked what he had done. *I have never been kissed by a man before, not even Dr. Murphy.* Feeling guilty, she had taken the easiest route out of the situation by avoiding Dr. Mastoras all morning.

They crossed a ravine and stream. To their right was a grove of olive trees, and after several minutes they ambled across a bridge over a gorge. Dr. Mastoras rode ahead silently. It seemed that he was avoiding her also.

The group ascended and descended a few hills, passing villages along the way. Two hours later, they stopped for a break.

Helena gazed around her and spied some ruins in the distance. "What are those?" she asked Yianni, pointing to them.

"Those are the ruins of the ancient city of Kleones," Yianni replied. "We are about an hour away from Nemea."

Helena sat on a large rock and drank some water. She chewed on figs and biscuits while the men took care of the mules. It was quiet here, with bucolic scenery that beckoned, but she could not relax.

"Would you care to go for a walk, Miss Cadfield? There's something I need to talk to you about."

Helena looked up at Dr. Mastoras, but the sun was in the way. She shaded her eyes with her hands. He appeared remorseful and sincere enough, but she wasn't going to fall for it.

"Whatever it is, you can tell me here," she replied firmly.

"I hope you didn't think me forward last night, Miss Cadfield."

"Your actions provided ample cause to believe that," she retorted. She jumped up, brushing her clothing nervously. "I have just met you, Dr. Mastoras, and expected more civility on your part." She marched to the wagon, not waiting to hear his response.

They left shortly after that.

At noon, they rode past the little village of Kutchukmadi. About a mile and a half from there, Helena noticed a magnificent structure consisting of three columns, while the remainder of its columns had been torn down.

"What is that structure?" she asked, admiring it.

Yianni slowed down. "That's the temple of Zeus," he told her.

They passed through a green valley. The farmers and their families steadily whacked the olive branches, causing the olives to fall. She knew that they were harvesting them to make cured olives and olive oil. Off to their left, in the distance, she could make out the domed top of a church. She wondered if it was Agios Giorgios, the one from which the attorney had obtained her father's death records.

"Petri is up ahead," Yianni said.

They had arrived to her home town.

Their wagon ambled down the dusty road and into the village. It had a single shop, a small courtyard with a fountain, a couple of buildings, and a few houses scattered here and there. An elderly woman, dressed in black, sat in front of a house, under the shade of a tree. She looked up and waved to them as they passed her.

They took a tree-lined path that led upward and then swung left on a fork. Going up the hill, Helena could see to her left several rows of olive trees that swept down to the valley below.

The property sat on a ridge, and when they reached the open space, the fierce wind wrapped itself around her. Helena held onto her large hat, battling with the wind, while loose strands of hair circled around her face.

Her heart leapt when she spied Grandfather's stone cottage. She knew it was his because he had described it to her. It faced a large courtyard to the right with a stone well in the center. To the far left, behind the cottage, she glimpsed the open, excavation site. Helena took a deep breath, trembling from excitement. She was finally here.

Yianni rolled the wagon to a stop in front of the stable and jumped off. He helped her down.

"Welcome home, Miss Cadfield," Yianni said, smiling broadly.

Helena bowed her head.

Yianni unloaded her luggage from the wagon and placed it in front of the cottage, then joined Dr. Mastoras at the stable to take care of the mules and the wagon.

Feeling thirsty, Helena walked toward the stone well. Her dress billowed around her from the strong wind. At the well, she found a wooden bucket attached to the rope and dropped the bucket inside it, and heard it splash. Moments later, she pulled the bucket up and drank the icy cold water, soothing her parched throat.

Dr. Mastoras approached her. He pulled out a key from his pocket.

"This is the key to your cottage, Miss Cadfield. Guard it well. I will take everything that belongs to me out of the cottage later. Yianni and I will be resting in the back."

She took the key and their fingers brushed. His eyes pleaded silently for forgiveness. She glanced away, fighting the urge to surrender to his magnetism. She was here with him on business, and nothing more. He had Miss Heinz and she had her Dr. Murphy.

After the men left, Helena strolled around. She pictured her grandparents and her mother and family living here, with their goats, sheep, and grape vineyards. It must have been a peaceful life. Beyond, she could see the wonderful view of the verdant valley opening like a green fan, and the majestic, gray mountains.

Helena returned to the cottage and unlocked the door. Small and cluttered, the one room house held many books and pottery. A table with two chairs sat in the middle, and behind it sat a cot. She placed her luggage down and stood there, gazing at everything and feeling a sense of nostalgia. It reminded her of her father.

The square, wooden table in the center of the cottage, held ceramic plates, loaves of bread, round cheese, a glass jar of olives, a wine bottle and water jug, along with some books. A long bench spanned the front wall and held a water basin, jug, and more food supplies. Above the bench was a window.

To her right, on the floor along the side of the wall was a row of various ceramic fragments and pottery. Next to the cot, against the wall sat another wooden chair with several books stacked precariously on top of it. Piles of books on the floor reminded her of her father's disorganized habit of collecting books. She smiled.

Against the wall rested a cane made of olive wood, with an eagle's head that her grandfather had carved. She pictured him walking slowly with the cane, accompanying her on her walks around Cadfield House, stopping occasionally to tell her stories. She would be mesmerized not only by the dramatic manner in which he told them, but also by his powerful memory. He knew all of Greek mythology and spent hours recounting the stories of Hercules, Zeus, Athena, Demeter, Ares, and Poseidon. He could recite many of Homer's poems. Although he had never achieved the education that her father had, in her mind, Grandfather was as learned as Papa.

No more sounds would come from them. No hugs or kisses. No smiles. No stories. Tears welled up in her eyes. Helena shut the door behind her, seeking privacy. Inside the cottage, after a brief mourning period, Helena went to work. As she removed the linen from the cot, she felt it unnerving knowing that Dr. Mastoras had slept here.

Trying to erase him from her thoughts, Helena searched the cottage for clean linen. She discovered a wall lined with shelves filled with folded sheets, wool blankets and food supplies in the small room to the side. A wood stove stood opposite the shelves. She prepared the cot, covering it with the clean linen.

Helena brought some water into the cottage and washed. She tried to sleep on the cot, but could not. Instead, she lay wide awake, reflecting on her trip. She thought about how different this life was to her structured life in England. England had been her home all these years. Even her father's digs, confined to the summers, did not keep him away from England, where he would teach students and cure patients. *Yet Mother was from here.*

Her parents came from two different worlds. Their love must have been great for her father to marry a Greek woman. Her mother had left Greece to live in England. *Would Dr. Murphy leave England to move here with me?* For some reason, she could not picture him here.

She remembered the treasures that her father wrote about and became excited. Jumping off the bed, Helena strode out of the cottage, intent on exploring the rest of the property and seeing about the treasures. Should she ask Dr. Mastoras to join her? She didn't feel comfortable going to the back searching for him. No, she would go alone.

CHAPTER 35

As Helena headed toward the excavation site, she passed a large, square veranda to her right, which sat behind the cottage. It had its own two-foot high, white boundary wall. In the center of the veranda was a large rectangular table under an enormous wooden trellis that spanned half the veranda. The table had two chairs and a few seats without backing.

Two old, gnarled grapevines sat on each side of the veranda. Their extensive branches, twisting through the trellis, provided partial shade for the table under them. Potted geranium plants, providing a burst of red color, stood in each corner of the trellis.

A wonderful scent wafted her way. It came from a large jasmine bush that grew along the back wall of the white cottage. A joyous feeling coursed through her body as she went and cut off a white jasmine flower and sniffed it, enjoying the sweet fragrance.

The fierce wind pulled her clothing in different directions. Shivering, Helena pulled her coat closer to her as she continued her stroll.

Up ahead, the remains of the grand mansion with its broken columns was a testament not only to the war that had ravaged the area, but also to the dreams that had been lost.

Her steps faltered as a wave of sadness enveloped her. She pictured the house standing tall, and being bombarded by all the ammunition, and the innocent victims caught in the onslaught. They must have felt helpless, unable to flee, she thought. She wondered where the churchyard was where her family had been buried. She wanted to see her parents' graves.

Helena tried to hold back her tears, but the intense pain released them without warning. She wept hard for her grandparents, her mother, her relatives, and for all the people who had died during the war.

"What's the matter with you?" Helena asked herself, sniffling and wiping away her tears. "You are becoming too emotional. Where is your reason and your logical thinking?"

She had reached the excavation site. She faced a long trench on the east end, about ten feet wide and nine feet deep. Along its side was a landing, about three feet deep. It held little baskets, tools, and pottery fragments neatly lined up next to them. She could picture the workers digging there.

Why had they excavated only the east end?

Her father's letter specifically mentioned that his discovery took place on the west side. Maybe her father had started digging there first, and Dr. Mastoras, unaware of the west end, continued the work.

She walked to the right, on the dusty marble foundation that spanned the perimeter of the house, heading toward the west end, toward the columns. Somehow, they reminded her of the columns in the dream she had, just after she received her father's letter.

A stone boundary wall extended the length of the back of the foundation and parts of each side. Most of the wall was intact, except for a few holes here and there. When Helena reached the columns, her eyes combed the area for a sign of her father's work. *If only he could be here to share it with me.*

She noticed a large pile of rocks behind the third column. The pile was much larger than the other piles and reached the height of her knees. Was it her imagination, or did these rocks appear more organized than the other piles? She stopped in her tracks, her heart pounding wildly as she studied them closely.

Could this be where Papa had excavated?

Helena bent down and shoved the rocks away from the pile, but the large ones took more effort. Panting, she arose and looked around for a tool. She found a shovel. With much exertion, she shoveled the rocks away and pushed them aside with her foot. She was sweating by the time she had reached the bottom of the pile.

Beneath the rocks lay a four-foot long, rectangular plank of wood, made of several beams nailed together. She pushed the beam with her foot, but it was wedged tight with all the rocks around it. Pulling a few rocks away, she then pushed the beam once more. It budged slightly and she could see the edge of an opening under it.

Her heart racing, Helena bent down and saw what seemed to be the shape of a stairwell. Eager to explore it further, she removed more rocks. After the plank was freed from the rocks, she yanked it with all her might. It popped up, revealing a hole big enough to squeeze through.

Papa must have found the treasures down here.

The hole consisted of many layers of soil and rock, giving it stability so that it wouldn't cave in. She could picture her father's lean frame going through the hole. It looked easy enough to go down there. Was she being too hasty? Should she wait for Dr. Mastoras to appear and help her, since he was an archaeologist, but could she trust him?

Helena managed to prop the end of the plank against the rock pile, careful not to fall into the hole. The raised plank would allow air and sunlight into the chamber below.

Kneeling on the ground, she braced herself and let her legs ease slowly down the hole. The wind struggled with her long dress, pulling it in all directions. She pulled it tightly around her. In doing so, she ripped a piece of the hem off. A part of her dress had caught under the weight of the rocks.

She held on to a large rock next to her, steadying her as her feet touched one of the stairs. The size of the hole allowed her slim frame to slip through it.

Her feet quickly settled on the staircase and she lowered herself onto the step. Once she felt the solid step, she twisted around and went down the steps, her arm groping the side of the wall. The dank smell of dirt was overpowering as her eyes met darkness. She panicked for a moment, her breathing coming quickly and shallowly. She shivered, feeling claustrophobic

"Now calm down," she said. "Remember, Papa used to do this all the time. I can do it, too."

Taking deep breaths, Helena moved cautiously, her heart pounding in her chest. She inched down the stone stairs, with one hand touching the cold, damp wall. The stone steps were about three feet wide and quite deep, deeper than regular stairs. They had been scraped, although bits and pieces of the rocks from above had fallen through when she had opened the hole. She could see her father at work here, with his meticulous method.

Helena almost reached the bottom, then jumped off. She turned and with the help of the sunlight that filtered through the open hole, counted thirteen steps.

The large chamber was symmetrically round, and the walls consisted of very large boulders. *Giants must have put them together.*

She noticed the broken pottery lying on the ground. Apparently, Dr. Mastoras had not discovered this place, for there were no tools or excavation supplies in sight. Several tall amphorae stood in a row next to the pile. She tried to open one of the jars, but it was tightly sealed. They were probably containers for oil or wine.

She entered a hallway. Even without much light, she could see frescoes on the walls. The painted wall on her left held images of life-like maidens with fair skin and dark, curly tresses. They were dressed in white Grecian robes and held purple grapes in their hands. The wall to her right revealed young nymphs dancing courageously around the dark shapes of bulls whose lowered heads suggested that they were tamed.

Feeling excited, Helena continued her exploration. So this was what her father was talking about when he felt as if he was reliving Homer's world, she thought. Could it be true? Could she be witnessing an ancient palace? Her imagination ran rampant.

She passed two columns, and entered a square, empty chamber and continued walking through it to another hallway that led into another similar chamber. There was hardly any light, but her eyes had adjusted. She reached a dead end, with a hallway spanning from her left to her right. Unsure where to turn, she turned right, and continued walking, looking for signs of treasures.

The blackness surrounded her. She needed more light. She stopped to pull out some matches from her pocket. She could hear her quick breathing as her fingers fumbled with the match, trying to light it. After a few attempts, she lit the match, but the flame fizzled quickly.

Helena leaned against the wall, breathing hard. Her fingers groped in her other pocket and found the wax candle that she always carried with her. She pulled on it, but it was stuck.

She muttered in exasperation. "Come on."

Her elbow jabbed the wall behind her as she yanked out the candle. The wall behind her groaned and shifted slightly. Excited, Helena turned and studied it, her fingers probing its surface. The smooth rock was the size of a large book. It was tightly wedged between the large boulders surrounding it. She pushed it, realizing that it might be some secret chamber. The left edge shifted inward. She pushed some more, but it didn't move. It needed more force.

Sweating from exertion, she rammed her shoulder against it, using the force from all of her body. It had pivoted several inches inward, forming an opening. Was there a secret chamber inside? She lit the candle, breathing deeply from the excitement, daring to peek inside the opening.

The chamber was larger than its opening and to her amazement, filled with treasures, including precious jewels, gold jewelry, and gold cups. Helena stood there, mesmerized by this tremendous amount of wealth. She had never seen anything like this before. She could picture Papa placing the treasures here, after what he wrote her about the thievery. No one must know about this, she thought.

With trembling hand, Helena reached in to scoop whatever jewels she could find. She heard a thud, followed by a slight tremor from the ground below her, as if something large had fallen. Startled, she pulled her empty hand back, her heart pounding in her chest.

Helena turned and looked to her left, in the direction of the sound. She moved forward a few steps to see if there was anyone there, but no one appeared. Turning back, she went to the small chamber, ready to resume her task, but her candle went out.

She fumbled with another match, but this time it didn't spark a flame. Panic seized her heart and she was momentarily frozen. She stood there, not sure what to do, but soon, logic kicked in. Could the sound she heard have come from the plank falling down and covering the hole, sealing her in? If so, that thought made her feel faint. Without enough oxygen, she would have no light. Without light, she could not see.

She must leave, she thought desperately, but she had to shut the chamber door first. No one must know about it, not yet. Taking a deep breath, Helena rammed her shoulder against the opposite edge of the stone of the chamber, sealing it shut. Her shoulder felt bruised.

The smell of dampness was suffocating her and she felt as if she were going to pass out. *She must get to fresh air.* She had waited too long. In a state of panic, Helena dropped her candle, panting and stumbling in the dark toward the stairwell.

Her eyes adjusted to the darkness, allowing her to see the outline of the stairs ahead. The open hole had vanished.

"Dear God." She sobbed as she stumbled up the stone steps. Reaching the top, she pushed desperately against the heavy plank. She felt unusually exhausted as she strained against it. She could see a sliver of light, but her arms began to burn from the pain, and she could not lift it high enough for her to get out. Something was holding it down.

"Help, help," she cried out. Her legs and arms gave out.

She tumbled backward, and then there was darkness.

CHAPTER 36

Helena found herself in a chamber filled with treasures. Rays of light streamed in from somewhere. Her hand brushed the silk white robe she was wearing. Her golden hair, pulled upward and back, hung like a long mane. A fair-haired, handsome man with a beautiful figure moved toward her and embraced her lovingly, gazing at her with admiration. She trembled under his bold gaze. He glowed, surrounded by a golden aura. Helena moved back to have a good look at him. She had never seen such beauty in a man before. She felt as if he knew her, inside out.

"Helen," he said, pulling her closer to him. "We are finally alone. Now that Meneleus is away, I will take you back to Troy with me."

"Paris?" Helena squeaked, feeling weak as she realized that Homer's Paris was holding her in his strong arms. "But..."

"Sshh," he said, kissing her. "We don't want anyone hearing us leave. I have a boat waiting. We will take the treasures that we stored here with us. They will be safe in Troy."

Helena trembled, feeling the pull of the irresistible Paris, whose face was so handsome. His beautiful eyes spoke of such potent love that her heart tugged. Their eyes locked.

She shivered at the sensual feelings coming from his warm and inviting body, and she softened in his embrace. Without warning, he bent down and kissed her passionately. Then he carried her away.

The moon shone above them, and all her senses were alive as he carried her to the boat. She felt the wind caressing her and heard the lapping, rhythmic sound of the sea as she waited for him to return with the treasures.

* * *

Aristotle and Yianni sauntered toward the cottage after having rested a couple of hours. Yianni had brought his backgammon game with him. Without the workers and their families, the place felt deserted. Even worse, there was no sign of Phillipa or his brothers. Aristotle realized that they were not as reliable as he would have liked them to be. Had he made a mistake in hiring Phillipa? He had promised Miss Cadfield that her property would be secure under his leadership. He must definitely have a talk with him.

"If you see Phillipa, tell him I want to speak to him. Meanwhile, I will check up on Miss Cadfield."

"Alright, boss. I'll be on the veranda," Yianni told him and left.

Aristotle knocked on the door of the cottage. He was eager to see Miss Cadfield again, even though he risked being spurned by her cool behavior. She did not answer the door.

He knocked once more. Silence.

Aristotle walked away feeling troubled. Was she still upset with him after his attempted kiss at the Corinthian Inn? How could he work with such a willful, stubborn woman who was unapproachable? Although she owned the property and her father had been a physician and archaeologist, her actions reminded him of a spoiled child. Anger consumed him.

Yet she was kind. She had provided food and shelter for the poor women and children at the inn a few weeks earlier. His heart softened a bit. Had he ever known Miss Heinz to do a charitable act?

Aristotle joined Yianni on the veranda.

"Where's Miss Cadfield? Still asleep?" Yianni asked.

"I knocked on the door, but she didn't answer," Aristotle replied, shrugging.

They began to play backgammon. Yianni threw the dice, then took a couple of wooden, round pieces, sliding them together to form a line. Aristotle's turn was next. They played quietly for a few minutes.

"I'm pretty sure Miss Cadfield would want to look around the excavation site," Yianni told Aristotle.

Aristotle moved his game piece. "I hope she gets up soon, before it gets dark, so I can show it to her. Tomorrow, once the workers arrive, it would be difficult to find the time to do it."

"I can do that, boss," Yianni piped up. "I know all about the digging done on the east end." He waved his burly arm around, pointing to the east end, and then pointing toward the west end. "And I will tell her to be careful on the west end where the rocks are." He stopped, his eyes bulging.

"What's the matter?"

Yianni arose and stared where his hand had been pointing. "Look, boss. The rocks near the columns. They are gone!"

Aristotle turned in the direction that Yianni was pointing, where the mound of rocks should have been. They had disappeared. Blood rushed into his head. They had not begun work in that area. *Someone had been digging here, and Phillipa was nowhere in sight.*

He jumped up. Rushing to where the pile of stones used to be, he saw that someone had removed them, exposing a dusty, wooden plank. A piece of gray fabric, caught underneath it, fluttered in the wind.

"Look!" Aristotle exclaimed, reaching down and pulling the cloth. He showed it to Yianni. "This is the same color as Miss Cadfield's dress. She must have been here."

Aristotle searched the excavation area and called her name, but there was no sign of her. He returned to the plank and yanked it up, revealing a hole. He gazed into the hole and froze. A sinking feeling descended on him when he saw Miss Cadfield's prone body lying face down. She was motionless.

Aristotle jumped into action. "Yianni!" he shouted. He waved to him. "Come quickly!"

Yianni scrambled toward him, stumbling and almost falling down in his haste. "What happened?"

"Miss Cadfield has fallen in the hole. Stay here and keep an eye on her. I'll get the emergency supplies."

Aristotle sprinted to the trench and grabbed the emergency supply bag. It included a rope, scissors, tools, and emergency medical accessories. He raced back to where Yianni stood.

"It does not look good, boss," Yianni said, shaking his head. "She is not moving."

"I must go to her."

Aristotle peeled off his outer coat. He swiftly tied the end of the rope around a column and pulled the remaining rope toward the hole. He securely wrapped the rope around his torso, under his shoulders, down his back, and under his leg. His years digging in Egypt had taught him survival techniques.

"Hold this."

Yianni took the rope. "What are you going to do, boss?"

"Bring her up. Meanwhile, you hold on to the rope and help me down."

Aristotle sat down on the edge of the hole, his long legs dangling through the hole. Sweating, he moved his large frame slightly to the side, trying not to disturb anything. He wasn't sure if the soil he sat on was stable enough to accommodate his weight.

Yianni had wrapped the rope around his thick hands. "It doesn't look steady."

"Keep a tight hold," Aristotle ordered.

With his strong arms supporting him, Aristotle carefully eased himself into the cell and slowly inched downward.

"Give me some slack," Aristotle commanded.

His head was still outside of the hole and he could see Yianni as he gave him more rope, but he couldn't go down. His shoulders were broader than the hole. He twisted himself so that he managed to squeeze his body farther down the opening. He had been in tighter spots than this.

"You are stuck, boss?" Yianni remarked, chuckling at the image before him.

Aristotle smiled tightly. "Hah! Watch this."

With a twist of the shoulders, and his arms gripping the ground on top of the hole, he lowered himself. His feet landed on a step, steadying him. The ray of light streaming down the hole showed a flat, open area, where Miss Cadfield lay.

He speedily descended the stairs.

Midway, he felt the rope tighten.

"Give me more rope!" Aristotle ordered.

He glanced around at the chamber, his excitement building up. Could it be a tholos, or tomb, or even a palace?

He swore when Yianni let go of the rope too quickly, causing too much slack and forcing him to drop to the ground abruptly. Yet his well-trained, athletic body was used to these situations from previous excavations.

He righted himself and flew to Miss Cadfield.

Miss Cadfield had a gash on the side of her face and the red blood was trickling and pooling around her ear. Her eyes were closed. He touched her wrist and was relieved to feel a faint pulse.

Aristotle untied the rope from his body. He would use it to help bring her up. He stood up.

"Yianni! Drop me my emergency bag," he shouted. "Miss Cadfield seems to have fallen and is knocked out. I will try to revive her."

Yianni dropped the bag, nicking Aristotle's head.

Aristotle swore.

"Sorry, boss!" Yianni called down the hole.

Aristotle rubbed his head, then bent down and tapped Miss Cadfield's smudged face a couple of times.

"Hello, Miss Cadfield. Miss Cadfield!"

No response.

Working quickly, Aristotle pulled out a roll of linen cloth from his bag and tore off a long strip. He wound it around her head to stop the bleeding. He checked her limbs for broken bones. Except for her swollen ankle, everything appeared intact. The many layers of clothing under her dress must have helped cushion the fall.

Aristotle arose and called out. "Yianni!"

"Yes, boss." Yianni's concerned face peered down the hole.

"She fell and hurt her ankle and is still out. I will tie her with the rope and carry her up the stairs. When I reach the opening, you will help me pull her out."

With Yianni's help, they lifted Miss Cadfield out of the hole. Untying the rope, Aristotle carried her light and limp body to the cottage.

CHAPTER 37

"Miss Cadfield. Miss Cadfield," Aristotle said, hovering over her as she lay on the cot. Her eyes were still shut. He pulled the strands of hair gently from her grimy and bloodied face. He noticed that his shirt had blood stains from carrying her.

"Yianni, bring me a clean shirt and a small clean cloth. You will find them over there in that bag. I'll go and fetch water."

When Aristotle returned with the water, he found Yianni hovered anxiously over Miss Cadfield's prone body, calling out her name, but she did not answer. The clean shirt and cloth were on the table.

Aristotle stripped off his shirt and donned the new one. After washing his hands, he sat on the edge of the cot, wiping Miss Cadfield's dirty cheek with a wet cloth, gently moving in small circles, admiring her fine-boned features. Soon, her clear complexion had returned. He rinsed the cloth in the bucket of water, then continued his cleansing, avoiding the bandaged area.

"You do a good job, boss. You are gentle, like a doctor. Why didn't you become a doctor?"

"Once I had entertained the thought of choosing that field, then after a few courses, decided to switch to philology. I couldn't stomach working on the cadavers."

Aristotle was relieved to see Miss Cadfield open her blue eyes. She blinked, then stared at the ceiling. As she focused on him, he found himself staring into their beautiful pools of blue.

"Miss Cadfield."

She licked her chapped lips. "What happened?" she whispered.

Her question filled him with joy. She was alive and she was responding.

"You must have fallen, and we found you and brought you back here," Aristotle said. "You have a cut on the side of your head, and I bandaged it. It seems to have stopped bleeding."

"I fell?" Miss Cadfield said, looking bewildered, her hand going to her head. "I don't remember anything."

"You fell in a hole at the excavation site," Yianni said. "Dr. Mastoras rescued you and brought you here and cleaned your face."

Miss Cadfield gazed at Aristotle in awe. "You saved my life," she said gratefully. She tried to sit up, but sank back down wearily. "I feel my head spinning."

Aristotle's mind raced as he watched her lay there with shut eyes. Should he let her sleep or try keeping her awake? He was worried about her head injury.

"Miss Cadfield," he said softly.

She opened her eyes and tried to sit up a second time.

"Please, take my hand," Aristotle said, gently pulling her into a sitting position.

He brought her some water in a cup and watched her drink it.

"I think you need to be careful when you move around," he said. "You were completely unconscious when I found you."

"The good thing is that I'm conscious now." She smiled at him. "May I have some more water? I feel thirsty."

"Yes, of course."

She drank the cup of water he gave her. She smiled. "I feel much better, thank you. Now I would like to wash and change clothing."

"We will be outside if you need anything," he told her, feeling relieved.

Fifteen minutes later, Aristotle knocked on the door. He had been sitting outside with Yianni, anxiously wondering about her.

"Please come in," she called out.

Aristotle was surprised to find Miss Cadfield sitting and reading. Her hair was pulled back and she was dressed in clean clothing. She almost looked normal except for her bandaged head.

"Would you like some tea? I had brought some with me from England," she asked, rising.

"That would be wonderful, but you stay right there. Yianni and I will take care of it. Yianni, please bring some fresh water. Meanwhile, I will light the oven. It will also help heat the cottage."

Aristotle went to the small room, whistling cheerfully. The oven jutted out of the wall and had a metal door, and on top of its flat surface sat a shiny, brass kettle. He filled the oven with the firewood and lit it. He wiped his hands.

Yianni arrived with the water. "Did you want anything else, boss?"

"Thanks, Yianni. That will be all."

"I'll be in the back."

Minutes later, the tea was ready. As Aristotle poured the tea into the cups, he felt her eyes on him.

"Dr. Mastoras."

He turned and looked at her. "Yes?"

She appeared apologetic and her hands were nervously playing with the edge of her blanket. "I wanted to thank you for rescuing me," she said softly.

He continued filling the cups with tea, feeling warm all over. "It was my duty as a gentleman," he replied quietly.

The cottage had become warm and cozy. Aristotle felt content, as he watched Miss Cadfield arise and sit at the table. They drank their tea.

"I also want to tell you something else," she said, and blushed.

"Yes, Miss Cadfield?"

"That I have forgiven you, Dr. Mastoras, for what happened the other night."

He felt light as a feather as he grinned at her. "You can call me Aristotle," he said softly.

"Aristotle," she said slowly, "but isn't Aris the name that Miss Heinz calls you by?"

"Ah, Miss Heinz," Aristotle said. "She picked it up from her brother, and has taken liberties with it. I don't particularly like it, and haven't the heart to scold her for it."

"She seems to be on pretty familiar terms with you," Miss Cadfield said, studying him. "Do you mind my asking how you met her?"

"I met her brother at university and he invited me over for dinner. She was twelve years old at the time. I've known the family since then."

"She is pretty," Miss Cadfield admitted, looking away.

"Yes, she is, and she also attracts many beaus," Aristotle said ruefully.

"She traveled to Greece to see you. That means you are special to her."

Aristotle furrowed his eyebrows at her astute remark. *She noticed Miss Heinz's interest in me.* "I don't know if she came because of me or just wanted to see Greece with her brother."

Miss Cadfield turned and looked at him with wide eyes. "Oh."

He grinned. "More importantly, I was a little taken aback by your prim and proper behavior the other night."

"The reason I was so upset is because I have Dr. Murphy waiting for me in England."

The light feeling that Aristotle had experienced fled as quickly as it came and disappointment settled in its place. He became solemn. "How did you meet your Dr. Murphy?"

"He was my father's medical student. When I was fourteen, he visited the house, and my father tutored him. He came often, and he'd tease me because I was a tomboy and used to wear my hair in braids."

"Hmm. What happened next?"

"Papa sent me to a boarding school in Paris, because he felt my behavior was not ladylike. When I returned three years later, Mr. Murphy had become a physician and his mother was looking to find him a wife."

"And you are one of the prospects?" he asked stiffly.

She nodded. "He showed interest in me."

"He agreed for you to travel to Greece?"

"He questioned my decision, but he really had no choice. I insisted that I needed to see about the property. He said he would wait for me."

Aristotle's heart, that delicate instrument that poets wrote so much about, had thrived under Miss Cadfield's attention, from the first time he had met her. The thought that someone else had already claimed her heart was a blow. Yet Aristotle could not, would not, let her go so easily.

She belongs here.

"Let me tell you something, Miss Cadfield. This is your property you are talking about. This is not just a home, an orchard, or an archaeological site. It is your family's heritage. If you leave and return to England, you will risk losing it to the state. Think carefully what you will do about it."

Miss Cadfield was quiet. "Thank you for your concern, Dr. Mastoras," she finally said. "I will deal with it as it comes."

She shut her eyes and touched her head.

"What is it, Miss Cadfield?"

"I have a headache."

Aristotle left her to rest.

An hour later, Aristotle returned to check on her. He knocked on the door, and she answered. He found her sitting up in bed, reading a book.

"Dr. Mastoras." She placed the book down on her lap.

"I came by to see how you were doing."

"Thank you." She smiled. "I still feel weak, but became bored, so I began reading."

"Do you recall the reason for your fall, Miss Cadfield?"

"No. I have tried to retrace in my mind what had happened, but I draw a blank." She shook her head. "My father used to say that after a fall, some amnesia may result. The memory usually returns if something from the past triggers it."

"If I showed you where you fell, do you think that might help you remember?" he asked.

"Yes. We can try now."

"Are you up to it? It will be dark soon." Aristotle looked at her skeptically.

She swung her legs over the cot and stood up. "Yes, it was just a little head wound, and my ankle is a little swollen."

"Dress warmly, then. It gets cold here in the evenings. Meet me outside in ten minutes."

Miss Cadfield joined Aristotle and Yianni, wearing her coat and limping with the help of a cane. They walked slowly toward the west end. The sun was beginning to set.

When they reached the area, they stood there, looking down the hole.

"You fell down there," Aristotle told her. "It had been covered with rocks. Did you remove them?"

"Yes."

"I wonder why you went there. We had not worked in the west end."

"The west end," Miss Cadfield repeated. Her hand rubbed her forehead. "I think my father had been working there, and I was curious to see it."

"He had been working on the west end?" Aristotle asked, feeling stunned by this and realizing the implications.

"Yes, you see the way he does his excavations is that he'll try one place, like the east end, and if it doesn't give him anything, he'll try another spot, like the west end. I was curious when I saw the rocks piled over here in an organized fashion. They were not randomly placed, which suggested that someone had been working here systematically. So I pulled them away and found the hole."

Aristotle nodded, appreciating her logic. "Do you remember anything else?"

Miss Cadfield shook her head. She leaned heavily on her cane. "All I remember is falling from the steps. I don't remember anything else."

"The boss brought you up with a rope. You were fortunate that I noticed that the rocks had been moved and he went to look. You may have died there if we didn't come looking for you," Yianni told her.

"Thank you Yianni, and thank you, Dr. Mastoras. I owe you both for saving my life," Miss Cadfield said.

Yianni beamed at her, and Aristotle smiled. They walked to the cottage.

Aristotle's mind was racing. If Dr. Cadfield's discovery came from the west end, then why had he told Dr. Kostakis that he had found the gold cup on the east end? This piqued his curiosity. From now on, he would concentrate his efforts on exploring the west side.

"Please, get some rest, Miss Cadfield. Tomorrow morning the workers will arrive and it would be good for you to make your presence known."

"Before you go, could you collect your belongings from the cottage?" she reminded him.

With Yianni's help, Aristotle took his valise, books, and excavating tools to the wood hut, where he would sleep with Yianni.

* * *

When Aristotle arrived on the work site the following morning, Wednesday, he was pleased to see Phillipa's brother, Nikos, guarding the site.

"Did Phillipa guard the site while I was away?" he asked him. "He wasn't here when we arrived Monday afternoon."

"Sunday afternoon, the priest came around to get some well water, and Phillipa's horse got excited and stomped on Phillipa's foot. Phillipa complained about the priest bringing him bad luck. His foot is so swollen that he could not walk. He said to tell you when he gets well he will come."

Aristotle asked Nikos if he could stay longer until Phillipa returned to work.

Nikos nodded, then scratched his head. "But I don't know whether I can be here all day. My brother needs me to help with the chores."

"Do the best you can."

Aristotle stood watching the workers toiling away. The cold wind was brisk, ruffling his hair, and the sun's rays warmed his head. He must think about working on the west end from now on, but first, he needed to check on Miss Cadfield.

Aristotle knocked on the door of the cottage. "Miss Cadfield."

Miss Cadfield opened the door and greeted him with a smile. She looked pale, but her eyes were large and bright.

"Good morning, Miss Cadfield. Would you like to meet the workers?"

"Yes! I'll be only a minute."

Aristotle escorted her to the site. He could see the eagerness in her shining eyes, and this gave him a measure of confidence. He had been anxious to please her after he learned that Dr. Cadfield had been working on the west end and not the east end. Why hadn't he seen the pile of rocks on the west end all this time? A young woman had to come all the way from England to uncover the chamber in west end. *Yes, but she is no ordinary woman. She is the daughter of the distinguished Dr. Cadfield.*

The Albanian workers consisted of men and women who appeared strong, healthy, and in good spirits. They greeted Aristotle with smiles. They looked curiously at Miss Cadfield.

Aristotle smiled back, realizing that the group was becoming like a big family to him.

Lucas and his sons came to greet him.

"Miss Cadfield, Lucas Vratsis is my foreman. He had worked for your father," he explained.

Miss Cadfield greeted him politely. Aristotle noticed a look of surprise on the man's weathered face. Lucas muttered a greeting, and then moved on.

Aristotle raised his arms. "Please, listen everyone. I would like to introduce Miss Cadfield, the daughter of the late Dr. Cadfield, and the rightful owner of this property." He gestured toward Miss Cadfield. "She has given her consent for us to continue the excavation."

There were startled looks at first, followed by chatter as everyone stared at Helena.

"Most of you will continue to work on the east side of the foundation," Aristotle continued. "We discovered an opening in the west end that had been excavated by Dr. Cadfield. I will take a few men to help me expand the hole, so please do not walk in that area, particularly the children. Also, remember, any valuables found must come directly to me."

Aristotle asked Miss Cadfield to sit at the table on the veranda. "From there you can watch the people working. If you will excuse me, I must attend to my work."

Aristotle called Lucas, Alexander, and a few other helpers. They chiseled and carved the one edge of the hole, and in the process, uncovered more of the stairwell, but did not find anything of importance.

By noon, the hole had opened considerably, and they had to watch that no one fell in. They made a small fence around it and a makeshift tent to place over the hole later.

Aristotle grabbed his supply bag and stepped carefully down the stairs. Lucas joined him. The stairs led into the large chamber. When he had rescued Miss Cadfield the other day, Aristotle had been in a hurry for her safety and had not noticed his surroundings. Rubble littered the ground from the digging and opening of the hole. *I must get the workers to clean it up.*

Aristotle gazed around him, studying and taking everything in, and was amazed at the size of the round chamber and the polychromatic designs on the walls.

"They probably stored wine there," Lucas said, pointing to one of the ceramic, amphorae.

"Or oil," Aristotle said.

Lucas grabbed several old rags that lay next to the amphorae, and then dropped them with disgust when a mouse scampered from the pile and vanished into the dark.

"This is remarkable," Aristotle said, studying the colored images of bulls and athletic lads on the wall. He took out some paper from his bag and a pencil and sketched the designs. "These paintings are thousands of years old and have been well preserved. There obviously has been an influence by the Minoan age here, with these bulls, which were a Cretan symbol."

Aristotle thought about the gold cup in Athens and the similarity of its design with the painted walls.

"There's more in here," Lucas said, walking into the recesses of the place.

"Have you been down here before?" Aristotle asked, suddenly alert.

Lucas turned and looked at him. "Actually, yes and no," he said slowly. "I was one of the workers that helped Dr. Cadfield excavate the stairs and clean up the dirt and stones that had piled up, then suddenly we were let go. I returned to see if he needed help and learned that he had been working alone, but did not need my help."

"I'm surprised that you did not mention this before," Aristotle said, tensing. He thought about the considerable time and money he had wasted on the east end.

"I thought you already knew about this area," Lucas said, shrugging his shoulders.

Aristotle stuffed the paper and pencil back in his bag. He will finish this later. They walked farther down the long hall. The walls consisted mostly of limestone boulders. Oxen or other large animals must have hauled them here. Aristotle wondered where the hallway led and if there would be an opening somewhere farther ahead. As he continued walking, it became increasingly dark. He took out a candle from his bag and lit it.

Lucas walked quietly ahead of him.

They entered a square room, then another hallway. At some point, they went around the bend and the walls were still made out of the same boulders, but nothing of importance showed up. They reached a dead end. It looked as if it led somewhere, but the wall had collapsed, closing it off.

Once they returned to the outside, Aristotle told the workers to take a break and afterwards, to clean the rubble in the chamber. He washed before going to see Miss Cadfield.

CHAPTER 38

Helena sat on the veranda all morning, wearing a large hat and gazing at the workers and enjoying the panoramic view of the valley below. She watched the children carrying buckets of water to the women who dipped the artifacts into the water, washing them. The men shoveled dirt and rocks into buckets, while a few others scraped and chiseled the ground.

She settled her gaze on the charismatic and enigmatic Dr. Mastoras. He was busy with his workers, directing the opening of the hole on the west end. She was in awe of him, because not only had he saved her life, but also had brought her to Nemea so easily and quickly, something that she had wanted to do for months.

Dr. Mastoras glanced her way and smiled, and she blushed, nodding her head. Embarrassed that she had been caught staring at him, she turned her gaze away. Her thoughts wandered elsewhere. Soon, she would be returning to Athens, back to the Stirlings and to Catherine. *Back to Dr. Murphy.*

England seemed so far away.

At one point, Helena noticed the foreman, Lucas, whispering to one of his sons. When someone came into view, they moved away. A young man with a swarthy complexion swaggered toward Lucas and shot him a mean look. He wore weapons in his belt.

Yianni stopped by and Helena asked him about the young man.

"He's Nikos Mavros. He's supposed to be guarding the place," Yianni replied.

Feeling pleased that Dr. Mastoras was looking out for her welfare, Helena nodded. "Good."

After watching Dr. Mastoras and Lucas disappear into the hole, Helena was tempted to join them. She tried to picture what could be down there, but couldn't remember anything that happened before her fall. Feeling annoyed with her memory loss, she worried that something important had escaped her. Besides, the wooden chair had become uncomfortable.

Helena stood up eagerly, intending to walk to the hole, but a sharp pain shot up her leg. She stumbled and lost her balance, smacking her hip on the table.

"Ow!" she cried, and grabbed the edge of her chair for support. She sank down shakily, rubbing her hip and leg.

Yianni hurried to her. "Are you all right, Miss Cadfield?"

She nodded. "I'll be fine," she mumbled. After Yianni left, her head began to throb. She lowered her head and shut her eyes.

"Miss Cadfield."

Helena awoke to Dr. Mastoras's deep voice. Had she been napping?

"Yes?" she answered, gazing up at him from under her hat. He was glorious to look at with his ruffled hair and beautiful, dark eyes that glowed with excitement.

"We found a chamber of some sort. Very large boulders make up its walls. It may be a mansion or a palace."

"A palace? That's wonderful!"

"In all honesty, I don't know yet. It appears to be thousands of years old, and the paint is still visible on the walls, which is probably due to the sealed chamber being protected from the elements. I know that wealthy merchants were in this area, probably involved in trade in Corinth, and had built large mansions such as this one. There were even amphorae down there, used for storing oil and probably wine."

Helena tried to picture all of this. Her headache returned, and she shut her eyes, feeling faint. Her head felt as if it would split open.

"Are you alright?" Dr. Mastoras asked.

"I seem to have developed a strong headache," Helena said, with a pained expression. She touched her forehead.

"Some rest should help."

"Yes." She arose shakily, her knees feeling weak. The wind pushed her and she clutched the table for support. She felt as if she were a hundred years old. As she grabbed the cane, the wind whipped her hat from her head and carried it a few feet away. It landed on the ground.

Dr. Mastoras leapt forward and grabbed the hat. He shook the dust off of it and gave it to her.

"Hold on to it. It's windy," he said.

They walked slowly to the front of the cottage.

"I wish I could remember what I had seen and what happened before my fall," she said wistfully.

"When you feel better, I will take you down there," Dr. Mastoras promised.

"I would like that," Helena said, perking up. They had reached the door to the cottage. She licked her dry lips. "Could I trouble you for some water from the well? I don't think I'm feeling up to hauling it."

"Do not worry."

Dr. Mastoras brought her two buckets of water and placed them on the counter top.

Helena thanked him. After he left, she took care of her needs. She drank some water, washed, and ate some food, thinking about what he had said. Her mind went in circles, as she tried to picture the chamber. When she sank into the small bed, she went immediately to sleep.

* * *

When she arose, Helena felt much stronger and refreshed. Her headache was gone.

She noticed the dirty plates on the table. While washing them, Helena thought about how Dr. Mastoras was businesslike and engrossed in his work, giving commands to his crew. He was different from the man who had strolled with her and tried to kiss her the other night in magical Corinth. He had two sides to him.

"Aristotle," she whispered, liking the way his name sounded. Then she remembered Dr. Murphy and wondered what he would have done under the same circumstances. Would he have rescued her? Would he have tried to kiss her if they had been strolling on a moonlit night?

"Helena Cadfield, you get those thoughts out of your mind," she said aloud.

She almost dropped a slippery plate and caught it in time. As she placed it down, she noticed that her hands were still white and soft, yet she knew that they would change from the harsh life here. This was a different world than the protected one at Oxford.

If only they might find the treasures down there. Then she would be off to England, living the rich life and becoming a physician's wife. After she finished her task, she wiped the spilled water from the bench with the cloth.

Later, she sat and read an archaeological book. She was fascinated by the finds that had been discovered in Egypt. She wondered if there were any tombs with skeletons in the west end and shuddered.

The sun had set, and she had difficulty reading. She rose and lit the lantern.

Someone knocked on the door.

Thinking it might be Dr. Mastoras, Helena's hands unconsciously fluttered to her hair, making sure everything was in place.

As soon as she opened the door, the forceful wind wrestled with her hair. She held the handle tightly.

Two women stood there in the dark, smiling at her. The older woman's gray hair was severely pulled back. She held a round loaf of fresh bread and a block of white cheese. The younger one was beautiful, with large, doe-like eyes and long black, braided hair. She held two bowls.

The wonderful scent of the bread caused Helena's stomach to growl. "Hello," she said.

"I am Mrs. Selmani and this is my daughter Lule. We brought you some food," the older woman said politely, in a language that was similar to the Greek language.

Helena strained to decipher the woman's guttural words as she fired them in rapid succession. She could understand most of the words and sensed that the woman was speaking in some type of Greek-Albanian dialect.

She thanked her and welcomed them into the cottage.

Mrs. Selmani smiled warmly and placed the bread and cheese on the table. She turned and looked around. "I see the dishes have been washed, did you do them?"

"Yes," Helena said.

The older woman appeared grateful.

"Sometimes we wash them. We also brought you some bean soup," said Lule, the younger woman, placing the two bowls on the table.

"The men and women are eating dinner outside, but I thought you probably would want to eat here tonight," Mrs. Selmani said.

Helena thanked her, sensing the respect that Mrs. Selmani held for her, for she did not stay to chat, but did her job and left quickly.

Afterwards, Helena cut off a small corner of the fresh bread and dipped it in the soup. Her stomach growled. She had not realized how hungry she was. She was ravenous.

The Albanian workers talked and laughed outside the window that faced the veranda. She recognized Dr. Mastoras's voice as he conversed with them. After she finished eating, Helena washed the dishes, and then changed into her nightgown and went to read some more. It was half-past nine o'clock when someone knocked on the door.

"Who is it?"

"Dr. Mastoras. I came to see how you are doing."

Helena felt warm all over and was about to get up to open the door, when she remembered that she was dressed in her nightgown with her hair braided.

"Just a minute, please," she called out.

CHAPTER 39

Helena grabbed her night robe and threw it over her, then limped to the door. As she went to touch the door, the wind blew it open.

Helena's breath caught in her throat as Dr. Mastoras struggled with the door, laughing. The wind had ruffled his dark locks and she could see the angles of his chiseled face defined by the light of the lantern.

He looks so handsome.

A warm feeling, deep inside, threatened to overcome her. She could not place it, for she had never experienced this feeling before.

She pulled her robe protectively closer to her. She intuitively knew that if she let him in, she didn't know what the consequences would be. That attempted kiss at the Corinthian Inn was still fresh in her mind. She was in love with Dr. Murphy, and she must remember that.

Dr. Mastoras shut the door behind him.

"I apologize for calling on you at this late hour," he said, smiling. "I noticed you didn't come out for dinner and wanted to be sure you were all right."

Her knees felt weak. *Why does he have this effect on me?* Trying to remain calm, she turned and limped to the table and sat down.

"Yes, thank you," she said shakily. "Mrs. Selmani and her daughter brought me dinner. I feel much better."

"Good. Maybe you might join us tomorrow for dinner?"

"I would like that."

"I also wanted to ask you about the west end. After we spoke this afternoon, have you been able to recall anything?"

Relief flooded Helena when he changed the topic to business. She relaxed. *He came to discuss business after all.* "No, sorry."

He had a thoughtful look on his face. "Maybe tomorrow, if you are up to it, we might go down to the west end chamber."

She shook her head. "I'm not sure if it would do any good. I don't remember anything."

"I understand, but it might trigger a memory," he insisted. "At least give it a try."

Negative thoughts coursed through Helena's mind, insisting that not only was it improper for them to be alone in the cottage without a chaperone, but also that she shouldn't go alone to the west end chamber with him. *Yes, but if you don't go and have a look, you might never remember anything.*

"All right, on the condition that you will behave the perfect gentleman," she said firmly.

"You have my word, Miss Cadfield," he said softly.

After he left, Helena lay on the bed thinking about him and about the west end. She fell into a deep sleep and dreamed that she had gone into the chamber and had found the treasures.

Early Thursday morning, Helena left the cottage and limped to the excavation site. The wind was brisk. She had not worn her hat, but was carrying it with her, afraid it will fly away again. The sun's rays felt pleasantly warm on her face.

The Albanians worked steadily, yet would talk and laugh sporadically, breaking the monotony of the routine. Some people looked at her and nodded, and she smiled back.

Helena's eyes searched for Dr. Mastoras. She wanted to tell him about the dream last night, where she had walked into the west end chamber and had found treasures behind a rock in the wall. Although it was a dream, it felt so real.

At the east end, she found Mrs. Selmani and Lule steadily scraping the ground with picks in their tanned hands. They dipped the artifacts in a basin of water, cleaning the fragments. Other workers were either busy working along the landing, or at the bottom of the ditch.

Helena sat next to Mrs. Selmani and pitched in, scraping and brushing the dirt. She unearthed some objects, recognizing them to be fragments of pottery. Mrs. Selmani tried to have a conversation with her, by asking about her background. Helena told her about her life in England and her father's interest in archaeology.

At one point, Helena looked up and saw Dr. Mastoras gazing at her. He stood tall above the other men who were working at the west end. He approached her.

"Good morning, Miss Cadfield. How is your foot?"

"Better," she replied, looking at him and sweeping back a bang that had fallen on her forehead. "It doesn't hurt as much today."

"That's good."

"Will I have a chance to visit the west end?"

"Unfortunately, much rubble fell down when we enlarged the hole, and we're trying to get it cleared. Hopefully, it'll be ready later this afternoon. I will let you know," Dr. Mastoras said, smiling. He turned and spoke a few moments with Mrs. Selmani and Lule, looking at what they had been working on.

Helena stole glances at them. She couldn't ignore that Lule beamed back at Dr. Mastoras, as he talked with her and asked questions, yet he didn't seem to look at her in that special way he had looked at Helena. He was intent more on the objects that she had cleaned than with her.

After he left, Helena was quiet the rest of the morning, sitting in her spot, scraping and sifting, and thinking. She wondered if she were doing the right thing, working here like the workers. Should she be acting more like the owner, being in charge and leading? A part of her rebelled at the menial, labor-intensive work, yet another part of her enjoyed the feeling of being useful and doing something she had always wanted to try. This was a new role for her, and so different from life in Oxford and Paris.

Whenever she rested her eyes on the panoramic view, Helena felt peaceful. For years, she had pictured Papa digging for treasures in the dust and the heat of the day, but realized there was more to it. Without having experienced this, she would never have known this feeling of bliss that embraced her as tightly as the wind.

Helena gazed at the families, recognizing their faces. At first, all the men seemed alike, with their long, beak-like noses and tanned, angular faces, and the women with their scarves and layered clothing. Mrs. Selmani had told her that most of the workers were related, except a few Albanians. Most of them had moved from northern Greece. Six of the men were the Kraja brothers, and their families had come along. Then there was the Greek foreman, Lucas Vratsis and his two sons, and another Albanian, Alexander and his two sons.

A jug of water was passed around and a cup along with it. Helena didn't drink from it, having learned from by her father that drinking in other people's cups was a way of catching disease. She must remember to bring her cup.

As the day progressed and the afternoon had arrived, Helena wondered when Dr. Mastoras would come and get her to visit the west end. She had considered strongly the idea of going to him, but something held her back. *He did say that he would come for me.*

Around four o'clock, the workers lined up in front of Dr. Mastoras. Yianni and the young guard, Nikos, checked their pockets. After they were paid, the group sauntered down to the camp to rest. Dr. Mastoras had not said anything to Helena about going to the west end, so when Mrs. Selmani invited her down to the camp, she went with her.

Her foot felt better, although she still used the cane. The camp sat in a clearing, nestled in a wooded area. It held several tents, and in the center was a round, stone campfire. Next to the lit campfire, an older woman stirred a big barrel of water with a long ladle.

"Is she making soup?" Helena asked Mrs. Selmani.

"No. She is washing clothes. We have to wash clothes daily because the work is so dirty. The boys bring down water from the well and we heat it up. Then we fill the barrel with hot water, soap, and dirty clothes."

"Could I bring my clothes down here to wash?"

"Of course. Give them to me whenever you like, and they will be washed and dried by the next morning."

Helena stepped in a puddle caused by the water in the barrel that had splashed out. She shook the water off of her wet slipper.

"Miss Cadfield, excuse me for saying this, but your shoes are too soft for the work we do. You need hard shoes, like these." Mrs. Selmani lifted her skirt and showed her the dark, leather shoes that looked like a man's shoes. "I am wearing my late husband's shoes. God rest his soul. I have another pair that you could use. They might be big on you, but if you wear extra stockings, they should fit."

Helena rarely received gifts. Besides Papa, the only person who had given her any gift was her Nana. "Thank you, Mrs. Selmani for your kind gesture."

Mrs. Selmani went inside her tent and returned with a pair of black shoes. "Here you are. Wear them in good health."

Helena put on the shoes. Thy were large and sturdy. "They will do. How much do they cost?"

"You do not need to pay me. These shoes are old. I do not throw anything away. I am glad that you can make use of them."

Helena hugged her thankfully, then left the camp and returned to the site. As she came up the path, she spied a lonely figure at the west end of the excavation site. It was Lucas, the foreman, looking around furtively. When he saw her, he put his hands in his pockets and turned and went the other way. She tensed, wondering what he would be doing there alone. Maybe she was overreacting. Dr. Mastoras seemed to be on good terms with him.

Helena turned and headed toward the cottage. She spied Dr. Mastoras getting water from the well. He had his back turned to her.

"Dr. Mastoras," she called.

He turned and saw her, his handsome features lighting up. "Ahh, there you are, Miss Cadfield. I was looking for you." He placed the bucket down.

"I apologize. I took a walk down to the camp and Mrs. Selmani gave me a pair of sturdy shoes to wear. My slippers were not equipped for this heavy work."

"Good. The shoes will come in handy. It will be dark soon. Do you still want to go to the west end? If so, we need to move quickly."

Helena appreciated that Dr. Mastoras had remembered to take her to the area. "Yes, of course."

Dr. Mastoras called Yianni to his side. "Yianni, start gathering today's crates filled with artifacts for inventory. Place them on the veranda and we will count them later. Ask someone to help you. Miss Cadfield and I are going to look down in the west end. If I call for help, you know what to do."

CHAPTER 40

Helena walked with Dr. Mastoras to the west end. The hole to the chamber had been enlarged and she did not have to gather her dress close to her as before. He descended it first, then gave her a hand, making it easy enough for her to walk down the steps.

"Be careful of the rubble down here. We are not finished cleaning it." Dr. Mastoras pointed to the large mound of dirt in the middle of the room.

Helena looked around eagerly, nodding. "I recognize the designs on the walls. I saw this in a recent dream I had."

"Oh? Do you remember anything else? Did you go in here?"

"Hmm, let me see." Helena started walking forward, while he followed her quietly.

Helena hoped to see more familiar signs. The increasing darkness made her anxious. They had reached a fork.

"I remember turning right here, but can't remember why...." she stopped, feeling bewildered. She shook her head. They turned right and continued walking. She stopped, looking around.

"What is it?"

"Somehow, I remember a small, irregular rock, stuck in between some larger ones on the wall." She touched the wall, but didn't find anything.

"Maybe it's farther down," Dr. Mastoras suggested. "Most of the walls are made up of large, irregular boulders, but I have also seen a few smaller stones in the wall."

As they walked forward a bit, passing a square chamber, Helena became even more nervous. Not only was it dark, making it difficult to see, but she was alone once again with Dr. Mastoras.

As if reading her thoughts, he took out a candle from the bag that was slung over his shoulder. "Here, let me light a candle."

The light helped a little, but it did not ease the mounting fear that was consuming her as they moved forward. She trembled. *Why am*

I reacting this way? She stepped on something and thinking it was a creature, she screamed.

"Sshh, it's all right, nothing to be afraid of." Dr. Mastoras said soothingly, touching her shoulder. He bent down, picking up the object. "It's a candle."

"A candle?" Helena became excited. "This must be the candle that I had dropped the other day. The stone must be here, above it somewhere."

"Why are you so interested in this stone?"

"It conceals a chamber filled with my father's treasures."

Dr. Mastoras grabbed her arm, looking stunned. "Do you mean you found treasures here?"

"Yes! I saw it in my dream," Helena sang out. She frantically searched the area above where the candle had lain, pressing on them. "It's here somewhere. I can't see that well. Could you light another candle?"

"Yes."

Dr. Mastoras gave her his candle and lit another one. The extra light helped as she continued her search.

At one point, she pushed against a small stone and it moved.

"There it is," she said excitedly. "Here, can you push the stone from this end?" She showed him.

Dr. Mastoras snuffed his candle, stuffing it in his bag. He pressed against the edge of the stone until it creaked, moving slightly. With his strong arms, he moved it even more, shifting it to the side.

Helena brought the candle forward, revealing the chamber inside.

Dr. Mastoras sucked in his breath in amazement as he reached in and pulled out a horde of gold jewelry. "Whew!" he exclaimed.

Helena gazed in appreciation at the jewels. "These are the treasures that my father had found," she said with pride.

"Here, take some." Dr. Mastoras gave them to her.

Helena stuffed her pocket with them. "Isn't this wonderful?"

He gave her more jewels, and then started filling his bag and pockets. "Yes, but this is too much for us to carry. I suggest that we take some of it, and then return for the rest another time."

Helena was beginning to feel out of breath and for some reason, felt dizzy. She leaned against the wall, feeling weak.

"Are you alright?"

"I feel light-headed."

"Then we should leave immediately. You go ahead and get some fresh air. I will seal this," he said. He pushed the stone to seal the chamber.

Helena walked toward the entrance hole, eager to get outside. After that fall, she did not feel comfortable spending time down here. When she arrived at the steps, she was startled to see a dark shape looming at the foot of the steps. Her heart quickened.

Helena recognized Lucas's small head and large, pointed ears and tensed. Her hands clutched her filled pockets protectively.

"Yianni said that you were down here, so I came to see if you needed any help," Lucas said gruffly.

"I had walked down the hall and felt out of breath, so I came to get some air," Helena replied. There was something menacing about the way he stood looking at her. She shivered, feeling fearful.

"Did you find anything?" Lucas growled. He moved closer, looking at her pockets

His rough tone disturbed Helena. She felt indignant and moved back.

Dr. Mastoras joined them. "Oh, there you are, Lucas," he said. "Let's get the tent set up. It's getting late."

Lucas nodded and left.

After they returned to the outside, Helena saw Yianni seated at the table on the veranda, playing a game of backgammon with Nikos Mavros, the guard. Several containers filled with artifacts found that day sat neatly stacked next to them.

Helena watched as Dr. Mastoras, Lucas and his sons, closed the hole with the plank and set up the tent.

"Did you find anything down there, Dr. Mastoras?" Lucas asked Dr. Mastoras pleasantly.

Helena was disturbed by the foremen's change in tone as he spoke respectfully to Dr. Mastoras. He had spoken in a surly manner to her. She wasn't sure about Lucas's intentions.

"Lucas, the reason we went down there was to have Miss Cadfield see if she remembered anything that happened before her fall," Dr. Mastoras said.

"It looks as if you also found something of value down there," Lucas said slyly, pointing to Dr. Mastoras's bulging bag and pockets.

"We found some artifacts down there, similar to the gold jewelry you sold to me," Dr. Mastoras admitted.

Helena froze. She stared at Dr. Mastoras, stunned that he would confide in this man. *Couldn't he see that Lucas is not to be trusted?* He was looking steadily at Lucas, as if waiting to hear what he said. Maybe she had trusted Dr. Mastoras too much. Maybe she should have a talk with him about guarding her treasures more carefully.

"Ahh, that's wonderful," Lucas said, easing his face into a smile. He nodded pleasantly. "Treasures will bring us more work. *Eh*, Dr. Mastoras?" He then winked at his sons.

"Tomorrow, we will go down and retrieve the rest of the artifacts," Dr. Mastoras said carefully. "Meanwhile, don't say anything to anyone. We don't want to tempt the workers."

Dr. Mastoras turned to Yianni, who had been standing nearby. "Did you gather all the containers of artifacts to take their inventory?"

"Yes, boss. Lucas and his sons helped me."

"Good. Lucas, come around eight tomorrow morning with your sons. Again, don't tell anyone."

Helena watched with increasing uneasiness as Lucas and his sons left. She felt thirsty and hungry, and wanted to go over the treasures in her pockets, but at the same time, was upset at Dr. Mastoras for confiding in Lucas.

"How could you tell Lucas about the treasures?" she hissed.

"First of all, he saw that our pockets were filled, so I could not lie. Besides, I sealed the chamber, and you know how difficult it is to find it. I have already been down there with Lucas and we could not find it."

"If you'll excuse me, Dr. Mastoras," she said curtly. "I will retire to the cottage to rest before dinner."

"Before you go," he said, leaning toward her and speaking in a low voice, "please put your assets in a safe place. We will pool all the resources together at some point to see what we have. Until I reveal the discovery of the treasures with anyone, let us use the word 'artifacts' for now."

Helena nodded curtly, too upset with him to say anything. She could feel his eyes on her as she hurried away to the safety of the cottage. She wondered what he would do with the treasures in his own pockets. She should have insisted that he give them to her. How did she know that he was to be trusted? She hoped he wouldn't show the treasures to Lucas. She was going to study the ones in her pockets, then rest. But first, she needed to get some water.

When she had quenched her thirst, Helena locked the door of the cottage, and washed and changed into a clean dress. Removing the jewelry from her pockets, she carefully placed them on the table, then bundled her dirty clothes and put them in a canvas bag to give to Mrs. Selmani to wash later.

Lighting the lantern, Helena sat at the table, studying the jewelry, admiring their beauty. They were different shapes and sizes, from a shiny, gold necklace with bright emeralds and intricate designs, to several gold earrings with jewels, and a few gold hairpins. There were also a few jeweled brooches.

Helena wondered if they had been found in tombs, for she knew that they put treasures in tombs of the dead, or if they had been found elsewhere. She put the exquisite gold and emerald necklace around her neck and went to the mirror that hung on the wall. Pulling her hair back to reveal her slender neck and the necklace, she gazed at herself, amazed at the transformation. The necklace was magnificent on her and gave her a regal appearance. It even made her blue eyes glow. Did Helen of Troy feel this way when wearing riches like these in her possession?

Feeling special, Helena carefully wrapped the treasures in a linen cloth, placed them in an inside pocket of her luggage and pushed it under her cot. She pulled the wool blanket down the side of the cot so that it hid the valise. She then lay down and put her arm under her head, thinking. If her father had found these treasures, he would have had some book that logged them, for he was meticulous about logging these things. At least that could give her a clue of what he had done.

Excited at the thought, Helena jumped up and started going through the books piled up in the cottage. She found at least a hundred books of various sizes and topics, ranging from archaeology and anatomy, to Greek philosophy and Greek history. She discovered an English version of *The Iliad*, which made her smile.

Helena finally found the logbook wedged between a stack of books lined against the wall. She sat back on the cot and read it. Her father wrote each day in it, jotting down the date and time, and where and what he had found. He also had drawn a sketch of each item. She became excited when she came across the passage where he had found the treasures on the west end.

His descriptions and sketches were similar to the jewelry that Dr. Mastoras had given to her. Papa had chronicled everything. *He had found them in the same chamber as I had.* His plan was to give the Archaeological Society a portion of the treasures and keep the rest for himself and for his daughter. She could not decipher the scribbling farther down the page, for his writing had deteriorated. It seemed as if he had been writing in a hurry.

According to her father, it was not clear how the treasures had gotten there in the first place, although he believed that they were thousands of years old, and from the same period in time as Homer's *Iliad*. He guessed that these treasures were looted from nearby ancient tombs and never retrieved.

Helena had grown tired and could not keep her eyes open. She fell into a deep sleep.

CHAPTER 41

When she awoke, Helena was shivering from the cold that had crept into the cottage. She peeked out the window. The sun had already set. She noticed her father's logbook by her side. She must have fallen asleep while reading it. Remembering what she had read, she felt a need to speak to Dr. Mastoras.

As she put her coat on, Helena spied her bundle of dirty clothes and took them with her. Locking the door, she went outside in search of him.

Someone had built a campfire in the middle of the veranda. The fire provided not only heat to cook the food with, but also sufficient light. The workers sat along the boundary wall and the edge of the veranda, talking. Some were singing and laughing.

Helena saw Yianni sitting at the veranda table talking with Alexander, a reliable and hardworking Albanian worker. The crates with the artifacts were all gone. She wondered where they had stored them.

She approached them and greeted them. "Have you seen Dr. Mastoras?"

"He'll be here soon, miss. He had to see about the tent, and then probably will wash before dinner," Alexander said. He arose and bowed. "Please, you can have this chair. They will be serving dinner soon."

Mrs. Selmani had told her earlier that the women ate together and she did not want to stand out. "Thank you, but I will sit with the women tonight."

Helena walked toward the veranda's boundary wall where some women sat, and joined them, placing her bundle down. She did not see Mrs. Selmani or her daughter.

Panos, an older Albanian worker, greeted Helena. "Miss Cadfield, we were wondering about harvesting the olive trees on the property," he said to her. "It is that time of the year, and it would be a shame not to collect them. The olives and the oil are valuable."

Two other men joined them and started talking with Helena about the olive trees. They told Helena that the olive trees were ripe for picking. They asked her if they could make olive oil.

"I like the idea," she said, "but if you are busy gathering the olives, who will do the excavating?"

"We can do it on our free time. Instead of resting, we could gather olives for a couple of hours each day. We could even gather them on the weekends when Dr. Mastoras is away," Panos said.

"I will think about it. Thank you for bringing it to my attention."

After they left, Helena thought about what they had told her. It would be good to produce olive oil and olives and earn money. This was what her family used to do. She was feeling better already. She liked that they were coming to her for advice. They were treating her the way she deserved to be treated.

Mrs. Selmani arrived with her daughter and some other families. They brought lanterns and plenty of plates. The veranda became full. The children ran around the campfire, shouting and playing. It was busy here, Helena thought.

Dr. Mastoras appeared, freshly washed and dressed. His white shirt, open at the neck, revealed his strong, tanned neck. He seemed relaxed, standing there talking quietly to Yianni and Alexander. Helena had learned from Mrs. Selmani that the Albanian women had washed Dr. Mastoras's clothes down at the camp.

After Yianni left, Dr. Mastoras sat with his long limbs stretched out before him. The shine on his boots glowed from the flame of the campfire. He conversed with Alexander.

A short time later, the women served the rabbit stew in bowls and cups, and everyone used their bread to eat the soup, scooping up the chunks of meat with it. One of the Albanian women served Helena a steaming bowl of soup and warm, crusty bread. She thanked her.

Mrs. Selmani, Lule, and young Arian came and sat next to Helena on the boundary wall. She liked that. They had become comfortable with her. They were silent, eating their meal. Afterwards, Helena gave her bundle of dirty clothes to Mrs. Selmani to take down to the camp to wash. "Thank you, Mrs. Selmani."

"Miss Cadfield, would you like another bowl of soup?" Mrs. Selmani asked, rising. "There is plenty."

"Yes. Please," Helena said, handing her the empty bowl. Mrs. Selmani returned shortly with the bowl of soup and bread. As Helena ate, she observed the shadows playing on the features of the people, as they talked and moved their heads. One minute, their glowing profiles almost appeared angelic and the next minute, when they turned their faces, the dark shadows had ghoulishly replaced them. Was she also seeing two sides to Dr. Mastoras?

As if sensing her thoughts, Dr. Mastoras came to her. He bowed politely.

"Miss Cadfield," he said, "would you do me the honor of sitting at the table with me?"

"Mrs. Selmani said that the women ate together and I didn't want to disturb their order," she replied.

"I cannot see how this would affect you, the lady of the house. Did you normally eat with the servants when you were living in Oxford?"

Helena knew he was right. She blushed at the thought. He was honoring her place at the table as an owner, and she secretly admired that. It was a noble gesture on his part.

A momentary hush settled in the air as she walked with him to the table. Alexander arose from the table, excusing himself and leaving them alone.

Helena and Dr. Mastoras ate silently for a few minutes, and then everyone went back to talking normally.

Helena remembered her father's logbook. "Regarding the artifacts, I have something to tell you. It has to do with my father."

"This is not the best place to discuss this, Miss Cadfield. Too many ears," he warned her.

Helena was silent, realizing that he had a good point. Then she remembered about the olive trees. "The workers spoke to me about harvesting the olive trees. I think the olives would be a good source of food, both as olives and olive oil, and also a way to earn some money. The workers are eager to get started."

Dr. Mastoras nodded. "It has already come to my attention. I do not see a problem, so long as you approve, and the work at the excavation site is not affected."

Afterwards, he arose and lifted his arm for attention. "Listen, everyone. I will be needing a few extra men to help clear the pile of dirt that had fallen inside the west end hole. Then I want to expand that opened section." He paused. "It has also come to my attention that the olive trees on this property are ripe for picking." He continued, telling them that Miss Cadfield had agreed for them to harvest them and make olive oil from them. Everyone cheered.

Soon, the men were joking, telling stories, and drinking the wine. Someone brought a violin and began playing music. In no time, a chorus of singers joined him, all wrapped up in their song.

Helena listened, trying to make out the words of the singers. The song must be Albanian, she thought, for she could not understand all the words, but she felt their emotions. She relaxed a bit, savoring the moment.

Later, the women began gathering the children and the couples slowly left for the camp.

Mrs. Selmani and Lule came and wished Helena a goodnight.

"I will have these cleaned for you by tomorrow," Mrs. Selmani said, showing Helena the bundle of clothes.

Helena thanked her, then arose, ready to retire.

"Did you like your meal, Miss Cadfield?" Dr. Mastoras asked.

"Yes, thank you, although it is getting late and I must retire. I also need to light the fire in the cottage, yet I am not sure how this particular oven works."

"I would be happy to assist you."

Dr. Mastoras followed her into the cottage and went to the small room. He opened the oven door, and then showed her where the woodpile was kept in the corner of the small room.

"See, it is quite easy. The wood goes in here and then you light it. The smoke goes out that chimney. When you run out of wood, come and ask me. I will cut some more for you."

He lit the fire.

"Thank you."

He arose, wiping his dirty hands on a nearby rag. "That should be sufficient wood for tonight to warm the cottage."

"I feel the heat already," Helena said, smiling. She needed to discuss with him the treasures. "Aristotle, before you leave, I would like to have a word with you."

Helena was stunned with herself. *Did I just call him Aristotle?*

CHAPTER 42

Aristotle joined Miss Cadfield at the table as she lit the lantern. Her face glowed from the light. Mesmerized by her ethereal beauty and graceful movements, Aristotle could not tear his gaze away. Had she bewitched him? Could he truly be observing a Greek goddess?

"Is it about the artifacts and your father?" he asked softly.

"Yes. I looked at my father's logbook today. He sketched the same treasures that we discovered. They came from the same place."

"It does not surprise me."

"What I'm trying to say is that he did not discover them elsewhere on the property. He discovered them inside that small chamber, untouched all these years. He writes that someone may have looted some ancient or royal tombs nearby and placed them here as a hiding place. He logged them in his book before he died and returned most of them to the small chamber for safekeeping."

"So he thinks they may have come from lootings of royal tombs. May I see that book?"

She retrieved the logbook and they sat next to each other at the table, their bodies almost touching as they bent their heads over the book. He leafed through it slowly, studying the sketches of the jewelry.

"I have that necklace in my possession," she said, her long, slim finger pointing at a sketch of a necklace.

Aristotle gazed at the drawing and nodded appreciatively. "Intricately beautiful," he observed.

He saw a sketch of a gold cup with the bulls and the inscription. "Ah, yes. I have seen that cup before," he said softly, turning and gazing into her shining blue eyes. "It was in Dr. Kostakis's basement, in Athens. Your father had given it to him."

"Yes, isn't it beautiful?" she said, lowering her eyes to the picture.

He silently read Dr. Cadfield's notes next to the picture of the gold cup. "According to your father, he believed that this cup belonged to King Meneleus," he remarked.

She looked at him, her eyes large with wonder.

"Do you realize what that means if he is right?" he asked.

Miss Cadfield nodded. "My father was always going on and on about King Meneleus and Helen of Troy, and how Paris stole her away with the treasures. He even had me read all of Homer's books and translations."

"Very interesting, but there has to be more proof than that cup."

Miss Cadfield was silent. She shivered.

"What is it?" Aristotle asked her.

"I remembered a dream I had, when I fell down at the west end. It's almost prophetic, really."

"Tell me about it."

"I saw Paris in my dream. He treated me as if I were Helen of Troy. Could all of these treasures be tied together with the dream?"

Aristotle whistled. "I thought your father had a strong imagination, but you surpass him by leaps and bounds."

"I am serious. This is not something I am making up," she retorted.

"Well, if Paris came to you in your dreams and there were treasures, then you are Helen of Troy and I am--" Aristotle laughed, then stopped.

"Paris," she whispered. "Aris, your name sounds like Paris. Don't you see? Someone is trying to tell us something."

Aristotle rose abruptly. "I think it's late, and if you don't mind, I'd like to take the logbook and study it more. Tomorrow I would like to explore the west end for the rest of the treasures."

"I have more to tell you," she said, her eyes pleading. "In that book, my father said that there were more treasures than what was down there. You see, he had removed a few of them from the chamber and stored them in the cottage. One of the treasures was the gold cup which he gave to the Archaeological Society, but the other treasures in the cottage were stolen."

Aristotle's eyebrows furrowed. "Stolen?"

"Yes. He circled the ones in the book that had been stolen. His last letter that he wrote to me states something to that effect. Here, I will show you."

She went to her luggage and pulling out her father's letter, read it aloud. "However, as I write to you, dark forces have already stolen the precious treasures that I had stored in the cottage two days ago. They stole them while I slept during the night. I am having difficulty retrieving them. My inquiries have produced no results; either they don't know about them, or have decided not to tell me the truth."

Aristotle silently digested this information.

"Lucas had worked for my father during that time, and that is the reason I did not want him knowing about it," she explained.

"I understand your concern, but just because Lucas worked for him does not mean that he was a thief. I have placed him in a responsible position as foreman, because I have never seen him do or say anything to raise any suspicion in my mind that he is a thief."

"I have seen him snooping around, and that has raised my suspicions," Miss Cadfield said, sighing. She folded her father's letter.

"Phillipa and his brothers are guarding the place. If they see anything, they will let me know," he assured her.

"Please, one more thing before you leave. Could we go over the treasures? I feel this is the only time we can do this, with no interruptions." She went to the cot before he could reply. Bending down, she pulled out her luggage and retrieved the bag of riches.

He sat back down, watching her graceful movements, curious to see what she had in her possession.

They slowly went over each piece of jewelry, comparing them to the sketches in the logbook.

"I recognize these. They were in my father's logbook, and these, and these," she said, handling the gold jewelry and showing him the sketches in the logbook. They went over them for a few minutes, putting the pieces in separate piles. The ones that had the same stones or design were placed together. Many had intricate designs.

Aristotle was troubled when he saw Dr. Cadfield's sketches of the stolen pieces in the logbook. One drawing reminded him of the necklace that Lucas had sold to him. *Maybe Miss Cadfield is right.* Yet Lucas had said that it was a gift from Dr. Cadfield. Maybe it was a duplicate. He had seen a few duplicate jewels in the logbook. He did not want to alarm Miss Cadfield any further.

When they finished, Aristotle somberly helped put them back in the bag.

"Where did you put the jewels that you found the other day?" Miss Cadfield asked.

Aristotle heard a scraping sound outside the door and jumped up, staring at the door, his hands clenched.

Miss Cadfield also became alert. "Who goes there?" she called out.

The sound happened again.

Aristotle rushed outside but didn't see anyone. He checked around, and then returned to the cottage.

"Maybe it was one of the Mavros brothers doing guard duty," Miss Cadfield offered, standing at the door

"If that's the case, he would have responded to you," Aristotle countered.

He entered the cottage and shut the door. "We must talk softly. The treasures you inquired about are stored in a safe place. You do trust me?" he whispered, resuming their conversation.

Miss Cadfield had the decency to blush at his challenging question. "I only asked because I want to be sure they are safe," she whispered.

"Yes, they are in a safe place," he said softly, sighing and rubbing his neck. "It has been a long day for both of us. I would like to borrow the logbook, if I may."

She handed him the book. "Tomorrow we will continue, then?" she whispered.

"I will make sure that someone guards the cottage tonight."

Aristotle bowed and left, taking the logbook with him. He didn't want to scare Miss Cadfield, but his gut instinct made him believe that someone had been outside earlier, listening to their conversation, and he didn't want them to learn more than they already knew.

Aristotle checked the surrounding property, but there was no sign of a Mavros brother. He muttered to himself that he needed to have a talk with Phillipa. Nikos, the youngest Mavros brother, was the only one that he had seen these last few days.

Aristotle asked Yianni to guard the cottage that night, promising to pay him double. He could not risk the treasures being stolen while under his watch. He had promised Miss Cadfield that much.

CHAPTER 43

Friday morning, Helena locked the cottage and walked to the work site. The workers were already hard at work and she could see Dr. Mastoras going among the workers, talking with them. The treasures they found had given Helena a satisfactory feeling of financial security. Once all the treasures were removed from the west end chamber, she would be rich and would not need to work.

Although she had pictured herself returning to England and eventually becoming Dr. Murphy's wife, after last night, she had a hard time keeping Dr. Mastoras out of her thoughts. She stayed up a long time, thinking about him.

She had noticed the special way he looked at her last night as she lit the lantern. She had inwardly trembled under his virile presence, but her outward composure was commendable. Her calmness was all an act. A finely orchestrated act, ingrained in her from all those years at the boarding school. Always hide your emotions, they taught her.

She could still remember the warmth emanating from his body when they sat together at the table going over the jewelry. How could she not notice his gentle touch when he handed her the jewels? This strong man had the touch of a baby. If he had tried to kiss her last night, she knew that she would have let him. His eyes had said it all.

England felt so far away up here on the mountain.

Helena sidestepped some children carrying buckets. She greeted Mrs. Selmani and Lule cheerfully and sat next to them. Mrs. Selmani's young son, Arian, scuttled back and forth, carrying small pails.

Helena chatted with the women as they worked. She had become familiar with their dialect. Helena learned that Lule was seventeen and did not know how to read or write, but knew how to cook and sew well.

Helena also learned that Mrs. Selmani's father was Albanian, and her mother Greek. Helena reached over to get a tool and her hand brushed a bundle that sat next to Mrs. Selmani.

Mrs. Selmani handed her the bundle. "I have brought your clean clothes," she said.

"Thank you," Helena said, taking them. She took out some coins from her pocket and gave them to her.

Mrs. Selmani thanked her.

After Helena deposited the bag of clothes in the cottage, she returned to the work site to continue her work. She did not want her washed clothes to get dusty.

Prepared for the strong sun, Helena wore her large hat. She studied her tanned hands as they steadily worked. Their dirt-crusted black nails and blistered fingers were a testimony of the hard work these past few days. They were the hands of a worker and not a lady, but she did not mind. She had wanted to experience digging for artifacts, and she finally was doing it.

Helena looked up, her eyes combing the area for a sign of Dr. Mastoras. He stood by the west end, talking with a few men. There was something reassuring about seeing him there. He appeared smart, confident, and in charge. He gave them his full attention, and he smiled often. The workers were constantly going to him for answers.

"Look what I can do!" Arian called out. He danced and pranced around them, juggling rocks with other boys, and earning scolds and slaps from his mother.

"Go and play on the hill," Mrs. Selmani commanded.

The boys chased each other down the hill.

Helena plied a few objects from the dirt when Mrs. Selmani nudged her.

"The men are going down the hole," Mrs. Selmani told her, nodding toward Dr. Mastoras.

Helena appreciated the woman's concern. She saw Dr. Mastoras descending into the west end with Yianni, and wondered what they would find. It was good that he didn't take Lucas with him. Her anxiety returned when she saw Lucas working near the entrance. Would he go down there?

* * *

Aristotle descended the stairs of the west end with Yianni. He had decided not to bring Lucas with him so as not to fuel Miss Cadfield's fears. Aristotle had been troubled all night with what he had heard from Miss Cadfield and read from Dr. Cadfield's logbook. It was rare to find so many ancient and valuable treasures in one place. It was unheard of.

What Dr. Cadfield had suggested could not be denied. Even if Homer's story of Helen of Troy was legendary, there was some truth in it. Miss Cadfield's dream with Paris was also thought provoking. It appeared that she had thought of herself as Helen of Troy and him as Paris, stealing her and the treasures. Then he reminded himself that it was only a dream.

Aristotle and Yianni walked through the large chamber and into the hallway. He groped his way, touching the boulders on the wall, and looking for the irregular shaped stone. It was not as easy to find this time. He should have brought Miss Cadfield down here.

They wandered down the hallway for a while, then went back to the stairwell, then returned. After a few attempts at pushing some stones and not getting anywhere, he finally found the irregular stone.

"Here it is," Aristotle called out. He gave it a resounding shove and it moved. He pushed harder and it opened. Panting, he reached in, his fingers probing until they touched cold, hard objects.

Yianni rushed to his side.

Aristotle began emptying the contents of the small chamber into his canvas bag. It filled quickly with jewelry. He handed the bag to Yianni. "Give me your empty bag," he ordered.

"Yes, boss."

By the time that they had finished emptying the chamber of its treasures, they had filled the two bags.

Shutting the stone door, Aristotle and Yianni headed for the stairwell. They walked to the stairs, their bags filled with treasures. Out in the sunlight, they stopped to catch their breaths. Lucas and the other workers were eyeing them curiously.

"Come with me," Aristotle commanded, feeling exhilarated.

Yianni followed him to the cottage. When they arrived, Aristotle reached into his pocket and remembered that Miss Cadfield had the key. "I don't have the key. Miss Cadfield has it."

"I don't think she locks it," Yianni said, checking the door. "See, it is unlocked."

Aristotle muttered to himself that he must remind Miss Cadfield to lock the door. They dumped the bags on the table.

"This will keep us working for quite a while, boss," Yianni said proudly. "Should I tell Miss Cadfield?"

"Yes, then round up everyone. I need to speak to them."

A few minutes later, Miss Cadfield entered the cottage.

"Miss Cadfield, I must remind you to always keep the cottage locked. The treasures are in there."

"Oh! I had locked it this morning, but when I came to drop off the clean clothes, I must have forgotten." She gazed in awe at the bags of treasures. "Thank you for retrieving them. Should we go over them?"

"I suggest that we do that later. We do not want to attract too much attention to them. This is a rare collection, worth thousands, if not millions of drachmas."

"Oh!" Miss Cadfield's mouth was wide open. "I had no idea that they were so valuable."

She shut the door nervously, locking it behind her.

"At some point, we need to go over them and compare them to the ones in the logbook to make sure we have all of them."

"I'd be willing to do it," she said. "Please make sure that it is guarded."

Aristotle frowned, remembering last night's sounds outside the door. "I will see to it. If needed, Yianni and I could do guard duty."

After Aristotle left the cottage, he went to the workers. He raised his arm. "Listen everyone, since we didn't work last Monday, we will be working tomorrow, Saturday, half a day only. Plan to be here at seven. We should be finished before twelve. I will pay you extra."

When he paid the workers at four o'clock, and they had left for the camp, Aristotle decided it was time to visit Miss Cadfield. He wanted to check on the remaining treasures.

First, he arranged for Yianni and Alexander to work on the veranda, emptying the containers of pottery shards and small tools, and listing the daily inventory. Then, he visited Yianni's hut. He shut the door and then pushed his cot to the side, revealing his valise that was under it. He placed the valise against the door. Taking a tool from his tool kit that sat on the side, he dug carefully where the valise had lain, unearthing the bag of jewels he had buried previously in the ground.

Refilling the hole with dirt and placing everything back in its place, Aristotle left for the cottage carrying the bag of jewels and the logbook he had borrowed from Miss Cadfield.

"Miss Cadfield, it is me, Aristotle," Aristotle said, knocking on the door.

She unlocked the door. "Please come in."

The sight of all the glistening treasures on the table raised Aristotle's interest. It appeared that Miss Cadfield had been studying them.

He gave her the logbook.

"Did you bring the other treasures?" she asked.

He opened his bag and spilled its contents onto the table. "Not one was lost," he said proudly.

"Good." Miss Cadfield lifted a gold cup from the pile on the table and studied the images on it. "This looks like Hercules battling the lion. I wonder if these cups were made here in Nemea."

"Anything is possible. As you know, Hercules was a legend here. I was told by Yianni that the wine made in Nemea has been labeled the blood of Hercules," Aristotle replied.

Two other gold cups had bulls on them, and were similar to Dr. Cadfield's cup. They studied them some more.

They agreed that Aristotle would give the Archaeological Society half the treasures.

"The remaining treasures go to you, Miss Cadfield. You will be a rich woman after we take these to the antiquities dealer."

She appeared pleased, and then a shadow crossed her face. "Are you sure they are safe here?"

"I will personally guard the cottage tonight if Phillipa doesn't show up."

"Thank you."

"This one would suit you." Aristotle handed her a beautiful, gold necklace with many intricate designs that formed an upside pyramid. Their fingers touched.

She clasped it around her neck.

He gazed at the necklace, then at her. He caught his breath at her transformation. Was it the trick of the eye, or was the beautiful Helen of Troy staring back at him? In that priceless moment, he realized she meant more to him than the treasures that surrounded them. Her irresistible eyes, the color of a shimmering ocean, drew him to her. He leaned toward her, wanting to take her in his arms and kiss her.

Miss Cadfield stared at him with wide, startled eyes.

Someone pounded on the door, interrupting them.

Aristotle tensed, returning to reality. "Hide the treasures, quickly," he told her.

They shoved everything back into the bags.

"Boss!" Yianni was yelling and knocking on the door. "We have company."

Aristotle strode out of the cottage, shutting the door behind him. "Who is it?"

"The bandits. Somehow, they learned about Miss Cadfield and came to visit her. Phillipa just rode in with his brothers."

"I will inform Miss Cadfield," Aristotle said. When he returned to the cottage, he found Miss Cadfield standing, and clutching the table.

"Did Yianni say bandits?" she cried.

"They are not really bandits, just Phillipa and his brothers, but Yianni likes to call them bandits."

"Why are they here?"

"They came to see you," Aristotle said. "Let's get those treasures out of sight. They are not safe there."

"What about the oven? It is large enough to hold them."

The pounding on the door had her rushing to the oven with a bag. Aristotle took the other bag.

"Boss, don't leave them waiting!" Yianni shouted from the door.

"I'll be right there," Aristotle called out, feeling annoyed. He realized that Yianni was still fearful of the brothers, ever since their first meeting.

He swiftly helped push all the bags into the oven's cavity. He shut the oven's door. "This is not the safest place, but will do, until we leave for Athens tomorrow."

As they went outside, Miss Cadfield locked the door.

In the courtyard, Yianni was talking with the three men. They were dressed in dark clothing and stared at her boldly, almost akin to admiration. When they saw them, Yianni and the three men approached them.

"This is Miss Helena Cadfield," Aristotle said tightly. "These are our three guards; they are brothers. Phillipa Mavros is the oldest, and then there's Markos and Nikos."

Miss Cadfield bowed.

Phillipa took her hand and bent down gallantly, kissing it. She blushed, pulling her hand away.

Aristotle became uncomfortable. "How's your foot doing these days?" he said dryly.

"My foot? Hahaha," Phillipa said, grinning slyly. "Much better." He gazed boldly at Miss Cadfield. "Miss Cadfield, did you know that we are related?"

She shook her head, looking dazed.

"Your grandfather Nickos and my mother's father were first cousins. My grandfather was Phillipa Kallodaftis."

"Oh, I didn't know that," Miss Cadfield exclaimed, clasping her hands and appearing delighted. "Would you like to come in and have some tea?"

Everybody broke out laughing.

She laughed nervously also. "I'm sorry. Here, they don't drink tea, they drink coffee."

"It's somewhat late for that, anyway," Aristotle said dryly. He turned to the men. "Why don't you visit Miss Cadfield tomorrow for tea? We still have much work to do today."

"Yes, why don't you visit tomorrow late morning and we can talk about everything," Miss Cadfield said, smiling at them.

The three brothers came to her.

She held out her hand graciously, bowing as they took it.

"Pleased to meet you, Phillipa, and Markos, and I already have met Nikos." She shook hands with them.

Phillipa pulled Aristotle to the side. "Now that you are here, there's a matter I want to discuss with you," he said to him.

"What is it?"

"I came to get paid," he declared, puffing his chest like a peacock. "You only paid Nikos."

"I paid him because he was the only one working," Aristotle retorted. "You two have been shirking your duties."

"How can I help it? I had my lousy foot to take care of, and with Nikos coming here, Markos had to stay to take care of me and to do the chores around the house," Phillipa countered. "Besides, now that you've found the gold riches, there's enough money to go around. Eh, *Afenti*?" He winked.

"Who told you about the treasures?" Aristotle asked sharply.

"Do you think we are stupid?" Phillipa said, looking offended. "The word spreads around here like wildfire. Nikos may be young, but he is sharp. He has eyes and ears. Now that you have treasures, you will need to pay us double to guard it. You see, it is not safe here. I can easily go and steal it from under your nose, just like that." He snapped his fingers, his eyes gleaming.

"Yes, and I can notify all the antiquities dealers in Athens to be on the lookout for it, just like that."

"Hahaha. I like you, and won't do it. You need someone sitting outside the door, guarding it. You need someone like me."

"It'll be only for tonight. Tomorrow we are leaving for Athens in the afternoon."

"I'll guard the place tonight, and I can come with you when you go to Athens, for there are bandits on the roads. The word gets around quickly," Phillipa said, winking at him. "My brothers can guard the place while you are away."

After much haggling, Aristotle and Phillipa finally agreed on a price.

After the brothers left, Yianni joined Aristotle and Miss Cadfield. "Sorry, boss, but they somehow found out about it. I didn't tell them, I swear."

"That's all right. Nikos was working here, and he saw everything. Eventually, they would have found out. Have you finished your work?"

Yianni left to finish his work on the veranda.

"They're not that bad," Miss Cadfield said to Aristotle. "Just a little untamed."

"Just a little untamed?" Aristotle muttered. "They steal and are too friendly with their guns."

"Yes, but you hired them to guard the place," she reminded him.

"I know, and sometimes I think it was a mistake. It's like asking the wolves to guard the chicken coop," Aristotle grumbled.

"Oh, I wouldn't say that," Miss Cadfield said.

"I'd like to give you some advice, Miss Cadfield, about those boys. I wouldn't get too friendly with them. I don't know whether they're telling you the truth or not about their relation to you."

She appeared thoughtful. "My grandfather used to tell me stories, and I do remember hearing about a cousin named Phillipa."

"I have made arrangements for Phillipa to guard the cottage tonight. I will also check up on it periodically. Tomorrow, we will leave in the afternoon, after the workers finish. Phillipa offered to travel with us to Athens, to guard the riches."

She nodded.

He took her hands in his and looked earnestly at her. "You look worried."

"You know, having all this gold jewelry here is not easy. It is also a big responsibility transporting them to Athens. What if we get stopped by bandits during the night?"

"With Phillipa, Yianni, and me keeping guard, there shouldn't be a problem. You get a good night's sleep. Tomorrow will be a busy day."

CHAPTER 44

After Dr. Mastoras left, Helena packed her luggage for tomorrow, then dressed for bed, thinking about the treasures. She had never had so much gold in her possession before. With it came great responsibility. She was nervous about this night, and wondered if Phillipa would show up to guard the cottage. Lying on the bed, she reflected on all these things. Then she thought about Dr. Murphy.

If all went well, she would be rich when she returned to him in England. He would court her and then they would marry. It seemed so simple, but another thought clamored for attention. Who would take care of the property after she was gone?

As she dozed off, a tapping on her door aroused her awake. "Miss Cadfield," a man called out.

Helena arose, her heart beating rapidly. Could it be Dr. Mastoras? Or could it be a thief? She couldn't be too sure. She grabbed the cane that was near the bed, then hurried to the door and listened. She was not about to open the door at this time of night.

"Miss Cadfield?"

"Yes?"

"It's Phillipa. I will be outside guarding the cottage."

"Thank you, Phillipa. Goodnight."

She found it difficult to sleep after that, especially knowing that she had treasures in the cottage and a guard that could easily pass for a bandit guarding the cottage.

Instead, she paced the room, her anxiety mounting. She knew without a doubt that she should not have shown the chamber to Aristotle until the last minute. That way the treasures would have stayed safe in the west end all this time and no one would have known about them. She wouldn't have to worry about someone stealing them. That was probably the reason her father left the treasures there in the first place. She had not carefully thought out the consequences of her actions.

After much thought, Helena knew what she had to do. She took the bags of treasures out of the oven and spilled the contents on the table. According to Aristotle, half of them belonged to her and the other half belonged to the Archeological Society. Why not choose what she was to keep? Why wait until they went to Dr. Kostakis in Athens to separate them? According to the law, she had a right to half of them.

Helena separated the treasures, deciding what to keep and what to give. She noted everything that she did in the logbook. Afterwards, the two bags of jewels went back into the oven. Now, she had to find a place for her own treasures. She searched the cottage for places to hide them. It was a long time before she returned to bed.

* * *

Saturday morning at seven, Helena locked the cottage and trudged toward the excavation site. She was acutely aware that Phillipa was not around. She found Dr. Mastoras hard at work with the other workers at the west end. She approached him.

"How are you this fine morning, Miss Cadfield?"

"I had a difficult time sleeping last night," she admitted. She glanced around her. "Phillipa guarded the cottage last night, but I did not see him this morning."

"I came by twice last night to check on things and he was there, watching the place. He left a few minutes ago."

Helena felt relieved. "Oh, thank you."

"Did you lock the place as you left?"

"Of course."

He reminded her that she had invited Phillipa and his brothers for tea, and that this would be during the time that the workers were working.

"I am aware of that. I will work for a while, and then prepare the tea when they get here."

"Afterwards, we need to leave for Athens with the treasures. It will be a busy day today."

Helena joined Mrs. Selmani and her daughter, who were steadily working. They greeted her with smiles. Soon, Helena was hard at work. Her mind raced ahead, planning the trip back to Athens.

Around ten o'clock, Yianni came and spoke to Mrs. Selmani and Lule. "The boss asked that you work at the west end. The pieces need to be finished before we leave today."

"Yes, we can do it," Mrs. Selmani replied, nodding.

"I will help also," Helena offered, dusting her hands.

Yianni helped them carry the tools and necessary supplies to the west end and then left.

The women settled down to work.

Helena tensed when she saw Lucas approach Dr. Mastoras, who was working nearby. She overheard their conversation.

"Dr. Mastoras, I learned that an uncle of mine died, and we need to be at the funeral today," Lucas told him. "We cannot stay longer."

"May his memory be eternal," Dr. Mastoras said. He dusted his hands and paid them.

Shortly after Lucas and his sons left, there was some commotion and someone shouted. Helena looked up.

A man dressed in a brown suit had arrived, and Dr. Mastoras had gone to greet him. They stood on the veranda, laughing and talking. Helena recognized him to be Dr. Ludwig Heinz. He was deep in conversation with Dr. Mastoras and did not notice her or glance her way. She realized that she probably looked like all the other workers.

After several minutes, she saw the two men walking toward her direction. They were discussing archaeological topics in German.

* * *

Aristotle was surprised to see his friend Ludwig. They talked about the excavation site, but soon the conversation had veered toward Miss Heinz. Her name always seemed to creep into their conversations.

"Ever since you left for Nemea, Greta has been moping. I think she is in love with you, my friend, but don't let her know I told you," Dr. Heinz said.

Aristotle was struck by the admission. "Come now. You said the same thing about all my female acquaintances, that they were in love with me. Be serious. This is your sister you are talking about. She who has had several beaus and an equal number of offers of marriage."

"Yes, and she did not accept any. You are the reason why. I do not lie. You seem to have this effect over women," Ludwig said, laughing, "but I have news for you."

"Yes?"

Ludwig's eyes twinkled. "Greta is here."

"Here? Where?" Aristotle glanced quickly around, then caught Miss Cadfield's gaze. It was apparent that she had been staring at them. He realized that he had been in his own little world and had forgotten all about her. He would need to introduce her at some point.

Dr. Heinz laughed. "Yes, she will be here any minute. I rode ahead. She is coming with a guide and Aunt Frieda and Uncle Gustav. You remember them. They were at the ball last week. Everyone heard about your dig at Nemea and wanted to see this ancient site of yours. We only plan to stay a few hours and return to Corinth, and then Athens."

"Splendid. It would be good to see everyone again. We were planning to return to Athens ourselves and it would be good to have company." Aristotle led Ludwig to Miss Cadfield. "You've already met Miss Cadfield. She is now the owner of this property."

Dr. Heinz greeted Miss Cadfield, and Aristotle noticed her blushing as she meticulously wiped her hands on a wet cloth, then rose and curtsied.

"It is my pleasure to see you again, Miss Cadfield," Dr. Heinz said in English, appearing pleasantly surprised. "I was not aware of your affiliation with this property. So, you are the owner?"

She explained the connection. "I have filed the necessary papers to claim it."

"Ahh, that is good to hear," he said, smiling.

A group of people rode up with their horses, and Aristotle saw Miss Heinz in that group. "If you will excuse us, Miss Cadfield," he said, bowing.

* * *

Helena watched in dismay as Dr. Mastoras strolled from the work site, talking amiably with Dr. Heinz, heading toward Miss Heinz's group. Why did it bother her? Was she jealous of Miss Heinz, or was she feeling awkward that she was not dressed properly to meet them? If she had known that they would be visiting, she would have dressed in presentable attire and paid more attention to her hair.

She pushed the stray strands of hair away from her face, feeling perplexed. No, it was more than that. This man, Dr. Mastoras, had evoked some importance in her life, and she could not ignore the pangs of jealousy.

Had she constructed a world in which he had become its center? How foolish of her to be falling in love with the wrong man. Before she came to Greece, her thoughts had revolved around Dr. Murphy and living in Oxford. Dr. Mastoras did not really fit into that English world of hers, yet she had become comfortable with him, and with this place.

Determined not to let him and his friends upset her, Helena sat back down, resuming her work, while stealing glances at them.

Laughter erupted from the group as they strolled toward them, talking animatedly. Standing next to Dr. Heinz, was Gustav Heinz, a well-dressed older man and his wife, Frieda, an equally well-dressed plump woman. Helena had met them through the Stirlings, but they knew her as a governess.

Next to Frieda stood Miss Greta Heinz. She was dressed in the latest fashions and wore a large, white hat with yellow ribbons and yellow feathers, and her face glowed with health and radiance. She could easily have arrived from Paris. She smiled at Dr. Mastoras in an adoring manner as he walked alongside her, holding her elbow.

Helena stared in dismay at them. They made a handsome couple. Dr. Mastoras seemed unable to get his eyes off that woman. A small fire raged in Helena's chest.

"You are the woman of this place. You must go and greet your guests," Mrs. Selmani told Helena fiercely.

Helena shook her head, fighting an inward battle to remain calm. "They are Dr. Mastoras's friends. They came to see him, not me."

"It is not right for Dr. Mastoras to be making eyes at this woman. You love him and he loves you," Lule retorted. "If I were you, I would scratch her eyes out."

Helena smiled at Lule and Mrs. Selmani. "Thank you, but I believe that he is engaged to this woman, and besides, I have my own suitor back in England."

The two women fell silent and Helena resumed her work, trying to keep her emotions under control.

CHAPTER 45

Dr. Mastoras and his group approached Helena's area. They stood on the marble pavement close to her, talking.

"At first, we worked on the east end," Dr. Mastoras said, speaking in German, and pointing to that section, "and did not find much of value there, so now we are expanding an opening in this west end and are coming across promising results."

Helena was relieved that he did not mention her treasures. She noticed the clean hemline of Miss Heinz' pale, beige day coat with her chiffon, yellow dress peeking out from under it. Her dainty, white slippers seemed out of place in this rough, dirty area.

Helena looked down at her clothing and dirty hands. She tucked her big, old shoes under her dress.

"If you come closer, you can see some steps that have been excavated." Dr. Mastoras pointed down toward the stairwell that they had been working on. "There, do you see them?"

"Oh, how wonderful. What is down there?" Miss Heinz asked, peering down with the others. "I suppose some poor, dead soul."

Frieda Heinz tittered nervously.

"Actually, someone's tomb might be down there, probably of royalty because of the size of the chamber, but we haven't explored everything yet. We have found some amphorae and some artifacts. There are also beautiful designs of Minoan art on the walls."

"Minoan art? That dates it to thousands of years old. I would like to go and look at it," Dr. Heinz said, appearing excited.

"I would, too, but I'm afraid I'm not dressed for it," Miss Heinz said. She continued speaking in that confident air. "We can learn so much from the past. It is so exciting! If I were a man, I would have become an archaeologist, like my brother."

At one point, Helena sensed Miss Heinz's eyes on her and she looked up. Miss Heinz's contempt was obvious as she looked away. Helena's pride took over. She did not care what Miss Heinz thought. She was doing valuable work on her property.

"It is amazing how these simple people can work like this all day, doing so much labor," Miss Heinz commented in German.

"Not everyone has your wealth. They work so that they get paid, my dear," replied Mrs. Freda Heinz in German.

"Without their help, where would archaeologists like Aris and I be?" Dr. Heinz reminded his sister.

"I'm afraid that Greece doesn't provide many job opportunities, so they grab whatever they can get," D. Mastoras told her.

"Yes, any opportunity," Miss Heinz said, pulling her dress closer to her as she stared at Helena in a calculating manner.

Helena flushed when she heard Miss Heinz's remarks. *I need to make the introductions.* Mindful of Mrs. Selmani's nudges Helena wiped her hands on the wet cloth and arose. She realized that she probably looked like the other Albanian workers there, for Mr. Gustav and his wife had not recognized her.

Before she could say anything, Dr. Mastoras spoke to them in German, gesturing toward her. "I wish to inform you that Miss Cadfield is the new owner of this property. She has graciously allowed us to continue excavating and has even gotten involved in the project."

Miss Heinz observed her in a superior manner, raising an arched eyebrow.

Dr. Mastoras gazed at Helena. "Miss Cadfield, would you care to join us?" he asked in English.

Helena pulled her shoulders back and walked toward them as if she were dressed in the finest clothes and meeting guests at Cadfield House. Miss Heinz's supercilious expression was not lost on her. She curtsied elegantly.

"I thank you for visiting us today. I recognize all of you, although we met under different circumstances in Athens," Helena said in English, smiling. "Please excuse my appearance. I was working alongside the workers so we could finish early today and was not expecting any guests."

"If I am not mistaken, Miss Cadfield, weren't you Miss Stirling's governess?" Mrs. Frieda Heinz asked stiffly.

Helena ignored her question. "This property belonged to my family, and when my late father, Dr. Cadfield, passed away, I inherited it. Dr. Mastoras was kind enough to bring me here to see the work that was being done on it."

Helena glanced at Miss Heinz, expecting her to add some caustic remark. She did not have long to wait.

"How could this be? How could a mere governess turn around and own such a valuable piece of property?" Miss Heinz asked, appearing offended.

Helena felt her face flush, for she understood perfectly what had been said in German. She pretended not to understand.

Silence reigned for a few moments.

"Dear sister, don't you see? She is no longer the governess. She owns this property. Here in Greece, the property is handed down from mother to daughter," Dr. Heinz told his sister.

"He is right, Miss Heinz." Dr. Mastoras turned and spoke to the group. "Feel free to walk around, but please be careful not to fall into the trench."

Everyone laughed.

Helena was reminded of her duties as a hostess. In England, she would have been busy serving tea, and why not here? This was her home. "I must see about the refreshments," she told Dr. Mastoras.

"Thank you."

"Would you like coffee or tea?" Helena asked him, feeling subdued.

He asked the group.

"Oh, you have tea!" Miss Heinz exclaimed, clasping her hands.

"Yes, and some nice refreshments to go along with it," Dr. Mastoras offered.

"Tea would be wonderful," Mrs. Frieda Heinz replied, and everyone concurred.

"Aris, can we go down and have a look?" Dr. Heinz asked him.

While the group strolled around, the two men went down the stairwell to see the chamber.

* * *

Helena asked Mrs. Selmani and Lule to help with the refreshments. "I will also need to change into something more presentable."

As they walked to the cottage, they discussed what they would make for the guests.

Once in the cottage, the women began preparing the refreshments.

Yianni pounded on the door. "Miss Cadfield!"

Helena went to the door and greeted him. "Yes, Yianni?"

"You have more visitors," he said, nodding his head toward the courtyard.

In the courtyard, still on their horses were her cousins, the three bandits. She had forgotten that she had invited them over for tea.

Feeling flustered, Helena wiped her hands and went out to greet them.

Phillipa and his brothers were in a good mood, joking and laughing. They wore better clothing today and their weapons were hidden under their vests. They had even shaved their faces.

"Hello, sweet cousin," Phillipa said, grinning at her as he came and smacked a kiss on her cheek. "We came for tea."

Before she could say anything, he thrust a bunch of dead rabbits at her. Their legs were tied together with rope. "They make good stew."

"Thank you. Why don't you see to your horses? We will be serving tea on the veranda shortly," Helena said, trying not to recoil as she took them. *Why me? Why now?*

She fled into the cottage before Phillipa could respond. Although she had hunted rabbits with her father, the cook had cleaned and skinned them. She knew nothing about preparing and cooking rabbits.

Mrs. Selmani and her daughter were working steadily, slicing the cheese and bread, and arranging the appetizers on the plates.

"Mrs. Selmani, could these rabbits be used for the meal tonight?" Helena asked her, lifting up the rabbits.

Mrs. Selmani gave her a pleased look. "They would make a nice rabbit stew. We will take these down to the camp. I will also bring you some yogurt cake for your company."

She left with Lule and the rabbits.

Helena scrubbed her hands clean, trying to remove the smell of the dead rabbits. She washed and dressed into her formal, black dress in the small room. She combed her hair, sweeping it up. Feeling a little bit better, she focused on making the tea. First, she must heat the oven.

She opened the oven to place the wood in it and saw the bags of jewels there. She sucked in her breath. She had forgotten all about them.

What was she going to do? The German group and her cousins were expecting tea. She could not leave the treasures in the oven. The oven would get too hot. They had to be removed.

Helena locked the door. Her heart pounding, she removed the bags of treasures from the oven. She must think quickly where to put them. The cottage was small and concealing the bags would be difficult.

Someone knocked on the door. "Cousin!" Phillipa called.

"I'll be right there!" Helena called out, feeling frantic. She turned and thrust the two bags in the linen shelf behind her, burrowing them in between the blankets and linen that was there. Sweating, her hands clammy, she straightened the blankets and the linen.

Taking a deep breath, she calmly went and unlocked the door.

Phillipa gestured to the horses in the courtyard. "Those are fine horses. Are they yours?"

"No. They belong to friends of Dr. Mastoras, from Germany. Meanwhile, could you and your brothers carry the two benches from the stall and place them on the veranda?" Helena asked Phillipa.

Phillipa complied.

Mrs. Selmani and Lule returned with a tray of yogurt cake, and helped Helena prepare the table on the veranda. They carried trays filled with cups and plates, goat cheese and crusty bread, yogurt cake, grape jam, biscuits, honey, olives, and sweet figs. Helena noticed that Dr. Mastoras and Dr. Heinz had not come out of the chamber and Miss Heinz and the others stood chatting near the west end.

Meanwhile, the cousins had brought the benches to the table and were already seated. Yianni had joined them. Phillipa gazed boldly at Lule, as she helped prepare the table.

Helena talked with Phillipa. "Grandfather Nickos mentioned a cousin Phillipa, who fought in the war. Was he related to you?"

"That was my grandfather." Phillipa talked proudly about him.

At some point, Helena asked Yianni to inform Miss Heinz and her group to meet them on the veranda for tea.

CHAPTER 46

The table was laden with refreshments and tea by the time Miss Heinz and the group arrived on the veranda with Yianni.

Miss Heinz immediately became the focus of attention, as all three brothers ogled her, grinning wickedly. She stared crossly at her plate, ignoring them as they tried in vain to gain her attention.

Dr. Mastoras and Dr. Heinz returned shortly from exploring the west end chamber and joined them.

Helena introduced the brothers to their guests, and Dr. Mastoras translated her Greek introduction into German. He then introduced his guests to the brothers.

Helena served the tea as graciously as she could, aware that Dr. Heinz was gazing at her appreciatively, as she served him the warm brew. "Thank you, Miss Cadfield."

"It is so beautiful here and refreshingly simple. Don't you feel as if you are living your life in the past, and not in the moment?" Miss Heinz asked Dr. Mastoras in German, batting her long eyelashes at him.

"Yes, you can say that," Dr. Mastoras replied, "but I have a responsibility in unearthing our heritage and bringing it to the present moment. Remember, I am part Greek."

Phillipa jabbed Dr. Mastoras. "*Eh,* what did she say? We don't understand her language."

Dr. Mastoras translated her words, and the three brothers nodded appreciatively at Miss Heinz.

"You must love your work, Dr. Mastoras," Mrs. Frieda Heinz cried, clasping her plump hands. "Being away from all the troubles and sorrows of our world and escaping for a while. This is truly a utopian world." She received the tea from Helena. "Thank you, my dear."

Dr. Mastoras translated what Mrs. Frieda Heinz had said to the bandits. "Yes, Mrs. Heinz, as a matter of fact, it is a utopian world," he answered.

"It's wonderful up here," Phillipa said, flourishing a knife from his belt. He stuck its pointed tip into the round cheese and popped the cheese morsel in his mouth. He then pointed the knife up in the air.

Everyone gasped. Helena stopped pouring the tea and stared with mouth wide open. Her cousin's crude behavior shook her to the core. All her sensibilities were being challenged today. *First, the dead rabbits, and now this.*

Phillipa paused and then chuckled wickedly. He jabbed the knife in the air once more. "There is nothing better than this sky. On a clear day, you can see far and wide."

Phillipa's brothers nodded, and took their knives and jabbed at their cheese, relishing the food.

Helena finished serving the tea, trying to remain composed after her cousins' behavior. Her knees were about to give way. *Am I going to faint?* She nervously glanced around for a seat.

"*Xadelfaki*, come, sit here," Phillipa said to Helena, gesturing for her to sit next to him.

Trying to act calm, Helena sat gingerly on the edge of the bench. On her other side sat Dr. Mastoras.

"I would love to live here for a while and get away from it all. It's terribly romantic," Miss Heinz was saying.

"Oh, Greta, you've been saying that ever since we came to Greece," Dr. Heinz retorted.

"Ludwig!" Mrs. Frieda Heinz scolded him. "Your sister is a sensitive soul and appreciates things more deeply than others."

"I thank you, Aunt Frieda, for coming to my aid," Miss Heinz said, laughing prettily. "I'm afraid both of you are right. Aris, what do you think? Should I remain here and learn to become a Greek peasant, like Miss Cadfield?"

"Greta." Dr. Heinz glared at his sister.

Helena looked sharply at Miss Heinz, realizing that her dart was intentional. Feeling humiliated, she lowered her eyes, pretending she had not heard it.

"*Eh*, cousin, what's the matter?" Phillipa asked Helena in Greek, poking her with his elbow. "Why aren't you talking? Why are you letting this princess lead the conversation?"

"It's all right," Helena answered him quietly, trying to remain calm as she sipped her tea. "This is how we treat our guests in England, with respect."

"Oh?" Phillipa said, jabbing a piece of bread with his knife. "Your people in England are too soft! We do not do things that way around here. If someone insults us, we kill them."

Helena winced at Phillipa's vulgar boast, realizing that even without understanding Miss Heinz's foreign words, he had picked up her barb.

"German society would surely miss you," Dr. Mastoras was telling Miss Heinz, "but I wouldn't call Miss Cadfield a Greek peasant, but rather a Greek goddess."

Everyone laughed and Helena blushed once more.

"*Eh*, cousin, why are they laughing?" Phillipa said, chuckling.

Helena explained it to him.

"He is right. You are a goddess!" Phillipa cried in Greek. He jumped up and beaming, lifted a cup and faced Helena. "Let's give a toast to Helena, for her beauty, and her grace!" He downed the brew and smacked a kiss on Helena's cheek.

Helena blushed at this public display of affection by her cousin. Dr. Mastoras translated Phillipa's speech to the Germans. Everyone lifted their cups, except Miss Heinz.

Alexander came and spoke quietly to Dr. Mastoras.

"Phillipa, you and your brothers go and line up the workers," Dr. Mastoras said to Phillipa.

"Don't forget, you pay us double from now on," Phillipa said to him, leaving the table and heading for the site with his brothers.

"Who were these men, Aris?" Miss Heinz asked in German, shuddering. "I mean, jabbing the cheese with the knife? How vulgar and disgusting. Who knows where that knife has been?"

Helena felt the blood rise to her head when she heard this. Miss Heinz had gone too far.

"These mountain men are survivors of the revolutionary war. They lost their families and had to be tough in order to survive. Because of men like these, our country is free," Dr. Mastoras replied tightly. He arose. "Now I must excuse myself. I need to take care of the workers. I'll be back soon."

After finishing his task, Dr. Mastoras returned promptly to the group and began a discussion with Dr. Heinz in German.

"I was amazed at the frescoes down in the west end. You mentioned that they were Minoan. What have you concluded about their origins? According to the philologist, Karl Hoeck of the

University of Gottingen, he coined the Minoans, or ancient Cretans, as non-Hellenic in origin," Dr. Heinz said.

"Yes, but another esteemed scholar, Karl Muller at Gottingen, believes that the Minoans were Greek and had migrated from Thessaly to Crete and then to the Aegean. I tend to think the same. As we gain more evidence, we can make better decisions."

They continued their discussion.

"During the Bronze Age, I believe that not only the Minoans existed, but also the Mycenaeans, as described in Homer's epic poem, *The Iliad*," Dr. Mastoras said.

"Do you think King Meneleus and Helen of Troy really existed?" Dr. Heinz asked him.

"Why not? The kings often built fortified palaces on top of hills, as is obvious here, for we are up on a hill and there are signs of fortification here," Dr. Mastoras replied.

"Like the Acropolis in Athens," Helena said.

The men turned and looked at her with surprise. She realized that she had spoken in German.

"Do you speak German?" Dr. Heinz asked her in German.

"A little. My father taught it to me," Helena replied.

"I would like some tea," Miss Heinz told her coldly in German.

As Helena poured the tea into Miss Heinz's cup, she was so tired that her hand trembled and the tea spilled on her beautiful clothing.

"How careless of you," Miss Heinz retorted, jumping up and wiping her dress furiously.

"I'm terribly sorry. I will bring a cloth to wipe it with," Helena cried. She had done her first gaffe as a hostess, something that would have earned her a frown by the mistress in the boarding school in Paris.

When Helena returned with the wet cloth, she was feeling troubled. She had found the cottage unlocked, and could not find the key. She had searched frantically for it, but to no avail. Even worse, what she saw had made her sick to her stomach. *Someone had removed the linen and blanket. The bags of jewels were gone.*

CHAPTER 47

Helena gave the cloth to Miss Heinz, who was having a conversation with Dr. Mastoras. Miss Heinz took it without thanking her. All the workers had left, including Mrs. Selmani, Lule, and the bandit brothers. The only people remaining were the guests on the veranda.

It is imperative that I speak to Dr. Mastoras.

"Where are you staying while working here?" Miss Heinz asked Dr. Mastoras, dabbing her dress with the wet cloth.

"We've built a wooden hut behind the stall. Miss Cadfield is using the cottage while she is here."

"Dr. Mastoras, I need to speak to you," Helena said, but he did not seem to hear her, having his undivided attention on Miss Heinz. Helena bit her lip, wondering how she was going to get through to him.

"What about the workers? Where do they stay?" Dr. Heinz asked him.

"Down in the camp." Dr. Mastoras pointed in the direction. "Most of them live in Nemea and beyond, but remain at the camp during the week. On the weekends, when I leave for Athens, they return to their homes or visit family."

"Dr. Mastoras, if you don't mind my asking you, where do you live when you're not working on this site? Do you have a familial home somewhere?" Frieda Heinz asked him.

"In Athens, a few minutes from the Acropolis. Unfortunately, it was torn down during the revolution with the Ottoman Turks, and a friend of the family, Barba Manolis, took me there to see it recently. It is like this area, mostly rubble. I have already begun the process of rebuilding it," Dr. Mastoras said.

"How exciting!" Miss Heinz exclaimed. "You could probably see the Acropolis, being so close by. I would love to see it again."

"Dr. Mastoras, I must speak to you," Helena repeated. She needed to inform him about the lost treasures in private. She was beginning to feel invisible.

"I'm pleased you can come to Athens with us," Miss Heinz said to Dr. Mastoras. "We're only here for a fortnight and then back to Germany. It would be a shame to leave without spending more time with you. Do you plan to visit Germany soon?"

"To be honest, it may be some time before I visit Germany again."

"We'll have to visit you, then," Miss Heinz said playfully.

"It looks like rain," Dr. Heinz said, looking at the gray clouds. "We should prepare to leave."

Dr. Mastoras turned to Miss Cadfield. "Miss Cadfield, I think you had better get ready for the trip," he said to her.

"Oh, she's coming, too?" Miss Heinz asked, looking surprised.

"Dr. Mastoras, I need to speak to you," Helena said to him, her mouth forming a thin line.

"All right, Miss Cadfield," he said, with furrowed brow. He excused himself and walked with Helena to the cottage. She opened the door.

"Why is it unlocked, Miss Cadfield? We had an agreement to keep it locked."

Helena quivered under his troubled gaze. "I don't know how it happened, but I lost the key, and the treasures are--" She couldn't finish her sentence, but broke down crying.

He grabbed her arms. "Tell me, what happened?"

"The treasures, they are gone," she said, sobbing.

"They are gone?" he shouted, appearing dazed. He hastened to the oven and swung the door open. He stared at the empty oven. "Why didn't you have the place locked?"

"I did. At first. But I had to make the tea for your guests. Remember?" she said,

"My God, the tea!" he shouted. "You had to remove the bags to heat the oven. Where did you put them?"

"In the linen shelf, across from the oven. I had covered them with linen and blankets, but when I came to get a cloth to clean the spill from Miss Heinz' dress, I found the door unlocked and the key was missing. That is when I found the treasures gone.

Angry emotions played on his face, his jaw clenched. "You were supposed to lock the cottage," he growled, his fists clenched. "What an idiotic thing to do."

Helena felt the blood rise to her head. *How dare he say that about me?*

"If you had kept your promise to guard this place, none of this would have happened. Only you were too busy serenading Miss Heinz and her group to notice if anyone stole anything."

Dr. Mastoras sighed, looking defeated. "You are right," he finally said. "I should have been more careful in guarding this place. Their visit caught me off guard."

"It was premature for us to have taken the treasures out and stored them inside the cottage."

"Maybe," he said. "Will you forgive me, Miss Cadfield?" He gazed at her apologetically. "I will do my best to retrieve them. You have my word."

Helena's anger dissipated when she heard his admission. "I also am sorry for my unladylike outburst," she mumbled contritely.

She was aware of his body close to hers, and his beautiful eyes tenderly gazing back at her. He leaned toward her. Helena could not ignore the rush of warmness coursing through her body. She shivered slightly at the power this man had over her. If they hadn't exchanged angry remarks moments ago, she would have thought that he was going to kiss her. She stumbled backward.

He grabbed her, breaking her fall.

Dr. Mastoras pulled her close to him, embracing her. "I guess my anger got the best of me, too," he whispered, nuzzling her neck.

Helena trembled in his arms as he slowly turned his face toward her and kissed her softly, causing her knees to weaken. It was a pleasant feeling to be kissed, she thought. Then his kiss became more urgent and she felt his body pressing against hers. Her breath became shallow. She felt hot all over. *What was happening to her?*

She had never felt this way about a man before.

Helena wanted to be with him forever and talk about the sun and the moon, about Homer and about medicine. She wanted him to tell her that he loved her. She wanted him to be her friend, someone she could turn to, and someone she could love.

Then she remembered Dr. Murphy and her plan to return to him.

"Please," she said, pulling away shakily. A part of her felt guilty because she wanted to remain in his arms. "You forget that I have Dr. Murphy waiting my return."

"Ah, yes, Dr. Murphy," he said bitterly." Miss Cadfield, you cannot ignore what just happened between us."

Helena blushed, her eyes gazing into his angry eyes. She could not deny it. "I…I have developed feelings for you," she said shakily.

Dr. Mastoras's face softened. "I also for you," he said, looking hopeful. "Don't go back. Remain here with me. We can make a life together."

Helena stared at him. "Are you proposing to me?" she asked.

He nodded slowly, smiling that special way.

Helena felt light as a feather. She pictured herself with him, and then reality hit. *I have loved Dr. Murphy all these years, and he's waiting for me.* "I thank you for the proposal of marriage, and I will cherish this moment for the rest of my life, but I must honor my promise to Dr. Murphy. I met him before I met you."

She glimpsed the hurt in Dr. Mastoras's eyes before he averted his gaze. His show of pain pierced her heart. She did not want to hurt him, but what else could she do?

"I am sorry," she mumbled, feeling sad. *Everything was going wrong.* "It's an English thing."

"Let's not talk about your English ways," he countered. "How will you return to England without your treasures?"

She blinked, her mind racing ahead. "Oh! I forgot about my treasures. I forgot to see if they were still here."

"Please explain yourself," he said warily.

"Last night, I had the foresight to separate *my* half of the treasures from the state's treasures. I placed the state's treasures in the oven, and put my half in my luggage," she informed him. "I logged them in the book, so we know which ones are mine."

Feeling excited, Helena rushed to the bed and looked underneath. "I don't know if they are here. They might also be stolen." She pulled the valise from under the bed and opened it.

"You stored your share of the jewels in there?" Aristotle asked, looking incredulous.

"Yes," she said, searching inside.

CHAPTER 48

Helena pulled out the wrapped jewels from the valise and triumphantly showed them to him.

Dr. Mastoras appeared stunned. "Congratulations, Miss Cadfield, for your carefully designed plan," he said bitterly. "Your intuition served you well. Now you can return to England after this."

Helena suddenly felt the weight of the lost treasures' burden on this man's shoulders. He had paid everything out of his pocket, and on top of it, was responsible for the stolen treasures.

"The missing jewels belong to the Archaeological Society, and I must be off to search for them," he said tensely, heading out the door.

"Wait," she said, bounding toward him. "We can split these treasures. This way I can pay you for your services and you have something to show the society for your efforts."

He turned to look at her, their eyes locking.

"You should be paid for your work," she insisted.

He looked down, appearing thoughtful. He slowly shook his head. "No, these belong rightfully to you. I promised you that they would be safe under my care, and I intend to keep that promise. I will search for them until I find them. I will receive my payment only then."

Helena handed him the logbook. "This will help you. It lists all the treasures I kept and which ones belong to the society."

He thanked her as he took it. Their fingers touched.

"Should I wait until you find the rest of the treasures?"

"That is my responsibility. You will return to England with your wealth and marry your English doctor."

She felt elated at his noble gesture and deflated at the same time. For some reason, she did not want to leave him like this. Not under these circumstances. "What would you do if you did not find the remaining treasures? Would you come all the way to England to claim your half?" She waited for his answer.

His jaws tensed. He appeared as if he were trying to control some emotion. "Please do not tease me, Miss Cadfield," he retorted. "I will arrange for you to travel with Yianni. Pack your valise well and get ready to leave for Athens. Do not mention anything about your share of the treasures to him. I don't want him or anyone else knowing that you have them."

Dr. Mastoras left before she could respond.

Helena's heart tore in little pieces as he walked out the door. *I might never see him again.* Besides, if she were in England, how would she learn whether he had retrieved the treasures? What a mess she had made of things.

* * *

Aristotle strode to the group on the veranda, feeling shaken from the emotional encounter with Miss Cadfield. He had felt her body trembling when he took her in his arms. His pent-up emotions for her, buried these days under layers of formality and societal norms, were finally released. She said that she had feelings for him, yet she had spurned him for Dr. Murphy. He not only had lost the treasures, but he was also losing her as well.

"I'm afraid I won't be able to travel with you today," Aristotle said to his German friends. "Something serious has come up and I must stay here."

Miss Heinz appeared furious. "Aris, could I speak to you for a moment?" she asked. "Privately."

"I don't have much time, really I don't," Aristotle said.

She pulled on his arm. "This is important."

They walked away from the group toward the site. When they reached the border of the property, she stopped and looked at him.

Aristotle felt Miss Heinz's eyes sizing him up, and at the same time, his thoughts were on Miss Cadfield and the stolen treasures. He was anxious to go after the thief, but Miss Heinz's anger deserved attention. He had never seen her this agitated before.

"Am I to suppose that you are staying behind for that vixen?" Miss Heinz asked. Her voice was shrill and her eyes flashed.

Aristotle tensed. "She is not a vixen," he said tightly.

"I came all the way to see you from Germany and this is the way you treat me? You know that I have loved you all these years, and you led me to think we would be married one day. Why, Aris, why are you doing this to me?"

Aristotle was surprised by her outburst. "It was you who had said we would be married, not me," he said. "How could I take you seriously when you were always flirting with other men? For all I know, you may have told them the same thing."

"Flirting is harmless," she said, shrugging, "but marriage is another thing. We have shared many good times together and laughed so much together. How could I not believe that you were the man for me?"

Aristotle's jaw tightened. He noticed the tears in her eyes. She was making it difficult, for he did not want to hurt her feelings.

"Yes, we've known each other for many years, and I've always been fond of you, but--" he said.

"I knew you had feelings for me," Miss Heinz interjected, clinging to him.

"Yes, but not the way you think. All these years I saw you more as a younger sister, the sister I never had. It has been a good friendship." He put his hand up to his eyes, remembering his little sister who was lost in the war, trying to check his emotions.

"Oh, Aris, I know about your little sister, you had told me about her once," Miss Heinz said, suddenly softening. "Is that how you've felt toward me all these years, only as a sister? All you had to do was ask for my love, and I would have flown willingly into your arms. Can't you see that I have loved you all these years?"

Aristotle gazed into her beautiful eyes realizing that she really meant it. He could feel her soft body pressed against his and it was difficult to tear his gaze away from hers. She leaned closer to him, as if to kiss him. He had never kissed her, other than a peck on the forehead or cheek. The temptation was great, but Miss Cadfield's kiss was fresh in his mind. *I know what I must do.*

He pushed Miss Heinz gently away from him.

"Please, let us remain friends."

Her face appeared distorted as she shed angry tears.

Aristotle turned and strode away.

Ludwig approached him. "We must be going, Aris. Is everything all right?"

"I'm sorry, my friend, but I cannot stop to talk. Something urgent has arisen and I must attend to it immediately. Have a safe journey, and please take good care of your sister."

Aristotle headed toward the stable. He wanted to catch Phillipa and his brothers before they left. They were talking with each other in the courtyard.

He told Phillipa about the stolen treasures.

"How dare they? Right under our noses," Phillipa said, scowling. "Lucas and his sons are the culprits. We'll take care of them, for sure."

"Wait, we are not certain who did it. First, you and your brothers go down to the camp and ask around. I will join you shortly." Aristotle looked around for Yianni, but didn't see him. He hurried to the hut and found him preparing his luggage. He told him what had happened.

Yianni broke out in a sweat, his eyes bulging with fear. "Oh, boss, that is bad news."

"Did you see anyone or anything suspicious during that time?"

"No, boss," he said shaking his head. "I always thought it was Lucas."

"Hmm," Aristotle said, recalling Miss Cadfield's similar suspicions about the man and thinking about what Phillipa had said earlier. Maybe he should have listened to her. "I will round up some men to search for the thief and the stolen treasures. Have you prepared the artifacts? Is the wagon ready?"

"Yes, boss. I placed the artifacts in the wagon this morning, and even covered everything with a blanket, in case it rained."

"Good. Listen to me carefully. First you will take Miss Cadfield to Athens and drop her off at the Stirling residence and--"

"Oh, boss," Yianni interjected. "Do I have to?"

"Yes, and you must hurry before it rains. Traveling becomes almost impossible on these dirt roads. You will help her with her baggage, and then unload the artifacts in Dr. Kostakis's storage facility." Aristotle pulled out some notes from his pocket. "Here is extra payment for your help."

Yianni took the notes and counted them. He whistled his appreciation when he saw the amount.

"That also includes the fare for you and Miss Cadfield's stay at the Corinthian Inn. You make sure she has her own room. When you reach Athens, you will drop her off at the Stirling's. Do not try and have a conversation with her, since she will be unchaperoned, and promise me that you will behave a perfect gentleman."

"Of course, boss, and after that, I am to take the artifacts to Dr. Kostakis to store in his basement," Yianni said, pocketing the money.

"Good," Aristotle said, patting him gratefully on the back. "Don't tell Dr. Kostakis about the stolen treasures. Leave that up to me. Now I must hurry."

CHAPTER 49

Aristotle met Phillipa and his brothers down at the Albanian camp. There, he interrogated Mrs. Selmani and her daughter Lule. The mother appeared distressed and did not know what was going on.

"I know nothing about the treasures," Mrs. Selmani pleaded. "Miss Cadfield was in charge of the oven. We did not go near it. We were only preparing the plates and the food. Please, believe me. We had nothing to do with it."

They searched the tents and everyone in the camp. It had begun to drizzle as Aristotle exited one of the tents.

"Dr. Mastoras, Dr. Mastoras."

Aristotle turned and saw Lule approaching him. She held a pair of long, gold earrings in her hand.

She handed them to him.

Aristotle whistled when he saw what Lule had given him. He recognized them. *A pair like these belonged to the stolen treasures.*

"I was given these earrings by Stephanos, the older son of Lucas, as a gift right after we returned from the site. When I asked him where he got them from, he just laughed and told me not to worry. Then he and his father and brother left."

"When was this?" Aristotle asked.

"Not too long ago. Maybe a half hour ago?" Lule said, looking worried.

"Yes, I remember," Mrs. Selmani said. "I was surprised to see Lucas and his sons here when we returned. I thought they had said they were going to a funeral, but they were still around. When I saw one of his sons approaching my daughter, I did not like that, so I hurried toward them, but he had already left."

She turned toward her daughter, appearing distraught. "Lule, why did you not tell me that he had given you a gift?"

"He made me promise not to tell anyone, but--" Lule looked at Phillipa, as if seeking his forgiveness. "I don't want stolen gifts."

Phillipa grinned at her. "You did the right thing."

"Come, Phillipa," Aristotle said with renewed energy. "We have no time to waste. Let's round up some men and go to Lucas's house."

"Yes, and we'll teach that thief a lesson. I know where he lives."

"We will come with you," Alexander said. "My youngest son is friends with Lucas's youngest son, Giorgios. Maybe he can talk him into telling the truth."

In a short amount of time, Aristotle, the three bandits, Alexander and his sons rode on horseback into the rain heading toward Lucas's house, intent on capturing him and the treasures.

It was a difficult journey for the group, for Lucas lived on the other side of Nemea. They were soaked from the rain and the small mountain roads were muddy from all the rain and in a few cases, impassable, so that they had to find other routes.

The rain continued to beat a steady rhythm that Saturday evening when the seven, wet and exhausted men arrived at Lucas's house.

Aristotle was determined to get the treasures back. He and the men tied their horses to the trees and walked to the front door.

They pounded on the door, and after some time, Lucas opened it. He gasped, his eyes bulging when he saw them. He went to shut the door, but Aristotle grabbed his collar while Phillipa shot his gun up in the air. They forced their way into the house.

"Why are you here?" Lucas shouted. Behind him stood his two sons, looking bewildered.

"You know why," Phillipa said knowingly, swaggering toward him, aiming his gun at him. His brothers had also aimed their weapons at them.

"Phillipa," Aristotle warned. "I don't want any blood on my hands."

"Don't worry. We'll just teach this thief a lesson," Phillipa drawled, and spat on the floor. His gun was still aimed at Lucas.

Aristotle turned to Lucas and faced him squarely. "Lucas, I trusted you as my foreman and gave you and your sons decent work. The treasures we found in the west end are missing, and we believe that you and your sons took them. I did not expect this from you."

"We didn't take anything," Lucas growled, his hands up in the air.

"I saw the gold earrings. According to Lule, one of your sons gave them to her. I recognized them. They belong to the treasures," Aristotle said firmly. "If you hand them over, there won't be any report to the government that they were stolen."

Lucas turned and shouted at his son Stephanos. "You dog! Why did you give them to her?"

Stephanos remained silent, his hands clenched, his face turning a beet red. He went to leave, but Phillipa shot his gun in the air.

Chaos struck as Lucas and his sons scrambled for the front door. Aristotle grabbed Lucas, while Alexander and Phillipa jumped on Lucas's sons.

"I'm afraid you're making it difficult for us to talk with you," Aristotle said, panting. He had wrapped his arms around Lucas. Although he was shorter than Aristotle, Lucas fought hard to be free.

"Let's tie them up," Phillipa said.

Aristotle hesitated, unsure if this was the right thing to do.

"They did it, I tell you," Phillipa said. "They stole the treasures."

"If I let you go, will you cooperate with us?" Aristotle asked Lucas.

"We didn't do anything!" Lucas shouted, struggling to be free.

Aristotle nodded to Phillipa, and he went to get the rope.

Soon, Lucas and his sons were tied up in their chairs.

Aristotle watched with apprehension at the three men sitting in the chairs. Phillipa had gone too far. But Lucas was not cooperating.

"You're not going anywhere until we learn what happened to those treasures. We can stay here all night, looking for them, or you can tell us and we will be on our way. We're not leaving until we find them," Aristotle said.

"We don't have anything," Lucas muttered, his eyes downcast.

Alexander's son spoke to Giorgios, the youngest son of Lucas. "Why don't you tell the truth? Do you want to go to prison? It will remain with you all your life. Come clean."

Giorgios was about to speak, then became silent, when his father stared at him.

Phillipa winked at Aristotle. "Now, we must eat. You don't know how bad the wet roads were getting here, and we're tired and hungry." He went with his brothers into the kitchen.

A short time later, Aristotle and the men had filled their stomachs with bread, cheese, olives and water. After providing Lucas and his sons food and water, Aristotle, Alexander, and Phillipa searched the house looking for the treasures. They found nothing.

Aristotle was beginning to wonder if they had been wrong about Lucas, but he remembered the gold jewelry that Lule had received from Lucas's son. It renewed his determination to get to the truth.

Aristotle, Alexander and Phillipa arranged to sleep in the room with Lucas and his sons, while the others slept in the bedrooms. Lying on the floor and covered with a thin, wool blanket, Aristotle listened to the rain pounding the roof and windows, thinking about Miss Cadfield and hoping she had a room at the Corinthian Inn tonight.

Scraping sounds coming from the room awoke Aristotle in the middle of the night. He saw Lucas struggling in his chair, trying to make an escape.

"No, you don't," Aristotle said. He leapt to his feet and seized Lucas by the arm.

Phillipa and Alexander awoke at that moment and jumped up, helping detain Lucas. They tied him more securely to the chair.

Lucas groaned. "I can't sleep in this chair," he complained.

"You can have a nice, soft bed to sleep in if you would only tell me where you've hidden the treasures," Aristotle said firmly.

That silenced Lucas.

Alexander stayed awake after that and kept an eye on them.

* * *

The next day, Sunday, Helena and Yianni arrived in Athens. As the wagon ambled through the streets, it began to drizzle and when they finally rolled to a stop in front of the Stirling house, it was raining steadily. It had been an uneventful journey. They had not come across the Heinz family at the Corinthian Inn. They must have stayed elsewhere.

Helena had taken her luggage with her to her room and early Sunday morning, after a light breakfast, they had embarked on the journey to Athens.

Yianni had been silent throughout the whole journey.

Helena reflected on what had happened the past few days. A sadness blanketed her heart, pressing on it heavily and squeezing out a few tears. She was leaving her home in Nemea. She was leaving Dr. Mastoras and all the memories. Forever.

The wagon stopped, and Yianni jumped off. Helena looked up numbly. They had arrived at the Stirling house

Yianni placed her bags at the door.

Helena hurried to the door, trying to get out of the rain.

"Will that be all, Miss Cadfield?" Yianni asked.

"Yes, thank you, Yianni," Helena said, wiping her wet face. Were those tears she was wiping away? "Please go quickly, before everything gets wet." *Before he saw the tears streaming down my face.*

She watched as his wagon clattered away with the artifacts, feeling broken like the pottery shards in the wagon. Helena tried to shake off the sadness that had swept over her at the choice she had made. A chapter in her life was closing and a new one was beginning. She must remember that.

* * *

That same Sunday, Aristotle could see the men tied up in the chairs becoming tired and worn out. He knew that eventually, they would give out.

Finally, in the middle of the afternoon, Giorgios, the younger son broke down. He was no more than sixteen. Giorgios told them where the treasures were. "They are hidden in the stable," he cried out.

"No, you swine, don't tell them!" Lucas screamed. His tied feet pounded the floor.

Giorgios swallowed hard and turned toward his father. "I'm sorry, Father, but I don't care about those treasures!" he said. "I never did. You and your greed is going to ruin us." Then he wept hard.

"If you are telling the truth, then you will all be set free," Aristotle said to him, untying the boy.

They went outside. It was a cloudy day and the damp ground was soft under his feet. It gave a pungent scent as Aristotle and Phillipa followed Giorgios to the stable. Inside, Giorgios walked to the corner wall and looked up at the beamed ceiling, his arm trying to touch it. He was too short.

"It's up there," Giorgios said, pointing to the ceiling.

Aristotle, who was taller, went and pushed each wooden beam, until one creaked and gave way.

"There, that's the one," Giorgios said excitedly.

Aristotle shoved the beam aside, exposing an opening. His hand groped around and touched rough fabric. It was one of the bags with the treasures. He pulled it, careful not to spill the contents, giving it to Phillipa to hold. He then retrieved the other bag.

Aristotle opened the bags and counted the treasures. Everything seemed to be there. Later, he would check them off in the logbook. Feeling relieved, he placed them back in the bags. He thanked Giorgios. "You did the right thing," he told him.

"Can I come with you?" Giorgios pleaded." My father will surely kill me once you leave."

Aristotle slapped him playfully on the back. "I do not think your father will do that, but you can go with Alexander and his sons until your father calms down."

They entered the house and Aristotle spoke to Lucas. "We found the bags of treasures. I am sorry that things turned out this way. I thought we were friends, but I was wrong. You have a good son, though."

Lucas silently turned his head away, tied up in his chair, the tears streaming down his face.

CHAPTER 50

As they were leaving the house, Aristotle heard his name called. He turned around.

"Dr. Mastoras," Lucas began, his eyes pleading, "I'm, I'm sorry for what I did. I cannot live with myself if I do not tell you the truth."

Aristotle sighed wearily. "I am also sorry, Lucas. I thought highly of you. What made you do it?"

"Dr. Cadfield had promised me that I would be rewarded after I helped him find the treasures," Lucas said, shaking his head in a daze. "Then he let us go, for no reason. He had promised me that I would get part of the treasures, but he didn't give me anything, not even any money. I was very angry, and I went to see him about getting paid."

"Yes?"

Lucas licked his chapped lips. "He was ill, and got up to answer the door. I asked him for payment, but he said he had no money. Then I asked for him to tell me where he put the treasures, but he didn't--"

Lucas stopped speaking, and hung his head in shame.

"And?"

"I shouted angrily at him, but he refused to answer. I kept shouting at him." Lucas's face twisted into an ugly mass of anger. "Then I pushed him, and he fell backward, hitting his head. I searched his place and left with whatever I could find."

"Father, you never told us this. You killed him!" Stephanos shouted.

Lucas stared at his son, his eyes glassy, looking dazed. He let out a loud groan and buried his head into his hands, weeping bitterly. "I don't know. I don't know if he died because of me."

"You need to see Elder James," Phillipa said knowingly. "He'll take care of you."

Aristotle had mixed feelings about Lucas. He felt both revolted and sad at the same time. "Whatever Dr. Cadfield had promised you was between you two. Although you felt he owed you money, you should not have stolen the treasures. Meanwhile, I paid you and your sons well for your work. Did I not?"

Lucas became silent, his head down. He sniffled, and nodded unwillingly.

"I do not want to see you at the excavation site or anywhere near it."

Outside, the sun was shining as Aristotle, the men and Giorgios rode away.

When the group entered the main road, Aristotle stopped and paid them. "Thank you. Now go to your homes. Phillipa and I will travel to Athens."

As Aristotle and Phillipa headed for Athens with the treasures, his heart was heavy from what had transpired. Could he have avoided it if he had paid more attention to Phillipa's and Miss Cadfield's warnings?

* * *

Aristotle and Phillipa traveled for two days. Monday afternoon, they were near the outskirts of Athens and stopped for a break.

"Dr. Mastoras, are you going to tell the authorities about Lucas?"

Aristotle was silent. He had thought about it long and hard. "No. We got our treasures."

Phillipa spat on the ground. "You are too soft," he scoffed. "Why didn't you let me take care of him?"

"Because I don't work that way," Aristotle said firmly.

Phillipa scowled. "He deserves hanging. What about Dr. Cadfield? He killed him."

"We don't know what really happened, whether Lucas killed him or not."

"He said he pushed him."

"There really is no evidence that he died of the fall, is there?"

When they reached Athens, Aristotle paid Phillipa well, thanking him for his help. "You might rest here a day or two before heading back," he told him.

Phillipa grinned. "I plan to do that. I want to buy something for Lule."

After returning the mule to the stables, Aristotle strode to Demosthenes's café, carrying his valise. He had hidden the jewels and treasures inside the valise, safely wrapped in clothing.

He would wash and shave, eat something, then look for Dr. Kostakis. To his surprise, he saw Dr. Kostakis sitting outside the café with Demosthenes.

Aristotle greeted the two men.

"I can tell whenever you return from Nemea," Demosthenes said jokingly. "You look like you need a shave and a wash."

Aristotle smiled. He turned and looked at Dr. Kostakis. "I have something to show you. Can I meet you in your basement in an hour?"

"I will be there."

After Aristotle washed in his room, he sat down and logged all the jewelry from the bags. Everything was there.

An hour later, he met Dr. Kostakis at the storage room of the Kostakis basement. "I think you will be pleased with what I have to show you," he told him.

Aristotle cleared a part of a table from pottery and placed his valise on the table. He opened it and carefully unwrapped the jewels.

"Congratulations, you have truly outdone yourself, Dr. Mastoras," Dr. Kostakis said, appearing excited. His hand trembled as he lifted a jeweled necklace, admiring it. "This is so beautiful and exquisite."

"Yes, and it's thousands of years old."

Dr. Kostakis carefully placed it back with the others. "Where did you find all these treasures?"

Aristotle told him about Dr. Cadfield's letter to Miss Cadfield and alerting her that the treasures were in the west end.

Dr. Kostakis nodded knowingly. "Smart man. He didn't trust anyone. We must secure these valuable treasures at all costs. The society will be excited to learn about your remarkable discovery."

Dr. Kostakis excitedly helped Aristotle place everything back into the valise. They walked to the hidden room together, talking about the discovery and the potential monetary value.

"Has Miss Cadfield received her share?"

"Yes, and she left me the responsibility to bring these here," Aristotle said. He purposefully did not mention the theft. "She plans to return to England."

Dr. Kostakis raised an eyebrow. "I presume she has family there?"

"She has a young suitor waiting for her," Aristotle said dryly. "Now, the matter of my future funding...."

"Rest assured," Dr. Kostakis said, "that any future projects in Nemea will be paid by the society. I will see to that."

Aristotle helped Dr. Kostakis place the treasures in the secure room, next to the gold cup that was already stored there.

"These treasures need to be catalogued along with the others," Aristotle said. "During the winter months, I plan to work here in the basement, organizing and labeling these, along with the artifacts we've accumulated. It will be too cold to have my workers working up on the mountain in Nemea. I will probably need some help here. Someone to be trusted, and more educated than the workers."

Dr. Kostakis nodded his head. "I will bring one of my best students from the university to help you," he said.

They locked the door and pushed the table back. They walked through the storage room, past the tables and the pottery, heading for the stairs.

Dr. Kostakis stopped abruptly, as if thinking. "I forgot."

Taking a key from his pocket, he locked the door to the room. "I need to keep this locked, to be safe," he said.

"Yes," Aristotle said, nodding knowingly. "Please keep it locked."

They slowly walked upstairs and out the door, discussing things.

"It would be good for you to give a presentation to the society. Mr. Pittakis and the society members will surely be impressed with the treasures," Dr. Kostakis said. He looked at his watch. "Now I must excuse myself. I have a meeting at the university."

An hour later, a shaved and washed Aristotle left his room and stepped outside. He found Barba Manolis seated at a table, having coffee. He greeted him and joined him.

"*Yiasou*, Aristotle. How is everything?"

Aristotle told Barba Manolis about Miss Cadfield and Nemea, but was careful not to bring up the stolen treasures.

"So you went up to Nemea with this young woman, Miss Cadfield. I think I remember her from the court ball. She is an attractive and nice young woman."

Aristotle nodded. "She is returning to England. She has a suitor there."

"Ahh, another man," Barba Manolis said, pulling on his white mustache thoughtfully. "I presume that you've fallen in love with her?"

"What gave you that idea?"

Barba Manolis chuckled. "I have lived a long life. I could tell the way you danced with her at the ball that you were interested. You did not show the same interest with the German girl."

Both men were silent.

"You are right. I don't know what to do," Aristotle muttered.

"Listen to me, my son. I call you son because you are like a son to me. Go after her. Let her know that you care about her. If you really love her, you must fight for her and don't let her leave for England."

"No." Aristotle slowly shook his head, remembering their kiss. He had shown her how he had felt about her with his proposal, yet she still wanted to go to England. "For her to want to leave for England, means that she loves him."

The door to the coffee shop opened. It was Demosthenes. "Dr. Mastoras, I forgot to tell you earlier that a letter arrived for you from Germany. It came a few days ago, while you were away in Nemea," he said.

Aristotle took the letter and thanked him. He looked at the address. It was from his attorney in Germany. "Demosthenes, one coffee with a biscuit, please."

"Right away," Demosthenes replied, going back into the coffee shop.

As Aristotle read the letter, he became troubled. "I can't believe it."

"What is it?" Barba Manolis asked.

"It is from my attorney. I need to leave for Germany right away."

"Tell me, why do you need to go to Germany? Is it the university?"

Aristotle explained to Barba Manolis that the letter had to do with his grandfather's grocery store and some legal issues. "The attorney says I must be present to sign the papers before I can sell it."

The coffee and biscuit arrived, but Aristotle could not eat anything. He was too disturbed.

"Why can't you do it from here?" Barba Manolis asked.

"I am late already. If I don't leave right away, I may lose the grocery store."

"Hmm," Barba Manolis said, his fingers pulling on his white mustache.

Aristotle arose, his hand combing back his hair, feeling frustrated. "I have no choice. I must leave today. If you happen to see Miss Cadfield before she leaves for England--

"Don't worry," Barba Manolis said, waving his hand. "I know what to say. You go finish your work in Germany. I'll keep an eye on your property, too, if you wish."

"Barba Manolis, thank you!" Aristotle said, going to him and hugging him.

CHAPTER 51

Athens, Greece
November 1837

Helena settled once more into her role as a governess to Catherine. When she returned from Nemea a couple of days ago, Mrs. Stirling and Catherine showered her with questions about her property.

Helena told them that it was a harsh life and she was thankful for the workers who helped her with her chores, including cooking the meals. She was careful not to tell them about the treasures, and kept the jewels hidden in the valise, under her bed.

On Thursday, Helena slipped away when Catherine was out visiting with family. Filling her purse with treasures, she took the carriage to town, and asked the driver to wait for her. She strode around town, visiting a couple of antiquities shops, selling her wares to the dealer who gave her the best price. Afterwards, she opened a new account in the bank, depositing her money. An hour later, finished with her chores, she returned home with the carriage.

Helena did this over several occasions, so as not to raise suspicion. Mr. and Mrs. Stirling must not know about this. She wanted so much to return to England a wealthy woman, and to prove herself worthy of marrying Dr. Murphy, but the image of Dr. Mastoras's angry face kept popping up in her mind. Was she doing the right thing by deserting him and running back to Dr. Murphy? Dr. Mastoras had proposed to her, but Dr. Murphy had not. One thing her father had taught her was to honor her promises and she must keep her promise to Dr. Murphy. *I had said that I would return to him.*

A week later, when Catherine was out with Mrs. Stirling, Helena went and sold the remaining treasures to the antiquities dealer, then deposited the final funds into the bank. She had been eager to unload them since her return to Athens and had taken great pains to keep the treasures hidden. After she finished, she checked the balance in her book. She had several tens of thousands of drachmas in her account. She toyed with the idea of confiding to Dr. Murphy about her newfound wealth. That had been the plan, to return to England wealthy. But this presented a new problem. She didn't want Dr. Murphy to court her for her money. *I want him to court me because he loves her.*

As she was returning home, she started devising a plan of what she was going to do when she returned to England. She also wondered what had happened to Dr. Mastoras and whether or not he had found the treasures. She passed through a crowd of people and bumped into Barba Manolis, Dr. Mastoras's friend.

He stopped and greeted her delightedly.

"Ah, Miss Cadfield, it's a pleasure to see you again," he said, his eyes twinkling. "I remember how well you danced at the court ball with Dr. Mastoras. You made such a handsome couple."

"Thank you, Barba Manolis," she replied, blushing. "You also danced well." She paused, thinking about Dr. Mastoras's relationship with Barba Manolis. Maybe the old man knew what had happened to him. "I was wondering whether I may ask you a question."

"Yes, of course."

"Have you seen or heard from Dr. Mastoras recently? He seems to have disappeared."

He nodded, appearing as if he had expected her question. "Yes, yes. I saw him about a week ago at the coffee shop. He said that he had to leave for Germany right away."

Helena furrowed her brows, wondering whether or not he had gone to Germany to marry Miss Heinz after all. "Thank you," she mumbled.

"Miss Cadfield, in case you would like to know, on the same day he returned from Nemea, he received news from a lawyer in Germany. We were sitting together at the coffee shop and I saw him read the letter. He had to leave that same day. I am sure he would have contacted you if he had time. He asked me to tell you when I saw you."

Helena thanked him and left, feeling perplexed. Given that Barba Manolis had seen Dr. Mastoras last week, then Dr. Mastoras must have found the stolen treasures. The only person who could verify that, would be Dr. Kostakis. She changed her route and headed toward Dr. Kostakis's building, determined to learn the truth.

She entered the building and was fortunate to find Dr. Kostakis in the basement. He was busy moving some vases around.

"Miss Cadfield, what brings you here?" he asked, beaming at her. He dusted his hands.

"Dr. Kostakis, could you tell me whether or not Dr. Mastoras visited you recently? I have been looking for him." She wasn't going to ask about the treasures, for she didn't want to arouse his curiosity if he hadn't received them.

"Yes, he did. He brought us the treasures from your property in Nemea, just before leaving for Germany. We are excited about the outcome. We thank you for your cooperation in this important matter." He smiled broadly.

"I'm glad," she said, feeling relieved. *He did find them after all.* "Could you please not mention this to anyone, I mean, particularly Mr. Stirling? You see, the treasures found on my property are a private matter. I don't want them or anyone else knowing about it."

"I understand your concern, but you need to know that the ancient treasures we received are in public possession by the state. This is something that cannot be hidden forever. I have asked Dr. Mastoras to make a presentation. His presentation of the jewels will ensure funding for the project."

"Do you know when Dr. Mastoras will return from Germany?"

Dr. Kostakis shrugged his shoulders, shaking his head. "I have no idea. I learned about his trip to Germany just the other day through Barba Manolis."

She thanked him and left for the Stirling house. She was excited that Dr. Mastoras had retrieved the treasures and wondered how he had gotten a hold of them. If only he were here, so she could talk with him and thank him. Maybe he would finish quickly with his business in Germany and return soon.

A few days later, Helena visited the attorney. He told her that the papers for ownership of the Nemea property were still being processed, and if there were more funds, it would help speed up the process.

"How much more is needed?" she asked.

"One hundred drachmas," he said.

She promptly paid him. "Please do your best."

Two weeks after her return from Nemea, Helena received a letter from Dr. Murphy.

Dear Helena,

I hope you are well. I received your letter today and thank you. It sounds as though you are having quite an adventure there in Greece. I must admit that I felt a little envious learning about this Dr. Mastoras working on your property. I presume he is much older, around your father's age?

My work here continues to fill my time considerably, although Mother still manages to host dinner parties in hope of finding me a suitable, wealthy wife.

Upon closing, I'd like to ask, when will you return to England?

I remain steadfastly yours,
Allan Murphy

As she read it, she felt guilty for having written too much about Dr. Mastoras in her previous letter to Dr. Murphy. This apparently had aroused jealousy in him.

That same day, as Helena sat on the veranda with Catherine, painting, Catherine told her that she had received a letter from Miss Heinz. "You know that she's in Germany, don't you?"

"No, I hadn't heard," Helena replied, painting the canvas.

"Well, she says that Aris is also in Germany. She has seen him a few times."

Helena stopped painting, feeling disturbed by the news. "I presume she is still interested in him?" she asked bitterly.

"I'm pretty sure. She said that she wants to marry him," Catherine said, nodding.

Helena continued painting, trying to ignore the sinking feeling in her stomach. Why did it bother her so much that Miss Heinz wanted to marry Dr. Mastoras? She had Dr. Murphy waiting for her in England. She had stayed here in Athens too long, hoping Dr. Mastoras would return shortly.

That evening, Helena had made a decision. She approached Mrs. Stirling and told her that she had received a letter from Dr. Murphy and wished to return to England.

"Oh, my," Mrs. Stirling said, appearing thoughtful. "I have been thinking about leaving for England myself, before the cold winter hits, and then returning in the spring time. Maybe we can travel together."

Helena liked the idea. "That would be nice," she said.

"I will approach Mr. Stirling about it."

After much discussion, Mr. Stirling finally consented to Mrs. Stirling's wishes to leave for England with Catherine and Helena. Helena learned that the Stirling flat in London had been let to someone else. Mr. Stirling made arrangements for them to stay with his sister, Mrs. Weldon, and her family in Oxford.

CHAPTER 52

Oxford, England
1 December, 1837

Helena's carriage arrived in Oxford on a cold, December day. As she sat alone in the carriage that held the Stirling luggage, she remembered her trip to Oxford several months earlier that summer. So much had happened since then. She was returning not as a daughter to Dr. Cadfield, but as a governess to the Stirlings. She could see the Stirling carriage ahead.

Soon the carriage entered the grounds of Cadfield House.

Helena wondered if Papa's servants were still there. To her delight, Mr. Barton, the butler, opened the door. She greeted him and he beamed at her. She followed the Stirling family into the house. Mrs. Barton and Mrs. Rotcliffe came to greet them and appeared happy to see her.

Helena was relieved to learn that the Weldons were visiting friends in Yorkshire and would be returning in a week. Without the Weldons around, the house felt almost as she remembered it.

After supper, Mrs. Stirling, Catherine, and Helena retired early for the evening. Everyone was tired from the trip. Helena's room had already been prepared for her and was warmed by the lit fireplace. She smiled when she saw the tub in the center of her room.

Mrs. Rotcliffe, the housekeeper, came by shortly with the maid, carrying buckets of warm water. Helena thanked them.

"Everything's been so different since you went away, miss," Mrs. Rotcliffe told her as she poured the water in the tub. "Jon, the footman, was replaced, and Nana's been gone all this time. I'm right glad to see your friendly face, miss."

"Yes, I have missed you, too." Helena watched her going about her tasks, and realized what a spoiled life she had lived. These servants had taken care of her in all aspects of her life, whereas in Greece, the roles had been reversed. She had witnessed the stark poverty of people in Greece and had worked hard alongside the Albanians in Nemea. She had felt alive, being with Aristotle and doing things on her own, whereas here, she felt that the comforts of a good life could easily dull her senses.

The maid poured the rest of the warm water into the tub, and then left.

Mrs. Rotcliffe tested the water. Appearing satisfied, she placed a towel on the chair "Ye better take your bath before it gets too cold, miss."

"Has anyone come calling for me since I went away?"

"Dr. Murphy came once, and we made sure to give him your address in Greece, miss."

"Thank you, Mrs. Rotcliffe."

"I don't know whether I should be telling you this, miss, but I heard from me cousin, whose husband works for his family, that his mum has found him a good match. Someone wealthy. They're secretly engaged."

"Secretly engaged?" Helena's heart sank at the idea that Dr. Murphy would be engaged to another. She had been hoping to see him again.

"Well, almost."

Helena felt relieved.

"She will bring ten thousand pounds a year, I hear. Her name is Miss Balfrey, I think."

"Miss Balfrey," Helena whispered, remembering the young lady that she had sat next to at the dinner party that the Murphy's had invited her to. It seemed so long ago.

"Yes, miss. I hear he had been writing secretly to some woman from a foreign country, and his mum saw the letter and tore it up, and said she would disown him if he didn't marry Miss Balfrey. Quite a scandal it is."

After Mrs. Rotcliffe left, Helena numbly took her bath, feeling stunned at the turn of events. After she slipped into a night robe, she combed her hair and braided it, then unpacked her valise. She shook out her dresses, one by one, and hung them in the closet. Everything she had dreamed about was turning into a disappointment. She realized that the secret woman that Dr. Murphy wrote to was none other than herself.

It was inevitable that his mother wanted him to marry someone with money, given his own standing in society, yet he had waited all this time for Helena to return to him. He wrote to her knowing that she had no money. Did that mean he loved her? Her heart swelled with hope.

She dreamed that she would return to him and tell him that she was wealthy and they would marry and she would live happily ever after. But Miss Balfrey's ten thousand pounds a year was not something to take lightly. *How could I compete with Miss Balfrey?* She had brought half of the money with her to England, and left the other half in Greece.

She needed someone to talk with. She wished Nana would be here so she could talk with her. She wrote to her before she left Greece.

Trying to find peace, Helena searched for her father's logbook that she had brought back with her from Nemea. She read it in the privacy of her room, reliving those days in Nemea, hoping to feel better.

Instead of finding peace, Dr. Mastoras's handsome image kept filling her mind. She pictured him the first time she met him that rainy night at the Corinthian Inn, and then when he stood at the carriage in Athens, dressed smartly in his suit. Also, when they danced together at the court ball, and later, when they travelled to Nemea. She thought about the time he had rescued her, and when they sat together in the little cottage, poring over the different treasures.

Then she remembered his kiss, and his proposal. She paused, shutting her eyes and savoring the moment. *Was he the one all along?* Is that what he had tried to tell her afterwards? How could she believe him? He had been seeing Miss Heinz in Germany. He probably was engaged to her by now. With those sad thoughts, she slowly put the logbook away and drifted to sleep.

* * *

The next day, Mrs. Stirling and Catherine went shopping. Helena took the opportunity to slip away and go downtown. There, she visited the bank that her father used to do business with. She showed the check to the bank clerk. It was a large sum. He rushed to the back and called the manager.

The manager, Mr. Burns, came and spoke to her personally. He appeared tense, requesting identification. She informed him that she was Dr. Cadfield's daughter, and he relaxed.

"I have done business with your father, Miss Cadfield. A good man he was. Sorry to hear about his passing."

She told him that she had inherited some wealth in Greece, and decided to bring it to England with her. "I would like to open an account."

"I'd be happy to assist you," Mr. Burns said.

An hour later, she left the bank feeling joyful. With three thousand pounds a year coming to her, she would lead a comfortable life in England. It was more than enough for her.

Later that same day, Helena wrote a letter to Dr. Murphy, informing him that she had arrived.

CHAPTER 53

Two days later, on Sunday, the Weldons returned from their trip. Much commotion and emotion ensued as they greeted Mrs. Stirling and Catherine fondly. Helena received a lukewarm greeting, but she did not mind. She watched the two women warmly catch up on their news and realized that they were on good terms with each other.

Mrs. Weldon asked Helena that evening whether or not she could be governess to Willy. "I heard so many good things about your ability as a governess from Mrs. Stirling, my dear, and feel that it would benefit him the few months that you will be here."

Helena was surprised at the woman's request, but felt comfortable with the idea and agreed to it.

The next day, Monday, she taught her two pupils in the same class, covering a number of topics. The classroom was on the second floor, similar to the one at the Stirling's house. Willy seemed to be comfortable with her, and would talk with her easily, yet had a difficult time with Catherine. It did not take long before Catherine complained about his unruly character and about his jumping out from behind doors and scaring her.

On Wednesday morning, Helena and Catherine were having lessons in the classroom. Willy was still in bed, which did not surprise her. A late riser, he often arrived after the lessons had begun.

Mrs. Rotcliffe came to announce that Dr. Murphy was in the parlor. "He asked about you, so I thought you should come down to see him. Mrs. Stirling is out shopping with Mrs. Weldon."

Helena's heart pounded in her chest. She had been waiting for this moment since her return to England. He had come for her. The old, familiar tender feelings for him arose in her.

"You may take a break, Catherine." Helena excused herself and went to her room. She nervously dressed into one of her good dresses, then combed her hair carefully. A part of her felt enthusiastic to see him, as if it were like old times, when he would visit Papa, but then she remembered about his secret engagement. She hoped it was not true.

As Helena entered the parlor, she saw Dr. Murphy seated at the couch. Her heart pounded in her chest. *He came for me.*

He saw her and arose, smiling that winsome smile. She smiled as she approached him and curtsied.

He took her hand. "Helena, it truly is a pleasure to see you again."

She thanked him, noticing for the first time how pale and thin he looked, almost frail. Was she comparing him to Dr. Mastoras's tanned and well-built frame? "Please have a seat," she told him.

After Helena ordered tea, she joined him on the sofa.

"I must admit that I was surprised to receive your letter. You had returned so quickly to Oxford. I wanted to ask you--" he said.

"Dr. Murphy, fancy seeing you here!"

Helena looked up in dismay as Mrs. Weldon entered the room.

Dr. Murphy shot up, looking embarrassed. He bowed politely.

"I'd like to congratulate you, Dr. Murphy," Mrs. Weldon said, her eyes flashing. "I just learned from a trusted source, that you are engaged to Miss Balfrey."

Dr. Murphy appeared uncomfortable, turning different shades of red. He glanced nervously at Helena, then back at Mrs. Weldon.

Helena was numbed by the news.

"I, well, it's not exactly true," he began awkwardly. "You see, my mother has been eager to marry me off for some time, and she took it upon herself to make that decision for me by publicizing it in the newspaper."

"Oh, so then it's not true," Helena said, wondering if she could believe him or not.

"If you could, Mrs. Weldon, excuse us for a minute? I would like to have a word with Miss Cadfield alone," he said sharply.

Helena noticed the knowing glance Mrs. Weldon gave her as she slipped away, leaving them alone.

Dr. Murphy sat back down on the sofa. "Helena, I was about to ask you how your trip to Greece went before we were interrupted by Mrs. Weldon. The letter you wrote to me from Greece sounded as though you were having an adventure of your lifetime."

"In a way, it was." Helena told him about life in Athens and Nemea, avoiding mentioning Aristotle. "Living in Nemea was totally different from England."

"I can only imagine."

She explained the life there and the archeological process, but did not mention the treasures.

"To be honest, at first I couldn't understand why you would leave here to go to some war-ridden country for some property that was in shambles," he drawled, "and when I learned about this Dr. Mastoras, I was frankly disturbed about it."

Helena felt insulted about the way he described Greece, yet understood his concern about Dr. Mastoras. This was not the time to tell him that Dr. Mastoras had proposed to her, not until she found out what Dr. Murphy's true feelings were for her.

"You know that I needed to see about my family property," she replied. "And regarding Dr. Mastoras, I assure you, we were well chaperoned. There were forty workers there during the whole time I was there."

That seemed to appease him.

"Now that you are here, I have forgiven you and couldn't help but come see you."

"I am glad to be back," she murmured, feeling relieved that he had changed the subject.

He moved closer to her. "Sweet Helena, I thought about you often all these months you were away."

"I also thought about you," Helena said, feeling pleased by his show of interest. This is what she had come to England for.

He took her in his arms and embraced her warmly, and then kissed her.

Helena had been waiting for this moment for a long time, ever since she was in boarding school. She had expected her heart to race and her breath to become shallow when he kissed her, just like the way she felt when Aristotle kissed her, but it didn't happen. Instead, his kiss felt hard and wet. Was it because Dr. Mastoras's kiss was still fresh in her mind?

"Dr. Murphy, please," she said, pushing him away and feeling slightly uncomfortable. Why was she reacting this way? *Wasn't he the man I want to marry?*

"Helena, if only you knew how many days I thought about you while you were away. Did you think about me?" He looked into her eyes.

At that moment of weakness, where his tender, brown eyes bored into hers, Helena slowly nodded her head.

He swept her into his arms again, murmuring words of endearment, and was about to kiss her again, but she had come to her senses and had turned her head to the side.

"Please, Dr. Murphy," Helena said. His kiss ended on her cheek. She felt shaken by her mixed emotions. One minute she wanted him and the next, she was spurning him.

He appeared confused. "I don't understand."

"I, I need some time to get to know you better."

"Ahh, yes, that makes sense," he said, appearing satisfied with her response. "I will call on you whenever I get a chance."

Dr. Murphy visited her almost daily after that. Mrs. Weldon and Mrs. Stirling chaperoned them. The two women seemed to be on good terms with him and Helena. They encouraged Helena to look her best for his visits.

Helena often wondered what Dr. Murphy would have thought if she told him that she had spent much time alone in that small cottage with Dr. Mastoras and without a chaperone. She also wondered what he would have thought if she told him that she had been kissed and proposed to by Dr. Mastoras. No, it would not do. *He would probably think the worst of me.*

Helena kept her feelings for Dr. Mastoras buried deep, only revisiting them in the privacy of her room and during the stillness of the night.

Whenever Dr. Murphy visited, they would sit together in the parlor, and he would hold her hand. He would share with her his medical work and his patients, and she would nod, telling him that Papa would have done the same thing.

He hadn't kissed her again after that first time.

One day in the middle of December, he had just finished telling her about an appendicitis case. She told him what Papa would have done.

"You know so much about medicine, Miss Cadfield. Sometimes I think you know more than I do," he teased.

"It's probably because that's all Papa talked about when he was around. That, and archaeology," she responded, smiling back.

She felt comfortable when Dr. Murphy reminisced about the past. He talked about those days he spent with her father and how he would tease her. "You were so young and tomboyish."

"Every time you showed up, you would always pull my braids," she said smiling. "Of course, you made sure my father wasn't looking."

He grinned. "I think he knew."

They both laughed.

"Who would have thought that one day you'd be traveling to Greece to excavate for lost treasures on a mountain? Too bad that you didn't find anything," he said softly, playing with her hair.

"What makes you say that?" Helena asked, her heart racing.

"It is obvious," he said, gazing at her knowingly. "If you had returned a wealthy woman, I would have expected you to be dressed differently, smartly, more like Miss Balfrey. Maybe you would have bought a place of your own. You undoubtedly would not have been a mere governess living here."

Helena sucked in her breath when she heard Miss Balfrey's name. *He was testing her.* She must tread slowly. "What would you have done if I had found treasures on my property?" she asked him. She wanted to tell him the truth, but something held her back.

"What would I have done?" he asked, blinking.

"Yes, what if I had found treasures and returned back to England as a rich woman, instead of being penniless?"

Dr. Murphy looked annoyed. "Please don't play with me. My mother would have married us on the spot, but let's not talk about Mother," he replied. His fingers stroked her cheek.

Helena enjoyed the attention he was giving her. This was not the first time that he had fondled her cheek.

"You know you have the most beautiful, blue eyes," he whispered.

She realized he had adeptly changed the subject. He pulled her head slightly toward him so that she could feel his warm breath as his lips touched her cheek.

She trembled when his lips found her mouth. He pulled her to him and kissed her passionately.

Helena felt hot all over from his ardent kiss, yet an uneasy feeling settled in her stomach. This was not a tender kiss. It was demanding and she didn't like it.

She tried to pull away, but he held her tightly.

"Please," she said, pulling away. Her hand went to smooth her disheveled hair.

"That is something to remember me when I am not here," he said, his eyes gleaming. He arose and bid his leave.

After he was gone, Helena thought about their discussion and the uneasy feeling returned. After she asked him that question about her wealth, and he replied promptly about his mother marrying him, she realized that he had not pursued the topic further. Instead, he had kissed her. Had he done so to change the subject? Or was it his way of telling her that he desired her? She was confused. She had wondered several times whether or not his mother knew that he was seeing her.

There had been no invitation to the Murphy house.

The next day, Dr. Murphy wrote her a hasty note that he was busy with patients and could not visit her. Helena was not surprised. She knew that doctors had busy schedules. The following day came and went and he did not visit or send her a note.

CHAPTER 54

As the days sped by, Helena became increasingly troubled by Dr. Murphy's absence. She kept busy with the lessons and with stitching handkerchiefs for Christmas presents. She wondered why Dr. Murphy couldn't tear himself away from his patients for even an hour to see her.

One day, while Catherine and Willy were doing their lessons, Helena stared out the window, her thoughts wistfully turning to Dr. Mastoras. How would he be spending his Christmas? Was he still in Germany seeing Miss Heinz? *What are you thinking? Push him out of your mind and your life! You are in England, seeing Dr. Murphy.*

"Miss Cadfield, Willy took my pencil!' Catherine shouted. She smacked his arm. "Give me that."

Helena sighed, turning her thoughts back to the children. "Please stop, you two. Willy, you can ask for the pencil. And you, Catherine, it is not ladylike to hit him. You will be an adult soon."

On Christmas day, a light snow powdered the ground. Everyone was in a festive mood as they ate the large breakfast. Later, the families gathered in the parlor for the handing out of presents. Helena presented her gifts to the Stirlings and the Weldons. For Catherine, she gave her a portrait, which thrilled her. Willy received a pair of knitted mittens. In turn, Helena received a painting from Catherine. She recognized the potted flowers on the Athenian veranda.

"Thank you, Catherine. I didn't know you had brought this painting with you."

"No, I made a new one. I wanted you to remember Greece."

Helena hugged her, smiling.

She also received a jeweled hairpin from Mrs. Stirling and a white shawl from Mrs. Weldon. They had a few visitors, but Dr. Murphy did not appear.

The Christmas meal, held later in the day, included roast beef and turkey, vegetables, stuffing, mince pie, and Christmas pudding. Afterwards, Helena entertained them by playing the piano.

That evening, in the privacy of her bedroom, Helena held the handkerchief she had stitched for Dr. Murphy, wondering what had happened to keep him away. A melancholy feeling set in her bones as her fingers brushed his initials on the handkerchief. She had hoped he would visit today, even for a short time. She had wanted to give it to him, although she still had mixed feelings about him.

She replayed the times they had spent together and realized that the best moments she'd had with him were when they discussed her father. She'd feel a sense of comfort flowing through her veins as memories of her father would wash over her. Yet when Dr. Murphy tried to kiss her or demanded more from her, she balked.

I had associated Dr. Murphy with my father.

Helena blinked, stunned by the revelation.

By having Dr. Murphy in her life, someone who had associated closely with her father, it had allowed her to keep a part of her father's past alive. *But was that true love?*

Helena sadly knew the answer, but a part of her pushed it way. She didn't want to accept it.

The next day was Boxing Day, and the celebration continued. The staff were given their gifts. Dinner consisted of leftover food from the previous night.

Helena continued to hope that Dr. Murphy would visit, but he did not.

That evening in her bedroom, Helena became reflective again. Was Dr. Murphy really that busy? Was it something she had said? Or was it another woman, like Miss Balfrey? She wondered how she would have reacted if she had been expecting Dr. Mastoras instead. Would he have come today? Something inside her said that he would. Had she made a mistake in coming to England, back to Dr. Murphy? Had she been chasing a childhood dream all these years? Was she infatuated by him and not really in love with him? Was Dr. Murphy in love with her? Was her infatuation enough to sustain a long-term relationship? It was time to grow up. With these thoughts swirling in her head, she finally went to bed.

As the New Year came and went, Helena became increasingly troubled by Dr. Murphy's absence. She wondered if he had been taken ill. On a cold, January day, she sent him a note, inquiring if everything was all right, for she had not heard from him.

The next day, Helena and Catherine, Mrs. Weldon and Mrs. Stirling took the carriage to Oxford. The clouds had gathered overhead as they entered the town.

"We must move quickly," Mrs. Weldon fretted, peering out the window. "It might snow later, and you know how difficult it is to travel in the snow!"

Helena left the two older women at the fabric store and strolled briskly with Catherine to the shoe store down the block.

"Your feet are growing so fast," Helena told Catherine. "This is the second pair--"

"Look, Miss Cadfield," Catherine interrupted, excitedly pointing across the street.

Helena turned and stared in the direction that Catherine was pointing.

Across the street, in front of the pharmacy was Dr. Murphy. He looked as if he were deep in thought. He had not seen them. Her heart skipped a beat when she saw Miss Balfrey descend from a nearby carriage and rush toward him. He embraced her warmly. The couple stood there talking softly, their heads close together. The couple entered the pharmacy together.

Helena looked away, feeling the pain of betrayal cut holes in her heart.

"Miss Cadfield, are you listening?' Catherine said, tugging at her sleeve. "Did you see Dr. Murphy and--"

"Don't pry into other people's affairs," Helena snapped.

Afterwards, they returned to the fabric store. Catherine entered first, and as Helena was about to follow her, she overheard Mrs. Weldon and Mrs. Stirling talking excitedly about Dr. Murphy. She stopped in her tracks, standing there listening, hidden from their view.

"Imagine my dismay when I saw Dr. Murphy coming out of the pharmacy with a young woman, but he did not see me. I wonder what he was doing with her," Mrs. Weldon said.

"Oh, she probably was his patient," Mrs. Stirling said.

"I don't know, not the way he was holding her," Mrs. Weldon said, wagging her head. "He hasn't visited Miss Cadfield for several weeks."

"*Ja*. That is true."

"The way Dr. Murphy was holding the young woman, it made me think it might have been that Balfrey girl."

"Oh, you should not tell this to Miss Cadfield," Mrs. Stirling said conspiratorially. "It would hurt her."

"Better for her to know than to be led on like this," Mrs. Weldon insisted.

"Oh, there is Catherine. Where is Miss Cadfield? Come, my dear, we have some fabric for you," Mrs. Stirling said.

Helena took a deep breath, trying to remain calm before entering the store.

* * *

It wasn't until the middle of January when Helena finally heard from Dr. Murphy. He sent her a note explaining that the holidays were the busiest time of the year for him and he hoped to see her soon.

She tore the paper into shreds.

One day in late January, during dinner, Mrs. Stirling brought up the subject of returning to Greece.

"I am missing my husband," Mrs. Stirling explained. "Not that I don't like being here, but it is different without him. I wish to start making plans to return sometime in March."

Mr. Weldon coughed politely. "You are always welcome here, but I agree with you. You should be with your husband."

Mrs. Stirling continued talking about the subject.

Catherine was sitting next to Helena. "Miss Cadfield, do you miss Greece?" she whispered to her.

Helena was silent. As she thought about the trip, strong feelings surfaced. She had truly missed that country, and Dr. Mastoras even more.

"Yes," she finally said. "What about you?"

"In a way I do," Catherine replied. "I had more fun there. Felix was there, and I danced with him. Here I am stuck with Willy all the time in this house. He is no fun and leaves me no peace."

"It seems that you will be returning to Greece soon, so you won't have to worry about him after that."

"Yes, but you will remain here, won't you? You will marry Dr. Murphy."

Helena did not reply. These past few weeks she had thought about Dr. Murphy's absence and the incident with Miss Balfrey at the pharmacy. She was sure his mother's plans to marry him to Miss

Balfrey were working well. But that wasn't the only reason that she had made her decision not to see him again. It was because in her heart, she knew that he did not love her. If he did, it should not have mattered if she were a mere governess. It should not have mattered whether she had wealth or not. Love surpassed all that. He should have proposed to her if he loved her, and then she would have told him the truth about her wealth. But it didn't happen that way. She sighed.

Another thought intruded. *If Dr. Murphy had proposed, would I have accepted?* Deep in her heart, she knew the answer. Maybe it was better that it happened this way and that he sought Miss Balfrey's hand after all, for Helena did not love him.

CHAPTER 55

In late January, Willy caught a cold, and Dr. Murphy was called in to see him. When he arrived, he went immediately with Mrs. Weldon to the boy's room.

Helena sat in the parlor, having tea with Mrs. Stirling and Catherine.

Mrs. Weldon entered the room with Dr. Murphy.

Helena tensed when she saw him. She had expected him to leave right away after treating Willy. Mustering her energy and remembering her resolution to act civilly toward him and not show her feelings, she relaxed. *I must remain calm.*

Dr. Murphy bowed his greeting and sat down.

Mrs. Stirling served him tea.

"Miss Cadfield, I hope you are doing well. I apologize for my absence these past few weeks. In addition to all my patients, my mother has taken ill. I have become not only her doctor, but also her nurse." Dr. Murphy sighed, and sipped some tea.

Helena wanted to believe him, but her heart refused to yield. After seeing him with Miss Balfrey, and making her own decision about him, she could not thaw her heart. Feeling numb, she nodded. "I am confident that you are giving *her* the best of care."

He smiled at her. "Thank you." He placed his teacup down and turned to Mrs. Weldon. "Before I forget, Mrs. Weldon, I wanted to ask you what has been done about Dr. Cadfield's medical books?"

"I think they are still in the library, if I'm not mistaken," Mrs. Weldon replied.

"I presume no one is using them. Could I possibly ask if they are available to read, Mrs. Weldon? Various medical conditions arise and I find it useful to refer to them."

"They are available, indeed," Mrs. Weldon replied. She left the room.

Helena felt uncomfortable at Mrs. Weldon's eagerness to please Dr. Murphy with her father's books, knowing that he expected them as payment for his services. Mrs. Weldon quickly returned with five books.

Dr. Murphy took them, thanking her. He gazed at their titles, and nodded. "I am much obliged."

Helena watched him with growing apprehension. Why did it bother her? Was it because her father's books were a part of her, and she had already severed her relationship with this man in her heart?

He took his leave after that with the excuse that he had many patients to look after.

The next day, Dr. Murphy visited again to check on Willy.

Afterwards, Mrs. Weldon and Dr. Murphy joined Mrs. Stirling and Helena in the parlor for tea.

After a short time, Mrs. Stirling excused herself, saying that she had something to attend to.

A few minutes later, Mrs. Weldon excused herself.

Helena blushed, knowing that they were leaving them intentionally alone.

Dr. Murphy arose and sat next to Helena on the sofa.

"I was counting the minutes they would leave," he said, taking her hand and kissing it before she could remove it. "I've missed seeing you."

"It has been several weeks," she admitted, pulling her hand away.

"You know that I was busy with patients," he countered.

Helena studied him. He seemed sincere enough, as he took her hands once more in his. She began to melt under his gaze, but she could not ignore the image of him with Miss Balfrey at the pharmacy. She needed to know the truth.

"Dr. Murphy, I need to ask you a question. How do you feel about me?"

"You know how I feel about you." He leaned forward and kissed her.

Shaken by his bold kiss, she pulled away. "That is *not* what I meant."

"What is it, then?" he demanded. "Do you want more? Is it a house you want?"

"A house?" Helena gazed at him in wonder, her heart quickening. "Are you proposing marriage?"

She watched the emotions playing on his face. He became silent, his eyes avoiding hers.

Nausea threatened to overcome her as she realized how quickly her decision not to commit to him had weakened after he dangled the idea of marriage in front of her. She was sickened not only by her weakness, but also how he had toyed with her like a cat toying with a mouse. Was she such a feeble-minded woman after all? Wasn't it Dr. Mastoras that she loved?

He slowly looked at her and smiled. "You can have anything you want, darling," he said playfully. "No one need know about it." He pulled her to him once more, attempting to kiss her.

"No one need know about it?" Helena pulled away, feeling outraged. She arose, trembling. "The Weldons and Mrs. Stirling have known about your courtship. Meanwhile, you have been seen around town with Miss Balfrey. Please clarify yourself," she said, brushing the loose strands from her flushed face.

"You are a governess, a servant, without a pound to your name. Miss Balfrey has wealth. Need I go further?" he retorted.

"How dare you say you care about me and at the same time insult me like that?"

"Let's not be hasty in judging me. I was merely stating the facts."

"The facts are, that you're in love with money." *And Miss Balfrey.*

He laughed nervously. "Maybe. Maybe not." He went to her and put his arm around her shoulder. "Come, let's not argue over this, my sweet. I do have feelings for you. I have waited for you all this time. Haven't I?"

She shrugged off his arm and turned her back on him, crossing her arms and tapping her foot nervously. "You waited because you thought I'd return with all those riches."

"Yes, it was an attractive idea at the time." He stroked his chin, sighed and moved away. "You did leave me to go to Greece, spending all that time with Dr. Mastoras." He turned and glared at her. "What was I to think?"

The blood rushed to her head. "How dare you imply that I did anything improper!" she retorted. "I never want to see you again!" she said heatedly.

He left abruptly.

* * *

Two days later, the unusually fair weather pulled Helena out of her melancholy mood and she took a stroll down the tree-lined path, away from Cadfield House. Catherine had not joined her as she was having one of her sulking moods because Willy had stained her good dress.

The afternoon sun felt warm and inviting as Helena's feet took her away from the mansion. She gazed at the birds flitting around in the nearby trees and wondered how it must feel to be free like them, having no worry or care in the world. Her mind wandered toward Dr. Murphy and a knot formed in her stomach.

Earlier that day, she had learned the news about him while having tea in the parlor with Mrs. Weldon and Mrs. Stirling.

"We received a wedding invitation from Mrs. Murphy this morning," Mrs. Weldon informed her. "Dr. Murphy will be marrying Miss Balfrey in two weeks."

"That does not surprise me," Helena said stiffly.

"To think I gave him those books of your father's," Mrs. Weldon continued, shaking her head. "Here we thought that he had good intentions for you, Miss Cadfield. Just think the scandal it would have caused and the loss of your reputation if people found out that he was seeing you all this time while engaged to Miss Balfrey."

"Yes, my dear, it would have caused a scandal," Mrs. Stirling said, nodding her head.

"Luckily, he came several times for our Willy, so that it did not raise suspicion," Mrs. Weldon said.

Helena had reached the end of the path. She turned around, her eyes combing the expansive property, a sense of nostalgia coursing through her. This had been her home for so many years, where she and her father had lived, yet it seemed so foreign to her. She knew that her home belonged in Greece.

Had she made a mistake in believing that she was in love with Dr. Murphy? Had she made a mistake in returning to England, thinking naively that he loved her for herself and not for her money? The tears welled up in her eyes. Everything was going wrong for her. Or wasn't it? *He was a spineless man ruled by his mother and his passions.*

Maybe she needed to experience this.

Helena strolled back to the house, deep in thought. She knew in her heart what she had failed to see earlier. She had thought she was doing the right thing by returning to Dr. Murphy. She was fulfilling a promise, and in the process, had left behind not only her house in Greece, but also her heart. What a fool she had been. She had let Dr. Mastoras slip away because of her perceived rules about propriety. She had denied her real feelings about him, thinking that by doing so, she was doing the right thing, that she was being a good woman.

Based on his actions toward her, Dr. Murphy appeared disinterested in propriety. Marriage to him was a means to more money. He was not marrying for love. Helena was sure of that. It was a matter of time before he would find a mistress, she thought bitterly.

Helena realized that she was a product of a society that placed women in inferior roles. Her role as a woman had been sealed when she attended boarding school. There, she learned what was proper and right, and how to dress and act like a lady. She learned to keep her thoughts hidden and not to reveal emotion. She learned to suppress her true self. She had trusted the very system that threatened to topple her own happiness.

If only she had let her heart rule, instead of her brain.

Was it too late to return to Greece and to the man she truly loved?

CHAPTER 56

Nemea, Greece
29 March, 1838

On a fine, spring day in late March, Helena arrived at the dock in Nafplio, Greece with Mrs. Stirling and Catherine. The air was crisp and breezy, and the cloudless sky was a sea of blue as they descended the plank. Mr. Stirling was there to greet them. It was an emotional reunion for the Stirlings.

Although tired from the trip, Helena felt particularly charged in being in Greece. She was returning home.

After stopping for the night at the Corinthian Inn, they reached Athens the following afternoon. Mrs. Fournos and Koula were glad to see them. For dinner, Mrs. Fournos served baked lamb with potatoes, dolmades, steamed greens, and spinach pies. For dessert, she served baklava and koulourakia.

"I did miss your cooking, Mrs. Fournos," Catherine said, enjoying her meal.

"Eat well. Soon it will be Lent, and we will have to fast," Mrs. Fournos said.

The following day it was Saturday. Mr. and Mrs. Stirling were out visiting, and Helena took Catherine shopping for a new dress, for Felix had promised to visit that evening for dinner.

Afterwards, Helena deposited her home to rest.

"I'll be back before dinner to help you with your dress," Helena promised Catherine. "I have some errands to attend to."

Before leaving England, Helena had made it clear to Mrs. Stirling and Catherine about her intentions of terminating her employment with them and returning to her home in Nemea. She felt it was the right thing to do. At first, Catherine had balked at the idea. However, once they arrived in Greece, Catherine's attention had immediately shifted to Felix, while Mrs. Stirling attended to Mr. Stirling. They were adjusting well without her.

Helena headed for Dr. Kostakis's building, eager to speak to him. It was a twenty-minute brisk walk. She was going to ask him if he had heard from Dr. Mastoras. She would also ask him if he knew how to get a hold of Yianni. She wanted him to take her to Nemea.

Her excitement grew as she approached the Kostakis building. The memories of Dr. Mastoras were stronger than ever. Her heart sang at the thought that he might have returned from Germany. At the same time, she steeled herself for the possible news that he might still be in Germany and had married Miss Heinz after all.

Whatever the news, she must be prepared to accept it.

Helena entered the building and walked down the stairs to the basement. She could hear the sounds of hammering. Good. It sounded as though Dr. Kostakis would be here. When she entered the storage room, she immediately noticed how everything appeared more organized.

A young man was seated at a table in the bowels of the room, hammering away, his back turned to her. She could not see him clearly, due to his body being hidden by the piles of vases on the tables behind him and the dim lighting. She stood quietly at the door, disappointed that Dr. Kostakis was not here. Should she disturb his work and inquire after him?

"Hello," she called out.

The young man turned and hurried toward her. He was short and thin, and wore spectacles.

"May I help you, miss?"

"Could you tell me where I can find Dr. Kostakis?"

"I'm afraid he will be away for a few days," he said.

"Oh. I was hoping to see him."

"Who is it, Costa?" a man called out from the back of the room.

Startled by the familiar deep voice, Helena peered anxiously toward the back, her heart beating wildly. Could it be *him*? She couldn't see anyone. Then a tall man rose out of nowhere from behind a pile of vases. He must have been bent over his work, and his body had been obstructed by the vases.

He stared at her, and then dusted his clothes and hair, and strode purposefully toward her.

Helena's heart leapt with joy when she recognized him. How could *he* be here? *He was supposed to be in Germany, with Miss Heinz.*

He seemed just as surprised to see her.

Their eyes locked.

"Hello, Dr. Mastoras," she said shakily, attempting a smile.

"Hello."

Her eyes soaked in his gloriously handsome features, his large eyes, firm chin, and sensuous lips, as she tried to rein in her joy. He was here, she thought, in real life and not in a dream. In that infinite moment where truth, life, death, and meaning all merged together, she knew without a doubt to whom her heart belonged. *How could I have been so blind?*

He glanced behind her apprehensively. "You came alone?"

"Yes."

His smile lit up his face and settled in his eyes. "Wait here one moment."

He went to the young man who had been standing discreetly to the side. "Costa, you are free to go. I will let you know when I will need you again."

Costa thanked him, dusted his clothing, and then picked up a few books and left.

"Costa is from the university and helps us a few days of the week," Dr. Mastoras explained.

He brought two chairs, and wiped them with a cloth before they sat on them. "What brings you here?" he asked cautiously.

Helena felt shy under his questioning gaze. "I, well, I, I just returned to Greece and came by to see Dr. Kostakis," she stammered, feeling her face become hot. *How silly it must sound.* Her hands clutched her purse close to her chest. What was happening to her? She really wanted to know if Dr. Mastoras were still single, but didn't have the nerve to ask him.

"Dr. Kostakis is not here."

"I wanted to ask him if Yianni could take me to Nemea."

Helena felt her face become hot when he did not respond. He *appears cold, almost indifferent. How could I get through to him?*

She continued. "Before I left for England, I visited Dr. Kostakis and was glad to hear that he had received the treasures from you. Please tell me what happened. Who was the thief?"

Aristotle crossed his arms. "Lucas. You were right all along about him."

"So it was Lucas after all. Please tell me how you discovered this."

Dr. Mastoras told her how Lule's daughter had received stolen jewelry from Lucas's son and how they went to his house and how his son helped them find the bags of treasures.

"I am glad that Lule told you," Helena said. She looked down. "I also learned from Barba Manolis that you left for Germany right away."

"Yes, on the same day that I returned the treasures to Dr. Kostakis, I received a legal letter regarding the grocery store that my father owned there. There was a possibility that I might lose it. I was already late. I had to leave right away."

He explained the ordeal he had to go through in Germany, but in the end, he had successfully sold the store.

She couldn't help noticing the guarded manner in which he spoke. Her eyes glanced down to his hands for signs of a ring, but he had crossed his arms. *Could he be married, or did he think I was married? Something was not right.*

"I returned a few weeks ago," he continued. "As you see, I am trying to organize and label all the fragments and artifacts found in Nemea. It is tedious work, but necessary." He looked at her. "I also took the liberty of purchasing some of the treasures you sold to the antique dealers. This way we have the complete set. There is more value when everything is together."

She nodded, feeling pleased. "I would be interested in seeing your work."

They walked together toward the tables and he politely pointed out different artifacts and the periods to which they belonged. He handed her a metal object, their fingers touching.

"This is a tool we found, and dates from the bronze age. Careful, its edge is sharp."

Helena studied it. "Amazing. I can't wait to return to Nemea and continue where we left off."

She handed it back to him and noticed the surprised look on his face as he placed it back on the table.

"Will you be returning to England any time soon, Miss Cadfield, or should I call you Mrs. Murphy?" he asked cautiously.

"No, I will *not* be returning to England, and I am still Miss Cadfield."

He stared at her, appearing puzzled. "Are you sure you will not be returning to England, Miss Cadfield?"

"Yes, I am quite sure. That phase of my life is over," she said firmly. "I wish to return to Nemea. To my home."

His beautiful, expressive eyes gazed at her for what seemed like eternity, and he smiled in that special way that she loved. The room faded away, and all she could see was Dr. Mastoras. She could not get enough of him. She wanted to melt into his arms.

"When do you plan to leave for Nemea?" he asked softly.

Warm, kind Dr. Mastoras had returned to her.

"As soon as possible."

CHAPTER 57

Two days later, on a Tuesday afternoon, Aristotle, Miss Cadfield, and Yianni arrived at the Corinthian Inn. After dinner, Aristotle invited Miss Cadfield to take a walk outside with him. He needed to speak with her, alone.

The two strolled down the moonlit path. The spring breeze caressed his hair like a lover, and Aristotle felt the same enchantment in these surroundings as a few months ago. Only it was slightly warmer, and there was no Dr. Murphy lurking in the background to snatch Helena away. *This time, I am not going to let her slip away from me.*

"Five months ago, we walked along this same path," he remarked. "I remember it well. It feels like it was yesterday."

Miss Cadfield's eyes flew open. She gazed at him with those large, blue eyes. "Yes, doesn't it?"

"I also remember feeling disappointed when you left for England to go back to your Dr. Murphy," he said softly.

Her eyes dipped down, hiding her emotions.

He had hoped she would open up to him, but she remained silent. It was not enough to have her near him. *I need to know if she left her heart behind.* "Tell me, Miss Cadfield, are you still in love with him?" he asked guardedly.

She stopped and turned her full gaze on him. Her eyes, illumined by the moon, held unshed tears. He felt that special attraction that only she could elicit in him.

"No. I *thought* I was in love with him, but it was not true love."

His heart soared with joy when he heard this. *Could it be true?* "What made you decide that?"

"Let's say that his character was lacking and left much to be desired."

"But if one is in love, wouldn't they overlook it?"

"That's the problem. I could not forgive his faults." She looked out into the darkness. "No matter how much I tried, I could not see myself spending the rest of my life with him. Besides, he was courting Miss Balfrey at the same time."

They resumed their stroll.

"That must have been difficult for you."

She sighed. "His mother was involved. They thought I was rich, but when I implied to him that I was not, he did not offer a proposal of marriage. At the same time, I was beginning to realize my error in returning to him, and had made up my mind not to pursue this path. I believe that he courted Miss Balfrey because she was rich, not because he loved her."

Aristotle was surprised to hear that. "You didn't tell him about your wealth?"

"I was about to, but something held me back. I wanted to see if he really loved me for myself and not for my money." She looked at him. "Does that answer your question?"

"Yes," he replied, his voice low and mellow. "So he ended up marrying Miss Balfrey instead, who was wealthy?"

"Hmmm. They deserve each other."

He burst out laughing.

"If you don't mind my asking, what happened to Miss Heinz?"

"She was more like a younger sister to me," he said. "She thought she was in love with me, but I think she was in love with being in love." He paused.

"She might have been infatuated with you, like I had been with Dr. Murphy," Miss Cadfield remarked.

"Yes. It's quite possible, and I made it clear to her that I was not interested in marrying her." He looked at Miss Cadfield in earnest. "If it means anything to you, she met someone else in Germany and became engaged."

"Oh," she said, appearing relieved. "From the letter that she sent to Miss Stirling, I was under the impression that she was seeing you and planning to marry you."

"Ahh, so you have been keeping up on her news," he teased.

"I happened to overhear the conversation," she mumbled, looking guilty.

"I assure you that I was living by myself in a small apartment, lonely and miserable in Germany. All I could think of was returning to Greece." He paused.

"Yes?"

"After I returned, I visited Nemea, hoping to resume where I left off," he said, shaking his head, "but it wasn't the same. Without you."

He stared out into the darkness, recalling how lonely he had felt on his recent trip to the mountain in Nemea. Everywhere he would turn, he expected to see Helena before him, but instead, a stark emptiness greeted him. How he had hungered for the sight of her beautiful face and the sound of her lyrical voice. Now she was here, by his side.

Miss Cadfield was unusually silent.

"So, I decided to remain in the storage room, organizing the artifacts instead," he continued.

"And that's where I found you."

"I even thought about coming to England to try to change your mind," he teased.

"Why didn't you?" she whispered.

"I felt that you must have loved him enough to want to go back to him," he muttered darkly.

"I was wrong. My home is here in Greece, Dr. Mastoras. I belong here."

Aristotle was pleased to hear that. His hand found her warm hand. "Is that the only reason you returned?" he teased. He saw the answer in her eyes before she spoke.

"To be honest, I was hoping to see you again, and even if you were married or hadn't returned, it would have sufficed for me to live on the mountain, in Nemea, reliving the time we spent together."

Intense feelings swept over him as he pulled her to him.

"My dearest Helena, my darling. You must know that you are the one I have loved all along."

She trembled like a leaf in his arms. "I have also loved you with all my heart."

Overcome by joy, he embraced her softness. "Dare I ask once more if you can accept me and my faults for the rest of your life?"

"Are, are you proposing to me again, even after what I did?" she stammered.

"Yes, *agape mou*, my love. I love you even more than ever, for your honesty, your fairness, your intellect, your values, and just as importantly, for your love for Greece."

"Yes, I will marry you."

His hear was bursting with joy. He kissed her passionately.

"You do not know how much this means to me. You have made me a very happy man."

"I feel the same way. It is as if I have known you all my life. We have so much in common."

"Yes," he whispered, nuzzling her neck.

"To think a few weeks ago I was living in another world. Was it Pericles who said no man steps in the same river twice?"

"For it's not the same river, and he's not the same man," Aristotle finished. "It looks like your father schooled you well."

She smiled at him as he gazed at her lovingly. "I have so many things I want to talk with you about."

"Hmm," Aristotle said, kissing her on the tip of her nose, and then kissing her lips fully, savoring the moment. "Me too, dearest, and we'll have a lifetime to discuss them all."

THE END

Acknowledgements

I would like to thank Professor Montesonti and all my professors at National University that guided my writing to greater heights, and gave me many opportunities to apply my critical thinking skills to their challenging questions and assignments for my MFA degree.

I also am grateful to the following members of the Hellenic Writers' Group of Washington DC, who read *Helena's Choice* and offered insightful comments: Maria Antokas, Stella Lagakos, Hoda Makar, Dr. Peter Paras, Dr. Christine Saba, and Calliopi Toufidou.

I would also like to thank Professor Kim Shelton (Univ. of CA, Berkeley), for her advice on the Nemea region of Greece, and Herta Feely and John DeDakis for their editing feedback.

In addition, I would like to thank my son, Anthony, for his useful comments and enthusiastic support. Finally, I would like to thank Joanna Vasilakis for her wonderful cover art.

About the Author

Patty Apostolides is a biologist, author, poet and classical musician. She has written five novels and a poetry book. When she retired as a cancer biologist in order to stay at home and homeschool her son, her second career as a writer began. She holds a BA in Biology from Case Western Reserve University, with minors in music and theater, and an MFA in Creative Writing from National University. She founded and is the director of the Hellenic Writers Group of Washington DC. In addition, Ms. Apostolides has performed as a violist for the Cleveland Philharmonic, the Cleveland Women's Orchestra, and the Fairfield Symphony Orchestra. More recently, she has played as a violinist for the Frederick Symphony Orchestra and the Eklektika String Quartet. She lives in Maryland with her son.

Visit her website at: www.pattyapostolides.com

CPSIA information can be obtained
at www.ICGtesting.com
Printed in the USA
LVHW041447060819
626725LV00012B/658